PRAISE FOR FARAH HERON

"The exact kind of YA fiction I would've loved to read in high school when I was shaping my ideas about love and who I wanted to be. Heron's newest book is filled with great lessons about staying true to yourself and what you want."

—*USA Today*

"As she does in her books for adults, Heron draws on her own Indian Tanzanian Canadian Muslim identity, and details of close-knit, transnational community enrich this YA debut. The book's memorable secondary characters—including Nilusha, Tahira's wise and compassionate mentor, and Juniper, Rowan's sweet younger sister—help Tahira stay true to herself in this entertaining enemies-to-lovers rom-com."

—*Publishers Weekly*

"Heron has penned an enjoyable coming-of-age romantic comedy. Touching on the pressures of social media, discovering your passions, and staying true to yourself, your morals, and your real friends, the book offers readers characters whose feelings and insecurities will resonate . . . A sweet read filled with fashion, flowers, and romance."

—*Kirkus Reviews*

"With well-rounded supporting characters and a polished narrative, this is a natural choice for Sarah Dessen and Sandhya Menon fans."

—*Booklist*

"Small-town fun, flower arranging, and summer crushes are all at the forefront of this winning YA novel."

—POPSUGAR

How to Win a Breakup

ALSO BY FARAH HERON

How to Win a Breakup

a novel

FARAH HERON

SKYSCAPE

Published by Skyscape, New York

www.apub.com

Amazon, the Amazon logo, and Skyscape are trademarks of Amazon.com, Inc., or its affiliates.

ISBN-13: 9781542036085 (hardcover)
ISBN-13: 9781542036092 (paperback)
ISBN-13: 9781542036108 (digital)

Cover illustration by Christina Chung
Cover design by Faceout Studio, Jeff Miller

Printed in the United States of America

First edition

This book is for all the Brown gamer-girls trying to find their place in the world. But mostly, this book is for Anissa.

1

It's All about the Gamer-Boys

Everyone had a type.

I'd had only one serious boyfriend . . . Devin Kapadia. Honestly, one boyfriend total, since it probably doesn't make sense to count Jordan Nguyen, my boyfriend from kindergarten. And I supposed a pattern of one wasn't really a pattern. But I was pretty sure my type was gamer-guys. Because even though Devin had above-average intelligence, a great sense of humor, a respectful attitude, and good hygiene all going for him, nothing had affected me more when we were together than watching him, or his playable character at least, slay a horde of dragons and orcs in less time than it took my sister to pick an outfit.

And now a new guy was making my knees weak, and he was also a gamer-guy. LostAxis, the person who had inspired this self-discovery, was *skilled*. Watching his fully decked out Dark Mage thoroughly decimate all the green enemies on his way to the center of the dragon's nest made my insides turn completely into goo. I forgot where I was, who I was, and even what I'd eaten for breakfast. I hadn't felt this immersed playing *Dragon Arena* since I'd played with the aforementioned ex. But never mind Devin.

The best part of this near-religious gaming experience was that it wasn't *just* LostAxis expertly obliterating the enemies on the way to the Obsidian Egg at the middle of the nest; instead it was *both* of us. Me and LostAxis played better together than anyone I'd ever raided with.

Like right now. I was gaming in my room, and we'd been working through this quest for hours. There was hopefully just enough time to finish it before Mom called me for dinner. LostAxis cued up a fireball spell at the orc pounding at him, and I hit him with a restore the second his spell landed. It was a tricky sequence—if I didn't time it right, my spell would piggyback off his and end up healing the orc instead. But that never happened when I played with LostAxis. Our battle maneuvering was like a symphony . . . but not like . . . orchestrated, or anything like that. More like . . . improvised. Like on those old jazz records my grandfather gave my dad. Dad said those musicians were *magic* when they played together. That's what me and LostAxis were together: *magic*.

We reached the dragon, and wasted no time and started pounding on her, too. LostAxis threw incredibly powerful destructive spells, while I watched our individual health points, ensuring we survived the dragon claws, fire breath, and tail whips that could take 75 percent of our health in one sweep. It was touch and go for a while, and at least three times I was sure LostAxis was going to be charred like a kebab, but after a complicated double spell maneuver, the dragon was turned to dust.

LostAxis approached the gleaming black egg the dragon had been guarding. The entire point of today's incredibly challenging quest was *this* egg—there was a 5 percent chance that it would contain an Obsidian Staff, a rare and powerful weapon that could be used by either Dark or Light Mages. And since he was a Dark Mage and I was a Light Mage, we intended to keep repeating the Obsidian Dragon quest every weekend until we each had a staff. He opened the egg, and the loot spewed in a plume above it before falling to the ground. I saw a bag of gold, some random jewels, a few potions, and most importantly . . .

The in-game chat lit up with a message.

LostAxis: Holy shit. 3 obsidian staffs!

My hands shook with excitement as they flew over the keyboard.

GreenEggsAndSam: Is that a glitch?

The chance of one staff was pretty slim, but three?

LostAxis: Hang on . . . Lemme look it up. Apparently, it's very rare. Called a hat trick . . . happens when the quest is completed with only a Light Mage and a Dark Mage, and they can't have more than a three-level difference between them, and they have to keep their health above 25% for the whole battle. Even then it's not a sure thing.

I was grinning ear to ear as I typed my reply.

GreenEggsAndSam: You mean we got three staffs because we're awesome?

LostAxis: Of course. You knew we were awesome. How about we sell the third staff and split the gold?

GreenEggsAndSam: Deal. Why is it called hat trick? Because it's like pulling a rabbit out of a hat?

LostAxis: Hang on I'm looking that up.

Still giddy from the drop, I moved my player to pick up one of the staffs. After equipping it, I started a spell to heal us both. The magic swirled a faint rainbow haze from the tip of the black staff.

LostAxis: Hat trick is a hockey reference. It's when three goals are scored by the same player in a game. Lol, why would they think people who play RPGs would know anything about sports?

I used the staff again, this time to cast a protective bubble around me and LostAxis.

GreenEggsAndSam: This thing is epic. I can't believe we got three.

LostAxis: I told you last night—we're the best team on the server. You and me, Sam? We're dragon slayer duo goals.

We transported back to the nearest village and were chatting about how cool that run had been, and about how every time either of us had a close call with an orc, the other was there to save them, when I heard my mother yell that dinner was ready.

GreenEggsAndSam: Dinner—I gotta go.

LostAxis: Damn—I didn't realize it was so late. Gold Aegean Dragon after dinner?

I logged in to the game's chat function on my phone so I could keep talking while I headed downstairs.

GreenEggsAndSam: Can't play late tonight. Mom says I have to rest my brain for the first day of school tomorrow. Shouldn't you, too?

I didn't know much about LostAxis, but he'd told me he was seventeen, same as me, and also starting grade twelve tomorrow.

LostAxis: Brains like ours don't need to rest. Tomorrow night? Now that we have our staffs, we can probably get the bonus egg in the Aegean nest.

GreenEggsAndSam: Tomorrow works.

LostAxis: Looking forward to it. Before you go—did you know that most power outages in North America are caused by squirrels?

GreenEggsAndSam: You're kidding.

LostAxis: Look it up. See ya tomorrow. 🖤

I was probably blushing when I got to the dining table. Actually, not even blushing, but full-on swooning, truth be told. It was the heart emoji. I was pretty easy to please . . . most of the time.

"Samaya, why are you looking like that? Who are you texting?" My mother was bringing a tray of biryani from the kitchen. I put my phone facedown on the dining table.

"No one. Just a friend," I said.

Last spring my parents, who had decided we all needed more family time, insisted that at least once a week, all four of us had to eat at the same time in the formal dining room of our two-story house. The "no phone" rule was new, too—and hard to remember.

Dad came up behind me and ruffled the top of my head. "Nice to see you laughing again," he said. Dad ruffled my hair a lot. Especially lately. I smoothed it back into place.

My sister, Tahira, joined us in the dining room, holding her phone. "You wouldn't believe who's in my tailoring class. Remember that reality show with the guy who—"

"Tahira," Mom interrupted. "No phones at the table. Sit, then talk."

Tahira rolled her eyes and tossed her phone on a side table. Tahira was a year older than me and had just finished orientation week at college. She was in the fashion program at the Ontario College of Art and Design and was exactly as dramatic as one would expect a fashion student to be.

When we were all seated, Mom started interrogating me.

"Did you find out who your physics teacher is?" she asked as she spooned biryani onto my plate. It smelled heavenly—rich with spices and fried onions.

"Not yet. The system still shows 'TBD,'" I said.

Mom shook her head. "It had better not be Mr. Weiland. He's a *gym* teacher. At parent-teacher night last year, he didn't know what an adiabatic process was."

"Mom, do you know what an adiabatic process is?" Tahira asked.

Mom was the director of HR for a hotel company, so no, she didn't know anything about advanced physics.

"I'm not claiming to be a physics teacher, am I? This year is too important for Samaya to blindly trust that all her teachers know what they're doing. That reminds me, Samaya: I made an appointment for you to talk to Mrs. Singh at ten tomorrow morning about your community service hours. You'll have to leave first period early."

Mrs. Singh was my guidance counselor. Mom had apparently been in contact with her a few times last week to "discuss" my "situation."

"That'll be good, Samaya," Dad said as he served his own rice. "She'll help you put a plan together to get back on track."

My family was very big on "making a plan," but even they'd been at a loss about how to fix everything after my life went so far off course last June. But I really didn't want to talk about (or think about) that right now. Time to try for a topic change.

I turned to my sister. "So, who's in your tailoring class?"

Tahira grinned. "Remember that show about the Northern Ontario sour-pickle dynasty? The son was—"

Mom interrupted, of course. "Samaya, tell Mrs. Singh that you're only looking for volunteer placements that will look good on your college application. None of these make-work-for-teens projects. I know you didn't have a lot of choice, but spending this summer scooping ice cream didn't help anyone. You need *leadership* experience. Something high profile. I hope you're also considering which extracurriculars to focus on this year."

"I know, Mom, I know," I said, glad that I actually had an answer for this. "I'm thinking of starting a game-dev club at the school. This organization called the National Youth Developers have this annual mobile-app competition—"

"*Starting* a club is a great idea, but I mean real clubs, Samaya," Mom said. "*Academic* clubs. Like math club. Not playing video games."

I frowned. I couldn't join the math club because Devin had been voted president at the end of the last school year. I'd helped my boyfriend campaign—and then he dumped me a week after the elections. "This isn't playing video games, it's *creating* them. I just need to find a teacher to be the adviser."

Dad smiled at me. "Oh, a club for coding games! That sounds fun!" Dad was a lawyer, but also a bit of a computer nerd. He was who got me into gaming when I was little. Dad cared about my academic achievement, but he wasn't near as pushy as Mom.

Mom ignored him. "Joining the physics club would be better for your scholarship applications."

I frowned. Mom knew Devin was the president of that club, too. He was the school's golden child. And she should have known that I wouldn't want to be in the club with him.

Maybe mentioning the physics club did remind her of Devin, though, because she suddenly grinned and said, "Guess what I saw on Facebook! Preeti Kapadia posted their vacation pictures from India! Did you see them, Samaya?"

No, I had not seen my ex-boyfriend's mother's Facebook. Everyone I knew had been shielding me from any news, or pictures, of the Kapadia family since June. Everyone except my mother. She didn't seem to have any qualms about mentioning the taboo family, despite the fact that it had been Devin who caused the derailment that required me to "get back on track" in the first place. Which meant family dinners had been a bit of a minefield for me during the last two months.

"The pictures from Preeti's cousin's wedding!" Mom continued, positively beaming. "The clothes! And you wouldn't believe the floral arrangements in the reception. It's been too long since our trip to India. We should plan another. What do you think, Tahira? I'll ask Preeti for recommendations where to stay."

"Yes! I want to go to India fashion week next fall," Tahira said. "There is this textile factory there that does custom screen prints . . . The colors are spectacular."

Thankfully, that shifted the conversation away from approaching the Kapadias for travel tips and toward my sister's budding fashion career. It was another one of my mother's favorite topics of discussion at dinner, so hopefully that was the end of all this talk about my ex's family.

But no. Mom threw another grenade a few minutes later. "Will Devin be back at school with you tomorrow?" she asked me. "There was some talk on her Facebook last year about him transferring to a private school."

"I have no idea."

"Which universities is he applying for?"

"Mom, how would she know that?" Tahira asked. "They broke up."

Maybe because she was still actually a teenager, my sister seemed to understand that when your long-term boyfriend dumped you publicly the last week of school, sabotaged your summer job, then took off with his family to India so he could "figure out" who he was "*alone*," that meant you were no longer privy to his academic plans.

Mom gave Tahira a look. "They're still friends, aren't they?"

No, no, we weren't.

Mom was still talking. "Now that Devin's back in our time zone, you can play that dragon-tournament game together again."

So now she was telling me I *should* be playing video games? I honestly didn't understand my mother. The only way to get through her talking endlessly about Devin or his family was to let my mind wander to something else. Like practicing pi in my head. I was trying to memorize the mathematical constant to two hundred digits and so far was up to one hundred and thirty-four.

Two years ago, when Devin and I started dating, I'd thought it was so cool that our families already knew each other—casually, at least. And I'd thought it was so cool that the casual acquaintance grew to family dinners together, picnics, and even trips to Little India on Gerrard Street for sari shopping. I'd been sure that the fact that our families were friends meant my relationship with Devin would last longer than the average high school relationship. And even though our backgrounds weren't exactly the same (my family was Indian but Ismaili Muslim, and my grandparents were from Nairobi, Kenya, while Devin's family was Indian but Hindu and his parents were born in Mumbai, India), I thought our cultures being so similar meant our connection was deeper. More profound. Maybe forever.

Boy was I wrong. But Mom seemed to be still holding out hope that one day an enormous, spectacular Kapadia wedding would involve our family, too. Which . . . ugh. I was *seventeen*. Could she please wait ten years or so before fantasizing about marrying me off?

I tried to keep my mind on the *Dragon Arena* battle, but my family was still talking about me, and they were hard to ignore.

"Sabina, Samaya's focus should be on school, not reconnecting with Devin by playing video games," Dad said.

I nodded. "Yes, *that*. It's my last year of high school. Right now, my focus is only on getting into university with scholarships and finishing my volunteer hours. And starting that game-dev club, which will help with my applications."

Well, maybe also finishing the Magic Guild questline in *Dragon Arena* with LostAxis.

Mom nodded. "Good girl, Samaya. Stay out of any drama this year. I know you'll keep the respect of your classmates and teachers, so you'll get glowing references for scholarships and awards. We're so lucky to have two daughters we can count on. Did you hear about that Vaughan girl from down the street? She was *arrested* for selling painkillers she took from her father. I can't even imagine!"

And the conversation shifted to Mom bringing out all the flaws in the kids who weren't her own, which was fine. It meant I could daydream about LostAxis and his wicked melee-spell skills.

A much better use of my brain space than thinking about Devin Kapadia.

2

The Last First Day of High School

Image: Smiling brown-skinned girl, chin-length black hair. Arm around the waist of a tall, brown-skinned boy. His wavy hair is longish and reaches the back of his collar. His expression is serious, and his head is tilted down to hear what the girl is saying.

Caption: When the school year ended last spring, Samaya Janmohammad and Devin Kapadia were the top grade-eleven students academically and all set to be Earl Jones Secondary School's golden couple this September. In fact, some students were taking bets on which of them would be named valedictorian this year, although most agreed the head of the math, physics, and debate clubs would take it. But all bets were off last June after a shocking breakup and Devin's unexpected relocation to India for the summer. Ears close to the ground have recently heard that Devin is back in Toronto and will be at Earl's this year. Does this mean a reconciliation is in the works? Only time will tell what's in store for what used to be the Earl Jones power couple.

"Don't read that," my best friend, Cass, said, pointing at the offending Instagram post on my phone. My friend since grade three, Cass always knew what was best for me. But—ugh. Ugh. Ugh. It was too late. What a way to start the first day of my last year of high school.

Cass and I were standing on a TTC bus on our way to school, and I'd given in to temptation and checked out the bane of our school's entire existence, the Earl's Whispers Instagram account. I should not have been torturing myself like this. Earl's Whispers had been a major contributor to my complete and utter downfall last year. The account had gone silent all summer—but was obviously back at full force for the first day of school. I hadn't got the distinction of being the first gossip of the day, though. That honor went to Abigail Schwartz, who was outed at six a.m. for lying about her summer job—she had not been working at a Yorkville Avenue boutique, but apparently at a Walmart across town. I didn't think it was much of a controversy, but Abigail's rep as the school's top fashionista was going to take a hit.

"I'd hoped this stupid account wouldn't be a thing this year," I said now, dutifully closing the page.

Cass snorted. "Of course it's still a thing. Earl's is the worst school in Toronto, remember? Ignore it. One more year, then we put this whole hellhole school behind us." They shifted closer to me as more people got on the bus.

I agreed with Cass. Honestly, I wished I could go back in time to grade nine, when Mom came at me with a plan to graduate high school in three years instead of four. My guidance counselor had talked her out of that idea. Mrs. Singh was big on school/life balance. But clearly, I should have listened to Mom.

And anyway, after a summer of hell, I was pretty sure school/life balance was a pipe dream. At our age, school *was* life, whether we wanted it to be or not.

The bus lurched to a stop—we had the thrill-seeker bus driver this morning—and I clutched the yellow pole tighter. My good friend

Aimee got on, and sat near where we were standing. Aimee was a school friend, but I hadn't really talked to her much over the summer. She'd been at a photography camp, and I hadn't been feeling very social. Cass and I were close with Aimee even though she was the only artist in our little math and science nerd crew. As she sat, her sunny smile attracted attention from several riders around us.

Or maybe it was her outfit.

"Looking good, Aim," Cass said.

I nodded appreciatively.

Aimee, as expected, had gone all out for the first day of school. Her long hair was dyed half-pink and half-black. She wore a black lace blouse with a high Victorian collar, a short black pleated skirt with lace edging, fishnet tights, and black boots. Plus elaborate dark eye shadow and black eyeliner, and a deep purple lipstick. She wore it all well—with her pale Irish skin, she looked like she'd been born in an Edgar Allan Poe poem. I loved her look. She'd even convinced me to start wearing dark eyeliner after Devin dumped me, telling me that a makeover was the best remedy for heartbreak. I wasn't sure just eye makeup could be considered a *makeover*, but it went with the black clothes I wore most of the time, and made me look closer to my actual age. Also? Devin hadn't seen the eyeliner yet, but I knew he'd *hate* it, and that was another good reason for me to start wearing it.

Aimee looked back at us, head tilted. "It's the first day of school? I don't get why you two didn't put more thought into your outfits. Cass, I understand: sweatshirts are, like, your uniform. But Samaya . . . you need to look good for . . ."

Aimee didn't finish her sentence. Which was good because I was pretty sure she was going to say Devin.

Cass was in their standard blue jeans and hoodie combo—this one in a bright teal that brought out their natural, pink-tinged cheeks. Cass was half-Chinese on their mom's side but inherited their father's blush-prone complexion. I always felt like the lone dark sheep when I was with my two closest friends.

"I *did* put thought into this," I said, indicating my clothes. I'd put on black jeans and Vans sneakers today, and the new black T-shirt my sister made me that was covered in math calculations in my own handwriting. And, of course, my new dark eye makeup. I thought I looked pretty good. And I didn't care at all what Devin would think about my appearance, anyway. Mostly.

My phone notification went off. It was the *Dragon Arena* chatting app.

LostAxis: Have a spectacular first day of school.

I smiled as I returned the sentiment.

"Is that the guy you've been gaming with?" Cass asked, hearing the notification.

I raised a brow. "You have your own phone. You don't have to read mine."

Aimee shook her head. "Besties don't have secrets. Are you seriously *still* talking to that guy? The Dark Mage you met online last winter, right?"

I nodded.

"You talk even outside of game?"

"Yes."

Aimee shook her head, disappointed. "You've been keeping this from us. Spill. I want to hear everything. Are you, like, *talking*, or just talking?"

Cass frowned. "What does that even mean?"

"*Talking* is like . . . you know, going somewhere. Flirting."

"There is no flirting," I said. Well, maybe there was *some* flirting, but not really. Calling us *duo goals* wasn't really flirting. "We've done a bunch of duo quests together. He's a Dark Mage, I'm a Light. We got three Obsidian Staffs yesterday."

"Shut. Up," Cass said. "For real? *Three* staffs?"

"Totally serious. We each kept one and sold the third."

"Jayden's gonna be pissed. He's dying for one of those," Aimee said.

Jayden was the Dark Mage in our regular *Dragon Arena* guild. Jayden was also one of Devin's best friends. The guild was a group of about twenty players, mostly from our school, who played together online last year. We'd even had a few in-person gaming sessions. I'd stopped playing with the guild last June after Devin dumped me, but Cass had told me the guild hadn't played all summer anyway, since everyone was too busy with camps and summer jobs. Last time I heard from Jayden, he accused me of breaking up the guild. I reminded him that since Devin was the one who dumped me, he should take it up with his best friend.

"I don't care if Jayden's pissed," I said. He wanted an Obsidian Staff, but there was no point in being mad that I had one. If he was jealous, he could just find someone to do the quest with to get his own.

"Yesterday he told me he's having a *Dragon Arena* party next month," Aimee said.

I raised a brow. "You're talking regularly to Jayden now?"

"Yeah. So?"

I frowned. I knew things would be awkward this year since Devin and I had so many friends in common, but I didn't think one of my closest friends would get *closer* to Devin's friend after we broke up.

"Are you, like, *talking*, or just talking," Cass said, mocking Aimee's earlier emphasis on the word.

Aimee waved her hand. "Enough about Jayden. I want to hear more about Samaya's mystery guy. You say there's no flirting, but would you even know flirting if you saw it? Because you and Devin were together a long time, so you might be a bit rusty—"

She had a point, but I hit her (gently) on her lace-covered arm anyway.

"Let me see his messages," Aimee said.

There really was no hiding from my friends. I opened the *Dragon Arena* message app and handed my phone to Aimee.

"He's into you," Aimee announced after three seconds of reading. "See this? He always makes plans to play again after a run. What's with the weird animal facts?"

I shrugged. "He's quirky."

"What do you know about him?" Cass asked. "He could be a forty-year-old in Florida or something. Did I ever tell you that kid I met in Arkansas, the one I've been playing *Fair Gems* with, isn't really a *kid* at all?"

I snorted. "What are they, a cat?"

They laughed again. "No, they *are* a person—just not a kid. Her name is Carol, and she's like a seventy-five-year-old grandma."

"Holy crap." Aimee laughed. "Are you still playing with her?"

"Hell yeah! TBH, her age only makes her cooler. She swears like a sailor and promised me she'd send some crocheted cozies for my game controllers."

I laughed. I did, of course, accept that LostAxis might not be who he said he was. What he'd told me was that he was seventeen, like me, and that he lived somewhere in Canada, but he didn't specify. We'd first met on a *Dragon Arena* message board, and there were lots of seventeen-year-old male players.

Aimee was still scrolling through my messages. It could take a while—there was a lot of in-game chatter between us. Out-of-game chatter, too.

"Holy shit, is this him?" Aimee said suddenly, holding up the picture he'd sent me several weeks back. He'd asked me what I thought my character would look like if they were in the real world, so as a joke I'd sent him a picture of Sam I Am, the main character from *Green Eggs and Ham*—which was where my character name came from. But he'd sent me a picture of himself.

It was a distance shot of him with some trees and an old concrete and rusted metal staircase behind him. Of course, I'd zoomed in when I first saw it—and saw that he was cute. Tallish. Broad shoulders. He had darker skin and looked like he could be southeast Asian. He was standing straight, looking down and to the right. One hand was holding on to a tall pole of some sort, and his other hand rested on top of it. I'd snorted when I first saw the picture—this was the exact pose in *Dragon Arena* that Dark Mages equipped with a staff would make when the character was in "waiting mode."

"He's *nice*," Aimee said, zooming in on the picture. "Are those dimples? Love it." She frowned, tapping her black-sparkled nail on the phone screen. "Where is this? Where does he live?"

"I don't know. Canada."

Cass huffed. "That narrows it down." They took the phone from Aimee, and zoomed in. "What's on his jacket? A duck?"

I shrugged.

Aimee frowned. "Why didn't you ask where he lives? If you both live in the same country, I would think you'd ask where."

"We game together. We have a lot in common. He's into math and coding, too. But we don't, you know . . . go deep."

Cass frowned. "Asking him where he lives is *deep*?"

"We only talk about gaming." I found it comforting that he didn't know me, or my baggage.

Since LostAxis and I had started gaming more regularly over the summer, I'd felt like . . . I don't know, my own person with him. Not Devin's girlfriend. Or Devin's *dumped* girlfriend. Not Cass and Aimee's friend. Not the top student in the grade.

I was just me. GreenEggsAndSam. An excellent Light Mage. And that seemed to be enough for LostAxis.

"Did you send him a real picture, too?" Aimee asked.

I shook my head. "He didn't ask me for one."

"He probably thinks you're a fifty-year-old housewife," Cass said. They paused, thinking. "Do you want me to ask my friend Carol for a pic you can send him?"

I laughed and shook my head as the bus stopped.

"You know what?" I said as we climbed off the bus. "It doesn't matter who either of us really are. I'm not interested in him as a *guy*, just as a gaming friend. In fact, I'm reclaiming the brain space that thinking about guys takes up in my head. Female-presenting and nonbinary folks are all I'm going to concern myself with from now on." I looped one arm in Cass's and the other through Aimee's after we got off the bus. "Maybe I'll join a convent."

"You're Muslim," Aimee said, laughing. "You can't be a nun."

"Fine. Send me to my grandmother's then. That's just as good."

~

"I'll be honest, Samaya," Mrs. Singh said. "I was surprised to see you're behind on your community service hours. You've always been steady and reliable."

"I was supposed to be a volunteer counselor at a math camp, but I had a difficult summer," I said. Understatement of the century. We were in Mrs. Singh's office, and she had my open student file on her desk. I'd come to our appointment right after meeting my advanced functions teacher and getting my locker for the year. Our school was semestered, so I had four classes right now, and we had a two-day schedule, which meant I had functions first period every other day.

Usually, I was called into the guidance office to talk about some new scholarship or academic competition that Mrs. Singh found for me—something that "has Samaya Janmohammad written all over it." This was the first time I'd been to the guidance office for something I'd done *wrong*. Although it wasn't entirely my own fault that I was behind on my community service hours. It was Devin's fault, too.

"I'm a little confused about that. You were supposed to volunteer as a counselor in a math camp, which would have given you your hours, right?"

"Yeah, but then I couldn't go. I broke up with my boyfriend right before camp." I was surprised Mrs. Singh didn't know this. She must be the only person at the school—staff or student—who didn't follow Earl's Whispers.

Mrs. Singh looked puzzled. "Aren't you dating Devin Kapadia? He's such a bright student. He finished his hours last year."

Yes, Devin was the perfect golden boy at this school. I tried not to roll my eyes. "Yeah, we broke up. We were supposed to go to camp together. But then he went with his parents to India for the whole summer instead. It was for a family wedding, but he wasn't supposed to go."

"I'm not following," Mrs. Singh said. "Why would that mean you couldn't go to camp? You needed that experience for your scholarship applications."

I sighed. I really didn't feel like telling her the whole story. What had happened was that when Devin dumped me, he made the camp admin switch me to counselor-in-training for the six- to eight-year-olds instead of the thirteen- to sixteen-year-olds that I was supposed to work with, so he and I wouldn't be working together. And because Devin had pretty much everyone wrapped around his perfect little finger, they gladly moved me to the less desirable age group. But I couldn't face a summer teaching simple arithmetic to kids while watching golden boy Devin work with teenagers on more complex equations, so I quit the job before it started. But then Devin changed his mind and joined his parents on their planned trip to India, so he didn't even go to camp, either. I'd tried to get my job back when Devin left, but they'd already filled the vacancies with counselors from the other age groups. And they wouldn't pull strings for me. I had no doubt they'd have done it for Devin.

So instead of even teaching simple math to kids, I spent the first week of my depressing summer in bed and the second watching movies in my pajamas. By the third week Mom was driving me up the wall with her disappointment that I wasn't making good use out of my time, so I got a job I hated in the ice cream shop near the mall. I ended up with a strong scooping ice cream bicep on my right arm, but without the community service hours I needed to graduate high school.

"It's complicated," I said.

Mrs. Singh looked at me skeptically. Like she wasn't aware that Brown kids ever let heartbreak get in the way of achievement.

"Well, I hope you're ready to apply yourself now," she said. "I know you intend to apply for some scholarships. Your mother tells me you have your eye on the Schaaf-Hanke leadership award. You know we had an Earl student win one last year."

Of course I knew. Mom wouldn't shut up about Tina Patel. Word around the school was that Tina's parents had paid a small fortune on an "achievement coach" to help with Tina's applications. My mother didn't believe me about that, though.

Mrs. Singh started listing similar awards, other scholarships offered by independent organizations, but she also talked about ones offered at universities with top math programs.

I'd heard all this from Mom before, so I zoned out a bit and looked through the window behind her desk, which faced into the quad. The quad was the unofficial grade-twelve chill spot in the school. I'd waited three years to be able to hang out there—and now I wasn't sure if I was ever going to. Not if Devin was there. Everyone would stare at us—especially after that Earl's Whispers post this morning.

I scanned the crowd. Aimee stood near the door talking to Jayden and another of Devin's friends, Omar.

Mrs. Singh was still talking about scholarships. "They'll be looking for excellence in STEM, and at your leadership experience, too. Winners must be resilient, well-rounded students who others look up to. Role models." She squinted at her computer. "Your grades are good enough. You already have three grade-twelve credits. Well done. Now, let's see. What are you taking this semester?" She glanced at her computer. "Data management, physics, advanced functions, and English.

20

Good. But what about extracurriculars? You could use some leadership experience. Have you ever taken a lead role in a club here?"

I cringed. No, not really. Devin was more the leader type. I told Mrs. Singh about my idea to create a game-dev team and enter the National Youth Developers competition I'd read about online.

"That's an excellent idea, Samaya. You can run it with Devin."

I shook my head. "No. We broke up."

She frowned. "Right. Ask Miss Zhao to advise the club. She's the new computer teacher. Are you still intending to study math at the University of Waterloo?"

"That's the plan."

"Excellent. Now, about those community service hours . . . You're aware that Earl's students need seventy-five hours to graduate, more than other schools in the area. You're only short twenty, so catching up shouldn't be a problem. But it's more than that. The summer volunteer position at the math camp won't be easy for you to replace. As well as giving you volunteer hours, the math camp would have provided you with a valuable reference and leadership experience for your applications."

"I am aware," I said. "My mother and I were hoping you would know of another similar opportunity I could do during the school year."

Mrs. Singh flipped through a binder. "The Scarborough Animal Shelter is still looking for volunteers."

"I'm allergic to cats."

"Many of our students work at the seniors' center. It's a little late, but I can probably get you in. Can you play euchre?"

I raised a brow. "Is that a game?"

She frowned, continuing to flip pages, then stopped on one. "What's this? The family shelter is looking for someone?" She stood. "Mr. Croft might know more about this." Mrs. Singh left the room.

While she was speaking to one of the other counselors, I watched my friends in the quad. Ugh. Aimee was now talking to Hana Dawar. I'd blissfully not thought much about that person all summer.

I'd been friends with Hana a long time. Hana and I, along with Cass and Aimee, had been inseparable in grade school, but Hana and I had had a special bond, probably because we were the only two South Asians in our friend group back then. Somehow in high school we'd shifted from friends to frenemies, though. I guess I was *technically* still friends with Hana, even though all through grade eleven, she'd been saying things like, "Wow, Devin has really filled out! He's borderline too good-looking for you now, Samaya!" and "It's not fair that you got the only decent Brown kid in the school—my parents would love it if I had a boyfriend like Devin."

Hana was at the top of my list of suspects for the true identity of Earl's Whispers, although she denied it. I thought she was full of shit— mostly because Hana and her friends were total mean girls and gossips, and Earl's Whispers had been calling Devin "Earl's most underappreciated hottie" for months, and Hana clearly had eyes for my boyfriend.

Ex-boyfriend.

I remembered what Cass said earlier and agreed again. This place was a complete hellhole.

Mrs. Singh returned smiling. "I got the details and it's perfect." She sat back at her desk. "So, do you know the family shelter over on Kingston? You remember—some Earl's students went there last fall for that multi-school build-a-playground project?"

I nodded. I remembered that project—but I hadn't gone. I wasn't exactly a DIY construction type. I was pretty sure Devin and most of his friends went, though.

"The shelter started a new fundraising initiative last spring," Mrs. Singh continued. "They use the big commercial kitchens in the facility to make cookies and pastries that they sell in a stall at a farmers' market downtown. It's all to raise funds for children's programming at the shelter. Two young people were heading the project, but one left for university, so they're looking for a new volunteer to bake and coordinate the selling efforts. It's minimum three hours a week, with the opportunity for more if you want it, and they're hoping someone will stay for the duration of the semester. This is perfect for you, Sam! Working at a family shelter will look *so good* on your application."

I frowned. I wasn't much of a baker. Or a cook, actually. "The culinary arts aren't really my thing." Or any arts, really.

"Let's keep an open mind, shall we?" said Mrs. Singh. "It's a great leadership opportunity. And it's just baking. You may have free time there, so you'll be able to use it to study. Like when cookies are in the oven! I'll call them and tell them all about you. At least check it out, okay?"

I knew I didn't have a lot of options left. I needed those hours. I put on my go-getter face. "Okay. I'll give it a shot."

It couldn't be that bad. No animals. No card games. And I might not be much of a baker, but I did like to *eat* baked goods. And with only one other "young person" to work with, at least I wouldn't be surrounded by other Earl's students.

I thanked Mrs. Singh and walked out of Guidance thinking maybe today wasn't turning out that bad after all. And walked right into Devin Kapadia.

Nope, today still sucked monkey balls.

3

The Golden Boy Makes Me Want to Puke

*D*evin. Was. Here.

Like, right here. Like, so close I pretty much slammed my head into his chest. Or at least I would have if he hadn't put his arms out to stop me, so now his hands were on my shoulders like we were dancing at the grade-ten fall formal again.

He dropped his hands and I took a step back.

My heart pounded. My hands curled into fists.

He was wearing a new loose linen button-up shirt and perfectly faded jeans along with gold-framed glasses that looked new, and expensive. Also, ugh . . . was he taller? His hair was still a bit long and wavy, and the (also new) messenger bag on his shoulder made him look . . . worldly. Sophisticated. *Hot.*

He looked like the king of the school. And of course, my body was still reacting to him. Stomach doing backflips. My stupid eyes were even watering. I quickly blinked before the tears could ruin my eyeliner—because the whole sad-clown look was not how I imagined I would look for this reunion.

Because, yes, I *had* imagined this meeting. Many times. For those first few weeks after the breakup, when I barely left the house, fantasizing about seeing Devin was a regular pastime, in between practicing pi, playing *Dragon Arena* with LostAxis, and watching the saddest Hindi romance movies on Netflix. At first, most of those fantasies were the same—he'd unexpectedly come back from India early. I wouldn't be wearing pajama pants and a stretched-out camp shirt. Nope. I'd be in something *sexy*—even though I didn't own anything that could remotely be called that. Whatever—fantasy Samaya was way cooler than real Samaya.

And Devin would take one look at me and . . . fall to his knees. He'd weep at the sight of me and beg for forgiveness for leaving me. He'd say he figured out who he was without me, and it was an empty shell of a seventeen-year-old nerd with nothing inside. He'd say he'd discovered that everything in his life was worthless without me standing by his side. The stars had lost all their shine. Music didn't sound melodic. Art looked flat. Food lost its flavor. (I confess the dialogue in my daydreams was mostly lifted from the grand gestures in the movies I was bingeing.) In the fantasies I'd put my hand out to wipe the tears falling down his cheeks, then sink to the ground and wrap my arms around him, burying my face in his neck, smelling that warm, spicy scent of Devin.

My first, and only, love.

However, after three weeks, when I traded my stained pajamas for an ice cream shop uniform, my fantasies changed. Maybe it was from having my arms deep in freezers all day, but my grief turned to anger. I stopped daydreaming in the romance genre and turned to the women-seeking-revenge one. *Kill Bill, Promising Young Woman, The Craft.* And although my daydreams started exactly the same, with Devin falling to his knees (now at the ice cream shop instead of my driveway), they ended with me flipping my hair (for some reason I had long, voluminous femme fatale hair in this fantasy) and giving him a bored look while he continued to apologize. I made him *work* for it. I told him how much he hurt me.

But in both fantasies, the weeping contrite Devin or the pleading apologetic Devin, two things were the same. Devin wanted me back, and I *took* him back.

And now? Now, he was in front of me for real, on a Tuesday morning in our high school hallway, and it felt nothing like the fantasies. He wasn't begging. Or weeping. I was wearing clean clothes. And he didn't look like my Devin anymore.

And now, I had no idea if I even wanted him back.

I waited for him to speak. Mostly because I was still frozen in shock, but also because *he* dumped *me*. He had the last word, so he got the first now.

He finally spoke. "Are you wearing makeup?"

I exhaled. "Hi, Devin. How was India?" My body was still in haywire mode, but I spoke in an annoyed tone. Because I *was* annoyed—I hadn't seen or heard from him for months, and he asked about my *makeup*?

"India was hot," he said. He looked up at the ceiling, then fiddled with the strap of that way-too-trendy messenger bag. "I have a bag of stuff we got you there."

He looked . . . uncomfortable. Awkward. Like he didn't know what to say to me. I wasn't surprised his mother had bought me stuff . . . She was like that. I liked Devin's mom. Mom liked Devin's mom even more. "Thanks," I said awkwardly.

He ran his hand through his hair. "Feels like we haven't talked in months."

I narrowed my eyes and crossed my arms over my pounding chest. "We haven't. And you were the one who said you needed space."

Devin exhaled. "I deserved that." He rubbed the back of his neck. "Look, I need to get to my class, but can we talk? Maybe at lunch? I need to tell you something. We could go for a walk by the bluffs."

Our high school was next to a park that ended at the edge of the Scarborough Bluffs, an impressive length of towering cliffs on the shore of Lake Ontario. I liked parks, but I usually stayed out of them in the fall because my tree allergies were no joke this time of the year. But the winding path overlooking the cliff with wide views of the lake stretching to the horizon was one of my favorite spots, so I was willing to put up with a bit of sneezing for it.

I knew we'd have to talk eventually. I was dreading it, but maybe ripping the Band-Aid off and getting it over with on the first day of school was the best way forward.

I sighed. "Fine. I'll meet you in front of the school at twelve." Without waiting for an answer, I turned and hurried down the hallway. I had physics before lunch—and even though I could do physics with my eyes closed, Samaya Janmohammad couldn't be late for class.

Devin was waiting for me on the steps of the school promptly at noon, and without saying much to each other, we walked over to the park.

It was chilly—as to be expected for early September, so I was glad I had my black bomber jacket. Devin was wearing a new denim jacket. Seemed he'd bought a lot of clothes in India. "This feels like Antarctica after a summer in Mumbai," he said.

I didn't know what to say, so I said nothing. This felt weird. We used to finish each other's sentences.

"India is always too much," he continued when I didn't speak. "My cousin's wedding was ridiculous. Did you see the pictures on my Insta?"

"No." Like I would torture myself with his Insta. Tahira made me unfollow all his accounts the day we broke up.

I stopped walking to look out over the bluff.

"I've seen yours," he said. "You haven't been posting much, though. How was your summer?"

My head shot around to stare at him. Had he really asked that? As if he didn't know that my summer was complete shit, thanks to him.

Whatever it was he was doing right now, I wanted no part of it. "What exactly did you want to talk about?"

"Samaya, come on. We were so close. Why can't we just talk?"

"*Were* close. Past tense. Now is a different story," I blurted out, surprising myself. Wow, I really wasn't at all like the girl in my first fantasy. I was becoming a bit of a badass. I mentally high-fived myself.

"I wanted to make sure you were okay," he said. "I'd heard you weren't happy over the summer."

I snorted. How exactly did he expect me to be? "I had a *wonderful* summer. I discovered dulce de leche ice cream and it changed my life. Why do you care?"

Devin ran his hand through his hair again. "Of course I care. C'mon, Samaya . . ."

I turned away from the beautiful view and faced him. "Devin Kapadia, you completely *blindsided* me when you broke up with me without warning. Then you pulled that crap getting me transferred at camp, which ruined my entire summer, all so you could 'see who you were without me in your life.' Like I was suffocating you or something. Like I was some sort of vampire stealing your essence. You *hurt* me." I paused. "And now you're back and you wonder if I had a good summer? And you want to, I don't know, pick up where we left off?"

Devin frowned, a deep furrow appearing between his brows. "I didn't mean to ruin your summer."

I glared at him.

"And I'm not expecting to go back to where we left off," he added.

There it was. He didn't want to get back together anyway. All he wanted was relief from the guilt after what he'd done. I knew Devin—he never wanted to be seen as a bad guy. He played a Paladin in *Dragon Arena*—the goodest good-guy class in the game. Now he wanted to continue to be the golden boy without worrying that he'd broken me along the way.

"So what is it you actually want from me, Devin? You hoping I'll be all fine and happy so you don't have to feel guilty for what you did?"

"Why can't we be friends? If we're not a couple, we have to be nothing?" He was looking at me with what looked like genuine sad eyes.

"How is that even possible after what you did?" I said. The fact of it was, Devin hadn't been just my boyfriend—he had been my friend, too. One of my best friends. He had to know that what he'd said and done last spring would hurt any chance of a friendship as much as it would hurt our relationship.

"I didn't even know you were having doubts." My voice cracked. I took a deep breath. "Maybe this"—I gestured between him and me—"was never going to be a forever thing, but friends would have had a discussion . . . instead of you just *telling* me we were done with no explanation. And friends wouldn't sabotage a friend's summer job because of their own . . . midteen crisis, or whatever happened to you."

"I didn't sabotage your job!"

"You told the camp you wouldn't come if we were working in the same team! They moved me to elementary grade, which you knew would be less valuable as experience on my university applications! And then you didn't even stick around and work at camp, so it was all for nothing!"

There was a time, early in the summer, when all I wanted was a rational explanation from him. All I wanted to know was why he did that to me.

Now I realized I'd wanted the rational explanation, and wanted him to *grovel*, so I could forgive him. But there was no point—I wasn't going to be friends, or anything else, with him again.

I gritted my teeth. "You were an asshole. And I am not in the market for assholes as friends."

Devin looked at me a few seconds. His eyes were still kind of sad, actually. "You've changed, Samaya," he said softly.

"Yeah, I have. I once thought I was so lucky to get to be in your orbit. But . . ." I shrugged. "But I just don't care anymore."

He didn't respond right away. Finally, he sighed. "I'm sorry."

Hallelujah. His first apology. But it was too little, too late.

He was looking at me with a familiar look. The one he used to give me right before kissing me. Or right before the first time he told me he loved me. I loved that look. Or I should say, I used to love it.

I turned and walked back toward the school. "Goodbye, Devin."

It was over. I couldn't believe it. No more fantasizing about him begging me to take him back. No more wishing I knew what was going through his head. No more Devin.

I didn't want him anymore. And I actually felt okay about it. Lighter.

I could start the school year without Devin Kapadia taking up any physical or mental space in my world. Which was great, because this year was way, way too important for me to have any distractions. My university acceptances, scholarships, and awards were all riding on this year—my final year of high school. It had to be perfect.

4

Sad Clown Is Not Cute

Officially getting over Devin on the first day of our last year of school was honestly the best thing that could have happened to me. I went to the quad for the rest of the lunch hour, not even caring a little bit about who would see me, or what they would say. I caught up with some friends, and even met a new transfer student. After data management last period, my teacher approached me as I was packing my bag. This was Mr. Persaud's second year at Earl's, and I hadn't had a class with him before. He was an older man with brown skin and a thick black beard.

"You look familiar. Did I teach a brother or sister of yours?" he asked.

I frowned, shaking my head. "My sister didn't go here." I was pretty sure he knew me because Devin had him last year, and I'd found Devin in his classroom a few times when he was supposed to meet me after school. But I didn't want to talk about Devin.

Mr. Persaud's face brightened. "I remember! You were with Devin Kapadia! My best student! He had the highest grade in my class last year, you know. And he wasn't even in grade twelve yet!" He smiled warmly. "That boy is going to go places. I'm writing him letters of recommendation for university. Be sure to ask him to help you with your coursework if you find it complicated."

I nodded, then left the room before the man could gush any more about Devin. Even if I had any intention of speaking to my ex again, like I would need his help, anyway. True, Devin was excellent at math. But I was better.

LostAxis and I played that evening, and as usual, we were unstoppable, plundering the hordes while barely breaking a sweat. We were both using our Obsidian Staffs, and the magic they wielded was stronger than anything I'd used before. But when we reached the dragon, the drop we were hoping for—the golden Aegean egg—wasn't there.

GreenEggsAndSam: Crap. There's no egg.

I knew this was a thing that could happen with some high-level dragons, but I'd never fought a dragon and not found an egg. What a waste of time.

LostAxis: Figures. With the day I've had, I should have known not to test my luck.

GreenEggsAndSam: Right there with you. I hate the first day of school. You wanna talk about anything?

I immediately wondered if I shouldn't have asked. As I'd told Cass and Aimee earlier, LostAxis and I didn't go deep. And I didn't really want to talk about what had happened to me today, either.

LostAxis: Nah. Playing with you now is helping. Did you know some snails can sleep up to three years?

GreenEggsAndSam: Really?

LostAxis: Would you do that if you could? Just sleep for three years and wake up twenty years old?

I thought about it a second before answering.

GreenEggsAndSam: I don't know. You only have seven years as a teenager—seems silly to sleep through 3 of them.

Then again, skipping high school wouldn't be a bad thing.

LostAxis: I'd do it. My head will be clearer when I'm 20.

GreenEggsAndSam: It's not clear now?

LostAxis: I feel like I can't see past the glasses on my face. I honestly have no idea what is happening around me anymore.

He sounded even more shaken up than me. Maybe he really *did* need a friend tonight.

GreenEggsAndSam: You sure you don't want to talk about it?

LostAxis: No. Just keep playing with me. Should we try this dragon again? The odds should be in our favor this time . . .

GreenEggsAndSam: Clearly you need to take data management. That's not how probabilities work.

LostAxis: I took data management last semester and got a 97, thank you very much. But practice and theory are noticeably different, don't you think?

We got the egg the second time around, but it didn't have the drop we wanted. We couldn't do a third round because I needed to log off soon for dinner. But Axis seemed to be in a better mood, at least. He seemed less bleak than when he'd mentioned sleeping for three years like a snail.

Before I logged off, he asked if we could play the next night but later, because he had math club after school.

LostAxis had mentioned he was into math several times. He even said he'd done the Math Olympics test last year—a province-wide math test you could take in grade eleven. I'd done it, too, and scored in the top five percentile.

GreenEggsAndSam: I'm not joining math club at my school this year.

LostAxis: Why not?

GreenEggsAndSam: Not feeling it. I need a change. No worries if you're a bit late tomorrow. Tonight was fun.

LostAxis: Honestly, the most fun I've had today. You and me, we're going to take over the world, one egg at a time. Did you know baby platypuses are called puggles? And so are beagle/pug mixes.

GreenEggsAndSam: Lol. Catch you tomorrow.

That night after dinner I did some research online on the game-dev competition so I'd be ready to ask Miss Zhao to be an adviser. I already knew my grades would be good this year—my grades were always good. And now I had a stellar extracurricular lined up. Even without math club. I could do this. I could salvage this year. A messy breakup hadn't derailed me at all.

Wednesday morning started out okay. Mrs. Singh came to my English class first period to tell me that the family shelter wanted me to come by after school the next day to start the baking volunteer job-thing. That was good—I'd get my community service hours sorted.

After second period, I was walking toward the quad when I got a text from Cass saying they were with Aimee in the cafeteria, and that I needed to go see them right away. And they said not to go on social media until I was with them.

Damn. What was it now? The social media comment made me think Earl's Whispers was posting about me again. But honestly, whatever the account was saying about me now didn't matter anymore. I was over Devin. I was still riding the high of telling him off.

But I changed course and headed to the caf anyway. I even made it as far as the cafeteria door before I couldn't resist and opened my Instagram.

And holy hell—I thought I was going to puke.

Earl's Whispers had a new post.

Image: Handsome Brown boy with gold-framed glasses and long legs sitting in front of one of the moss-green lockers on the lower level of Earl Jones High. Sitting on his lap is a small Brown girl wearing white jeans and a floral blouse. Her long, wavy dark brown hair is draped over the boy's shoulder, and she's nuzzled into his neck. The boy's arm is around her waist.

Caption: Get a room, kids! This is too much PDA for the first day of school. But is anyone really surprised at this outcome? With Devin Kapadia returning to the western hemisphere looking like a complete snack, we knew he wouldn't be Earl's most eligible single for long. Can't say we blame Hana Dawar for sinking her claws into that as soon as possible. New power couple? A pairing like this could catapult Devin, one of the top academic students at Earl's, to new heights of popularity. Could we be looking at both this year's valedictorian and prom king and queen? Or maybe being associated with Devin will bring Hana into the influential academic golden circle at Earl's. Look what Devin did for Samaya Janmohammad, after all. Only time will tell.

This school was easily the tenth circle of hell.

Cass and Aimee were suddenly in front of me, snatching my phone from my hands and guiding me to a table. My vision blurred. I started reciting the digits of pi in my head, hoping to tune out this whole situation.

"You weren't supposed to look at Instagram," Aimee said as we sat down.

I tried to think of a defense for myself, but instead wiped my eyes.

"Ugh," Aimee said, cringing. "Your makeup. Here. Let me fix it." She rustled in her bag and pulled out a packet of makeup-remover wipes.

"You carry those wherever you go?" Cass said.

Aimee nodded as she gently wiped at my eyes. "Makeup emergencies are surprisingly common. Why did you look, Samaya?"

I shrugged. "Eventually I would have seen it. Or heard about it." I took a deep breath. "What's going on in the quad? More of this?" I indicated toward my phone.

"I'm assuming. Hana texted me saying we should join the gang there," Cass said. "Suspicious to do that right after this post went up."

Meaning Hana was hoping I'd come and see her there with Devin. Which was why my protective friends had told me to meet them here.

"She's got some nerve," Aimee said with a final swipe over my eye, removing the eye makeup I'd done myself this morning. It was probably a good thing. Why the hell did I wear all this stuff anyway? Aimee held up an eyeliner pen. "This is brand new. You want me to reapply?"

"What's the point?"

Aimee shrugged. "I mean, it would distract attention away from the puffy-redness thing you've got going on."

I frowned, looking at Cass. "When was that picture taken?"

"No idea. Maybe yesterday after school?"

It figured. While Mr. Persaud was gushing about perfect Devin, Devin was apparently hooking up with my nemesis in the hallway.

Aimee was still holding up the eyeliner pen. "So . . . yes to more eyeliner, or no?"

I sighed. "Fine." I closed my eyes and let Aimee do her magic.

"How long do you think this has been going on?" I asked while Aimee worked. The scent of her strawberry hand sanitizer was filling my nose.

"No idea," Aimee said. "How long has he been back in town?"

I shrugged. "Don't know. Can't be more than a week."

"Hana moves fast," Cass said.

Clearly. Hana had obviously had a thing for Devin for a while, but seeing her draped on his lap almost the moment he got back into town hurt, even if I was over Devin. Hana and I weren't as close as we once were, but she'd been my friend. We used to play Barbies together, connect our Game Boys at school in grade seven, and we even did a science project together in grade nine on the cooling effect of South Asian spices.

It felt like Aimee was doing something much more elaborate on my eyes than what was there before. "I think he was trying to tell me this when we went for a walk yesterday," I said. "I told him off first, though."

Cass shook their head. "I still can't believe he expected you to forgive him."

"Maybe he wanted to smooth things over because Jayden wants to start up the *Dragon Arena* guild again," Aimee said.

I raised one brow at her. I'm not sure she noticed because she was working intently on my other eye. "First of all, no," I said. "I'm not going to play anything with my ex. Second, since when do I care what Jayden wants?"

Aimee put her hand down and gave me a look. "No one is saying you have to play."

"Then why do you keep bringing it up?" I snapped.

Cass tilted their head, looking at me. "This is upsetting you more than I thought it would. Don't tell me you wanted Devin back."

Aimee was still on pause, presumably curious to hear my answer.

"Believe me, I don't. I *am* over him," I said. "Seriously. This reaction is shock, not despair or devastation. We were together for *two years*; it's jarring to see him with someone else." Especially Hana.

Aimee nodded, then finished my eyes. She handed me a small mirror. "There. You look fierce."

"Nice," Cass said.

"Not bad," I said, closing one eye to admire Aimee's work.

Aimee tilted her head, smiling. "He's going to forget what's her name's face as soon as he sees yours."

"Nah. Remember? He always hated me in makeup." Me, on the other hand? I liked the new Samaya.

The Samaya who stayed up late last night texting a guy without even knowing his real name. I didn't need Devin anymore. I'd moved on. I opened the *Dragon Arena* messaging app and sent a quick message.

GreenEggsAndSam: We still on tonight?

The response came immediately.

LostAxis: Absolutely.

GreenEggsAndSam: Can't wait. Did you know there was a horse named clever Hans who was said to be able to do simple math?

LostAxis: Seriously?

"Who are you texting?" Aimee asked.

I put my phone away. "Just confirming that I'm playing with LostAxis tonight."

Aimee grinned. "Excellent. He's much better than Devin."

~

The rest of the day was hell. Everyone I saw asked me if I'd seen the Earl's Whispers account. People stared at me. Angela in my functions class asked me if Devin was already dating Hana when he dumped me. Andre in physics asked me if I'd had threesomes with Devin and Hana. And Britney asked me at my locker at the end of the day how it felt to be dumped for the most popular girl in the school. Britney was tight with Hana, so no surprise there. But the worst was the kid I didn't even know who asked me on my way out the door if Devin had done all my schoolwork for me last year.

I'd never been happier to be on a TTC bus when the day was over. Cass, Aimee, and I were sitting together near the last row.

"Shit," Aimee said, staring into her phone. "You're on another Whispers post."

"Fuck. Again? Can I get a restraining order against this account?"

It was a picture of me from today, standing in the doorway to the cafeteria at lunchtime. My phone was in my hand. And my eyes . . . they were a mess. Tears. Eye makeup smudged everywhere.

"Ugh," I said. "Who took this shot?" I tried to remember who had been in the cafeteria then.

Cass cringed. "Could be anyone."

I opened the post on my own phone. I looked horrendous. Devastated. Wincing, I read the caption aloud.

"As expected, Samaya Janmohammad, half of last year's hottest nerd couple, isn't taking the news of her former flame, Devin Kapadia, moving on very well. And it's no wonder—Devin had a major glow-up overseas. No one is surprised that he chose to upgrade his relationship, too. Samaya may be the top student academically, but academics aren't everything. And a little more eyeliner won't bring her back to Devin Kapadia's league."

"This is harassment," Cass said. "We need to report this to the school."

"I'm not going to do anything," I said.

Cass shook their head. "Why not, Samaya? You're going to let them do this to you?"

Aimee sneered at the photograph again. "We could find out who's behind this and ruin them ourselves. We'd be doing the whole school a service."

I shook my head. "No. I don't want to be labeled a snake on top of everything else. Earl's sucks. This Whisper person, or people, are right— everything at this school, even the blasted math and physics clubs, are popularity contests. You know how everyone thinks Devin's the golden boy. This is Earl's—here the smart kids are the popular kids. Now that they're in grade twelve, Devin, Omar, Jayden, and their crew are the most influential kids in the school. Even the teachers worship them."

"So?" Cass asked. "Who cares if you're popular?"

I didn't really care. Or at least I wished I didn't. "This is my last year of high school. Did you know that my sister was offered scholarships at three different schools when she was in her final year of high school? I was supposed to be at the top of my class, too, and Devin and I were supposed to get all the awards."

"So, you're upset that you won't be able to ride Devin's coattails anymore?" Aimee asked.

Cass scowled. "Samaya wasn't riding anything. She earned all her success."

I'd earned my *grades* myself. But my popularity? My friends? Other than Aimee and Cass, they were all Devin's friends. Hell, even teachers remembered me as Devin's girlfriend. Now he was the head of all the clubs, and I was the girl crying in the cafeteria.

"You have to do *something*," Cass said.

I shook my head. "I am not going to be the one who runs to the principal because her ex was getting a lap dance by a cheerleader on the first day of school."

"Hana's not a cheerleader," Aimee said. "Our school doesn't have cheerleaders."

I scowled. "If we did, she'd be one. I need to *increase* my respect at school, not make it worse. This is the second time Whispers posted a pic of me crying." The first was when I lost it at school when Devin dumped me. "I need to be the resilient role model, not the small girl who cries at school."

"Fuck gender expectations," Cass said.

I nodded. "I have to figure out how to get students to *respect* me, not just to get the awards at graduation, but also so this year isn't complete hell. Tattling on everyone's favorite gossip account won't do that. I need to rise above it."

We were all silent for a few moments.

"We'll fix this, Samaya," Aimee said. "Give us time to think of something. We got you."

I nodded. I had no idea how . . . but somehow, we had to fix it.

~

Later that night when I was getting ready for bed, a text came through on my group chat with Aimee and Cass.

Aimee: I've been thinking—the best revenge is living well, right?

Me: I guess.

Aimee: Send me that picture of LostAxis.

Me: Why?

Aimee: Right now Devin is winning your breakup. If you start winning, you'll get the respect. And I know how to turn the tables and make you the winner.

Win the breakup? And what did that have to do with LostAxis? Not understanding why, I added the photo to our group chat. In a few minutes, Aimee posted it back on our chat, except instead of standing alone, he was standing next to me. The pole he'd been holding was gone, and my head was tilted toward him.

Only that couldn't have really been me . . . because I'd never met LostAxis in person.

Aimee: Did you know photography camp included photo manipulation classes?

Cass: Holy shit Aim . . .

Me: . . . I have no words.

I zoomed in on the shot even closer. It wasn't the best photo manipulation—I looked like I'd been cut and pasted onto the picture with kindergarten scissors, and his arms were kind of awkward since the pole had been erased.

Aimee: Give me more time and I can do this seamlessly. No one will know it's fake. Post this on your Instagram, and everyone will think you moved on. You're not sitting at home crying over Devin. You're spending your time with this hottie you've been gaming with for weeks.

Me: But I've never met LostAxis. We're online friends only.

Aimee: No one has to know that part. I can even DM this photo to the Earl's Whispers account, claiming I took it over the summer. I'll tell them you were crying at lunch today because of allergies, and you can't possibly still be hung up on Devin, because you're with this guy now. This will work.

Me: I don't know.

Aimee: It's not even lying because you ARE actually talking to him. What do you think, Cass?

Cass didn't answer for a while. I could picture their dark eyebrows furrowed as they considered it.

Cass: I don't like lying but this is barely lying. You don't have to say you're dating the guy—just that he's someone you've been gaming with, which is true.

I chewed on my lip, thinking. Should I ask LostAxis before using him like this? Probably. He was my friend.

But I didn't like the idea of explaining to him why I was doing this. And he didn't like things getting personal between us.

Me: Okay. Let's give it a try. Added bonus is that it will piss off Devin. But don't say that we're like . . . dating or anything. Just talking and playing games together.

Aimee: Consider it done. I'll send you and Earl's Whispers the pic when I'm done. Stay tuned.

I zoomed in on the pic again. LostAxis and I did actually look good together. Better than me and Devin? I didn't know. Or care, honestly.

But I certainly looked better in this picture than the Samaya in the Earl's Whispers post—shocked, crying, and alone.

This was a definite improvement.

5

The Plan Works Spectacularly

Image: Smiling teenage boy with light brown skin and dimples, with his arm around a shorter teenage girl with chin-length, wavy hair. They are outdoors with trees behind them, and she is looking up at the boy.

Caption: Well, well. This is unexpected. A mysterious bird has informed us that we were wrong about Samaya Janmohammad's heartbroken mental state over her ex Devin Kapadia's shiny new relationship status. Seems Ms. Janmohammad only had some pollen in her eye, and was not distraught over learning that Hana Dawar had taken her throne as half of the school's "it couple." In fact, word on the street is that Samaya moved on with a gaming friend long before Devin even left his family's homeland. And judging by this anonymous pic, Samaya has not only moved on ... she's moved up. Devin may have had a serious glow-up in India, but this mystery gamer friend of Samaya's might even be an upgrade, in the looks department, at least. Nice.

I smiled. For the very first time, seeing my name on a Whispers post didn't make my chest tighten. "They took the bait," I said to Cass and Aimee. Today we'd all managed to get seats near the front of the bus instead of where we usually sat at the back.

"It's excellent," Aimee said. "I couldn't have written a better caption myself."

I read through the post again. "It's good. It's very good. Only thing better would be if it mentioned that LostAxis is a math whiz, too."

If I was going to use LostAxis as proof that I could move on from Devin, why not use him to prove I had moved *up* from him, too? I didn't want people to think I was only with LostAxis for his looks. Even if he looked like . . . that.

Cass raised a brow. "I know you only associate with geniuses, but honestly not everyone cares."

"I don't *only* associate with geniuses."

"Name one friend who isn't on the honor roll," Cass said.

I frowned, thinking. "Hana."

"You don't even like Hana," Aimee said.

"Yeah, well, considering we go to an academic-focused school, and I met most of my friends in my advanced classes, it's kind of unavoidable that they're on the honor roll, don't you think? I don't even have a lot of friends at all—just you two." I'd met most of my friends through Devin. "Anyway, at least it mentions I met LostAxis gaming."

My phone buzzed with a text.

Hana: You've been holding out on me. Is this the guy you've been gaming with all summer?

This was the first time I'd heard from her since the picture of her and Devin showed up on Whispers. Did Hana think we were still . . . *friends*? But Hana knew *everyone*. If I could get Hana talking about me and my new guy, then everyone would be talking about it. Even people who didn't follow Earl's Whispers.

Me: Yeah that's him. We have so much in common. He took the Math Olympic test last year, too.

Hana: Love it. You're made for each other. We should double-date.

I rolled my eyes. "Look, Hana wants to double-date."

Cass huffed a laugh. "Yeah, when pigs learn to skateboard, maybe."

I laughed. "I'm sure there is a skateboarding pig somewhere." I thought about it. "LostAxis would know."

"At least we know the picture is working, though," Aimee said. She paused, thinking. "Here, Samaya, give me your phone." She put her hand out.

Shrugging, I handed Aimee my phone. I was sitting next to her, so I'd be able to stop her from doing something I didn't want her to do with it. But all she did was set the picture of me and LostAxis snuggling up together as my phone home screen. She handed me the phone back. "There. Your relationship is now official."

When we got to school, Devin was on the steps to the front door talking to Jayden. I tried to quickly turn, figuring I'd go in the back door of the school, when he called out to me. "Samaya. Wait."

"What," I said when he reached us.

"Can we talk?" His expression was . . . strange. He glanced awkwardly at Cass and Aimee, clearly hoping they'd make themselves scarce.

"Sure," I said. "Cass and Aimee are staying, though."

He frowned.

"Or you don't talk," Cass said. "Your call."

Devin's brow wrinkled. "I'm not going to throw her over the bluffs or anything."

Cass narrowed their eyes menacingly. "I'm more worried she's going to throw *you* over."

I crossed my arms. "Go ahead, Devin. Talk."

He sighed, running his hand through his hair. "What's with the picture with that guy?"

I could see the vein in his forehead. I decided to try for coy. "What picture?"

"You're going to have to be more specific," Cass said.

"You know what picture. Why did you post that?"

"I didn't," I said. "Earl's Whispers did."

"Who is he?"

"Didn't you read the post? He's a guy I game with."

"Where did you meet him?" Devin's expression was more shocked than angry.

"In game."

He frowned. "How did you get this picture?"

"I took it," Aimee said. Devin's head whipped to look at her.

"Who posted it on that account?" he asked.

"Earl's Whispers is anonymous," Cass said.

Devin scowled. He was jealous. Devin had never been a possessive boyfriend. At least not when we were actually together. But this. This was new.

And completely uncalled for.

I stepped closer to him, going for menacing. "What, am I not allowed to date? You're allowed to practically impregnate Hana Dawar in the hallway, but I can't meet up with a guy I've been gaming with almost daily for months?"

"Samaya, I wasn't *impregnating Hana*. I have no idea who took that picture of her and me."

"Are you dating her?"

He didn't say anything. Just blinked at me with those coal-black lashes.

"So, if you *are* dating her, then why am *I* not allowed to move on, too?" I asked.

When he still didn't speak, I took a deep breath, trying to calm myself before I made a scene. The last thing I needed now was a pho-to-hungry bystander. "Who I associate with is no longer your concern,

Devin Kapadia. You and me, we're not a thing, remember? You told me that in the last week of grade eleven, and I repeated it back to you two days ago." I turned around and started walking away. "For the last time . . . goodbye."

~

I didn't see Devin for the rest of the day, which was great. Mostly. But still. I felt really weird about that whole conversation. I'd dated Devin for more than two years. Old habits die hard, and that seemingly genuine upset look on his face when I told him we weren't a thing was burned into my brain. I kind of understood his outburst. Hell, I'd also had a mini meltdown when I saw him with someone else. But I'd accomplished my goal. I'd wanted to upset Devin—the best revenge *was* living well. But that didn't mean it felt good.

As the day went on, it was clear the picture was not just successful at upsetting Devin but was also doing wonders for my reputation. It felt like *everyone* saw the Earl's Whispers post. Or spoke to Hana. And everyone wanted to say something to me about it. I got congratulations in class, high-fived in the hallways, and a standing ovation in functions. (That may have been a bit of a joke.) Anyone I was slightly acquainted with asked me who that mystery guy in the picture was.

I told everyone the same thing. Just a guy I met gaming. Yup, he's into math, too. Nah, we're not serious. Just having fun!

It was a 180-degree change from the day before. No more sideways looks in the hallways. I felt *respected.*

I could get used to this.

~

I didn't stick around after school to bask in my newfound glory. It was Thursday, and I needed to get to the New Beginnings Family Shelter for my first volunteer shift. The shelter was about a twenty-minute bus ride west from school on the edge of a residential area, near a large, forested park on the bluffs. It was a large two-story gray building with a grassy yard in front of it that was surrounded by a black iron fence. The yard had a little patio with outdoor furniture on one side and a large kids' playground on the other. That must have been the playground kids from my school built. I went through the gate and walked up to the heavy-looking front door. Was I supposed to knock, or just walk in?

"You look like a fairy," said a small voice.

I turned, startled. A cute little girl sat on a tricycle near the playground. She was Black, with hair pulled into puffy pigtails, and was wearing red pants with a pink T-shirt.

I looked down at her. "Why do you think I'm a fairy? I don't have wings."

She looked at me solemnly and pointed to her shirt. It had a faded graphic of that old Disney cartoon with Tinker Bell and her fairy friends on it. She pointed to a fairy with dark purple hair and winged eyeliner. "Your eyes are like hers."

I made a mental note to tell Aimee that her makeup lessons had impressed a preschooler.

"My hair isn't purple, though," I said. "And it's short." I touched the ends of my black hair.

She shrugged, then pointed to the token Black fairy. "I want to be this one, but I don't have a yellow dress. I've never seen a real fairy before. Have you?" she asked.

"No. I thought fairies were make-believe," I said, then cringed. Maybe I shouldn't have said that. I hope I hadn't crushed the belief system of a child living in a shelter. I was so not used to talking to little kids.

She shook her head. "Mama says fairies are pretend, but she's wrong." She leaned in close. "You have to be careful. Fairies don't like people. Unless people bring them candy. Then they let you see them."

I smiled. I liked this kid's imagination. "I'll make sure to keep candy in my pocket then. I have to go inside to speak to someone, but if I see you again, maybe you can tell me where to look for these fairies?"

The girl nodded. She had kind of serious eyes, but she smiled.

"I'm looking for someone named Muniba. Do you know where I'll find her?"

The girl got off her tricycle. "She's in here." She held out her hand for me to hold and guided me to the door. "Muniba doesn't believe in fairies, either," she said. "She gives me cookies. Daniel's are better, though."

The shelter wasn't what I expected inside. From the outside it looked like a simple, kind of industrial building, but inside it was bright, sunny, and colorful. The walls were each painted a different pastel color, the reception desk near the door was bright green, and a big living room–type space just past it had purple sofas and a red coffee table. There were people everywhere. A bunch of women on the sofas talking, some kids sitting on the floor around the coffee table, and three people talking at the reception desk, plus people in the hallway behind the sitting area. It looked like comfortable chaos here—not the depressing environment I expected in a shelter.

The little girl pointed me to the reception desk. "Ask there," she said, before running off to the other children at the coffee table.

I asked, but apparently Muniba wasn't one of the people at the desk. A woman led me to a room nearby and told me to wait.

I sat on a blue plastic chair in front of the messy desk in the tiny office overflowing with bookshelves and boxes. This room had white walls and looked like it had been forgotten when the rest of the place was decorated.

About three minutes later, a South Asian woman in her thirties and a tall Black man around the same age wearing a chef's jacket walked in.

Without even a greeting, the woman eyed me suspiciously. "How old are you? I thought they were sending over a grade twelve."

"I *am* in grade twelve. I'm seventeen."

She shook her head as she sat behind the desk. "Impressive. You're going to love those forever-youth genes when you're older. I'm Muniba, the executive director of New Beginnings, and this is Andre, the kitchen manager and head chef."

A family shelter needed a head chef? Andre perched on Muniba's desk, which made Muniba frown with annoyance as she shifted some files to give him more room. Andre had a short beard and longish dreadlocks pulled back, and one of those faces that looked like it smiled more than anything else.

"Do you have any experience working in a kitchen?" he asked.

"Not really. I sometimes help my mom make dinner."

"Okay, what about baking experience?"

I shook my head. "My sister got into cupcakes back when that *Cupcake Wars* show came on Netflix. I helped her a few times. I thought this job was more of a coordinating a bake-sale role than an actual baking thing?"

Muniba snorted. "It's both. Your teacher told me that you had baking experience."

I shrugged. I didn't put it past Mrs. Singh to embellish my abilities.

"Andre doesn't have the time to babysit teenagers. He's also in charge of our sister facility—a drop-in center downtown. You don't bake *at all*?"

I shook my head again. Ugh. Figured that this *not that much cooking* job was turning out to be a *very much about cooking* job after all. Was it too late to find another way to get my volunteer hours?

"It's fine," Andre said. "Daniel can teach her. Lord knows that kid knows everything and more about baking. You and Daniel will be pretty much running the bake-sale project. Deciding what to make and baking every Thursday evening. If you don't finish on Thursday, you come Friday, too. We won't need you for the selling day on Saturdays. Me and Muniba got that, but you're welcome to join us if you want to.

As long as you're not a complete kitchen disaster, you'll be fine with Daniel running the show. Seriously, never seen a teenager that gifted with pastry before." Andre chuckled. "Ice-cold hands. Probably from all the hockey."

I had no idea what cold hands had to do with baking, but I kept my mouth shut. I was pretty sure, based on her expression, that Muniba had no confidence in me, but Andre seemed easy to please. I couldn't say I loved the idea of working with a hockey player, though. In my experience, they were dude-bros dripping with toxic masculinity. But then again, the guy did bake—hardly a toxically masculine hobby.

We went over some details—with the number of hours they needed me each week, I'd finish my community service hours before the semester was done. But I told them if it worked out, I'd stay the whole semester anyway. I still needed the reference, after all.

"We'll check out your baking skills later," Andre continued with a mischievous smile. "But first, tell me this, Samaya: Can you count?"

I blinked. "I'm literally the top math student in my grade."

He lifted himself from Muniba's desk. "Excellent. We just got a massive donation from a restaurant downtown that had to close suddenly. It all needs to be inventoried. Leave your backpack here. Let's get you practicing those math skills." He grinned wide. So far, I liked him better than Muniba. Muniba seemed like a grump, while Andre's cheerfulness was contagious.

I followed him out of her office.

We walked past the front desk and through the sitting area. I noticed the children, including the small girl I'd been chatting with, weren't there anymore, but the women on the couch were. They smiled warmly as I walked past.

"All the stuff is just over here," Andre said as we headed down an empty hallway. We passed a room that looked like a day care that was filled with all the kids I'd seen earlier. Eventually we got to a small room and stepped inside.

"Welcome to the pantry," Andre said. Shelves lined three of its walls, and a row of glass-front fridges stood along the fourth wall. The shelves were stacked with cooking ingredients. Flour, bags of sugar, the biggest jar of cinnamon I'd ever seen, that sort of stuff. The fridges looked full, too, but I couldn't see what was in them from where I stood.

"The kitchen is there," Andre said, pointing to a swinging door on the facing wall between two columns of shelves. "When the donation from the restaurant came in, the items were all stacked before anyone inventoried them." He pointed to the three shelves that lined the wall with the door. "We need everything on these shelves, and in the first fridge, counted and recorded, then Daniel can decide what to make with all this stuff tomorrow."

He handed me a clipboard with a blank piece of paper on it. "List everything here. How many cartons of eggs, how many bags of flour, chocolate chips, you know. Also mark the best-before dates so we know when we need to use it by. When Daniel's done in the kitchen, he'll join you. Shouldn't take you more than an hour. You can leave when you're done and come back tomorrow afternoon to bake."

I took the pencil off the top of the clipboard. "Got it."

Andre shrugged. "Okay. I'll leave you to it. I'll be back to check on you in a bit."

I slipped my earbuds in, put on my favorite playlist, and drew a chart on the blank paper, using the side of a box as a ruler. Then I started counting.

I wasn't sure about the baking part of this job, but this was perfect.

I loved counting. Dad said once when I was a kid, he came to check on me well past midnight and found me still counting sheep—I was well into the thousands by then. Yeah, lately it had all been about complex math, theoretical equations, and of course, memorizing pi, but simple numbers—*counting*—were my first love. Honestly, I should have stuck with numbers instead of bothering with boys.

Three five-pound bags of all-purpose flour. Five ten-pound bags. Total of sixty-five pounds of flour. Twelve bags of white chocolate chips. Eighteen bags of semisweet chips. I counted to the beat of the indie music playing in my earbuds, smiling as the neat rows on my chart filled up.

Three bags . . . of . . . what were those? Unmarked plastic zipper bags . . . I picked up one of the bags. A powdery white substance was inside.

Of course, I didn't think there was anything shady about an unmarked bag of a white powder—this was a bakery. It was probably a type of flour or baking powder or something like that. Or maybe it was rat poison.

It wasn't cocaine. Or ricin. I was being ridiculous.

I gingerly put the bag away. I didn't know what it was, and I'd taken enough chemistry to know that something that looks inert might not be. I'd ask Andre about it when he came in. But it was bugging me. My list was so tidy, and I didn't have a place to put things I couldn't identify. I'd already written the number three in the column. Maybe I could leave it blank? I tried to erase the three, but the eraser at the top of the pencil Andre gave me was completely worn down. I picked up the bag again. Was there a way to search this on my phone? Google search for "white powder" or something?

I carefully opened the bag and held my phone up above it, ready to take a picture of the mysterious white substance, when something solid, like a wall, hit me in the back. The impact made one hand launch my phone in the air, and the other launch the bag into my face. I was engulfed in a thick white cloud of . . . sugar.

At least now I knew what it was—the powdery icing sugar used on doughnuts. I yanked out my wireless headphones.

"Oh my god, I'm so sorry," said a deep voice.

I turned and saw a big stack of towering, teetering white bakery boxes and someone's arms trying to steady them so they wouldn't fall. The boxes were all labeled on their sides: PIE.

I'd just been hit by a wall of pies.

The tower moved as the person—a guy—holding the boxes turned to put them on an empty shelf near the floor. I still couldn't really see his face, but he was big—not exceptionally tall, but with broad shoulders and *built*.

"That was my fault—I should have knocked," he said, his deep voice sending a shiver down my spine. That was a nice voice.

I looked down at myself. My black Fibonacci T-shirt was covered with powdered sugar. And I was pretty sure that my face was even worse.

I started brushing the sugar off my shirt, when the guy stood and handed me my phone. I took it, relieved to see that the screen hadn't broken in the fall—the lock screen picture looked flawless. I looked up at the guy to thank him and . . . I nearly fell into the spilled sugar around me.

It was LostAxis.

The warm brown skin. The dimples. The dark hair. This was the guy from the picture Aimee had photo manipulated. My gaming buddy. My friend.

I looked at my phone, and the fake picture with him with his arm around me was still on the screen.

Shit.

6

This Pie-Guy Looks Familiar

S everal thoughts went through my head quickly when I realized
I was standing in front of LostAxis. Well, more specifically, *four*
thoughts.

One—three seconds earlier, LostAxis had been holding my
phone, which had a picture of the two of us standing with our arms
around each other on it on the lock screen. Two—I *had* never sent him
a picture of me, so he likely didn't realize I was GreenEggsAndSam,
his gaming friend. I was just the random stalker who kept a picture
of him on her phone. Three—LostAxis was even better looking in
person than in his picture. His hair was ink black and shiny; his eyes
were wide set and large. His skin was a perfect warm, tawny brown,
and he wore a pristine Toronto Raptors shirt with jeans and sneakers.
But his cheekbones . . . those were what stole my focus. They were
utter perfection. Sharp, defined, and *stunning*. His lips were full,
wide, and . . . laughing. Which brought me to my fourth and final
thought—it was possible he hadn't looked at the picture when he had
my phone, because he was currently laughing at me. If he'd thought
I was some sort of stalker who copied herself onto a picture of him,
I would think he'd look horrified, not amused.

Andre came through the swinging door from the kitchen then, holding a green binder. He stopped short when he saw me. "Shoot, Samaya, you okay?" he asked, handing me the dish towel that was draped over his shoulder. He turned to LostAxis. "Daniel, I see you met Samaya."

So LostAxis was *Daniel*. The guy I was supposed to be working with all semester. Ugh.

"I don't know what just happened," Daniel said. "I came in from the kitchen, and suddenly there was a cloud of sugar. And under it was *her*."

I looked at him. There was no way he'd seen the picture on my phone. Of course he wouldn't have looked—that would have been super rude. And he only had the phone in his hand for maybe a second. I wiped my face with my arm and checked my phone. The screen had turned off. I slipped the phone in my pocket.

I didn't even know for sure that this was LostAxis. It was probably too big a coincidence. Yeah, LostAxis told me he lived in Canada, but this was literally the second largest country in the world. I needed to ask this guy if he frequented *Dragon Arena* message boards.

Andre raised one brow at me. "Bit of an incident with the powdered sugar?"

"You could say that."

LostAxis rubbed his chin, looking at me with a smirk on his face. Why was he looking at me like that? It was . . . sexy.

I suddenly remembered my black eyeliner—had it smudged again? With the white sugar on my face, did I now look like one of those sad white-faced clown figurines my grandmother had in her dining room? I wiped my face with the dry dish towel. My face felt hot. I was probably as red as a tomato, too. Or a raspberry. I was a big old half-rotted raspberry with smudged eyeliner. And this unsettlingly attractive guy who I'd been slaying orcs with all summer was laughing at me. I looked down and pretended to brush more sugar from my jeans.

"Do you need clean clothes, Samaya?" Andre asked. "We have a whole donation bin."

I found my voice. "No, it's fine. I'm fine. Just fine."

"All right then," Andre said. He handed me the slim green binder. "Here are the recipes for the bake sales. The ones that sell well are marked. After you've taken stock of everything, go through the binder to figure out what we could make with this stuff."

He headed out of the small room, calling out behind him without turning around. "I'll leave the kitchen door open this time, so no one sneaks up on you again. Let's try to prevent y'all wearing the ingredients before we can bake with them."

I rubbed at my face again. "Not the way I expected to meet you. But thanks for helping me inventory."

LostAxis grinned, then turned toward the shelves. "The restaurant donation was huge. Where are you with the counting?"

I nodded. "I've finished the first shelf."

"You want me to count, or write?"

I handed him the clipboard and pen. "I'll count, you record what I say, okay?"

My brain wasn't working right. This was *LostAxis*. Right here in front of me. I should be telling him who I was . . . but I couldn't. He may not have looked at the picture when he picked up my phone, but if I told him that I was his gaming friend, I would have to also tell him that my friend had manipulated a picture to make it look like him and I were dating. And that my whole school had seen the picture. I bit my lip. I could *not* admit that.

He took the clipboard. "Got it."

I turned back to the shelf. "Five bags of powdered sugar?"

He snorted, then looked at the now half-empty bag I'd dropped on the table. "Minus the one you're wearing."

I took a deep breath. This was mortifying. The guy in the picture was real, and he lived here in Scarborough, and he was going to discover what a loser I was. "Four and a half," I said.

He seemed to pick up from the tone of my voice that I wasn't looking for fun banter here. I kept counting—and thinking. It was clear that I couldn't keep working here—I needed to spend another hour pretending I didn't know that he was LostAxis, the best Dark Mage I'd ever seen, then never come back to the shelter or speak about this to him again.

"Four bags of raisins." I made a face. "Yuck." I hated raisins.

"What did raisins ever do to you?" Daniel asked.

I ignored him. "Eight tubs of . . ." I lifted the big white plastic pail, not sure what it was. I wrinkled my nose after reading. "Beef suet? What the hell is that?"

"Beef fat," he said.

"I thought these were baking supplies. Why is there cow?"

"Animal products are used in baking a lot. You do know that milk and butter are also from cows, right? Did you know it takes twenty-one pounds of milk to make one pound of butter? Good thing cows produce so much milk. Like seventy pounds a day."

If I'd had any doubt this cheekbone-forward boy behind me was the same person who I'd bonded with doing dragon-egg quests with all summer, that doubt flew out the window with that statement. Animal facts. This was totally LostAxis. I ignored my racing heart.

"What, are you, like, a cow expert or something?" I asked.

"I went to my ex-girlfriend's uncle's dairy farm once, and you wouldn't believe the output on those things. Hey, did you know that *heifer* refers to female cows that have not had a calf? So you can't milk a heifer."

LostAxis had a really nice-sounding voice. It made me wish I'd asked for his phone number weeks ago so we could have actually *talked* while playing. His voice was deep, kind of smooth, and had an undercurrent of mischief. I shivered, imagining that low voice asking me to heal him, or warning me about centaurs ahead, or telling me about the .22 caliber punch of a mantis shrimp.

Sigh. I should say something. He was my friend—he might not mind about the whole picture and Earl's Whispers situation. I decided to tell him after we were done inventorying. I inspected the jars on the shelf next to the beef fat. "Eight jars of maraschino cherries. This is such a weird assortment of stuff."

He nodded. "A trendy restaurant that had a pastry kitchen downtown closed and donated all this to the shelter. The shelter gets donations from bakeries and restaurants all the time, but not usually so much at once. They also donated a whole bunch of pies they had in their freezer. I was bringing in the last of them when we met. We're not going to sell them at the market, because we didn't actually make them. There's extra—if you want to take one home, you can."

"You should carry fewer pies at a time so you can actually see where you're going when you walk into a room." I sounded snarky. I didn't really mean to, but I was embarrassed and irritated and couldn't hide it.

He was silent a moment.

Ugh. This was so awkward. I should definitely tell him we were friends. We could laugh about meeting this way and go back to slaying dragons tomorrow.

This whole situation—this whole week—was doing a number on my nerves.

"Well, you shouldn't stand with your back to doorways and your face in a bag of powdered sugar." He was mimicking the annoyance in my voice, and yet somehow, he still sounded playful.

I turned to look at him. I absolutely had to see the expression that went with that tone of voice.

Daniel had kind of a smirking smile on his face while he was writing on the clipboard. And when he saw me looking at him, he grinned. A wide grin that somehow made his cheekbones even sharper.

I couldn't help it. I returned his smile. "Maybe I *wanted* to cover myself in sugar to make a memorable first impression."

He chuckled. "I love sugar, so you succeeded there. You exceeded my wildest fantasies." He said *fantasies* low and sultry. Flirty.

I quickly turned away from him again. "Dried cranberries. One-point-eight-kilo bags, two bags."

"Got it."

I kept counting, but my mind started to wander. Was I absolutely sure this was LostAxis? Because if I said something and it *wasn't* him, it would be even more embarrassing. I needed to work with this guy, Daniel, all semester. All I had to go on was one picture. Was it possible that there was more than one burly, sharp-cheekboned, hot Asian guy in Canada?

What was I saying? Of *course* it was possible. There were probably hundreds in Toronto alone. This was the most diverse city in the world. It was fine. This guy wasn't LostAxis—just someone who looked a lot like him. Maybe a relative.

"That's mixed peel," he said, pointing to the last stack of containers on the shelf.

"Huh?"

"You looked confused. It's not labeled, but it's mixed peel."

I nodded and counted the containers of whatever mixed peel was. "There's eight." I moved to the next shelf. Only one shelf left.

"What's this?" I said, holding out a block of . . . something.

"That's lard."

I wrinkled my nose. "Ew. Now pig fat. There's"—I did a quick count—"six of these blocks." Nose still wrinkled, I put the block of lard back on the shelf.

"You vegan or something?" Daniel asked.

"What? Oh, no. I mean, I don't eat lard. I'm Muslim. But I eat beef and chicken."

"Just not in your baked goods."

"Preferably." I turned back to the shelf. "Thank goodness I didn't get a face full of this stuff." I made a disgusted face.

"Yeah. I like lard, but I wouldn't want to fall into a vat of it or any-thing. Powdered sugar, maybe. When I used to work in my aunt's bak-ery, I used to steal spoonfuls of the stuff when I was making doughnuts."

I saw a possible opening to find out if this *was* LostAxis. I moved some cans of sweetened condensed milk to the front of the shelf. "I've never had the time for a part-time job," I said. "I do a lot of extracur-riculars. Plus, my hobbies. Do you have hobbies?"

He looked at me, eyebrow raised. "Are you, like, interviewing me or something?"

"Well, if we're going to be working together, we should get to know each other, shouldn't we?"

He chuckled. "Fine. Let's cover all the bases, though. My full name is Daniel Alexander Ramos. I'm seventeen and in grade twelve at St. Francis Secondary. I'm an only child, and my hobbies include baking and hockey. Mostly hockey."

Right. Andre had mentioned Daniel was a hockey player. But also, if this guy was into hockey, then maybe he wasn't LostAxis? There's no way LostAxis played hockey. He was the furthest thing from a jock. And, also? He had to look up that hockey thing in the game—the hat trick. "You play on a team?"

"I know, it's shocking. I'm the only Filipino player my team has ever had. Scarborough Killer Geese. It's a rec league. And when I'm not playing hockey," he continued, clearly unaware about the internal investigation going through my head, "I'm usually gaming online. Oh good, we're almost done. We still need to decide what we'll bake for the weekend."

Gaming. Maybe this *was* him? No. Lots of guys gamed. This wasn't the coincidence of a century—this was just a guy who looked a lot like a picture my friend sent me.

We went back to counting. He'd finished the page on the clipboard, so I used a box again as a ruler to make lines on the next blank sheet.

"Why are you doing it like that?"

"Like what?" I faced him again.

He pointed to the shelf. "Like that. You're not just counting; you're tidying and sorting."

I frowned. "I don't do anything halfway. I don't know if I even know how to do that."

He smiled, shaking his head. "Man, my mom would *love* you. You ever rent yourself out to be a parent-approved date for holidays?"

"Like a rent-a-girlfriend situation?"

He nodded.

"You're a weird guy."

He laughed, then picked up the clipboard again. "Nah, it's a good business plan. My mom has *hated* every girl I've dated. Want me to count for a while? You record?"

"No thank you," I said. "I'd rather count. I like counting."

"Now you're the weirdo. Who likes counting?"

"Me. I've always liked numbers. It's how I got into math."

He frowned. "Seriously? Who is *into* math?"

"Me."

"Yeah, Mom would *adore* you. I'm terrified of math. Seriously—I almost hyperventilated when I saw my calculus textbook yesterday. There is no way I'm going to pass that class."

This was definitely not LostAxis. Thank goodness.

Daniel looked toward the stack of pies on the shelf. "Hey, are you going to take a bumbleberry pie home? You didn't say."

"Bumbleberry? Did you just make up a fruit?"

He looked at me like I'd said I'd never heard of Taylor Swift or something. "You've never heard of the best pie in existence? Bumbleberry is not *one* fruit. It's many. Apple, rhubarb, strawberry, raspberry, and blueberry. *Bumbleberry* means mixed berry. Now you have to take one."

"Hate to tell you, bud: rhubarb and apples aren't berries."

"Hate to tell *you*, but technically, raspberries and strawberries aren't, either."

I frowned. "Then what are they?"

He laughed. "I have no idea. But you should take a pie. The pies from this place have, like, no right to be this good."

By the time he convinced me to agree to take a pie, we had finished counting. It was past five by then, so after going through the recipe book quickly to decide what we'd make, we made plans to meet here again after school the next day to bake. We decided to walk to the corner to the bus stop together, but I needed to say goodbye to Muniba and get my things out of her office first. I told Muniba that so far everything was great, and confirmed I'd be back the next day. I liked the shelter, and now that I knew this wasn't LostAxis, there was no reason not to come back.

When I went outside, Daniel was crouched talking to the little girl I'd met earlier. He was holding a backpack and jacket.

"Did you like the cookies I left with your mother?" he asked her.

She nodded. "They were better than Andre's." She shook her head solemnly. "I don't like grapes in my cookies."

He chuckled. "They're raisins, Yasmin. Not grapes. Did you meet Samaya? She's also anti-raisin." He indicated to me.

The little girl nodded, then leaned in to whisper something into Daniel's ear. Whatever she said, she took a while to say it all. I didn't hear, but it made Daniel smile. Actually, it made him smile bigger, because I don't think he'd ever *not* been smiling since I'd met him.

He looked at the little girl's face and nodded. "Don't worry . . . I'll be careful. Thanks for the warning. Enjoy your raisin-less cookies." He stood and waved. "And go back inside, you know you're not supposed to be out here alone so late."

She nodded solemnly and started walking toward the door.

As we walked out the gate, I couldn't help but ask: "What did she warn you about?"

Still smiling, he kept his eyes in front of him. "I don't know if I should tell you. She told me to keep it a secret."

I laughed. Daniel was really growing on me. I liked how earnest he was, unlike the other guys my age I knew. Devin and his friends were snarky and always trying to sound cool. I couldn't imagine any of them leaning down to hear a little girl's issues with raisins. Working with Daniel was going to be fun. I was so glad something was working out for me this week.

"Well," I said, smiling, "it will be hard to work together if we keep secrets."

Daniel looked at me impishly. He leaned close. "Yasmin said she thought you looked like a fairy when she first saw you. But then you said you didn't believe in fairies. So she looked at some books in the shelter library and decided that you are probably a vampire because you're wearing black and have black all over your eyes. She told me to be careful that you don't bite my neck. And don't worry, I resisted the urge to tell her that I happened to like my neck bitten."

I blinked a few times, then snort laughed. "That kid is something else."

He nodded. "She is. There's a decent number of kids here right now, but Yasmin's the youngest school-aged one. And, in my opinion, the best."

"Is there a school in the shelter?"

"Nah, they all walk to a nearby school. There's an on-site preschool, though. And after-school programs."

That was interesting. No one had told me why any of the specific people I'd met were staying in the shelter. I hoped Yasmin hadn't suffered too much before getting there. We were at the bus stop by then. Daniel was going in the opposite direction and pressed the button to cross the street.

"Have a good night," I said, walking toward the bench at the bus stop. "It was nice meeting you."

"You too!" Daniel unrolled the navy jacket he was holding and started putting it on. With horror, I realized I'd seen it before. There was a logo of a duck in the corner. Only I now realized it was a goose, not a duck. As in, the Scarborough Killer Geese, Daniel's hockey team.

"That jacket," I said, voice cracking.

"It's great, right? I love our team merch. Only players get this jacket." The light changed, so he started walking. "See ya, Samaya!" He waved.

It all became clear as Daniel crossed the street.

Daniel played hockey. He hated math. LostAxis didn't know anything about hockey. He was great at math. Daniel was *not* LostAxis.

But also, Daniel *was* most definitely the boy in the picture. His face matched the one in the photo, but the pic wasn't a close-up. Many guys' faces could probably seem to match it. But having the same face and the same (rare) jacket as the guy in the photo? That was too much of a coincidence.

Which meant . . . LostAxis had sent me a fake picture. I had been *catfished*.

And . . . also? I was now *working* with the guy my whole school thought I was dating.

I fell onto the bench at the bus stop and put my face in my hands.

7

Pi or Pie to the Rescue

The moment I was on the bus, I texted Cass and Aimee, asking if they could meet me for an emergency meeting at the playground in my neighborhood in fifteen minutes. I added that one of them needed to bring spoons. Since it was past six, I also texted Mom to tell her I wouldn't be home for dinner.

Cass and Aimee beat me to the park and were sitting in our favorite spot at the top of the slide when I got there. I climbed up the ladder with my pie in one hand. It was a cooler September day, and the clouds looked a little ominous, so there were no kids in the park. Good. I'd deal with the rain if it came.

"So, you saw it, then?" Cass asked as I plopped myself on the metal platform next to them and unboxed the pie. It was stained red from the hole in the middle.

I frowned. "Saw what?"

Aimee blinked. "You haven't seen it? Why do you have cherry pie?"

"It's bumbleberry." I placed it on the floor between us. "Dig in, folks. I have a major crisis we need to deal with."

Cass raised one brow, then handed out spoons. Their hoodie today was a rich burgundy color. And as usual, Aimee was fully decked out with elaborate makeup, including black lipstick, a short pink-and-black plaid skirt with black fishnets and thigh-high socks, and a snug black crop top. If that little girl Yasmin thought I was a vampire or a fairy, she should meet Aimee.

I plunged my spoon into the middle of the pie, exposing the deep, glistening red filling. "I didn't think the bumbleberry would be so red. Did you know bumbleberry means mixed berry? Even though some of the fruits in it aren't even berries at all."

Aimee followed my lead and scooped some pie for herself. "What's going on, Samaya?"

I took a breath. This was complicated. "Okay, so you know how my shelter volunteer job thing is, like, a baking thing, right?"

Cass nodded, chewing. "I am completely in favor of you bringing us a pie every time you work there."

I shook my head. "Yeah, well, I'm not sure I'll be going back."

I explained in great detail how I'd come to discover that the photo LostAxis had sent me was a fake—that it was a picture of Daniel, my new volunteer coworker.

Aimee shook her head. "*Shut. Up.* Seriously?"

Cass's eyes were even wider than Aimee's. "Are you sure? That can't be possible."

I opened the picture on my phone and zoomed in on his jacket. "This logo is for the Scarborough Killer Geese hockey team. A team Daniel plays on."

"Holy shit," Cass said. "But are you absolutely sure it was him?"

I nodded, zooming in on the face. "This was his face. But weirdly, he looked . . . hotter."

Cass snorted.

I threw my hands up in frustration. "Look, I didn't expect it. He was, like, bigger in person, too. Broader."

"A hockey player," Cass said.

I winced. "Yes."

Cass frowned. "So what's wrong with that? Hockey players are hot."

I raised a brow at Cass. "Um . . . they're jocks? I thought you hated jocks." Cass had often said that the only good thing about Earl Jones was that since the school was academically focused with no decent sports teams, there were few jocks there.

Cass shrugged. "They're not all bad. Anyway, I don't think it's LostAxis. It's too big a coincidence."

"It's him. That's his team logo, and he said he's the only Filipino player they've had."

"We don't know that the guy in the pic is Filipino," Aimee said.

I nodded. "True, but I'd put money on it being him. Or a twin brother, which he doesn't have because he told me he's an only child."

"Okay, then how do you know that this Daniel guy isn't LostAxis? Maybe Daniel actually is the guy you've been gaming with."

"LostAxis told me he hates sports and took the Math Olympics test. Daniel is obsessed with hockey and is worried about failing calculus."

Cass gave me a knowing look. "Can't say I'm surprised LostAxis sent you a fake picture. I warned you, didn't I? You were catfished."

I exhaled. Yeah, Cass did warn me.

"Kill me now," I said, taking a large spoonful of pie. Thank goodness for pie, at least. Ironic, though. Pi had been a big comfort for me for years. Good to know pie worked, too.

"Death by pie seems a good way to go," Cass says.

"Agreed." I put another spoonful in my mouth.

"This is unreal," Aimee said, taking my phone to look at the picture. "What are the chances? Well, I suppose at least it's a good thing you get to work with the hot guy, not the lying, probably-a-basement-dwelling, neck-beard, catfishing guy."

"Yeah, but did you forget about the Earl's Whispers post? The whole school thinks I'm *dating* the guy in this picture. The picture that is actually of the shelter guy, Daniel, not LostAxis, whoever that really is."

Aimee shrugged. "Daniel probably won't see it. St. Francis is on the other side of Scarborough—I doubt he follows an Earl's gossip account. And if he does find out, just tell him that you had no idea the picture was of him."

"Yeah, and embarrass myself even more to the cool and very hot guy." I liked Daniel so far, but I didn't really know him well enough to trust him yet. What if he told Muniba and Andre about the photo manipulation and me pretending he was my boyfriend? Would they think less of me for lying? Maybe I'd lose this volunteer job. And I *needed* a reference from them.

"Are you going to confront LostAxis about him sending you a fake pic?" Cass asked.

That was a good point. I *should* say something to LostAxis about the fact that he sent me a fake picture. Confronting Devin the other day had made me feel so much better . . . Maybe telling off LostAxis for getting me in this mess in the first place would be cathartic, too.

But . . . what LostAxis had done to me wasn't nearly as bad as what Devin had done. Devin broke my heart and ruined my summer. All LostAxis did was lie to me about what he *looked* like. Maybe he was self-conscious about his looks, which was fine. Not everyone gets to look like Daniel. I was the one who had Aimee make the picture and effectively tell the whole school I was dating him, so what right did I have to tell him off?

I needed to deal with the fact that I was now working with the guy in the picture. And I needed to deal with everyone at school thinking I was hung up on Devin. "I should just block LostAxis," I said. "If he was dishonest about this, what else could he have lied about? Was he seventeen at all? Is he even in Canada?"

"I mean, you lied, too, though," Cass said very gently. "You basically told the whole school you were dating the guy in the picture, and you're not."

"I know." I'd created this mess. I took another spoonful of pie. Bumbleberry was now my favorite.

"Samaya, you really should at least tell Daniel about the picture," Cass said. "That's his face—he deserves to know you're using it."

I sighed. Cass was right, as usual. I would be mortified, but I had to tell him. "Ugh. Could this get worse?"

"Um . . ." Cass looked nervously at Aimee.

"What?" I asked. My friends were hiding something. "Crap. Why did you ask me if I'd *seen it* when I got here? Is there another Whispers post about me?"

"Well," Aimee said sheepishly. "Not really *directly* about you . . ."

I opened the Earl's Whispers account. After scrolling past the gossip about some grade ten who'd been caught cheating at e-sports, and some speculation that Genevieve Larocque in grade eleven was actually a thirty-year-old undercover reporter (*what?*), I found the post that my friends were talking about. It was a picture of a guy and a girl walking on the path near the bluffs. His hand was in her back pocket, and hers was in his pocket. I'd recognize those butts anywhere.

I winced at the picture. "Devin just went all caveman on me today about the picture of me and Daniel, and now this? Also, how is Hana's butt so . . . *perfect?*"

> Caption: Earl's newest it couple have confirmed that they will be attending the Nerd Prom together in November. To be honest it's shocking that Devin Kapadia would take anyone other than Samaya Janmohammad, even after their much-publicized split in June. Devin and Samaya will likely be awarded the top academic awards for their grade, and most assumed they would still go together—even just as friends. Clearly taking Hana to the Nerd Prom is Devin's retaliation for Samaya being seen with that mysterious

new gamer-boy. And what a retaliation it is! As of now, we deem Devin Kapadia the front-runner to win this breakup. All eyes are on Samaya to see if she'll up the ante with her new boy and inch ahead of Devin.

The Nerd Prom was what everyone called the school's academic banquet / fall formal, and it's where the academic awards from the previous year were awarded. Everyone on the honor roll got a free ticket, but anyone else could buy one. Devin and I had gone together for the last two years.

"They've turned our breakup into a sporting event," I said. "Someone needs to shut this account down."

"Nope!" Aimee said. "Look at the post after it."

I did—it was a close-up of Aimee's artfully applied eye makeup, reposted from her own account, along with a caption that proclaimed her to be the best makeup artist at Earl's.

Cass looked at me. "I don't think getting rid of the account will stop people gossiping anyway."

I cringed. Cass was probably right. True, Whispers was talking about me and Devin, but so was the rest of the school, too.

I thought for a second. "Do you think LostAxis is actually someone from Scarborough? Where did he get Daniel's picture?"

Aimee shook her head. "I doubt it. The picture was probably online somewhere, and LostAxis used it because Daniel was doing that Dark Mage pose in it."

"It's a hockey pose, too," Cass said. "That's how players hold their sticks sometimes."

"Then that makes sense. Daniel is obsessed with hockey. Hey, either of you want to do something scandalous so the gossip train will leave me alone and pay attention to someone else?" I joked.

Aimee gave me an annoyed look. Cass took a large bite of pie. "I might be willing. For pie, that is."

I laughed and took another big bite.

When I got home that night, the first thing I did was open *Dragon Arena* to see if LostAxis was there, but when I searched his name, it said *player not online*. One of the things I loved about this game was it was a bit safer for racialized, female, and nonbinary gamers, mostly because there was no audio chat. Neckbeards couldn't spew racial and gendered slurs at other players, and you couldn't see the history or stats of a player unless they were online. And you could block players, which meant they couldn't contact you or even see your character in the game at all. It was like you wouldn't exist to them anymore.

I blocked LostAxis and logged out of the game.

8

The Gamer-Nerd of My Dreams

I came very close to saying screw it all and skipping school the next day. But of course, I couldn't. One, it was only the fourth day of school and I didn't want to face the Annoyed Asian Mother face already. My parents were mostly cool—especially compared to some of my other friends' parents. Mine were more the "disappointed look" kind of parents instead of the grounding / taking-phone-away kind. But also, two, if I didn't show up to school after that picture of Devin's and Hana's butts was posted, people would talk.

I did go later than usual, though, skipping the bus ride with Cass and Aimee. And at lunch, I went to find Miss Zhao about that game-dev club. Partially to avoid seeing anyone, but also because I really did want to start that club. After all the research I'd done, I was genuinely excited about it.

Miss Zhao was a new teacher at the school. She taught computer studies and programming, and after knowing her for about three seconds, I wished she'd been my teacher when I took those classes instead of old "obsessed with Steve Jobs" Mr. Patel. Miss Zhao was chatty, enthusiastic, and excited to work with me.

I told her everything I'd learned about the competition, and together we looked at their website on one of the computers in the tech lab. "I love this!" she said, reading over the page.

The competition was for teams of five to ten students of any grade, who would create a mobile game, essentially a phone app, from the ground up, including all the scripts, graphics, and coding. There was also a business element—the teams had to put together a marketing and project-managing plan. The judging would happen in May. It could be a puzzle game like *Candy Crush*, or a word game like *Words with Friends*, or really any type of game. Teams would be judged on originality as well as sales potential, so it was advised to make something with a completely original game play instead of something similar to other games out there.

"I'll absolutely be your staff adviser," Miss Zhao said. "I wish something like this existed when I was a kid. Then again, if they had this in my high school, there is no way the guys would let a girl join. So, what's the plan then? You have a team already?"

I frowned. "Not yet. My friend Cass for sure. I think they're the best programmer in the school. I could ask my friend Aimee to do the art."

"You'll need more than just the three of you. Who else do you think you can get to join—and how? You'll need more students who can code. And it looks like you'll need to make a business plan to show them when you ask them. Do you have a concept yet? What kind of game are you thinking?"

These were all things that I should have thought about before now. I sighed. Mom and Mrs. Singh said I needed leadership skills for my scholarship application. I had to do better than this. "Maybe an adventure RPG?"

"Love it. Get a team together, and I'll look up what my requirements as adviser are." She glanced at her phone. "I'm free Mondays after school. How does that sound? You should be able to put together a team by then."

I nodded, but I wasn't optimistic about finding people so quickly. I could count on Cass and Aimee, but beyond that? Maybe my newfound respect, thanks to my hot gamer boyfriend, would help me.

I had to rush to the shelter to get there on time after talking to Miss Zhao. I considered skipping—calling Muniba and telling her that I didn't think the role would work for me after all. But if I quit, Mrs. Singh would tell Mom, and neither would be thrilled. Also, I didn't want to ditch Daniel on our baking day. It was only our second day working together, and I *did* still kind of like the guy, even if I hadn't decided yet how to tell him about the Earl's Whispers post with a picture of him. And I didn't want to let down Andre and Muniba, and the whole shelter, either.

Andre was standing behind the front desk when I walked in, talking to a woman there. Just like yesterday, the shelter was busy.

He grinned. "Ah, Samaya! Glad to see you back. This is Faduma."

I smiled at the woman behind the counter. She was Black, with big, serious eyes, and a gray hijab.

"I hear you met my daughter yesterday," Faduma said.

"Oh, yes," I said. *This must be Yasmin's mother.*

"I'm sorry she told you she thought you were a vampire. My girl has a wild imagination." She looked apologetic.

"Oh, it's no problem. She's adorable!"

She smiled. "She is a handful. You are working with Daniel, right?"

"Yes. We're baking today."

"He's a special boy, too. We are all very attached to him here. You will be good to him when you work with him, won't you?"

"Of course," I said. The way she said it made me think she thought I would hurt Daniel. Weird. I turned to Andre. "Um, should I go to the kitchen?"

He nodded. "Daniel is helping in the day care right now, but he'll be there soon."

I nodded and headed to the shelter's kitchen, smiling awkwardly at the people I passed.

The kitchen was empty when I got there. This was my first time in it, though I'd seen it through the swinging door from the pantry the day before. It was a standard commercial kitchen—to me it looked like a bigger version of the one at the back of the ice cream shop where I'd worked for the summer. There were several high prep counters, a big stove, some ovens, and a bunch of metal shelves holding pots, pans, baking trays, and bowls. I sat on a stool at one of the high counters and opened my functions textbook.

I was halfway through the first section of my homework when my phone dinged. I checked the screen. It was Devin. Ugh. Why?

Devin: I wanted to talk to you after school—I couldn't find you.

Me: I was busy.

Devin: What whispers said isn't true.

Me: What are you talking about Devin?

Devin: I'm not only with Hana as retaliation for you posting that picture.

I exhaled. Was he trying to make me feel better? Because telling me that his relationship with my frenemy was actually genuine, and not just a ploy to retaliate, was not making me feel better.

Me: So?

Devin: So you don't have to post more pictures of you and that guy.

Me: Devin I told you. I didn't post that picture. And you don't get to tell me what to do, anyway.

Devin: I thought we were going to try to be friends.

Me: Friends don't tell each other what to do! And you keep going all jealous caveman on me, so clearly we can't be friends.

Devin: I'm not jealous.

I sighed. Maybe I should take the nuclear option and block him, like I'd blocked LostAxis.

Me: We need a break, Devin. Maybe one day we can be friends again, but not now.

Devin: What does a break mean? We're not going to talk anymore?

Me: Pretend you don't know me. Until you figure out how to be normal with me.

Again, he didn't text for a while. Had I pissed him off enough that he'd leave me alone? I didn't know how I felt about that.

I wanted him to leave me alone, but at the same time, it felt shitty to say it. We'd been together for so long—I couldn't imagine not having Devin in my life.

Devin: Okay.

That was it. No arguing, no promising he'd do better. None of it. I had kind of expected him to fight me on this, but maybe he was finally respecting me. I stared at my phone, blinking. And then, before I could second-guess myself, I blocked Devin from my phone.

"So, do you think bars and squares are cookies or cake?"

I turned quickly.

It was Daniel. And he was, of course, grinning. I carefully used a paper towel to dab at the stupid tear falling from my eye so it wouldn't mess up my makeup.

Daniel frowned. "You okay?"

"Yeah, just something in my eye."

"I thought you were as deeply moved by the square/cookie/cake controversy as me."

I stared at him. It was extra cruel that the guy who was kind-of sort-of causing my problems right now was super cheerful and kind of silly.

"Excuse me?" I asked.

Now, Daniel grinned again. I was starting to suspect grinning was his resting face. "Squares and bars are pretty much cookies, right? Dense and dry. Ha! Sounds like my math teacher. But also, squares are like cake. You have to cut them into pieces to eat them. And they can be tender and moist, too. Whoops. Sorry. I should have asked if you were averse to the word *moist* before saying it. Anyway, squares are like if cake and cookies had a love child."

"Do you often have deep thoughts about baked goods?" I asked as I closed my math textbook.

He shrugged, then pulled out the stool next to mine and sat. Up close, he smelled clean and sweet—like vanilla. "I try not to have too many deep thoughts at all. But yes, when I do have them, they are often about baked goods. Or about the NHL draft, but I don't think you care about that as much as I do, so I decided to go with baked goods."

"Perceptive. I can't understand how anyone would be *that* into hockey."

"Oooh, savage . . . the Count is nerd-shaming me."

"The Count?"

He nodded. "I thought of that nickname last night. Yasmin called you a vampire, and you said you love counting. So you're the Count. You know . . . from *Sesame Street*? One! *One surly math-nerd.* Mwa-ha-ha!" He did a terrible impression of the *Sesame Street* character.

I scowled. I wasn't *surly*. I was in a serious personal crisis and had every right to be in a bad mood. Besides. That *Sesame Street* Muppet was never surly, either. He was positively gleeful about counting. That's why he was my first crush. "It's not nice to call me surly."

He winked. "You're right. I'm sorry. My bad. You don't mind if I call you Count, though, do you? I should have asked your preferred name. Do you go by Samaya, or do you like Sam? I don't like Danny or Dan . . . so I know what it's like to have a name that's easy to shorten. I kinda wish my mom gave me a name that is what it is, you know? Like I have this teammate . . . Graham. You can't call him anything but Graham, no matter how hard you try. *Gra* just sounds weird, and I called him Ham once and got cross-checked at our next practice."

I snorted a laugh. He was so much more talkative than he was yesterday, like he was trying to cheer me up. Which was nice.

"You have brothers or sisters?" he asked.

"A sister. Tahira."

"That'd be hard to shorten, too. I'm sure you don't call her Tah. I guess Hira would work. But you . . . you could be Sam, Maya, Sammy, even May. But . . . I'm guessing you like Samaya, right? You seem a purist."

"Yeah. Some people call me Sam, but I prefer Samaya." LostAxis called me Sam . . . but then again, my character name in *Dragon Arena* was GreenEggsAndSam, so it made sense. It was Devin who gave me the idea for that username back when we first started playing. He had also called me Sam a few times, but when I told him I didn't really like it, he stopped. He'd once been a good boyfriend. Until he wasn't.

And now he was gone from my life. I told him we couldn't even be friends. Nausea built in my stomach. I hoped I didn't start crying again. It wasn't that I wanted Devin back, because I didn't. Devin had been a huge part of my life for so long, and it was hitting me for the first time that this was the end of an era for me.

"Aren't we supposed to be baking?" I asked. Maybe that would take my mind off . . . everything.

He stood and opened a drawer in the kitchen cabinet near the door. "Yup. I get to rock your world with lemon squares today." He handed me an apron from the drawer, then took one for himself. "Did I tell you yesterday where I got this recipe?"

"No."

"Remember I used to work in my aunt's bakery?" he asked, slipping the apron over his head. "That's where I learned to bake. This little white lady, a customer, used to come in a lot—her name was Rose. She liked my aunt's pandesal—those are these little Filipino sweet buns."

Daniel tied the apron strings behind his back. "Rose asked me one day if we had any lemon squares. I said no, but the next time she came in, she asked again. Finally, after I said no three times, she asked me if I even knew how to make lemon squares. I also said no, and the next day she brought in a recipe to give to my aunt. She said this was the best lemon squares recipe in the world. She used to make them to have with her tea but didn't have the strength to bake anymore. My aunt handed me the recipe and told me to make them for Rose because she was our best non-Filipino customer. If Rose wanted lemon squares, then we'd have lemon squares. And oh my god, they really *are* the best lemon squares in the world. They became a top seller. Do you like lemon squares?"

"I don't think I've ever had them."

"You'll love them. I promise, Rose's lemon squares will make it all better." He smiled at me. He really had no business looking so good in a plain white apron.

I frowned as I stood to put on my apron. "Make what better?"

"Whatever got caught in your eye earlier." He paused. "But even if there is nothing wrong, lemon squares won't hurt. Unless you're allergic to lemons. Or dairy, because yikes, there is a lot of butter in them. Like so. Much. Butter. How many pounds of butter did we count yesterday? There was about two dozen, right? Hey, do you think it's true that people use butter as tanning oil? Can you imagine the smell?" He shuddered. "Butter-roasted human."

I raised a brow. "What do your teammates think of you?"

He laughed as he headed to turn on the ovens. "They think I'm weird. But I think everyone is weird. Sometimes it just takes longer to find the weird deep inside some people." Daniel took a bowl into the pantry and returned with it filled with lemons. "Shall we square, Ms. Count?"

I nodded. This dude's . . . *weirdness* . . . made me forget about all the weirdness about this situation with him. "I don't know a thing about baking."

"That's okay. I do."

Together, we followed the steps of white-lady Rose's recipe. "The base is pretty much shortbread," Daniel said as he measured all the ingredients into a big bowl. We weren't alone in the kitchen anymore. Andre and two others were cooking on the other side of the room. It smelled strongly of beef stew or something. I hoped the lemon squares wouldn't smell like beef.

"The filling is really where it's at," Daniel continued, pressing the crumbly base into a large pan. "And it's covered with powdered sugar, a sensation you're familiar with. I guess that's something that makes bars more like cakes than cookies. Cookies don't have toppings, but bars usually do. Like date squares, and Nanaimo bars and . . ." He paused and looked at me, a rare serious expression on his face. "Am I taking this too far?"

I blinked.

He tilted his head. "It's hard to know what to talk to you about, so I figured bars and squares would work since we're making squares. You want me to ease up?"

"Why is it hard to know what to say to me?"

"Because you're, you know. *You.* Cool. Smart. I'm not used to having genius friends."

I shook my head. "I'm not a genius." And I wasn't really that cool, either. I was a gamer, and a math nerd. Those were hardly cool-people hobbies.

He shrugged. "Okay, but you are a little intimidating." He took the pans to the oven and put them in. "Okay, let's make the filling. Can you zest those lemons?"

I wasn't sure what that meant, so Daniel showed me how to use this big, long grater thing to get the top yellow layer off the lemons. The bright, fresh citrus scent exploded as a little pile of yellow flecks collected on the wooden cutting board.

He put the bag of lemons next to me so I could zest them all. "Best thing about baking is that it makes me think about baking, instead of all the things that are bothering me. Like, I told you yesterday how stressful my first calculus class was?" He took a citrus juicer and put it on the counter. "Anyway, I went home and made peanut butter cookies. Now that's a cookie with a smell that eases all worries. We should make those for the market. Not this week; there was no peanut butter in that donation. Unless"—he cringed—"I should have asked you . . . you aren't allergic to peanuts, are you?"

"No. Was calculus upsetting you that much?" Poor guy. I turned to math for comfort, and he needed comfort from math.

"Yeah . . . the teacher gave this review quiz to make sure we had the skills to do the class, and I failed miserably. I am not numerically minded. Unlike you, Ms. Count. That sounds weird. What's the Count's first name? I don't think it's actually *The*, is it?"

I looked up from my lemon zesting. After I was finished with a lemon, Daniel cut it in half and pressed it into the sharp conical top of the juicer, his impressive biceps flexing under his thin Toronto Maple Leafs T-shirt. I think I abstractly knew that hockey players were built, but seeing one squeeze lemons like this was . . . well, it was something. What would it be like to have arms like that around me?

"You don't know either?" he asked.

"Huh?" What was he even talking about?

"The Count. What's his first name? Does he even have one?"

I shook my head. "I have no idea. Why are you taking calculus if you're not good at math? It's the hardest of the grade-twelve math courses." It was my favorite for that reason, but yeah. It was tough for most people.

"My uncle insisted. He's an engineer, and he wants me to be an architect or an engineer. I mean, there's no way that's going to happen, but Mom said I should at least take calculus since we live with him."

He lived with his uncle? It sounded like there was a bit of a personal story there. I didn't want to pry into his family situation, though.

"What do you want to study after high school?"

"Pastry arts." He smiled. "That probably doesn't surprise you."

I laughed. "Not one bit."

Daniel grabbed another naked lemon to juice while I kept zesting.

"It was my ex texting me," I said suddenly. I didn't know why I said it. Daniel's talkativeness was contagious, or something. "That's who was pissing me off when you got here."

He raised one eyebrow as he squeezed the lemon. "Bad breakup?"

"You could say that. *Unexpected* breakup, at least for me."

"Ah. Sorry. When?"

"Right before the end of the school year last year. I was pretty upset all summer. And because of him, I lost out on a summer camp counselor job."

He tilted his head. The expression on his face was so . . . compassionate. Almost caring. Which was weird because the guy barely knew me. I found it a bit overwhelming, so I looked down at my lemon.

"Is that why you needed to work here?" he asked.

I nodded.

"This is an improvement over camp, I hope," he said. "You get lemon squares here. I take it he's still bugging you now?"

"Yeah." I exhaled. "It's not like I want him back or anything, but he's being a jealous troll. I blocked him so he can't text me anymore."

Daniel smiled as his eyes traveled over me from head to feet. "He regrets breaking up with you."

Was Daniel flirting? I shook my head. "Nah. He's dating my friend now. She's been wanting him for a year, at least. They're going to the fall formal together."

"Then he's got no right to be jealous. Who is he even jealous of?"

"He thinks I'm seeing someone." There was more to it. So much more. But now that I had the chance to tell him about his own involvement in my drama, it was hard to say anything. Being dumped and then catfished was mortifying. My shoulders slumped. "Devin and I were together for *two years*. I would never have imagined this is how it would end."

Daniel shook his head. "*Two years?* I don't know whether to be impressed or terrified of you."

I shrugged. "I just . . ." I didn't know why I was telling him all this, but I couldn't seem to stop. It was nice to talk to someone who didn't know Devin or didn't know me when I was with him. All my friends had known us both since grade nine. Everyone assumed we'd be together forever. Hell, even I'd assumed that, too. And everyone knew Devin was the cooler one. The popular one. I was just his nerdy girlfriend.

But Daniel didn't see me as the nerdy girlfriend. He saw me as smart. As terrifying, for some reason. Even if that wasn't actually who I was, that's who I was to Daniel. It was kind of like LostAxis—he wanted to play *Dragon Arena* with me not because I was Devin's girlfriend who'd come along when he'd started the guild with his friends, but because I was an excellent player on my own. I was myself when I played with LostAxis—not Devin's other half. And it kind of felt the same with Daniel.

"Don't get me wrong," I said. "I *am* over Devin. He's being such an asshole. I even told him off." I sighed. "The breakup was rough, though. The whole school thought I was pathetic."

"Hopefully, now they realize you're kind of adorable," he said.

Daniel was definitely flirting. I swallowed. "I don't think you'd think that if you knew me better. I'm kind of seen as only a high-achieving nerd at school. I basically have two friends right now." I'd had more, but those were Devin's friends.

"Yeah, I figured out that you're a high achiever. But why would what others think of you affect what *I* think of you?"

I stared at him. Daniel was . . . perceptive. And very smart. "Don't you care what people at your school think of you?"

He shrugged. "I don't really have a ton of friends there. I'm closer to my hockey team. My school is pretty chill, though."

"Well, at my school people are taking bets on whether me or Devin is winning our breakup. And spoiler alert, it's not me."

Daniel looked up from his lemons and gave me a sympathetic look. I thought he might even put his hand out to comfort me. "Why would people do that? Breakups are not a game."

"This gossip Instagram account at my school keeps talking about me and Devin. They posted a picture with his hand on his new girlfriend's butt yesterday."

"Like on that historical Netflix show! Lady Whistledown!"

I raised a brow. "You watch *Bridgerton*?" I'd watched the series with Tahira when it first came out. I would not have thought a male hockey player would be into period romances. I handed Daniel the last lemon to juice and watched as he cut it in half and started juicing.

He nodded. "I watched it with my mom. She covered my eyes during the sex scenes. Hey, Samaya, you didn't tell me who your ex is jealous of anyway. *Are* you actually seeing someone?"

I chuckled. The irony was, Devin was jealous of *Daniel*. The very person who was asking who Devin was jealous of. When I didn't say anything, Daniel shrugged. "You don't have to tell me if you don't want to."

"Nah, it's fine. A gamer I played with online over the summer. LostAxis. We're not actually dating. But that gossip Insta account posted a picture of me with him."

"LostAxis? Your mystery dude has a secret spy-like code name?" He shook his head, impressed. "You know what? Nerds are so much cooler than civilians. So, someone posted a picture of you and this spy-guy on Lady Whistledown's Instagram, and your ex saw it and freaked out."

I nodded. If he looked up the account, he'd see the picture was of him.

"I say you post more pictures of the guy. Show the school that you're the one winning this breakup." He seemed so proud of himself for solving all my problems with that suggestion.

I had thought of that. It was the easiest answer—ask Daniel for a picture of the two of us together and post it. I could keep up the charade that I was dating LostAxis. I bit my lip. Would he let me do that? I'd have to explain everything to him. It was one thing to tell him about the picture, but completely another to insert him into my drama.

I looked at the now-empty bag of lemons. "What's next?"

He grinned. "Eggs. I'll get them."

I thought about it while we made the filling for the lemon squares. Maybe I *could* ask him to help me. Being catfished and randomly finding myself working with the catfishee (subject of the catfish?) wasn't a disaster. It could be an opportunity. If he helped me.

But I barely knew Daniel. Did I trust him enough for this? He could also ruin me. One DM to Earl's Whispers and the gossip would only get much worse.

Maybe I was looking at all this the wrong way. What if there was something in it for him, too?

"Um, actually, Daniel, you might be able to help me. Can you keep a secret?"

He grinned conspiratorially. "Absolutely. I'm excellent at secrets."

I took a breath. "Okay. So, this is going to sound super weird, but . . . the guy that everyone thinks I'm dating . . . it's you."

His eyes went wide. "What? We only met yesterday!"

I opened my phone and found the post on Earl's Whispers of Daniel and me together. I showed it to him.

"Shit. This *is* me! This is a picture of me!" He tapped the screen rapidly. "And you! It's a photo of us together!"

"Yes, that's why I am showing it to you."

"But how . . . why . . ." He pinched the screen with his fingers to zoom in. "This is behind the shelter. But I've never met you before."

I showed him the original picture LostAxis sent—before Aimee's manipulation. "A friend did it. She's awesome at photo manipulation."

He studied the picture. "I remember this day. It was when we built the playground, I think."

I looked at him, confused. "Last fall," he explained, "a whole bunch of kids from different schools and a bunch of the shelter volunteers all built that playground outside. It was funded by a bank. Were you there helping, too?"

Holy crap. "No. Kids from my school went to that, but not me." I bit my lip as a realization hit me. "Do you remember who took this picture?"

He shook his head. "I don't remember anyone taking my picture that day. But there were a lot of people here. At least sixty." He zoomed in on the manipulated picture. "It's a flawless manipulation. But I don't understand. Why did your gamer boyfriend send you a picture of *me*? And why did your friend add you into the picture?"

I shrugged. "It's a long story."

He blinked at me several times, then went to the pantry and returned with a block of baker's chocolate and some cocoa powder. "Okay. We'll make brownies while you explain."

I told him everything while we started on some triple chocolate fudge brownies. The story was completely unbelievable, but surprisingly, Daniel believed me. And to be honest, he didn't seem all too flattered that his picture had been used by a catfisher.

He shook his head. "I don't understand people. Why not send you his own picture? Or a celebrity's? And why lie to you? I feel violated. He stole my likeness."

I cringed. "I think he used this picture because you're standing like a Dark Mage."

He looked at me like tulips had just grown out of my head. "What?"

I pointed to the unmanipulated picture. "It's from the video game we play. You're standing like a Dark Mage holding his staff waiting for a battle to begin. LostAxis plays a Dark Mage in the game."

Daniel frowned. "That was one of the construction pieces. A pole from the slide railing. I was pretending it was a hockey stick. That's how I hold my stick when the clock's not running."

I nodded. "That's what my friend Cass said. Are you mad at me for doing this?"

He looked at me while stirring the melting chocolate in a glass bowl over a pot of simmering water. "No. Not really. You thought you were just posting a picture of you and your actual friend."

"It was actually my friend Aimee that sent in the picture, but yeah. I thought the picture was of LostAxis, not you. If I could go back, I wouldn't have told Aimee to do it." I sighed. "I was so frustrated then. Earl's Whispers had just posted a picture of me crying when I first found out about Devin and Hana. I really hated everyone talking about me all over again, and . . . I'm sorry."

"How many people do you think saw it?"

I shrugged. "A lot of people from my school. I'm not talking about thousands or anything. Couple hundred? Is it a problem if people see it? Technically, the post says I'm friends with this person, not dating him. And you and I *are* actually friends now."

"Are we?" He flashed an incandescent smile, then gave me a sultry expression that made it completely clear why any catfisher would use his picture. "I guess we are."

I laughed. "The account is @EarlsWhispers, if you want to check and see if you recognize any of the people that commented on the post."

He shook his head. "No, I can't. I don't do Instagram."

"You don't have an Instagram account? Do you have a phone? How old are you?"

"Seventeen going on seventy, or at least that's what the guys on my team say. And yes, I do have a smartphone. Social media isn't really my thing. And honestly, if you *had* actually asked me before using a picture of me as your fake boyfriend, I would have said yes. Show that school that Samaya the Count can get it! Hey, is that the favor you want? You want more pictures together?" He put down his spatula and picked up my phone, holding it in front of us like he was going to take a selfie.

I put my hand on his and lowered it, ignoring my stomach fluttering when I touched his skin for the first time.

"Actually, yes. More pictures would help. But I have an offer for you." I took a breath. "If I tutor you in calculus so you'll pass your class, will you pretend to be LostAxis, the guy I played online games with, in pictures and *in person*? Like, come with me to my school's fall formal in a month?"

Daniel blinked. "You want me to pretend to date you in exchange for math help?"

I nodded. Was I asking too much? All he knew about me was that I was a nerd who was dealing with gossip at school. Why would he do this for me?

"I'm an excellent tutor," I said. "I'm younger than my sister and I've helped her with every math class she's ever taken. And I've helped my friends . . . I was the top math student at my school last year."

He smiled. "So, you'd get your cred back at school, and piss off your ex? And I'd get a free calculus tutor, and I get to take you to a formal dance?"

I nodded again. "Yes. Exactly."

He grinned. "How can I say no? But hang on. Am I going to have to actually play this dragons and dungeons game?" Daniel asked.

"*Dragon Arena*. And no." I shook my head. "Don't worry about playing. You'll have to talk about it, but I'll teach you what you need to know."

There was no way I could turn a jock into a level-fifty-plus Dark Mage in a few weeks. Or a few months, for that matter.

I was asking a lot from him. He'd have to learn all about a game he didn't play, plus learn how to pass as a believable nerd, and pretend to be my boyfriend. All that just for some calculus help didn't seem worth it. But I didn't know what else I could offer him. I braced myself for disappointment. "So, seriously? You'll do it?"

He grinned, and I think it was his biggest grin yet. "Yeah, of course. Actually, there is almost nothing I would say no to if you could guarantee I'll pass calculus." He wagged his brows. "I'm all yours, Samaya. Turn me into the gamer-nerd of your dreams."

I grinned, too. I wanted to throw my arms around him and hug him, but I didn't. Honestly, though? This was going to be fun.

9

We're Not Going to Use the Word Rules, Okay?

While the brownies were in the oven, adding a rich chocolate scent to the citrus aroma (with a bit of beef stew) in the air, I ripped a page out of my notebook, took out a pencil, and sat at one of the high stools at a counter. If we were going to do this, we needed ground rules.

Daniel frowned as I wrote the title on the page. *Samaya and Daniel's Rules for Fake Dating.*

"Do we need *rules*? I hate that word," Daniel asked.

"You're a hockey player—you *must* be used to rules."

He put his hands up defensively. "I am, I am. That's why I hate them. It might be hard to make a relationship look real with rules. This is my 'worried about rules' face." He made a comical serious-confused expression. "Not very romantic."

I rolled my eyes and erased the title. I thought and then wrote a new one: *Guidelines, Parameters, and Framework for Fake Dating.*

Daniel laughed. "Better," he said.

"Parameter number one," I said, writing while I spoke. "Respect each other's boundaries." I looked up at him. "We are *pretend* dating only, and I am not looking to cross into *real* dating. I don't want you ever accusing me of leading you on, friend-zoning, or anything else out of the 'nice guys' handbook. I am telling you right now, I have sworn off actual dating for the foreseeable future. Don't fall for me. I won't date you."

He nodded. "I can handle that. We will resist each other's charms." He folded his hands on the counter, then made another of those sultry expressions. Ugh. He needed to stop that flirting or I'd be trampling all over my own no-falling-for-each-other parameter. I never would have thought I could have a crush on a hockey player, but here we were.

"I'm serious, Daniel!" I said. After *Parameter one*, I wrote *Fake dating only. No real romance.*

"*Parameter two,*" I continued, still writing. "*Results aren't guaranteed. Your grades are not my responsibility.*" I looked up at him. "I'm not doing your homework for you. I am an excellent tutor—but if you don't pass, it's on you, not me."

"And same goes here. I'll be the best fake-nerd-boyfriend you can imagine, but I can't guarantee that having a fake-nerd-boyfriend is going to miraculously fix all your problems."

"Okay, but I'm positive this will work," I said.

"I love your confidence." He gave me another glimpse of his smile, and I noticed for the first time that his left canine tooth was a bit crooked. Somehow it made his face even cuter—like he was more real instead of only perfect. "Can I make a parameter?" he asked.

"Of course." I wrote *Parameter three* on the sheet.

"Great." He exhaled, not looking at me. He bit his lip, looking unsure if he should say something. This was weird. Daniel not knowing what to say?

"So . . ." He hesitated. "If this were a real relationship, I would definitely want us to be honest and open with each other, but it's not. So my parameter is that we don't worry about that."

I frowned. "We aren't going to be honest?"

"No, no. We'll be honest, but not necessarily *open*. If I don't tell you something about me, or my family or anything, it's okay. Because we're not really dating."

I frowned. That was one hell of a parameter. What exactly was he hiding? We might not be dating, but we *were* friends. And friends were open with each other.

But were we really friends? We'd known each other for literally two days. We were working together—and maybe for Daniel, that was as far as he wanted this to go. He was putting a line in the sand here. We'd be casual friends, not close. And I needed to respect that.

"Okay. That's fair. I'll accept that." I had no choice. Daniel was literally my last chance to get some credibility back at school.

He handed me a big metal strainer-thing. "Sift the powdered sugar. It needs to be light as snow. Resist the urge to put it all over your face this time."

I rolled my eyes as I took a big bowl from the stack on the counter and set the sifter on top of it. I'd been assigned this job before—back when Tahira had her short-lived cupcake obsession. I poured some sugar into the strainer and started shaking it over the bowl, watching the fine powder mound below.

Daniel started cleaning the cracked eggshells and spilled chocolate from the counter. "Okay," he said "What timelines are we talking about here? When's the dance?"

I checked the calendar on my phone. "In six weeks. End of October."

"I'll be in calculus until the semester ends in January. Are you going to keep tutoring me after you don't need me as your 'boyfriend' anymore?"

I hadn't thought of that. I totally didn't need to keep the fake boyfriend that long—just long enough so people could see that Devin hadn't broken me. But I planned to work at the shelter all semester—so also until the end of January. "I'll tutor you all semester no matter how long our *relationship* lasts." I put down my sifter to add it to the list as *Parameter four*.

He nodded as he wiped. "That works. We can probably do calculus here after baking."

I nodded. "We'll break up right after the Nerd Prom, though."

I wrote *Parameter five: relationship will end after the Nerd Prom*.

He snorted. "Nerd Prom?"

"That's what everyone calls the fall formal. It's technically the academic banquet."

"Okay, that's funny. Your school sounds ridiculous. Next issue. I don't have a formal suit."

I frowned. "Like, at all? It doesn't have to be nice . . . What do you wear to weddings or funerals? Don't you have formal dances at your school?"

He shook his head. "I don't have a suit."

I cringed. That was going to be a problem. Especially with Devin's new fashion-forward look. It wouldn't impress anyone if I showed up with a guy (albeit a very cute guy) wearing jeans and a Leafs jersey. I was about to ask him how he could go through life without any formal clothes when I remembered his parameter. Maybe not having nice dinners or family weddings was his secret. I suddenly laughed. "I forgot. My sister's a fashion student. She'll find you something."

"Well, that fixes that problem. How many dates total? I'm assuming you want more than just the one?"

I thought about it, biting my lip. "Maybe two dates plus the dance?"

He nodded. "Works for me."

I was done sifting the sugar by then, so I jotted down parameter six. *Two dates, plus the Nerd Prom*.

"And pictures at each date?"

"More than that. People need to believe we're serious. How about one picture a week? We can take it here at the shelter. Plus, one picture at each date. Eight pictures total."

He nodded. "Fair."

I wrote: *Eight pictures together for social media.* "What else?"

"What about PDAs?" Daniel said.

Oooh, that was a good point. "I assume you mean public displays of affection?" I asked.

"Yup. At the dance, how handsy are you going to be? And how handsy do you want me to be?" He waggled his eyebrows.

I rolled my eyes.

He laughed. "Kidding, kidding. No one needs to be handsy. But . . . I assume we'll need to dance at this dance. Should we keep two meters apart?"

"No, of course not. How about two *normal* slow dances?"

"Works for me. Only PDA will be dancing," he said.

I frowned. "I don't think that will believable. Maybe . . ." I paused to think. I couldn't believe this was happening. I was supposed to be with Devin forever, or at least until university. Now I was negotiating physical contact for a fake relationship with a hockey player. "Holding hands?" I asked. "Anything else, we ask first. How does that sound?"

"Perfect." He grinned. The timer went off for the brownies, so he put on oven mitts and took the trays out. He put them on racks on the counter in front of me. They smelled like absolute heaven. "We need to let these cool a bit before we even think about cutting them," he said.

"The hard part will be not eating them."

He laughed. "I have great self-control. I worked in a bakery, remember? I don't think anyone's ever used me to be more popular before."

I frowned. That wasn't really what I was doing, was I? "It's not really to be more popular. More like . . ." I paused, thinking. "To not be seen as a loser. I really don't want to be single at the dance if Devin is there with Hana. Everyone will be staring at me to see if I'm crying again when they slow dance. Earl's Whispers said you were an upgrade to Devin Kapadia, so maybe they will stare at him when we dance instead." I shrugged. "Plus, this will make Devin mad."

Daniel grinned widely. "Ah. I love a little bit of pettiness."

"So we have a deal?" I asked.

He shook my hand. "This is going to be fun. We have a deal."

After the brownies cooled, and we'd sugared the lemon squares, we packaged them all up for Andre to take to the sale the next day, then said good night to Andre and Muniba.

On the walk to the bus stop, Daniel suddenly leaned close to me and flashed one of those whole-face, dimpled smiles. "Shall we get our first relationship picture with no photo manipulation needed? Lean in." He held his phone out in front of us.

He texted me the shot right after he took it. Our heads were almost, but not quite, touching in the picture. My smile felt a little out of practice, but I knew his would more than make up for it.

"One down, seven to go," Daniel said. "We should give this arrangement a code name in case we have to talk about it in front of others. How about . . . *Operation Lemon Squares. Lemon squares* for short."

I snort laughed at that. "Sure. Whatever."

"Yay! Okay, see you next week, Count!"

He headed across the street to catch the bus going in the other direction, that smile never leaving his face.

Once on my bus, and with shaking hands, I posted the picture on my Instagram. I didn't add a caption, though. Mostly because I didn't know what to say.

Also? I wasn't exactly sure what I was doing. But this, whatever it was, was happening.

10

Lemon Is the Answer

When I got home, my sister and her boyfriend, Rowan, were watching TV in our living room. Which was where they spent most Friday nights.

"Oh good, you're here. You got a delivery. Also, it's your turn to empty the dishwasher," Tahira said as soon as she saw me.

I frowned at my sister, then smiled at her boyfriend. "Hiya, Rowan. How's garden school? Did you play in the sandbox this week?" He was studying landscape architecture at University of Toronto, several steps up from *garden school*, but he knew I was teasing him.

He snorted. "How was your first week of grade twelve?"

"Horrendous," I said, sitting on the armchair in the living room. "I can't *wait* to be out of high school. Please tell me that postsecondary is better than this."

He laughed. "Not necessarily better. I will say that it's so much work that the drama kind of fades away."

"That sounds amazing."

Tahira shrugged. "There's still plenty of drama in fashion school. Besides, Rowan, you wouldn't know drama if it was right in front of your eyes." She kissed his cheek so he'd know she loved him anyway.

After my messy breakup, one would think being around such a perfect couple would be irritating. But I loved Rowan for Tahira. He was thoughtful, smart, and absolutely adored Tahira. Rowan was Black, and looked more like a fashion student like Tahira than a landscape architect student. He always wore super-stylish, botanical-themed clothes (he was a bit of a nature nut), and paired with my sister's tall gorgeousness, they were almost nauseatingly perfect together.

"Do you know when dinner is?" I asked.

"Mom's working late. We're supposed to put a pizza in the oven if we're hungry." She handed me a very full green plastic bag. "This was dropped off for you, and I'm dying to know what's in it. It smells like . . . *cumin*."

I took it, curious, and sniffed. It *did* smell like an Indian spice store. "Who dropped it off?"

"Devin," Tahira said.

I dropped the bag on the floor. "Seriously? He came *here*?"

She nodded. "I didn't see him—Rowan answered the door. Too bad, too, because I would have loved to give him a kick in the balls."

I looked at Rowan. "What did he say?"

"Nothing," Rowan answered. "He handed me the bag and told me to give it to you. I gave him a death glare if it helps."

"It does, thank you." I gingerly picked the bag back up. The scent of spices and incense was strong.

"You think it's biological warfare?" Tahira asked.

"His mother bought me stuff in India. Ugh. I can't believe he still brought it over. I specifically told him we shouldn't have any contact with each other."

"I can't believe his mother bought you stuff at all," Tahira said. "Glad Mom's not here, though. Then we'd have to hear how generous and thoughtful Preeti Kapadia is."

I didn't doubt that. I opened the bag.

Inside was a bright yellow and purple lehenga choli with the costume jewelry to match. I pulled the two pieces of the formal outfit on my lap. It was quite beautiful. The choli—the top—was sleeveless, cropped at the waist, and backless. It was covered in silver embroidery. The lehenga, the skirt piece, was long and flowy, also with rich embroidery. At the bottom of the bag, there was a small souvenir purse with an elephant on it, and several packs of Indian chocolate cookies. I had always loved those cookies, but the lehenga choli was a thing of beauty.

Tahira whistled low. "That's exquisite," she said, running her fingers over the embroidery.

I had never been one to wear fancy Indian clothes, even though I'd always loved looking at them. Tahira had the height and the figure to pull something like this off, not me. But seeing this beautiful outfit now brought a memory to the surface. A while ago, maybe a year back, Devin's parents and my parents, and Devin and I, of course, had all gone to one of those Indian buffet places on Gerrard Street together. While our parents were talking over chai, Devin and I escaped. We ended up at the sari shop next door, and he asked me if I would want to get married in Indian clothes. I was sixteen; I hadn't really thought about it much. But we went around the store, pretending to pick out wedding clothes. This lehenga looked a bit like the red bridal ones we looked at that day, except less ornate. And a much nicer color.

"It's gorgeous," Tahira said. "It's like the lehenga I wore to prom." Surprising everyone, my sister had designed and worn Indian clothes to her prom instead of a western dress. But she'd worn the lehenga with combat boots and simple western jewelry.

I shook my head. "I can't believe his mother bought me this."

Tahira frowned. "Does she even know you broke up?"

"I mean, I assume?"

"This is creepy," Tahira said. She looked at Rowan. "If you and I break up and your mother buys me formal clothes, I'm getting a restraining order."

Rowan chuckled. "My mom only wears pantsuits. I doubt she'd buy you a dress for any reason." He looked at the clothes on my lap and frowned.

Tahira held up the lehenga top. "Do you think this is a peace offering from Devin's mother because her son is such a douche?"

I shrugged. "I have no idea."

"Rowan, you should have told him Samaya was on a date when he was here," Tahira said. "With, like, I don't know. A famous hottie physicist or something. Are there hottie physicists?"

I laughed.

"I wonder if he saw the picture you posted on your Insta." Tahira looked at me, questioning, as I put the clothes back in the bag. "Who was that guy, anyway? He's really cute."

"He's . . . just a guy. He volunteers at the shelter." I looked at Rowan. "I'm volunteering for a weekly bake sale at a family shelter."

"That picture didn't look like *just a guy*," Tahira said. "Don't forget you told Mom your focus would be on school and nothing else for a while."

"Don't worry, he and I made an agreement with parameters and everything."

I gave them a brief version of my plan with Daniel. Without mentioning the catfisher or Earl's Whispers and their vendetta against me, I explained Daniel had agreed to pretend to be my boyfriend to make Devin jealous and stop the student body from thinking I was distraught over him. Tahira looked skeptical, and I fully expected her to object to the whole plan, but my phone buzzed before she said anything. It was a text from Daniel.

Daniel: You'll never guess what I saw on the way home . . .

A few seconds later a picture came through on my phone. It was a magazine ad for lemon liqueur or something. Basically, a picture of some bright yellow lemons against a black background. The text on the ad read LEMON IS THE NEW BLACK.

It made no sense, but it made me snort a laugh. This whole thing with Daniel could all go up in flames, but if nothing else, I kind of liked my new jock friend.

11

Everyone Wants a Piece of Me

Earl's Whispers, unfortunately, did not take the bait and repost that picture of me and Daniel from my Instagram. Nor did they even mention me, or Devin Kapadia, on their page on Monday. But that didn't matter at all, because even if the school's biggest gossip account didn't seem to care, enough people saw the picture to make posting it worthwhile.

"Did you see the way Jayden was looking at me in physics?" I asked Cass at lunch. We were sitting at a picnic table in the quad. I'd told Cass and Aimee about my arrangement with Daniel over the weekend.

"I did not," Cass said, barely looking up. Their thumbs were moving fast, texting someone on their phone.

I grinned. "He was giving me total dagger eyes. He probably thinks I'm, like, betraying his buddy or something. There were so many comments on my Insta—even a bunch from people I don't even know. And three people stopped me in the hall to ask about the guy on the post."

Cass looked up, eyes narrowed.

"Who are you texting?" I asked.

"Oh, it's—"

"Is it Aimee? Hey, do you know if she's moved from *talking* to, to maybe *seeing* Jayden? Because if so, I'd need to prepare myself. Jayden is totally #TeamDevin."

Cass put their phone down. "You do realize that your friends are actually independent people and not just members of your team, right?"

I blinked. "I was *kidding*, Cass." Was I coming off as self-absorbed? "Of course you guys can do what you want. I guess Aimee will tell us about her and Jayden when she's ready." I paused. "And I know she won't tell Jayden the truth about me and Daniel, right?"

"Of course she won't." Cass rolled their eyes. "Relax, Samaya. We're your friends. We'll cover for you. Oh, I asked Nabil in computers about the game dev. He's going to try to make it."

I exhaled. "Thanks. Aimee said she'd ask around, too."

I couldn't deny that I was worried about this club. I'd asked a few people I knew in math class but didn't get a committed answer from anyone. What if no one showed up?

Cass seemed to be reading my mind. "I wouldn't worry about the game-dev team. It'll be fine."

Cass was right. Everything would be fine.

And everything *was* fine. Sort of. I'd been worried no one but Aimee and Cass would show up to the meeting, but when I got to Miss Zhao's classroom after school, it was full—but it was all people I knew from the *Dragon Arena* guild. Jayden, Omar, and their friends. Even Hana was here, and sitting at the same table as Aimee and Cass. All Devin's friends were here. No Devin, thankfully, but still.

"There you are, Samaya!" Miss Zhao said from her desk near the door. "Great job assembling a team. Including you, there are exactly ten people here!"

Of course there were. If there were more than ten, I could have maybe kicked a few out. Like my ex-boyfriend's best friends. Or his girlfriend. But since the team could be up to ten people, I had no reason to get rid of anyone.

Miss Zhao spoke to the others. "Okay, Samaya here is in charge." She looked at me and smiled. "Go ahead, Samaya. I'll be here if you need me."

Okay. So I guessed this was it. I took a deep breath and walked to the front of the room. No one looked at me. Everyone kept talking to one another. I cleared my throat.

Kavita, a grade-eleven girl from the *Dragon Arena* guild, yelled, "Guys, everyone listen to Samaya!"

I smiled a thank-you to Kavita and looked around. Cass gave me a supportive nod. I took a breath. "Okay, so, thanks for coming. I am putting together a team to enter the National Youth Developers Mobile Game Competition. We'll need to come up with a concept, do all the design, and write the scripts and code for the game. Plus, we'll need a marketing plan. The competition is in May, so there is a ton of time. I'll start assigning people jobs. Does anyone have a preference for what they can do or—"

"Why do you automatically get to be leader?" Jayden asked. He was leaning back in his seat, next to Aimee, with his arms crossed on his chest.

I gave him a pointed look. "I'm team captain. This team was my idea."

He shrugged. "So? Take a finder's fee, or something. I don't know. We should run like a democracy, not a dictatorship."

I shook my head, getting annoyed. I needed to be the leader—this was for my scholarship applications. We hadn't even started yet, and he was already causing trouble? "Who said this was a dictatorship? This team was my idea! It wouldn't exist if it wasn't for me. We're going to all work together, but I've taken all the computer and coding courses the school offers, plus math and physics." I knew for a fact that Jayden hadn't taken computers.

"Game design is more than just coding. It's an art, not a science," he said smugly.

I gritted my teeth. I'd known Jayden as long as I'd known Devin, since they'd been friends forever. He hadn't seemed to have an issue with me when Devin and I were together. We played *Dragon Arena* together well enough. Dark Mages and Light Mages always had to work together to some degree, and even if we didn't gel as well as me and LostAxis, I did enjoy playing with Jayden. But he'd always been one of those "just playing devil's advocate" guys. I'd always found him a little annoying. Right now he was a lot annoying.

"I know game design is an art," I said. "That's why I asked Aimee to be here, too. This is a team effort. Cass can be in charge of coding, Aimee art design—"

"And you get to call all the shots."

I looked at Aimee, but she didn't meet my eyes. I couldn't believe she was actually into this guy.

I decided to move on. "So, I was thinking an adventure role-playing game with some puzzle element will really—"

"Why an RPG?" Omar said. "We should do a first-person shooter."

Several others in the room said *yesss*, or *that would be awesome*. Alex said RPGs were for nerds, which made me snort a laugh, since we *were* nerds, and Alex played a warrior on *Dragon Arena*—an RPG. Omar agreed and started talking about some mobile first-person shooter that I'd never played.

Omar didn't normally push my buttons like Jayden did, but still. I wouldn't have guessed they would have an issue with building an RPG, since that was the type of game we all used to play together. I was losing them.

Miss Zhao caught my eye. "Need help?" she asked.

I shook my head. "Nope. I got it." I was supposed to be the leader here. "What kind of game do you think we should make?"

Everyone started shouting out their favorite types of mobile games. Puzzle games, psychological horror games, word games, cat-collecting games. No one was stopping to listen to anyone else. It was getting louder. I was getting a headache.

Miss Zhao hollered for everyone to shush.

"I have an idea!" Kavita said loudly. "Why doesn't anyone who has a decent game concept do some market research and come back with a proposal? We can vote in a few weeks."

I smiled at Kavita, grateful. Maybe she should be in charge of marketing. "That's a great idea. Then once we have the game type finalized, we can pick a development platform, write and finalize scripts and concept art. Then after we code the thing, we'll—"

"I say whoever's concept wins the vote gets to be captain," Jayden said.

I glared at him. "I say whoever is an asshat for no reason gets booted from the group."

I cringed. Maybe I shouldn't be calling him an asshat with Miss Zhao right there.

Jayden raised one brow and sneered. "I don't think you're cut out to be captain. You're much too emotional."

I gritted my teeth. "No one is forcing you to be here, Jayden."

Aimee put her hand on Jayden to calm him. "Chill, guys. I think voting for captain is a good idea. What do you think, Cass?"

Cass, and pretty much everyone else in the room, all started talking at the same time again. Eventually, I managed to shush enough of them so we were able to have a functional conversation. We eventually agreed that anyone who had a viable idea could present it to the others here in two weeks. We'd then vote on the concept and captain.

I had a massive headache by the time we were done.

As I was putting on my backpack to leave, Jayden came up to me. "No hard feelings, Samaya? I just want to make sure our team wins this competition."

I nodded because what else could I do? I wanted to tell him that he was as transparent as glass right now, and I knew that he was only being an ass to me right now for retaliation for . . . actually I didn't know for what. Not playing in the guild? Not being Devin's girlfriend? Posting those pictures with Daniel?

Was all this just to make sure I knew my place?

"Oh, by the way," he said, leaning on my desk, "Aimee told me you have an Obsidian Staff. With that, we should finally be able to do the diamond egg run."

The Diamond Egg quest was this ridiculously hard quest that needed, like, twenty players to finish. Jayden had been trying to get the guild to try it again for months. We'd tried last winter and all died. Badly.

I shook my head, narrowing my eyes, suspicious. Did this have anything to do with him being such an ass to me at this meeting? "I don't really play *Dragon Arena* anymore," I said.

He shrugged. "We need a decent Light Mage, and you're good. I'll be having a gaming party soon. Your new hookup plays, too, right? You can bring him."

Jayden had a few of these gaming parties last year. Basically, we'd all bring our computers to his basement and do a quest with us all in the same room, so we didn't have to type in the chats. They *were* fun when Devin and I went together. But there was no way I'd go now. Or bring Daniel to one. Namely, because Daniel didn't actually play *Dragon Arena*. Also, Devin would be at Jayden's party. I shook my head.

Jayden smiled. "Too bad. Planning the diamond egg run would have taken up so much of my time. I wouldn't have had any spare time to work on a game proposal." He had a smug, punchable expression. "Hey, Aimee, we still getting coffee?" he called.

Aimee was still sitting at the table with Cass, Omar, and Hana. She grabbed her bag and headed to the door. I didn't think she heard what Jayden said to me, but she turned to give me a sympathetic look before leaving with him. "We'll talk tonight, okay, Samaya? I'll totally do concept art for your proposal."

At least Aimee would still help me, even if she had terrible taste in guys lately.

After everyone except Cass and I had left, Miss Zhao came and sat on the edge of my desk. "That was rough. That boy seemed to have it in for you."

I snorted. "Feels like everyone has it in for me, lately. I'm pretty sure he's doing this so I'll play in his *Dragon Arena* guild again." I frowned. "Or maybe he just doesn't want to be led by a girl in a game-dev team."

Miss Zhao sighed. "That's probably part of it. It's still so much harder for girls in tech."

"Why didn't you step in and help her if you knew they were being sexist?" Cass asked.

"I'm supposed to be an adviser here. It's *your* team," said Miss Zhao. "And the rules for this competition are quite strict—students must manage the teams and do all of the work themselves."

"It's fine," I said. If I was going to use the game-dev team on my scholarship application, I'd need Miss Zhao to give me a reference. She needed to see me handling this. "I'll put together the concept this week."

As Cass and I walked out of the tech lab, Hana was waiting for me right outside the door. Ugh.

"Hey, Samaya! I love the RPG idea." Hana was wearing high-waisted blue jeans and a floral sweatshirt. It looked like she'd been getting fashion tips from Tahira's Instagram. "You'll have my vote."

I raised a brow at her. She seriously thought we were still friends. "Uh, thank you?"

Her smile looked forced. "I . . ." She hesitated. "We're good, right? Still tight? I mean, you have that new guy now, so you're fine."

I didn't know why she cared. Did she feel guilty, like Devin did? I shrugged. "Sure, Hana. We're good." We weren't, but there were enough people around that I needed to pretend. I mean, my whole fake-dating plan was so I'd look like I was fine—about everything.

She grinned. "Yay! Because we go back so far, right? We can't throw all that away over a guy! Anyway, I wanted to tell you both, my mom is letting me have another backyard movie party before the weather gets too cold. We just got a high-definition outdoor projector. It's not as good as the projector in Dad's media room—remember last year when Omar spilled Doritos all over the white carpet?" She slipped her floral backpack over her shoulders. "I swear, my mom only agreed to the outdoor projector so I wouldn't have parties in the house anymore. We can watch the next Silverborn movie. You absolutely have to bring your new guy, Samaya!"

I blinked. Pretending to be cool with her was one thing; taking Daniel to a party where Hana would be hanging off Devin was completely another.

"Think about it! Talk soon!" She headed down the hallway before I could tell her there was no way I'd go to her backyard party.

I turned to Cass. "Why is everyone trying to torture me today?"

Cass snorted. "Actually, everyone seems to want a piece of you. I think your plan is working too well. Maybe we should go to Hana's. Don't you need to go on a date with the guy?"

I shook my head. "I can't bring Daniel to Hana's. I'd rather stay home and practice pi. Or eat pie. It would be a hell of a lot more fun than Hana's party."

∼

I had to take the bus home alone since Cass had plans, but when I was halfway to the stop, someone called my name. I turned and it was Devin. I wished there were a way to block people IRL and not just online.

"Hana told me you two talked," he said.

Every time I talked to him, it gave me a sour feeling in my stomach and a big lump in my throat.

"Devin, what do you want? We're supposed to be taking a break," I said.

He stared at me for several long seconds before speaking. "I just want to make sure you're okay. You should come to Hana's party. No hard feelings. It won't bother me if you bring that guy. I won't talk to you at all if you don't want me to."

"Yeah, well, I don't need your permission to do anything, do I?"

Without saying more, I turned and kept walking to the bus. Thankfully, he didn't follow me. I was tired of his mind games. Of his, of Jayden's, and of Hana's, too. Maybe I should change schools so I never saw any of these people again. I wiped a tear quickly before anyone saw it, because no doubt, with my luck, someone would take a picture of me and post it on Instagram.

My phone vibrated with a text. It was Daniel.

Daniel: OMG I need you.

I blinked at the screen.

Me: Excuse me?

Daniel: I'm freaking out here . . . my calc teacher sprung a test on us tomorrow. She said it's a redo of the one last week. I know you're supposed to tutor me Thursday after baking, but can we do it tonight instead?

Daniel: I'll owe you. You want more dates? PDAs? I'll let you take a picture with your hand on my butt. I'll have flowers delivered to you at your school.

Daniel: You into serenades? I can sing Harry Styles. I'll do ANYTHING . . .

I laughed. Daniel texted really fast. And he sounded exactly like . . . Daniel. I wrote back.

Me: Sure. How about FaceTime?

Daniel: I LOVE YOU.

Another text came through before I could respond.

Daniel: Please don't think I'm breaking your "no feelings for each other" parameter.

Daniel: I LOVE YOU in like a platonic and grateful, not creepy incel way. I like you a great deal. That's what I should have said, instead of bringing the L word into this. Let's start over.

Daniel: Now I'm worried that the reason you're not writing back to all this is because you think I'm nuttier than a snickers bar. I've ruined this, haven't I?

I laughed out loud, quickly typing.

Me: You're hilarious. You don't owe me anything for it. FaceTime at 8?

Daniel: 😊 😊 😊

Daniel: (I'm not going to say more because I'm afraid I will fuck this up.)

I don't think I stopped grinning at all the rest of the way home.

~

My FaceTime rang at eight o'clock sharp. And once the connection went through, I was met with Daniel's face. His hair looked wet, and he wore a plain gray T-shirt.

"My savior!" he said, smiling. "I had hockey practice today, and hockey days are hungry days. Let me eat this real quick." He took a huge bite of something.

"Oh. So . . . hi. How are you?" I held my phone out in front of me so he could see my face. I felt kind of awkward and didn't know what to say. Which was weird, because there'd been no awkwardness when we saw each other Friday. And I'd weirdly been looking forward to this call for the last hour.

"I'm superb, now that I'm talking to you."

"Um," I said. "It's no problem."

He grinned as he did something with his phone, propping it up on a table in front of him or something. He took another bite of what looked like a huge bun. I could make out that he seemed to be sitting sideways on a bed, which was neatly made with a white floral comforter.

"Okay," he said when he finished chewing. "So, I told you that I bombed that test last week. Well, it was more a nuclear disaster. I wish my uncle was into history or something instead of engineering. My brain isn't wired for this math stuff. Unlike you, Count."

"I don't get why you don't just tell your uncle that you don't want to study engineering or whatever?"

He shrugged as he took another bite. I watched his cheekbones move as he chewed. "It's a long story," he finally said. "Why do you take calculus? I mean other than you're so good at it. Where do you want to go for university?"

Right. Me asking about his family was overstepping his boundary. I was fine talking about myself, though. "I'm applying to University of Waterloo and University of Toronto. I'd probably prefer Waterloo, for either computational mathematics or software engineering." I bit my lip. I often got weird comments when I told people what I wanted to study in university. Things like *you don't look like a mathematician.* Or *girls always say they want to do coding, but it's so competitive.* Daniel wasn't like that, though. He seemed to accept me as I was. "You said you want to be a pastry chef?"

"Yup," he said. "George Brown College right here in Toronto has a great baking and pastry program. That's where my aunt went—the one who has a bakery."

I assumed his uncle wasn't pleased with this plan. I wanted to ask more, learn about his goals and what he wanted to do after college, but I also didn't want to. Both for his parameter, and a little bit for mine. I was determined not to develop a crush on Daniel, so keeping things professional was best. "So, what was your calc quiz on, anyway?"

"Limits. And that's the problem."

"Why?"

"Because I may be okay with all our parameters and guidelines, but *limits* makes no sense!" he said. "What the heck does it even mean? I thought math was all like . . . black and white. Concrete. Why am I trying to figure out the value of something as it approaches something else or whatever the fuck is going on? I swear, when my teacher explains it, she may as well be speaking Japanese . . . wait. First Hiroshima and now Japanese. My subconscious is on a Japan kick. I think I need some sushi."

I frowned. "Did you mention Hiroshima?"

"No, but that's what I was thinking when I said my test was like a nuclear bomb."

I laughed again. "Show me the quiz."

He texted me a picture of the quiz. I propped my phone up on my desk, and for the next hour, we went through each of the questions on it. It took him a while to pick up the concepts—I had to explain several times in different ways. But eventually he seemed to get it. He was, thankfully, capable of doing calculus; he just had to work at it a little harder. Which was fine. I totally accepted that math didn't come as easy to others as it did for me.

"You should be a high school math teacher," he said, after we finished the last question on the quiz. I couldn't see his face on the phone screen while he was bent and looking at his notebook. "Not study computer math . . . wait, what did you call it?"

I snorted. Like Mom would be okay with me being a teacher. "Computational mathematics. Basically, it's programming computers to do complex math."

He looked up at me, grinning. "Ooh, that's smart. Then people won't have to do it. Yes, do that."

It was so different from how others reacted to my career choices. Daniel was so refreshing. "So, you feel okay with this quiz tomorrow?"

He shrugged. "A lot more okay than I was earlier. I should change your name from the Count to the Math Goddess, but I don't want you to think I'm almost breaking parameter one again. Hey, how's my end of this arrangement working? Did you post that pic on your social last week? I thought about joining Instagram to see it."

"Maybe it worked a little too well. I would have tagged you in the picture if you weren't such a wannabe boomer."

"Hey, none of that. And you clearly haven't met any boomers, because my Lola in the Philippines is all about the Facebook. That's what she calls it. *The Facebook.*"

"So you don't have *any* socials?"

"I'm more into actually being social than social media. I hang out with my hockey teammates on Discord, but that's it."

"Okay, weirdo, not boomer then. But yeah, the picture worked great at school. You caused quite the stir. Ex got a little jealous. Okay, a lot jealous."

He must have seen something in my expression because his face washed with pure concern. "What did he do? I should have been there."

I waved my hand. "It's fine. I can handle Devin Kapadia. It's funny—he was never the jealous type when we were actually together. But he did not like seeing those pictures of us. He literally just stared at me, then insisted you and I go to a party his girlfriend's having. I think he wants to check you out in person."

"He wasn't jealous before because you were his. Now you're not," Daniel said.

I scrunched my nose. "Yuck. I'm nobody's."

He laughed, head falling back. "Yes, well, Count, you haven't been single for long, but if you ever start dating again, you may find that possessiveness is unfortunately a common flaw in many young men."

My eyes narrowed. I wanted to ask about his past relationships. He'd mentioned past girlfriends, and he'd said he'd never had a relationship as long as me and Devin's, but were his past relationships serious? Had he been in love before? I knew Daniel was seventeen—he'd told me his age, and Andre confirmed it. But sometimes—I didn't know why—he sounded a lot older. Wiser. He was both strangely open, and weirdly guarded, and that wasn't like any other teenager I knew. And yet other times, he was goofy and talkative. Daniel was kind of hard to figure out.

But I shouldn't be trying to figure him out at all. He had his boundaries, and I had mine. Our arrangement wasn't about being friends but only about what we could do for each other. "Um, are you good with your quiz tomorrow then? I should go see if my mom needs help cleaning up after dinner."

Daniel grinned. "Yeah . . . I think I can do some more practice exercises on my own now that they sort of make sense to me. See you Thursday! We're making scones!"

I smiled and said good night. I wasn't really going to ask Mom if she needed help—she hated anyone in the kitchen with her and was probably long done cleaning anyway. But I had to get off the call before it got even more personal. Doing calculus with him seemed safe. Baking with him was fine. Heck, pretending he was my boyfriend wouldn't be an issue at all.

But anything outside those parameters seemed risky. Because . . . Daniel was already becoming such a breath of fresh air. When everyone else seemed out to get me, and each day was more stressful than the one before, Daniel made me smile. And laugh. And he respected my abilities. I was afraid of growing attached to the handsome hockey player who borderline smiled too much.

The only way this was going to work was to remember Parameter one: no feelings. I was not looking to develop a crush on Daniel Ramos.

12

Scone to Be All Right

When I got to the shelter on Thursday, a bunch of kids were play-ing in the playground. Some adults, including Yasmin's mother, were on the picnic table near the swings watching them. Yasmin was on her tricycle, so I went over to say hello and ask her about her tricycle.

"It's the shelter's bike," she said. "I can use it whenever I want because there are no other little kids. Just big kids and some little babies."

I frowned. "That's a tricycle, not a bike. *Tri* means three, and it has three wheels. A bike is a bicycle. *Bi* means two. Bicycles have two wheels."

She looked at me blankly. "Daniel says you like counting."

I laughed. "I do! What do you like at school?"

"I like reading. But I'm not good at it, so I look at the pictures. I got a book about fairies from the library. They also had a video game about fairies, but the big kids don't let me use the PlayStation."

"Oh, that's too bad."

Yasmin nodded. "It's okay. I play games on Mama's phone sometimes."

"Those are called mobile games. I'm making a mobile game at a club at my school."

That made her eyes brighten. "Is it about fairies?"

I frowned. "Well, no. We don't know what it's about yet."

She nodded. "Then you can make it about fairies."

I smiled. "Maybe I will. I need to go inside and bake now."

"Okay. Goodbye. I'm glad you're not really a vampire."

She pedaled her little tricycle over to the playground, where the other kids played.

When I walked into the kitchen, Daniel was already there, using a small ice cream scoop to measure brown dough onto a baking sheet. The air smelled of brown sugar and cinnamon.

He grinned when he saw me. "Count von Count!" he said.

I laughed. "Count von Count?"

He nodded, a ridiculously pleased expression on his face. "Yes! I thought it was weird to call you *the Count*, even though a vampire that counts is, like, the *perfect* name for you, but calling you 'the' seemed a bit *extra*, so I looked up the Count's full name. It's also Count! Full name is *Count von Count*! Although . . ." He frowned. "You don't look very vampire-like today. You're wearing an actual color. Still spooky in the eyes, though."

I looked down at my clothes. I was wearing a red-and-yellow striped ribbed T-shirt with high-waisted black jeans. "Yasmin told me she doesn't think I'm a vampire anymore. You just caught me on some darker days last week."

"She's a smart kid. Things are brighter now?"

His grin was certainly brighter than anything I'd seen in a while. I quickly turned away from his face.

"We're making scones today, right?" I asked. "Are those scones?"

"No, we'll make scones next. I thought I'd get some cookies on first. These are a classic oatmeal, but with butterscotch chips instead of raisins since you're raisin-averse. Honestly, I don't get why so many people have such big issues with raisins. I mean, they're just grapes. I don't mind fruit in cookies. And chocolate is practically a fruit, right? Doesn't cocoa come from trees?"

I turned back to look at him, blinking. Chocolate being practically a fruit was a fact that LostAxis had once told me. It suddenly occurred to me that I still didn't know exactly how LostAxis got that picture of Daniel.

"Hey, Daniel, I was wondering, do you know how that guy I was gaming with got the picture of you from the playground build?" It was possible that LostAxis took it himself. The real LostAxis could be an Earl's student who'd come that day.

He shook his head. "No idea."

"Were there pictures from the event posted anywhere? On the website or newsletter?"

He shook his head. "Doubt it. Muniba is a bit of a stickler for pictures around here. It's a safety thing for the residents. She'd probably be pissed at whoever took that picture of me."

Maybe I could ask around at school to see who'd helped build the playground . . .

"So, Samaya, you ready to make some scones?" Daniel asked.

I nodded. I could figure out this LostAxis mystery later. "What exactly are scones, anyway?"

Looking excited, he put down his scoop and got up, returning a second later with a hardcover cookbook open to a page near the middle. He put it on the counter in front of me.

"Here. Read up. That's my favorite Martha Stewart baking book. My tita had the same one." Daniel returned to his bowl and continued scooping the cookie dough. "Scones are like biscuits. Maybe a bit denser. Last year Andre and I made a high tea for the residents here for Mother's Day, and we made these little orange cranberry scones. Hey, those have fruit in them! Do you like cranberries?"

I shrugged. "Yeah, I suppose."

"See? No one ever complains about cranberries in cookies—white chocolate cranberry biscotti are amazing. But god forbid someone puts a raisin in something. All hell breaks loose. Scones aren't cookies, by the way. I mean, really not a cookie—not like how a bar is not really a cookie but is kind of like a cookie."

I chuckled as I looked at the recipe. And now that I saw a picture of one, I realized I'd totally had a scone before. They were like biscuits.

After a few minutes of silence while I read the recipe (they looked easy enough to make) and Daniel finished the cookies, he came to stand next to me, a mischievous smile on his face. "You never asked me about my math quiz."

I shrugged. "I was waiting for you to tell me. Didn't want to traumatize you in case it didn't go well."

"Much appreciated. But I am in no distress whatsoever. And you can believe that—because I am very much a male human when I am in distress. You should see me with a cold."

"So that means you did well on the quiz?"

"Yes! Fourteen out of twenty!"

That grade wouldn't have been something I would cheer for, but he seemed thrilled with it. "That's amazing!"

"Thanks to your help! I'm going to pass this class. I can feel it, here." He tapped his hands against his chest. "So let's make scones to celebrate."

Scone-making went fine. Daniel walked me through the steps—grating the very cold butter, mixing it with the flour, sugar, and baking powder, then carefully mixing in the wet ingredients and the additions. We made two dozen orange cardamom, and two dozen pumpkin spice.

After they were out of the oven and cooling on the counters, Andre joined us in the kitchen. "These smell so good. This weekend's sale is going to be awesome." He looked at me. "You interested in joining us, Samaya? Since you made so many today, we won't need you tomorrow.

You can catch up on your hours on Saturday at the market. Daniel's coming this week."

"You should come," Daniel said. "We can get our selfie of the week there for . . . lemon squares."

I laughed at our relationship code name. He had a point, though. This fake relationship would look more real if we had selfies in a variety of places instead of all at the shelter.

I probably didn't really need the hours, but I did want to see the market. I agreed, and Andre told me to be ready at the shelter at seven Saturday morning.

Daniel and I headed for the front door. Yasmin was in the common room coloring at the coffee table with some older kids. She ran up when she saw us.

"Daniel! I was looking for you!" Yasmin said.

Daniel crouched down to talk at her level.

"Mama told me that you said you would make me a cake for my birthday. Can you make a raspberry one?"

He nodded. "I don't think I've ever made a raspberry cake before, but I think I could figure it out."

She beamed. "Raspberry is my favorite flavor." She pointed at me. "Did you know she's making a video game about fairies? It was my idea."

"Is she?" Daniel looked at me. "I'll bet it'll be amazing. Samaya is the smartest person I know." He stood. "I'll see you next week, Yasmin."

"Okay! Bye, Daniel! Bye, Samantha!" She went back to her drawing.

I chuckled as Daniel and I walked to the bus stop. It was a sunny day, but a bit chilly. I zipped up my hoodie. "Not the first time someone's called me Samantha."

He laughed. "She called me David for the first week I was here. Why does she think you're making a fairies video game?"

"Because I am. I mean, I'm making a game. It probably won't be about fairies, though." I told him about the game-dev club.

"Hey, that sounds cool. You *should* do it about fairies. An adventure game about fairies sounds awesome. Like those Tinker Bell movies!"

First, he talks about *Bridgerton*, then the Tinker Bell movies? "You have unusual taste in entertainment."

He shrugged. "You should at least look into this fairies idea. I think a cool, grown-up fairies game would be awesome. Why do elves get all the love? Fairies can fly! They can tie stiff leaves to their shoes as ice skates."

"Why would they need ice skates?"

"Canadian fairies would play hockey, wouldn't they?"

I chuckled. "That's nice of you to make her a cake for her birthday."

"She's had it rough. She's the youngest in a big family, and they had very little even before they ended up here. I doubt she's ever had a cake for herself. Not a decent one, anyway."

I was a youngest child, so I kind of knew what it was like to be an afterthought sometimes, but I only had *one* sibling. Being the youngest in a family with social challenges, whatever they were, had to be even harder.

Logically, of course I knew that the people staying at the family shelter were here because they had nowhere else to go, but their problems had been kind of vague for me. Not real issues that real people were dealing with.

I felt so bad for that little girl. Her family should have had their own home somewhere. Yasmin should have her own room, and a brand-new tricycle that was only hers and a cake every year with her name on it. Here I was complaining that some gossipers at my school were targeting me and I was catfished, all while working in a shelter full of people facing much harder challenges.

"That's tough. I wish there was something we could do for her," I said.

"Samaya, we are *literally* doing something here for the shelter residents. The money we raise at the farmers' market goes directly to children's programming at the shelter. The whole day care was just redone with bake sale money. And the playground was donated by a bank, but the mulch and landscaping came from fundraising."

Now that I knew how amazing the shelter was, I wished I had come that day to build the playground, but I'd been focused on other things. Myself, probably. I hadn't seen how assembling monkey bars could benefit me. Not that I was any better now. I'd only started volunteering here to get my volunteer hours to graduate, not to actually help kids like Yasmin.

And also, if I'd been here, maybe I could have met Daniel earlier.

"I can also help make her birthday cake, if you want," I said. "Not that I've made a cake before, but how hard could it be?"

He shook his head, laughing. "I'm not sure you're ready for frosted cakes yet, Count. You could measure the ingredients for me or something. Work within your strengths."

I playfully slapped his arm and tried not to think about how firm it was. So, so strong.

13

Samaya and Daniel Go to the Market

I had Mom drive me to the shelter Saturday since I had to be there so early. Daniel and Andre were in the parking lot when I arrived, loading the baked goods into the back of a white van. Muniba was nearby, talking on her phone.

When the van was loaded, we all hopped in, and Andre drove us to Evergreen Brickworks for the Saturday farmers' market.

I had only been there a few times before and never so early in the morning. This facility was apparently a former brick factory, hence the name Brickworks, but it had been turned into a green space with ponds, some walking trails, and an outdoor education area. There were a few permanent cafés, and the farmers' market, which was held in a big open-sided structure with a concrete floor and metal roof. The bright fall sun lit up the area as vendors and farmers set up tables around the perimeter of the space. The farmers had crates of fruits and vegetables, and the other vendors unloaded things like homemade jams and soaps. There were even a few other baked-goods stands.

We draped tablecloths over our tables and started arranging the food on them. In addition to the lemon squares, brownies, scones, and cookies, we had some fancy strudel things that one of the residents had made, plus a lot of muffins and cinnamon rolls that Andre had made the day before. We hung a large canvas sign behind the table that said all the proceeds were going to the New Beginnings Family Shelter, with some pictures of smiling families of all races.

"Why isn't Yasmin in any of those shots?" I asked Andre. "She's so adorable."

Andre shook his head. "These are stock photos. We don't risk putting the faces of our actual residents, past or current, on any of our materials. People have many reasons to be at the shelter, and we want to respect their privacy before anything else."

Right. Daniel had mentioned that Muniba didn't let people take pictures at the shelter. It made sense.

Business was steady all morning. Most of the customers were adults my parents' age or maybe a bit younger. And as expected most, but not all, were white. Farmers' market crowds usually were. But people were friendly, and many were chatty about the shelter. We sold out of the lemon squares first, which I felt weirdly proud of, even though I hadn't made this batch. And Daniel's fruitless oatmeal cookies were the next to go. I was actually having a great time. Andre kept challenging me to figure out the customers' change without using the calculator (which, of course, I was always able to do), and Muniba was so different when she was away from the shelter. Kind of sillier. More fun. She did the desi thing of asking me my specific South Asian background, and after I told her, she listed about five aunties from my community and asked me if I knew them.

But mostly it was fun because of Daniel. He was so mesmerizing to watch with the customers. Just as friendly and charming as he was with me, but also, so respectful. He wasn't the slightest bit awkward talking to adults, like many of my friends were. He was natural, kind, and playful.

His dimples were out, of course, since he was smiling so much, and his cheekbones looked like they could cleanly slice a lemon square in half.

"A master baker should never divulge their secrets," he said when a woman asked for the recipes for the scones. He then leaned close and whispered, "The secret is frozen butter, and very cold hands."

Ah! That was why Andre had made that comment my first day about Daniel having cold hands. I'd touched his hand a few times when cooking with him, and they had been cold! Our parameters allowed hand-holding on dates, so I'd presumably be holding his hand at some point. Were they always cold?

Daniel smiled at me, clearly noticing that I'd been watching him.

I quickly looked away. I really had to figure out how not to stare at the guy so much.

During a lull in the crowd, Andre insisted Daniel and I take a break. He gave us each a scone and some money and sent us to go find something more lunch-like to eat.

We ended up grabbing some Jamaican beef patties and sat at a table in the eating area at one end of the farmers' market. The market was still pretty busy, but it was quieter here. The area was set up with about ten folding tables with four chairs at each. It was near the side of the space, so the breeze from the open walls added a bit of a chill.

"This is good," I said, nibbling on the patty. "The beef patties I get near school are kind of bland. Super spicy, but nothing else going on."

"I like the patties at Warden Subway Station," Daniel asked.

I knew that his school was near Warden Subway Station. He'd also told me that his aunt with the bakery lived in Brampton—an hour from where he lived now.

"You ever try those?" he asked.

I shook my head. I wasn't in the habit of getting food on public transportation.

"Well, we're going to have to remedy that. The patties there are legendary." He described the perfect flaky pastry and spicy beef filling in detail, even speculating on the type of fat they used in the pastry and the spices in the filling.

I raised a brow. "You've given this a lot of thought. Did you make beef patties at your aunt's bakery?"

He shook his head. "Nah. She made Filipino empanadas, though. I mostly made the pies there. We even had some Filipino pies, like ube, egg, and coconut. I keep telling Andre he should let me make pies for the bake sales, but he doesn't think they'd sell well since some of the farmers make them, too. And for some reason, people trust fruit pies made by a white farmer more than a Filipino teenager."

He had a point. "Maybe if they knew you were a hockey player? People love hockey players," I suggested.

"That they do. Hey, remember our squares and bars conversation?"

"Uh, yeah? That was the only squares and bars conversation I've ever had."

"Ha. I know I said that squares are a cross between a cake and a cookie, but I've been thinking about pie. I found this recipe for an apricot square, and it had a lattice crust top, like a pie. And lemon squares—they're so close to lemon meringue pie, except, you know. No meringue. So maybe we need to add pies to the bars and squares family tree."

I shook my head, amazed. Where had this guy come from? Yeah, he wanted to be a baker, but still. What seventeen-year-old talked and thought about squares and bars this much? "You're a strange person, Daniel Ramos."

"What? I'm not strange for being Team Pie. Lots of people like pie."

"Yeah, but I doubt they think about how to classify baked goods as much as you."

"You having second thoughts about Operation Lemon Squares?"

I laughed. "Nope."

"That's good. Ready for our selfie, yet?"

The seating area had picked up with more people eating lunch now. I nodded.

He stood and came around to my side of the table. "Here, let's take one biting the patties."

With one hand, I held the patty near my mouth, but I put my other hand around Daniel's upper arm and pulled him closer. We needed to level up this fake relationship so we didn't just look like two friends hanging out. He seemed to get the idea and moved in closer. He snapped a few pictures—some of us holding the patties near our mouths with our eyes wide, some of us biting into them, some of us chewing while laughing, and some of us with my head rested on his shoulder.

The pictures were . . . perfect. Silly. We looked genuinely happy together. No one would look at these and think anything other than this was two teenagers in love.

This was what Devin and I looked like once. Maybe a long time ago.

Daniel tapped the screen with his finger. "These are, like, the most Toronto pictures ever. We're counting these shots as just one for the parameters, right? Is there a more Toronto food than Jamaican patties? It's too bad my aunt's empanadas never took off like these—she'd be a millionaire." He sat back across from me, popping the last bite of his patty in his mouth. "We should ask the patty shop if they want to use this photo in their advertising."

I laughed.

"Samaya?" a voice behind me said. I turned . . . and crap. It was Hana.

"Hey, Hana!" I stood. "What are you doing here?" Evergreen Brickworks was pretty far from our neighborhood in East Scarborough. I hadn't expected to see anyone I knew here today.

She pointed to a Brown couple a distance away at a vegetable vendor. I hadn't seen her parents in years, but I remembered them. "My parents are trying to be all *farmers' market bougie*, lately. They bribed me to come by promising we'd go for boba tea on the way home."

Hana sat in the seat across from Daniel at the table and turned to me. "Oooh, this is the gamer boyfriend."

I cringed. Of all the people at Earl's for Daniel to meet first, why did it have to be Hana Dawar? Daniel didn't know anything about *Dragon Arena* yet. And he was wearing one of his hockey T-shirts. This was a disaster. Our whole plan was about to go up in flames. I bit my lip, looking at Daniel, panicked.

Daniel took my hand in his. And wow. It *was* cold. But not in a bad way or anything. Just . . . *cool*. Smooth. I felt my breathing calm with the pressure of his cool fingers.

He smiled warmly at Hana. "I'm Daniel Ramos. Samaya's been talking about me?"

I nodded and found my voice. "This is my friend Hana from school."

Hana nodded. "What are you guys doing here?"

Daniel pointed to the shelter table. "We're volunteering at the shelter bakery booth."

Hana looked at me. "Ah! Cool! So adorable that you game together *and* volunteer together." She looked across the hall toward the shelter booth. "That's the shelter we had that class trip at, right, Samaya? The construction project? I still have a picture of me in a hard hat on my Insta."

I frowned. "I didn't go to that." If Hana was there, she could have been the one who took the picture of Daniel. "The shelter has a no-pictures policy."

She shrugged. "Everyone was taking selfies. It's not often we do, like, real construction work."

Seemed like there were a lot of rule breakers. I looked at Daniel, hoping he could help here.

"I was volunteering that day," Daniel said without skipping a beat. "I don't remember you, though. It was so awesome so many came to help out. The kids love that playground."

Hana swung her hair over her shoulder. How was it so shiny? Unfair. "I don't remember you, either. What school do you go to? Where do you live?"

Daniel squeezed my hand, and I knew what he was asking. He wanted to know if he could answer the questions. I barely squeezed back and nodded at him. He told her what school, and said he lived near it.

"How long have you played *Dragon Arena*?" Hana asked.

"Hana, what's with the interrogation?" I asked.

"It's not really an interrogation. I'm just curious. But whatever." She nodded toward his shirt. "Leafs fan, though," Hana said. "Dad would call you a glutton for punishment. Hey, aren't you a Dark Mage? What do you think about the new update that totally changed the—"

"I haven't really played much lately, not since the new update," Daniel said. He had a small, noncommittal smile on his face. How was he so cool when I was a bag of nerves? His hand was even still cold.

She frowned. "Oh, I thought you two still played together. Hey, did Samaya tell you I'm having a backyard party next week? We just had the yard redone. I swear, my folks must have spent a hundred grand on landscaping. You absolutely must come."

I winced. "Ugh. I don't know, Hana . . ." I still couldn't believe she wanted me to come to her party. She was literally dating my ex.

"Come on. My parents will be out." She grinned at Daniel. "It's going to be *lit*."

I'd been to a few of Hana's parties before. They were most definitely *lit*. Everyone would be there. Everyone . . . on the nerdier side of the school, that is. Which, for Earl's, was most of it. No one would be playing *Dragon Arena* at the party, but people would definitely be talking about it. And of course, Devin would be there. As Hana's date. Going was a terrible idea.

"That sounds awesome!" Daniel said.

I shot him a glare. Even if he didn't know who Hana was, he had to see how tense I'd been since she'd sat down.

"Excellent," Hana said. "I can't wait for Samaya to show you off." She looked over to her parents, who were talking to the squash seller. "I'm going to have to pry them out of there, or we'll never leave. Honestly, my parents are like . . . *obsessed* with farmers lately. You know they've even talked about selling the house and buying a farm? Can you imagine Pakistani farmers in rural Ontario?" She shuddered. "Not like they'd ever do it, though. There's no take-out delivery there. Great meeting you, Daniel. Can I take a shot of you?" She held up her phone to take a picture.

Daniel pulled me close before I could object so we were posed similar to how we'd been in the selfie, except we weren't eating.

"Awesome," she said, looking at the pic. "Y'all are too cute. See you Friday!"

She left. As soon as I was sure she was out of eyesight, I snatched my hand out from his. "We can't go to Hana's party. Why'd you say we'd go?"

He shrugged. "I'd love to see a hundred-thousand-dollar backyard. We can make an extra batch of cookies on Thursday and bring them. Are your friends #TeamRaisin or #NoRaisin?"

"Hana is Devin's new girlfriend."

"And Devin is . . ."

I titled my head sternly. "Devin is my *ex*."

"Shit." His eyes widened. "The jealous ex. Yeah, sorry about that. We don't have to go." He looked apologetic.

"It's fine; you didn't know."

"She seemed so nice. Was she being fake?"

I nodded. "Yeah, she most definitely was being fake. She's been after Devin forever. She's only being nice to rub it in that she has him now."

"Well, *you* have *me*."

I blinked. I did, but not really. "Yes, but I still don't want to go."

Daniel was silent for a few moments. "Won't all your friends be there?"

I nodded. "Yeah. Hana's parties are big." I thought for a moment. "Even if we did go, you couldn't bring cookies. You're supposed to be a hard-core gamer and nerd."

"Gamer-boys don't bake cookies?"

I put my hands up, frustrated. "Seriously, Daniel. A party with my friends isn't a good first date. You don't know a thing about *Dragon Arena*, and I guarantee that's what people will be talking about. My ex's best friend has been on me to rejoin the guild lately. He's the guy that was harassing me at the game-dev meeting. He'd bug me at the party, too. And he'd bug you. Plus Devin will be there." I sighed. "It would be better if we went bowling or for a coffee or something like that for our date. Maybe to the mall."

Daniel's eyes perked up. "Or skating?"

"I don't skate."

"I could teach you," he offered.

Daniel's expression was so helpful. Considerate. Like he cared that I was practically having a nervous breakdown at the thought of going to Hana's. And I felt terrible. Why was he doing all this for me? I was a grumpy negative Nancy, and he was literal sunshine in a jock's body who offered to teach me to skate. Was putting up with me and my judgmental friends worth a bit of calculus help? He deserved a tutor who only wanted pies or something from him, instead of someone who made him pretend to be in a relationship.

"I know about *Dragon Arena*," he said, breaking up my self-pity party.

"What?" I hadn't taught him anything about the game yet.

"It's a MMORPG, which stands for a massively multiplayer online role-playing game. I know it was released two years ago, on June fifth. I know that you have to choose your class when you start your character, which is different from other MMORPGs where you can change your class. I know there are eight classes—four offensive ones, three defensive, and one mixed. I know that it's the third most popular online RPG in the world right now and is the most popular with teens." He smiled proudly as he recited all these facts. "I know it was designed by a team out of Japan led by Hiruki Matusaki, and that he always intended the servers in the game to be geographically based so players could meet in game and become friends in real life, too."

I blinked. *Okay* . . . he might know more about *Dragon Arena* than I did.

"Where did you learn all that?"

"Wikipedia."

I frowned. He'd done his own research? "Okay, but knowing about the game is not the same as playing it. People are going to ask questions specifically about what class you play, maybe what weapon you use, or about that update Hana was talking about. You can't answer those questions from Wikipedia," I said.

Daniel's text tone went off then. "It's Andre," he said, looking at the text. "Break's over."

I exhaled. We headed back to the bake sale stand. Daniel was the same—cheerful, friendly, and enthusiastic as we continued to sell the baked goods. But my mind was reeling after the run-in with Hana.

I wasn't really afraid that Daniel wouldn't be able to fool my friends as a fake boyfriend, because clearly he could talk the talk, and him taking my hand there told me he'd be convincing in action, too. And I wasn't afraid of seeing Devin and Hana together, because I had to see that at school all the time.

I had another fear—a reason that was muddling my brain and making me dread the thought of taking Daniel to Hana's party. Sitting under the stars and watching a movie with him sounded intimate. Romantic.

And the goose bumps that erupted all over me when he squeezed my hand with his? The way my stomach did a little somersault when he said he'd researched *Dragon Arena*? My body's reaction was telling me it could be dangerous for me to be on a date, fake or not, with someone who I was becoming quite fascinated with.

I had no doubt Daniel and I could pretend to be really into each other in front of my friends. What scared me now was . . . I wasn't sure I'd be faking it.

14

Skimming Too Close to the Limit

B y three o'clock, we were sold out of food, so we had no choice but to pack up and leave the market. Andre drove the van again, with Muniba next to him. Daniel and I sat in the row of seats behind them.

"That was a success," Andre said as he merged onto the highway. "Three people told me they came specifically for our stuff. We'll have to make more for next week."

"Definitely," Daniel said. "Want me to come Tuesday after school, too? I can make pies."

"You're already coming Thursday and Friday," Andre said. "Balance, remember, Daniel? Anyway, no pies. The money doesn't work out. We can sell a whole pie for maybe fifteen dollars, but we can cut up a tray of brownies into twelve pieces and sell for three dollars each. How much is that, Samaya?"

"Thirty-six dollars."

Andre chuckled. "You should rent yourself out for party tricks."

"That's not a very impressive calculation," Muniba said. She looked back at me. "Not that I have any doubt you can do complex math in your head, but Andre is too easily impressed. Hey, I saw you kids talking to my niece at the market. Do you know Hana?"

I froze. What did she say? "Hana is your *niece*?"

"Yeah, her father is my second cousin. We're not super close, though. She's grown up so much since the last time I saw her!"

This was not good. "She goes to my school," I said, trying to sound casual. Why hadn't Hana said her aunt worked at the shelter when she mentioned she'd been there for the playground build? I looked at Daniel, panic rising. Hana thought Daniel and I were *dating*, and that we met playing video games before I started at the shelter. But Muniba knew we'd met for the first time at the shelter and that we definitely weren't dating. What if Muniba told Hana?

"We're going to a party at their house tomorrow," Muniba continued. "Which makes it even funnier that I saw them today. Haven't seen my cousin and his family in years, then twice in one weekend? Apparently, Hana was even at the playground build at the shelter last year, but I was at my sister's in Montreal that week."

Damn it. For sure Muniba would talk to Hana about me. Operation Lemon Squares was about to crumble, unless we extended our fake relationship to the shelter.

But how could I ask Daniel to do that? He'd been working there longer than me. He was clearly close with Andre, and even to some of the residents. I couldn't ask him to lie to them all.

I looked at Daniel, and he shrugged at me. "Hana invited us to a party in her backyard next weekend," he said.

"Oh, that sounds amazing!" Muniba said. "They have the best parties."

I shook my head. "We're probably not going."

"Samaya thinks a big party with all her friends is a bit too intense for our first official date," Daniel said. "She wants to go bowling instead."

I blinked at him. Was he really okay with . . . ?

Muniba laughed and looked back at us for a second. "Hah! I won that bet." She looked at Andre. "I told you there was romance blossoming between our young volunteers." She patted Andre's shoulder. "Andre and I first met volunteering at a food bank, and we're still working together. And still married."

Wait. *What?* "You two are married?" How did I not know that? "But you're so different!" I blurted out.

Andre huffed a laugh. "Married twelve years next month. We had an October wedding. And yes. We're like oil and water. But when you shake us up, we emulsify into a smooth, velvety salad dressing."

Muniba slapped Andre's shoulder. "That's gross. Samaya, careful getting involved with people in the cooking field. The metaphors are . . . colorful. And kind of disgusting, sometimes."

Andre chuckled, then lowered his voice to sound sultry. "We bring so much flavor to relationships. Sweet, and just the right amount of spicy."

"A real recipe for happiness," Daniel added.

Muniba groaned, and I laughed.

It was after four by the time we got to the shelter. Daniel and I helped unload the van before we went to the shelter dining room to go over his calculus for next week. His teacher said they would still be doing limits, so I went over the next lesson in his textbook with him. The dining room was a bright, large space with big round tables and plastic chairs, and one wall full of windows. Each table had a different colored tablecloth on it.

"I can't get over how much easier this is with you explaining it," he said. There were some women sitting at another table, and they'd brought us a full teapot and mugs when we first sat down. I was learning that the residents at the shelter had a tendency to spoil Daniel. Probably because he'd been working here so long.

"I'm really not anything special," I said. "Some people learn better one-on-one. Have you never had a tutor before?"

He shook his head. "Nah. Mom could never afford that. And I disagree. You *are* better."

I rolled my eyes and told him to do the next question on his own while I sat back with my tea. I couldn't tell if he was being flirty or friendly. That seemed to be a thing with Daniel. Watching him interact with customers today clarified this was how he was. His friendliness came across as flirty. He gave out compliments like other teens gave out snark. But it made me wonder, if he was so attentive to everyone he met, what was he like when he *really* liked someone?

He'd told Andre and Muniba we were together. Like, *together*. Why? Did he need the calculus help so much he was willing to do anything I wanted? Signs pointed to yes on that, considering he'd just called me the best teacher he'd ever had.

"Do you mind?" he said, pulling me out of my train of thought.

"Do I mind what?"

"I usually listen to music when I do homework. Do you mind if I put something on?"

I shook my head. "Go ahead. I usually have music on, too."

He fiddled with his phone a bit. A slow beat came out of the speakers.

"Nice. What is this?" I asked.

"Just some lo-fi jazz. I listen to different instrumental stuff when I'm studying, and this is my newest favorite."

I tilted my head, letting the music go through me. "It's kind of similar to the old jazz I study to. Most of my records are from the seventies or eighties."

He raised a brow, impressed. "Records? I'm surprised. You've never struck me as an old-school hipster."

I chuckled . . . and probably blushed. My old record habit was a bit quirky and sounded pretentious, which was why I rarely mentioned it to anyone. "They're my dad's old records. A bunch of jazz, and lots of classic Bollywood. Most were his dad's. When I was little Dad used to teach me to memorize math stuff by reciting it to the beat of seventies and eighties Bollywood music." I tapped my pencil along to the music. "I can still sing digits of pi to the tune of a bunch of old Hindi songs."

He smiled slowly, shaking his head. "That's so awesome. Now I want to get a record player to be as cool as you."

I blushed harder. "Don't be ridiculous. I'm not cool."

"You are! You wear math T-shirts and listen to jazz. You don't hide who you are. That's cool."

But I did hide. I was hiding right now, pretending to be the cool girl with the gamer boyfriend. That was the whole point of being with Daniel. To pretend I wasn't a mess who was still hurt by everything that had happened with Devin. My entire existence lately was pretending.

"You're cool, too," I reassured him. I sounded like a dork, though. I awkwardly took a sip of tea so he wouldn't see my face.

"I'm just a poor midrange hockey player who can't do math."

"You *can* do math. You're doing it right now." I paused. "What do you mean *midrange?*"

He refilled his mug with more tea before speaking. "It means I'm just okay at it. I'm pretty good for my rec team . . . maybe even one of the better ones on the team, but that's actually not a good place to be."

"Being the best on your team is great!"

"Not really, because people have nothing to compare you to. I'm not good enough for the pros, or hell, even the semipro team. I know that. The coaches know that, but every rando who watches me play only sees me play with my teammates, who are great guys, but not as fast skaters, or not as good at puck handling. Plus, everyone wants the feel-good story—the Filipino hockey player who came from . . . Anyway, this is probably my last season."

"Why?"

"I'm going to have college to pay for, and hockey is expensive."

Was it? I honestly had no idea. "I'm sure your parents will keep paying after high school."

"It's just my mom. And no, she can't afford it."

That didn't seem fair. He should be able to play as much as he wanted. I was about to tell him that when I saw he was looking down at his paper, focused on the problems.

I really shouldn't be prying into his personal situation anyway. That was his parameter. I refilled my tea and let him finish his work.

"There," he said a few minutes later. "I'm done. Check my work, Count."

I slid his notebook over and looked over his calculations. He'd done it perfectly. "This is right," I said. "See? You can do math. We have time for another one?"

"Nah, I think I got this. I need to get home, anyway."

As he was packing his books into his bag, I touched his arm. "Thanks, by the way. For . . . playing along with Muniba. I know we hadn't talked about what to tell people here at the shelter, and I know it's a big ask . . ."

He glanced around the room to make sure no one was listening, then smiled at me. "Not a problem at all. You're my math savior right now. I'd happily tell Taylor Swift that I was dating you if it meant I'd pass calculus. She'd write some song about teenage love and cardigans with combat boots, and it would be amazing. Hey, are you sure you don't want to go to that girl's party? You seem kind of torn about it."

"I don't know. Everyone will be there, so that would be good. You know, for people to see us. If it went well it could definitely help me win this breakup. But you're going to have to be a hard-core nerd to be believable. Some of my friends are annoyingly gate-keepery." Like Jayden. And Omar.

"Then why are you friends with them?"

That was a very good question. I mean, I wasn't really friends with them. Devin was. And I wasn't with Devin anymore. I couldn't answer, so I shrugged.

"Well, anyway, if you want, I think I can pretend to be *Mr. Count* in person," Daniel said. "At least enough to make these nerd-snobs accept me. It would be great practice for your formal."

"Yeah, but I don't think we need to practice for the formal. There won't be nearly as much talking there. It's a whole awards ceremony. Then dancing."

"Hopefully we'll talk to each other while we dance." His voice became playful. "Or are you thinking we'll gaze longingly into each other's eyes?"

He gave me a look then. A smoldering-eye, lowered-eyebrow, pursed-lips look that was so removed from his normal wide grin that my throat went dry. Oh my god, I would not survive the dance if that's how he looked at me. Because . . . I was pretty sure I was developing a small, tiny *thing* for Daniel Ramos.

I needed space. I exhaled and picked up my things.

"I need to run, too," I said. "My mom probably wants me home for dinner."

"Sure thing. Give me ten minutes and I'll walk to the bus stop with you."

I shook my head. "Google Maps says my bus will be there in three. I'm literally running. See you Thursday!"

I bolted out of the room before he could say anything else. And I didn't post our new selfie on Instagram. I needed to think.

15

He's More Myth than Boyfriend Now

I spent all Sunday working on my proposal for the game-dev project. My concept was still an RPG puzzle game in a modern setting. After jotting down my ideas and making some terrible sketches, I looked at my work. Was this idea unique enough? It needed to be amazing, not just to convince the others in the team to vote for it but also to make a splash in the competition.

In the evening I texted my friends.

Me: For the mobile game, what do you think about the characters being fairies instead of people? Living in the forest

Cass: Could be cute.

Aimee: I love it. I'll bring my sister's Tinker Bell books to school tomorrow. We can use them for research. Anyway, got to go! I have a date!

Cass: Yeah, I'm out too. We'll talk tomorrow.

I shrugged and put my phone away. I had time before I needed to finish this proposal, since the whole game-dev team wasn't meeting to vote on the game proposals for another week.

~

"You two look cute," I said to Aimee.

I was riding the bus to school with Cass and Aimee the next morning, looking at an Instagram picture of Aimee and Jayden that I'd missed from the day before. It seemed they actually went bowling for their date.

Aimee grinned. "Everything is going so well with him. I don't know how I never noticed how sexy he is. This year is going to be the best ever—mark my words."

Aimee looked so happy. Like, literally glowing. I found it hard to be mad that she was with the guy who'd been such an ass to me at that game-dev meeting. Cass raised a brow at me, though. I knew they didn't approve of Aimee brushing Jayden's bad behavior at the meeting last week under a rug.

"How come you don't have a selfie with Daniel from the weekend?" Aimee asked.

I cringed. I still felt weird about posting one of those pictures. I told Cass and Aimee all about running into Hana at the market and said I hadn't posted because I'd been hoping she would post the picture she took.

"Don't wait for others to tell your story!" Aimee said. "Control the narrative yourself! I mean, I think it adds to your credibility that Hana saw you in public together, but don't wait for her. Do it now. The hour before school starts is the busiest time on Instagram. Post something before Devin or Hana post something about their weekend plans."

She had a point. But still.

Maybe it was because I'd had such a great time on Saturday with Daniel, or maybe it was that weird moment when I was leaving the shelter and realized I'd developed a bit of a crush on him. Whenever I looked at the pictures we'd taken, all I saw was my smile. My joy at that moment. And I knew I wasn't feeling that way because of the Jamaican beef patty in my hand—or at least not *only* because of the beef patty.

Daniel's face? It was full of joy, too, but his face always radiated happiness. It wasn't because of me. I wondered if it was genuine, or was his constant cheerfulness a mask? Maybe he was pretending, like I felt I always was—except I hadn't been pretending when these pictures were taken.

It felt wrong to post this picture as part of our fake relationship when there was nothing fake about my feelings at that moment. But I had to.

Before I second-guessed myself, I uploaded three pictures, one of us before taking a bite of the patty with our eyes wide, one of us biting, and one of us laughing with my head resting on his shoulder and him looking down at me. Again, I kept the caption simple, just a heart emoji.

"There. It's done," I said.

And of course, Aimee was right: everyone seemed to be scrolling Insta right now. It got likes right away. Even a few comments. Things like, *Goals, awww*, and the heart-face emoji. Hana even commented something about how cute we were when she bumped into us that day.

It was fine. People were talking about me, but for good reasons.

That's when I saw a comment from someone whose name I didn't recognize.

I frowned. "Who's @GamesLost?" I asked my friends. "They commented *Nice hat trick.*"

Aimee looked over my shoulder at the comment. "I dunno. You aren't even wearing hats. I don't get it."

Cass shook their head. "A hat trick is a hockey thing. It means the same player scores three goals in a game. I'll bet it's one of Daniel's friends. GamesLost sounds like a hockey fan's name."

First, how did Cass know that obscure hockey thing? And also . . . I checked back to the last picture I'd posted—the one of Daniel and me walking to the bus stop. And yup—GamesLost had commented on that one, too. I hadn't thought twice about it since so many people had commented on that post.

All they'd written then was *for real* with no punctuation.

My stomach clenched in a knot. "Or sounds like a video gamer's name. I think GamesLost is LostAxis."

"*No. Shut. Up.*" Aimee took the phone from my hand and opened this GamesLost person's account.

I nodded. "There's a hat trick reference in *Dragon Arena*. It's what the drop was called when LostAxis and I got three Obsidian Staffs." I looked up at Cass. "This has to be him, and he's saying it now because I just posted three pictures."

"Or because this is the third time Daniel's on your Insta," Aimee said. "The account is private." She showed me GamesLost's profile picture. It was useless—a heavily blurred image that I didn't recognize.

I stared at the picture. Was this hat trick comment supposed to be a threat? I had no idea. What I did know was that LostAxis knew I, Samaya Janmohammad, was GreenEggsAndSam. Which meant it was very possible that my former gamer friend knew me in real life. "I need to figure out who was at the shelter on the day of the playground build. I think LostAxis is someone I know."

Cass whistled low. "That . . . wow. Who would catfish you? They're a Dark Mage, right? Maybe it's Jayden. He *does* play Dark Mage, and he seems out to get you lately." They gave Aimee a side-eye.

I frowned. Dark Mage was a difficult class to master, and Jayden was the only one I knew, other than LostAxis, who played the class well. I shook my head. "I don't think so. I've played with both Jayden's Dark Mage and with LostAxis's Dark Mage, and they have completely different playing styles. Jayden relies on solo spell combos, while LostAxis is amazing at bouncing off paired combos with me. They're both great mages, but completely different game-play styles. I doubt they're the same person."

"It's not Jayden," Aimee said emphatically. "I'd know."

Cass shrugged. "Yeah. I'm not sure Jayden has it in him to work *with* someone."

The bus was at the school by then. I was quiet, in shock as we walked into the building. I couldn't believe that LostAxis . . . my friend . . . could be someone I knew. One way or another, I needed to figure out who it was.

I had English first period that morning, and when class was over and I was walking out, I was stopped by Nabil, a guy in the game-dev club who I'd become friendly with in physics club last year. He was a bit awkward, but nice.

"Samaya," he said, looking serious. "It's completely unnecessary for you to get people to spread rumors about you. People should make their decision based on the *idea*, not because of who you're dating. This isn't a popularity contest."

"What are you talking about? Who is spreading stuff about me?" I asked, taken aback.

He looked at his phone. "Class is about to start. My French teacher makes anyone who comes in late sing Celine Dion in front of the class. I can't hit those notes."

With that he gave me a mock salute and headed down the hallway.

I checked the Earl's Whispers account—nothing there about me. I opened the chat group with Aimee and Cass.

Me: Nabil told me there's some buzz going around about who I'm dating.

Aimee: I haven't heard anything.

Cass: Could be a physics club only rumor.

Aimee: There are physics only rumors?

Me: The sciences are wild, Aimee. Let me ask someone else in physics club.

Cass: I'll ask around, too.

I wasn't in the physics club this year because Devin was in charge there, but I knew who was in the group. I sent an Instagram DM to Kavita, who'd helped me in the game-dev meeting and was in physics club.

Me: Nabil said someone was saying stuff about who I'm dating? Do you know what he's talking about?

Kavita wrote back right away.

Kavita: I've heard two things. One, that you're not going to do any of the work for the game dev, and that your new guy is like a hacker or something and plans to steal the code for a game from Russia and enter that into the competition. And two, I heard your new guy is secretly a super famous pop star in Asia. Britney swears he is bringing Jungkook and Justin Bieber to Hana's party.

Lol. *That* was the gossip I was so worried about? Where had that all come from?

Me: That's hilarious. None of it is true, by the way.

Kavita: Yeah, it's way too far-fetched to be plausible.

But even if it was untrue, this was proof that my plan was working. I was definitely the one winning the breakup right now.

I was also worried about being late for class, so I was rushing down the hallway while texting Kavita a thank-you when I walked face-first into a madras shirt.

Damn it. Devin.

"Did your cousin choose all these new clothes?" I asked instead of saying sorry for running into him. Before going to India, he'd always worn geeky T-shirts.

"What?"

I waved in the general direction of his outfit, then shook my head. "This new look is out of character for you. You said you needed to figure out who you were without me . . . Is this what you discovered? You're actually some preppy hipster?"

When he didn't respond, I looked at him. Stood and really looked at him, as this was the first time since he'd come back from India that I'd been this close to him without my hands shaking and my heart pounding. Yeah, his clothes were new, but that face was as familiar to me as my own. I'd seen him happy. I'd seen him so focused on a game or schoolwork that his coal-black eyes seemed to stop blinking. I'd seen him with that focus on me. He'd been my best friend. I'd loved him. And he'd loved me. But now, ever since he'd shut me out of his life without warning, all I felt was irritation. The shift in my feelings was kind of jarring.

But I still knew him. And I could see that Devin was miserable.

Why? Hana was still posting pictures of him all over her Insta, so in theory he was in a happy relationship. He was still president of the math and physics clubs. He hadn't become the loser crying in the cafeteria. Maybe it was the pictures of me and Daniel that were getting to him? Or was it all the hilarious buzz about Daniel being an international pop star?

I was winning the breakup at this moment, but I didn't feel all that great about it. And it wasn't fair. Why did he get to make me feel bad because he looked miserable when *he* was the one who had started this by hooking up with Hana?

"Devin," I said.

The annoyance I was feeling must have shown on my face because he recoiled.

"Are you going to tell me off again?" he asked.

"No." I sighed. "We're not supposed to talk to each other, remember?"

He stared at me for several seconds. Finally, he spoke. "Did you like the lehenga choli?"

I snorted. "I did. Your mother has impeccable taste."

He shook his head. "Mom bought the other stuff, but I bought you the lehenga. Picked it out when I was shopping with my cousin. It reminded me of the one that you liked on Gerrard Street that time we were there with our parents. There was a yellow one that you said was your dream prom dress."

I blinked. He remembered that? And he'd bought me a similar one?

153

I shook my head. "That's so weird, Devin. We broke up. Why are you buying me clothes?"

His hand shot to the back of his neck, and he bit his lip. "You always liked bright colors. You never thought you could pull them off, but I think it would look great on you." He shrugged. "Don't get mad at me—it's not a big deal. Stuff like that is cheap there."

I didn't say anything. And my stupid eyes started leaking again. Devin was like chemical warfare lately. Always making my eyes water.

"Again, we broke up," I repeated. "Why did you buy me clothes?"

"I assumed we'd still be friends when I came home," he said.

I shook my head. "It's over."

He nodded. "I know it's over. You don't have to keep saying that. I'm sorry. I bought it as a gift for a friend."

I wiped my eyes. These tears weren't even because I was sad this time. More like angry. But I was crying again. I fucking hated this was how my face reacted to him. I looked around quickly, hoping no one was around to see this, but since class had already started, the hallway was empty. And now I was late, too. Without saying a word, I turned and rushed to my next class.

During class, I texted Cass and Aimee for an emergency lunch meeting away from anyone else. We met behind the school, where Aimee used her ever-present makeup-removing wipes to clean my smudged eye makeup.

"I should stop wearing the stuff," I said. "This is the second time I've leaked all over my face at school."

"Which means you should stop talking to Devin Kapadia, not stop looking like a badass," Aimee said. "Have you heard the rumor that you and Daniel are doing an ad campaign for a hot new Toronto designer?"

I chuckled. Considering my sister was on the verge of becoming a hot new Toronto designer, it wasn't that far-fetched. But still. I was hardly model material. Daniel, maybe, but not me. "My 'dating Daniel' plan is working a little too well, I think," I said.

"Yeah," Cass said. "Tales of your legendary new boyfriend are being spread far and wide, and your ex looks like he's going to cry every time someone mentions you."

I snorted . . . and a snot bubble flew out of my nose. Wiping it on the tissue Aimee had given me, I shook my head. "I wish he *would* cry. And that someone would take a picture of him and post it on Whispers."

"Have you found out who made that GamesLost Instagram comment yet?" Cass asked. "I asked around a bit and no one knows whose account it is."

I shook my head. "It's LostAxis. I just know it." I sighed. "I'll bet he's someone from the guild. Hell, they could be the same person behind Earl's Whispers, too. Seems a bit excessive to have two secret saboteurs in my life, doesn't it?"

"Now you're reaching, Samaya. I doubt LostAxis is Earl's Whispers," Cass said. "Cuz whoever's behind Earl's Whispers is out to get you. But the gamer person was your friend. I mean, yeah, they lied about what they looked like. But that wasn't some giant plan to ruin you."

I shrugged. "A lie is a lie. I *know* I never told LostAxis my real name. If they're commenting on my Instagram, then they know me personally, and never mentioned that to me. That's a bigger lie than just lying about what they look like. They may not be Earl's Whispers, but they could be the one sending tips to them. And those comments could be a threat."

"And you think whoever it is, is an Earl's student?" Cass asked.

I nodded. "I mean, probably? Most kids I know go to Earl's." I didn't really know anyone that well who went to another school. Except Daniel.

"I agree. They probably go to Earl's and are in the guild," Aimee said. "And I think you should go to Hana's to find out who they are. For sure they'll confess when they see you brought the guy in the picture."

I shook my head vigorously. "No! I burst into tears whenever I talk to Devin. I'll make a fool of myself, and Hana will tell her aunt. I'll lose my volunteer job, and then I won't get any scholarships, and Daniel will see that I'm such a mess and he won't want—"

"You're catastrophizing, Samaya. Why would you lose a job because you cried?" Cass asked.

"And why do you care what Daniel thinks of you?" Aimee added. "He's going to help you no matter what, because you're helping him with calc."

Aimee was right. It shouldn't matter at all what Daniel thought of me. But it did matter. A lot.

"Look, if LostAxis goes to Earl's and played *Dragon Arena*," Aimee said, "they'll be at Hana's. Everyone will be at Hana's. You have to bring Daniel."

I bit my lip and shook my head. "He's such a jock, though."

Cass raised a brow. "Now you're looking for excuses. I happen to know several great jocks. One in particular—"

"C'mon, Cass. A jock wouldn't last an hour with our crew. Plus, I told everyone he was into math like me, and he actually hates math." I knew I was making excuses here. Daniel got along with everyone—he'd be fine. But I was so nervous about taking him to this party.

"He can fake it. We'll teach him to be nerdier. Come on, Samaya," Aimee said, rubbing her hands together. "This is the perfect opportunity to show them all how happy you are. Remember, the best revenge is living well. And most importantly it's makeover time! I can't believe I get to do this, but we get to turn a jock into a nerd."

I exhaled. "Okay. Fine."

16

Let the Nerd Lessons Commence

When I got home after school, I called Daniel to give him the news. We were going to Hana's after all, but I needed to give him a nerd-over first.

"Okay . . . *what*?" he asked.

I sighed. "I know, I know. You need a nerd makeover. And lessons. My friends will help."

"Nerd lessons," he deadpanned.

This was ridiculous. "Yeah, you know, we'll teach you more about the geeky stuff in case it comes up in conversations." Geeky stuff would definitely come up in conversations.

"But I thought you didn't want to go?"

"I don't. But this is the best way to figure out who LostAxis is. I think he's been commenting on my Insta and knows me IRL. We're hoping if I show up with you, he'll confess who he is. Anyway, you said you wanted to see Hana's house. My friend Cass can pick you up and drive you home . . . they have a car."

"Friday night?" he asked.

"Yes."

"I'll be baking at the shelter after school. Can they get me there?"

"Sure."

"But first I need nerd lessons?"

"If you don't want to go, that's fine—"

"No, of course I'll go. I'm just messing with you. I promised you three dates." I could hear the smile in his voice. "Turn me into the nerd of your dreams, Samaya."

~

Our first order of business had to be his clothing. Every self-respecting gamer-nerd needed a shirt that broadcast his fandom of choice. I had a few *Dragon Arena* shirts, and some math-themed tees, but there was no way Daniel would fit into them. And neither Cass nor Aimee had anything that would work.

Any decent shirt had to be mail ordered, and we couldn't get it by Friday. But thankfully, getting shirts quickly was one area where I had an advantage. I had a fashion designer sister who'd had her own little T-shirt e-commerce store for a year now.

I went searching for Tahira later that night and found her sewing in her room. I sat on her bed and hugged a pillow to my chest. "I have a T-shirt emergency."

She barely looked up from her machine. "Finally realizing that you need at least one shirt without a pun on it?"

I looked down at my shirt. It was a programming shirt that said {!FALSE} (It's funny because it's true). It wasn't my favorite shirt, but I thought it was witty.

"It's not for me, it's for Daniel."

"Your fake boyfriend. Aren't I already getting him a suit for your dance?"

I nodded. "Yes, and you're the best sister in the world and I appreciate you, but I'm also bringing him to a party on the weekend and I need him to look the part. All his clothes are, like, hockey jerseys. Or other sports crap."

Tahira laughed and turned her chair to look at me. "Yeah, I don't think anyone would buy you dating a sports nut. Go to the mall and get something nerdy."

"But I need him to have some real credibility—no local stores have any good *Dragon Arena* merch, and there isn't time to order online. Can you make a rush custom shirt that says Come to the Dark Mage Side . . . we have offensive melee spells? In like, *Star Wars* font."

Tahira frowned. "Are you sure you and I are related?"

"C'mon, Tahira. You're the only one I know who can do this. Hana's party is on Friday, and everyone will be there."

"Why are you even going to your ex-boyfriend's new girlfriend's party?"

"To figure out who was catfishing me in *Dragon Arena* all summer."

Tahira shook her head. "Samaya, did it ever occur to you that maybe you spend too much time focusing on things that aren't really important? Imagine what your grades would be like if you put all this energy into your schoolwork instead."

"You sound like Mom. Plus, I'm a high-nineties student—how high do you want my grades?"

She shook her head. "I just don't get why he can't be himself for your friends to approve of him."

"Yeah, maybe if we were really dating he could, but we're not, so what difference does it make if he's pretending to be someone else?"

Tahira sighed. "Fine. I have some yellow iron-on sheets for the printer. What size does he wear? Wait, this is the guy from your Insta, right? Those muscles need a large-size shirt. He's going to be the buffest gamer in existence."

"Hardly. Henry Cavill is a serious gamer."

"Yeah, but he's also Superman. Leave this with me, Samaya. I'll have a T-shirt for you by Friday."

Okay, step one of Daniel's makeover was done. Next up: teach him enough about *Dragon Arena* so he could carry out a conversation.

I wasn't too worried about math conversations. Yeah, most of my friends were into math, science, and computers, but it wasn't like we talked about functions and the Pythagorean theorem at parties.

But conversations about *Dragon Arena* were most definitely going to happen at this party. There was no way there was enough time to teach Daniel to actually play *Dragon Arena* well enough to convince the others he'd been playing for close to a year in a few days . . . but maybe I could stream for him while I played so he could see how the game worked?

I quickly sent Cass a few texts, and soon we had what felt like a workable plan. I'd start a Discord server for only me, Daniel, and Cass. Then Cass and I would do a duo quest and stream onto the Discord for Daniel to watch us. Maybe I'd even start a new Dark Mage character so he could understand that class. Since Daniel himself said that Discord was the only social platform he used, hopefully this solution would work for him.

~

Tuesday night, Daniel and I worked for half an hour over FaceTime on his calculus. He was understanding it . . . sort of. I did have to explain the new concepts to him a few times, but I was getting addicted to the look on his face when the light bulb lit and he understood. It was like his already-big smile got bigger.

"Man," he said, shaking his head as he wrote in his notebook. He'd propped up his phone on a dresser again, and I could see him sitting cross-legged on the middle of his bed with that floral bedspread. "I really think you should think about being a high school math teacher instead of a math computer."

"I don't want to be a math computer; I want to study *computational mathematics*." My phone was propped up on my desk for our video call.

"Whatever." He shook his head, smiling. "Well, hopefully part of that is showing others how to do complicated stuff. Because you excel at that."

"Well, considering the next thing I'm going to be showing you is how to fit in with my friends, it's a good thing you think I'm good at this. Are you feeling okay with the calculus for now?"

"Yes!" He exaggeratedly closed his notebook. "It's time to learn to nerd!"

I laughed. "Yeah. We have a lot to go over."

"I'm ready. You have no idea how much time you've freed up for me. This homework would have taken me three hours if I had to figure it out on my own," he said. "Okay, what first? Do I need to dress like a vampire when I come to this party? I have a black Toronto Maple Leafs T-shirt somewhere. I much prefer the traditional blue but—"

"No. No sports shirts. No jerseys. No hockey T-shirts."

"What about soccer?"

"Do you wear soccer shirts?"

"I'm literally wearing a Toronto FC shirt right now." He pointed to it. "The team is awesome."

I shook my head. "No sports. I already got you a *Dragon Arena* shirt. And you'll need to be able to talk about your fandoms."

"Fandoms." He shook his head. "Like *Star Wars* or some shit? Honestly, I'm not really into light swords or lasers."

I closed my eyes. This was going to be harder than I thought. "Light*sabers*."

He shook his head, disappointed. "I was making a *joke*. I know they're called lightsabers. I may not be into *Star Wars*, but I am a human being living in this century."

I exhaled. "Okay, so *Star Wars* isn't your fandom. Is there a fandom you *are* into? Like me . . . I like *Star Wars*, but I'm also into *Doctor Who* and She-Ra. And I like anime."

"You're, like, seventeen, and you still watch cartoons?"

"Yes. Now, there must be *something* you like." I crossed my legs on my desk chair. "*Lord of the Rings*, *Game of Thrones*, MCU?"

"What's MCU?"

"Marvel Cinematic Universe. The Marvel movies."

"Ah, like Avengers and Superman."

I shook my head. "Superman is DC. But yes, like the Avengers. Although DC would work, too. You into Batman?"

"No, but I've seen some of the Avengers movies. They're fun. Would this Marvel stuff be nerdy enough for your friends?"

I shook my head, laughing. What was I doing? This conversation was surreal. "Yeah, it would be fine. It's not like a super hard-core obscure fandom, but it works. If anyone asks, you're really into the MCU. Read the MCU Wiki, pick a favorite character and movie, and learn as much as you can about it. If anyone asks you something you don't know, we'll deflect. *Dragon Arena* is your main fandom, with a side of MCU. You'll need to know more about *Dragon Arena*."

"Okay. Should I start a character?"

"There's no point. You're supposed to be a level-fifty Dark Mage, and you'll never get that far. We just have to make people *think* you play. Cass and I are going to do a duo quest and stream it live onto a private Discord channel so you can watch us."

He shrugged. "Okay. Sounds like a plan. When are we doing this?"

I couldn't tonight—I had an English essay due tomorrow. "When can you do it? Tomorrow night?"

"Can't. I have hockey practice," Daniel said. "I can do Thursday night."

"We're at the shelter Thursday, remember?"

"After the shelter. How much time do we need?"

"Couple of hours?" He'd only be watching me play once, and somehow the next day he had to pass as a level-fifty Dark Mage.

"I'm free all night after the shelter."

"All right," I said. "Until then, you have homework. Calculus, and MCU and *Dragon Arena* Wiki."

"Got it, teacher. Talk soon."

I had no idea what I was getting myself into, but there was no turning back now. In three days, I was going to unveil my fake boyfriend to the world.

17

Nerd-Boy Interrogation

After I got home from the shelter on Thursday evening, I warmed up a bowl of leftover biriyani. Mom was working late tonight, so she told us all to fend for ourselves for dinner, which worked well for me. Daniel, Cass, and I were meeting on the Discord channel in about half an hour to start Daniel's *Dragon Arena* training.

I was in my room at my computer logging in to the game when I got a text from Daniel.

Daniel: Not going to be able to play tonight. Something came up. But still good for the party tomorrow. See you then!

I stared at my phone. He was canceling on me? Why? The party was tomorrow. Today was his last chance to learn about *Dragon Arena*.

I texted Cass, sending them a screenshot of Daniel's message.

Cass: Did you respond?

Me: I don't know what to say. He didn't even tell me why he's canceling.

Cass: Yes, he said something came up.

Me: I know. It's just he promised. I spent hours working on calculus with him this week.

Cass: And he's still coming to the party. We'll stay close to him and make sure no one interrogates him on the best armor for Dark Mages.

I sighed. Of course Cass was right. I'd already been worried that this arrangement was benefiting me more than him. I couldn't be mad here. When I didn't write anything back, Cass wrote again.

Cass: You're too hyper focused on the details here. No one will care about what he's into or what he's wearing. All that matters is that the guy from your insta comes to the party. He doesn't need Dragon Arena lessons.

I huffed at that. *Of course* I was focused on *details*. I was a math and programming nerd.

Me: Well, I don't have much of a choice now.

Cass: Write back to him. And be nice.

I opened the text to him.

Me: Okay, I understand. See you tomorrow!

~

"Is he going to change into that shirt in the car?" Aimee asked. She was sitting in the front passenger seat, while I was in the back of the car. "I wouldn't mind a peek of some hockey abs." She turned back to look at me, waggling her brows up and down.

"Don't objectify my fake boyfriend," I said.

It was Friday evening and we were ready for Hana's party. Cass had picked up me and Aimee, and we were on our way to the shelter to get Daniel.

Aimee turned back around and laughed. "Honestly, though, I'm excited to see if he's as hot in person as those pictures, right, Cass?"

Cass didn't say anything. Which didn't surprise me. I knew that deep down Cass didn't approve of this whole "turning Daniel into something he wasn't" scheme.

I sighed as I fiddled with the clasp of my bag. I was still feeling a bit off since he'd canceled on me the day before. And Cass's comment that I was hyperfocusing hadn't left me. The truth was, I didn't like *using* a good guy like Daniel. And maybe I *was* worrying about details too much. I needed to ease up a bit.

But I was still monumentally nervous about this party. So much could go wrong. Not even counting the part that Daniel was going to a *Dragon Arena* party when he'd never even seen game play, but also Muniba could have told Hana that Daniel was no math nerd, or that we met at the shelter, not online last year. Also, what would happen if LostAxis, whoever he was, was actually there and made a scene? I hated conflict. Maybe this plan of drawing out the catfisher by showing up with Daniel at a busy party wasn't such a brilliant idea.

Daniel was waiting outside the shelter when we got there, holding a huge reusable grocery bag. I hopped out of the car after Cass parked.

He looked exactly like he always did, wearing black jeans and a Toronto Maple Leafs T-shirt, but it still felt weird to see him. Maybe because it was evening. This was officially the first time I'd seen him after the sun had set. It was, of course, not the first time we'd seen each other this week—we'd been baking together only yesterday. To my relief, those weird twinges of a crush I'd felt at the market on Saturday hadn't made an appearance then.

But this *was* our first date. Even if it was a fake date. It was no wonder I had major stomach butterflies as I walked up to him. Without saying anything, I handed him the T-shirt my sister had made for him. In return, he handed me the grocery bag.

I took it and peeked in. It was filled with records.

"What are these for?"

He smiled. "They're for you! The shelter had a donation this morning and there was a stack of records, but there's no record player here. Andre got excited and took a bunch, but I snagged these ones for you. They're mostly movie soundtracks from the sixties and seventies. I know you said you were more into seventies jazz, but I thought you might like these, too."

I looked more closely at the album covers, recognizing a few movie titles. I smiled at him. "These are amazing! Thank you so much!"

"No problem!" He grinned, then held up the T-shirt I'd given him. He shook his head. "Ha! This is actually funny! I don't really get the appeal of broadcasting to the world what your favorite video game is on your T-shirt, but I like this."

I chuckled. "It's no different than you broadcasting your favorite stick and puck team."

"Touché. I'll go change . . . Back in five." He hurried back into the shelter, and I turned to head to Cass's car when a small voice startled me. "I think our forest is full of fairies like in the book."

I turned around and smiled at Yasmin. She stood in the light near the door of the shelter. "It's dark out," I told her. "Does your mother know you're out here?"

She nodded. She was wearing a green sweatshirt with blue sweat-pants, and her hair was pulled tight to the back of her head. "She said I could come out and say thank you for the book."

I smiled. "You're welcome."

Aimee had brought a couple of her sister's old Tinker Bell and other fairy books to school this week for inspiration for the game. One of them was a picture book written like a field guide to fairies in the wild, and I asked Aimee if I could bring it to the shelter for Yasmin. I'd given it to her mother the day before.

"Have you seen fairies in the trees before?" Yasmin asked.

I shook my head. "I don't go into forests very much. I'm allergic to cedar trees. Hey, Yasmin, I need to say thank you to you, too. You gave me the idea to make my video game about fairies, and now we might be doing that."

She glanced toward the forest. "You're welcome. Mama's going to take me to look for some fairies when she has time."

Daniel came back out with a gray hoodie zipped up over the shirt.

"We need to leave now," I told Yasmin, "but make sure to take pictures of fairies if you find any. I'll need them for research for my game." I waved goodbye, and Daniel and I headed to Cass's car.

Before Daniel got into the back seat, he unzipped his hoodie with a flourish and took it off. "Am I nerded up to your satisfaction?"

I laughed, then looked at him. And wow—I'd only ever seen him in colored shirts—red for the Raptors, blue for Leafs, and mostly jerseys. But this black T-shirt with a dragon on it? I would *not* have thought it would change him so much. But it did. He *looked* the part. The shirt stretched over his broad shoulders, so he still appeared pretty buff, but the dark color made him, I don't know, less bright and sunny, and more . . . complicated. Mysterious. And of course, less like a jock. He was now the kind of guy I would turn to look at twice at Comic-Con or something.

I nodded, smiling, then got into the car. "You're a perfect geek."

Once Daniel was in the car, too, I introduced him. "Cass, Aimee, this is Daniel."

They turned their heads to greet him as we buckled our seat belts.

"Ah. Aimee. You're the artist who first started my relationship with Samaya with your Photoshop skills," Daniel said.

"I am," Aimee said. "And wow, remind me to get some more pics of you tonight. You two look amazing together."

I frowned but didn't say anything. Our parameters had a strict number of pictures—if others took pics, would I have to subtract them?

During the twenty-minute drive to Hana's house in the posh Beach neighborhood of Toronto, the three of us gave Daniel as much *Dragon Arena* backstory as we could. Then Cass and Aimee took turns quizzing him on the kind of questions they expected he'd be asked at the party.

"How did you and Samaya meet?" Cass asked.

"On a *Dragon Arena* message board," Daniel answered. "I was looking for a level thirty to thirty-five Light Mage to do a Purple Topaz Dragon Egg questline with."

"You sound like you're reading from a walk-through. Call it a Purple Topaz run," Cass suggested.

"What level is your Dark Mage now?" Aimee asked.

"Fifty. But I haven't played much since school started."

We knew people would want to look up Daniel's character in game, and obviously, he didn't really have a level-fifty character to play with, so this was our solution. There was no way to look up a player unless they were online at the time. Daniel could say he rarely played during the school year, and if pressed, he could claim to have given up the game altogether.

"What's your character's name?" Cass asked.

"IceMagic, because it's my preferred magic class," said Daniel. It was dark, so I couldn't see his expression, but I could tell he was proud of that name.

"Nice," I said. "I assume *ice* for hockey?"

"Yup."

"Love the *Star Wars* joke on your shirt. What's your fav *Star Wars* movie or canon story?" Aimee asked, moving on to non–*Dragon Arena* questions.

Daniel shrugged. "Not a fan of the prequels, but the original trilogy is great. I don't acknowledge the existence of *The Last Jedi*."

I gave him an impressed nod. He'd done some research. "Well done," I said.

"I'm more into the MCU," Daniel added.

"Oooh, that's good," Cass said. "What's your fav?"

We passed under a streetlight, so I saw the ridiculously pleased grin on his face. "*Thor: Ragnarok*."

Cass laughed at that.

I shook my head at Daniel, grimacing. "No."

Daniel frowned. "Something wrong with *Ragnarok*? I thought it was hilarious."

"It was good, but it wouldn't be a *real* fanboy's choice," Cass said. "It's too silly. Not epic enough. Either *Avengers: Infinity War* or *Endgame* is your answer."

He frowned. "I haven't seen *Endgame*."

"I thought you were going to do homework?" I asked.

He glared at me. "I did. I looked up all the movies and characters. But I didn't have time to actually watch them because I had hockey practice and was baking twice this week."

I noticed he didn't mention the mysterious thing that made him cancel on me last night. I sighed. He was right. I couldn't exactly expect him to be, like, an MCU expert already.

"It's fine," Aimee said. "We can deflect any convo that's headed in the wrong direction. Do you have a favorite video game? Other than *Dragon Arena*. We can try to steer conversations to things you know."

"*HockeyStars 2016*. Not a fan of any of the more recent versions, but I play 2021 onlin e with my friends."

I raised a brow. "Why is your favorite the old version of the game?"

"Because that's the season Matt Dumba scored ten goals and sixteen assists."

"Who's Matt Dumba?" Aimee asked.

"Filipino-Canadian hockey player. But also, the controls are better in the old game. Not sure what they did with it after that year, but stick handling is not as sensitive anymore. I think maybe they outsourced to another studio, but of course it's not something they would admit. I'm a purist—I like the old play style." He continued for a while about the difference between *HockeyStars 2016* and later editions of the sports game franchise.

"I dunno, Samaya," Cass said with a laugh from behind the steering wheel. "He's already a total nerd. A makeover was not necessary."

I shook my head. "He can't talk about hockey games all night."

"Actually, I could," Daniel said.

"There's nothing wrong with hockey," Cass said. "Let him be himself."

"He sounds like a jock. I can't date a jock." I turned to Daniel. "No offense."

He shook his head. "None taken. I remember your boundary."

"Samaya, you're being elitist," Cass said, annoyed. "There's nothing wrong with jocks."

"I know there's nothing wrong with jocks," I said. I looked at Daniel. I mean, I'd had a crush on a jock for days now. It was this jock sitting right next to me. "You know how the vultures at Earl's are. I mean, can't you just see Jayden's face?" I paused. I kept forgetting that Aimee was dating Jayden now.

"Jayden hates hockey. He'd call Daniel vapid and say you're slumming it," Aimee said, proving my point. Which made me wonder again: Why exactly *was* Aimee dating that douche?

"Samaya, really," Cass said, her voice firm. "All this would be easier if you let him be him. Let him talk about *Dragon Arena* and MCU, but let him go on forever about the controls in his hockey game, too."

"Or about if bars and squares are cakes or cookies?" Daniel asked, hopefully.

I laughed, then thought about it. Both Cass and Tahira had now said I shouldn't care so much what people like Jayden and the rest of the guild thought about me. And maybe they were right.

I did want to impress the people here, but they were people just like me. And *I myself* liked Daniel just the way he was.

"Oh, I meant to tell you, Samaya," Aimee said. "Jayden's not submitting a game proposal for the game-dev club. And I don't think anyone else is making a proposal, so we can go ahead with the fairies game!"

"What? Why is he dropping out all of a sudden?" We were supposed to vote on Monday. I'd been working hard on my proposal, but Jayden seemed hell-bent on being team captain.

"Oh, because I said . . ." Aimee hesitated. I'd known her long enough—she knew I wouldn't like what she was going to say.

"Why, Aim?" Cass asked.

"Because I said you'd play Light Mage for the diamond run. He's having a party in a few weeks."

"Aimee!" I shook my head. "I already told him no! I'm not playing in the guild anymore!"

"But you said you really need to be captain for the game-dev team! Come on, Samaya . . . this helps everyone. You don't have to bring Daniel, but c'mon. Do it for the game-dev team. Do it for me! Jayden really wants to do the run, and you're better than the other Light Mages in the guild."

I frowned. Maybe I should do it for Aimee. If she and Jayden were going to continue to be a thing, then maybe I needed to suck it up and try to mend things with him to keep my friend. "Fine. I'll think about it. Just me, though," I added, looking at Daniel reassuringly.

"Yay!" Aimee clapped her hands. "It's going to be epic."

"We're here," Cass said, parking on the street in front of Hana's house. Aimee unbuckled her seat belt and turned to us again, smiling at Daniel. "Don't mind Samaya. She's feeling all nervous since her ex will be here, and Samaya gets controlling when she's anxious."

I rolled my eyes, then got out of the car.

Daniel got out and walked around to my side of the car. He held out his hand. "Would you like to hold hands as we walk in?"

I took his hand. I could do this. It would be fine. He squeezed my hand. I probably didn't deserve that squeeze. I wished there were a way to tell him that he was more than enough just the way he was, and that if this relationship were real, I would be proud to walk in with him in a Leafs jersey and carrying a bumbleberry pie.

But it wasn't real, so we couldn't be completely real, either.

18

The Party

My family was pretty comfortable money-wise, but Hana's family was capital-*R* rich, as far as I could tell. Her backyard was *fancy*. Most of the space was taken up by several decks at different levels, with huge rectangular planters lining the edges. There were lots of people standing around on them, talking and holding drinks. A large pergola strung with bright lights lit up the dark evening. And there was a huge U-shaped couch with a bunch of kids on it. Down a few steps was another deck, this one with a circular gas firepit in the middle and speakers playing loud pop music. Kids were sitting around the fire. I couldn't really make out who they were, but I could see Devin.

I could always find Devin.

Aimee headed down there right away—I assumed because she'd seen Jayden somewhere among the others.

"Samaya and Cass!" Hana came up to us exuberantly. She grinned widely. She was wearing a long, black floral dress with a cardigan, and her long hair was in a high ponytail. She looked like a goth-boho hybrid. And she was carrying a red Solo cup, the liquid sloshing onto the patio as she reached us.

"Ohhh, and Samaya, you brought your tasty new boy." She put her hand on Daniel's forearm. "I'm still dreaming about the cookies my mom bought from your shop. What were they called? They had a weird name . . ."

"Um. Oatmeal chocolate chip?" Daniel said.

"Amazing. A boy who can bake. Samaya, you have the best luck with guys. I mean, you can tell we have the same taste." She giggled and glanced to where Devin was talking with some others.

I suppressed an eye roll. She sounded drunk. "Nice dress, Hana," I said, hoping that would stop her from talking even more about Daniel. Or Devin.

"Isn't it amazing? I got it when Mom took me to buy a dress for the fall formal. Did you get a dress yet?"

"My sister ordered me one from a designer she knows. Wholesale." I knew that would impress her.

"Nice. You're so lucky. My sister's in law school—not as cool as fashion school. C'mon, let me get you a drink. Or snacks? My mom ordered a jumbo sushi platter. My parents aren't home, but my brother's inside. He's *chaperoning*, but don't worry, he's cool." Hana leaned in close. "He bought vodka coolers if you want one. Or there's some of those fruity soda waters, too. Or pop. Whatever!"

Daniel looked at me, brow raised. I didn't drink. But I'd been to parties with drinking enough times not to be surprised at Hana's offer. My group weren't hard-core drinkers. Most of the time. There was the time last year that Aimee and Omar got so drunk they fell into Jayden's pool together. But really, this was more of a play-board-games-or-video-games-and-watch-movies kind of crowd than a wild underage-drinking party crowd.

But still, I didn't know if people drinking here would be an issue for Daniel. I also didn't know if he was the rat-me-out-to-Andre-for-being-at-a-party-with-alcohol kind of guy.

"I'll have a Coke," he said.

I told Hana I'd have one of the fruity soda things, and Cass asked for the same. Hana disappeared to get the drinks.

"This party isn't what I expected," Daniel said. He swung his arm a bit, and I realized we were still holding hands. Should I take my hand back now?

I cringed. "Sorry . . . I should have told you there'd be drinking here. There's probably weed somewhere, too. I don't drink or anything else, but I really don't care if you want to."

He laughed. "It's not the drinking that's a surprise. It's just . . . the party isn't how I pictured it."

"What did you picture?" Cass asked.

He shrugged. "I don't really know. Not this."

We headed to the empty corner of the couch thing, and the three of us sat, with Daniel next to me and Cass across from us. Daniel and I weren't holding hands anymore. People were looking curiously at us, probably because of all the ridiculous rumors that had spread about Daniel this week.

Cass started talking to this girl from our physics class who was also on the sofa. Daniel leaned in close so no one would hear him. "You told me this was a geek party. This looks totally normal, except . . ." He looked around the yard. "Prettier. More posh."

I laughed. "Well, it's only pretty because Hana's mother's an interior designer. But what did you expect from a geek party? A bunch of neckbeards playing *D&D*?"

His face brightened. "I love *Dungeons and Dragons!*"

I looked at Daniel and blinked. Did he say what I think he said? "Excuse me? Do you . . . have you . . . how do you even know what *D&D* is?"

Oh my god, my jock-pretend-boyfriend who I was trying to turn into a geek played *D&D*, so he was arguably already even geekier than me.

But Daniel shook his head. "Last year Andre tried to teach a bunch of us at the shelter. Do you actually drink those fruit-water things? I'm not a fan. Drinks need some sugar, IMO."

I frowned. He clearly didn't want to talk about this *D&D* thing, even though I was fascinated with this new knowledge. This totally would give him credibility here.

But if he didn't want to talk about it, I would let it go. Because *parameters*.

"Here you go!" Hana called, hurrying across the patio with a can of Coke and a LaCroix. "Sorry it took me so long. I was talking to Aimee. We're going to put the *Dragon Arena* movie on soon. As soon as it's a bit darker out so we can see it properly. The last thing we need is to make that movie look even worse."

Damn. I didn't know we'd be watching that. I hadn't told Daniel anything about the terrible direct-to-streaming musical that the *Dragon Arena* game was technically based on. The movie was a running joke among players of the game. If Daniel were really a hard-core player, he'd have at least heard of it. More likely, he'd have seen it. Even more likely, he'd have participated in a rousing sing-along with a roomful of other fans watching the movie.

"I thought we were watching the new Silverborn?" I asked.

"Oh, we will. Probably. I doubt we'll get more than twenty minutes into *Dragon Arena* before we'll want to gouge our eyes out." She grinned at Daniel. "You're not one of those purists who actually likes the movie, are you? I think that would be a deal breaker for Samaya."

Damn it. I needed to change the subject. "Hey, Hana, what—"

Daniel put his hand on my arm, stopping me. "I *love* the idea of watching *Dragon Arena* outside. The last time I saw it was at one of those screenings downtown, and they had people shoot water guns at the audience when the matriarch dragon started crying after the hero stole her egg. Do you have water guns?"

Wow. He really *had* done his research. Also, the *Dragon Arena* Wiki was really thorough.

Hana clapped her hands. "Oh, of course I do. I'll pass them out with the kazoos for the final battle. I've always wanted to go to one of those screenings. You guys went before, right?" she said, directing the question to someone behind us.

It was Omar and Carson. "Yeah, last year," Carson said. "The theater smelled like cheese and bleach."

Omar and Carson sat next to Cass while Hana headed away toward where Devin was sitting. Omar immediately glared at Daniel, mistrust in his eyes.

Was it possible that Omar was LostAxis, and he was glaring at Daniel now because Daniel was pretending to be him? Omar was usually a good guy, but he had been Devin's friend first, and I'd barely spoken to him since the breakup. If Devin was at the playground build, Omar would have definitely been there, too, because Omar always did what Devin and Jayden did. He normally played an archer in the game and was quite good. I'd never seen him play a mage, so I had no idea what his game-play style would be with a magic class. I couldn't rule him out the way I'd ruled out Jayden.

But if Omar was LostAxis, I had no idea why he would pretend to be someone else to play *Dragon Arena* with me. It didn't make sense.

"How long you been playing, anyway?" Omar asked Daniel, his question sounding like some kind of accusation. *Suspicious.*

Daniel shrugged. "About a year. But I don't play much anymore. Not a lot of time lately. I volunteer with Samaya at the family shelter, and I play hockey. We've had a lot of practices as we gear up for the season opener."

"And you're a Dark Mage, right?"

Daniel nodded. My hackles went up. I glanced at Cass, but they were still talking to their physics friend.

Maybe I could draw out a confession from Omar? "I met Daniel questing," I said.

"When?" Omar asked, still looking at Daniel, and not me.

"Last March," I replied, "we played almost daily all summer. He's such a great player. Honestly, there are no better mages in the guild." I narrowed my eyes, waiting for Omar to confess.

"What level Dark Mage are you?" Omar asked Daniel.

"Fifty," Daniel said.

He scowled. "I'd like to see you play. You need to come to Jayden's party. We're doing the Diamond Egg quest. You ever do it?"

Omar was *definitely* LostAxis. It's the only reason he would be acting so menacing to Daniel. But I didn't know how to make him confess. Daniel shook his head. "Nope. Always wanted to. Maybe I'll come."

My head shot around to glare at Daniel. Why did he always agree to go to my friends' parties without checking with me first?

Omar practically growled at him.

This was starting to worry me. Omar was pissed. Which made sense if he was LostAxis, because Daniel had basically stolen his identity. Was Omar going to cause a fight? A scene? So soon after we got here? It was of course laughable that he would consider a physical altercation with Daniel—a hockey bruiser. Omar wasn't a small guy, but there was no way he'd win against Daniel. I'd never seen Omar look so angry.

Cass finally sensed the tension and stood. "Hey, guys," they said. "Let's get some food before it's all gone. Daniel, Samaya, come on."

Daniel looked at Cass blankly before getting up.

"Wait, Samaya," Omar said before I could stand. "Can I talk to you for a sec? Carson, could you leave us alone?"

I frowned. He was going to confess. I didn't like the idea of having this conversation alone. But maybe Omar wouldn't say anything with the others here. And I wanted that confession—it was the main reason I'd come to this party: to find out who LostAxis was.

I nodded, then looked at Daniel. "Can you grab something for me? You know what I like."

Daniel frowned. The look he gave me clearly said he was concerned about leaving me, and he'd stay if I asked him to.

I shook my head. "It's okay. Go ahead." I smiled.

Hana left with Cass and Daniel, leaving me alone with Omar.

The moment they were out of earshot, Omar said, "Where did you say you met him again?"

"In game." Which was not actually where I met LostAxis. We first met on a *Dragon Arena* message board. But I was curious if Omar would correct me, proving he knew it was a lie.

"When? And what's his name in game?"

I squeezed my fist. "Why are you asking so many questions, Omar?"

It had to be him. Which . . . *ugh*. Omar was LostAxis? *Really?* I had nothing against Omar. He was a bit of a goof, and always did whatever Devin did. But why would my ex-boyfriend's sidekick catfish me? It didn't add up. Maybe he had a crush on me?

I could not wrap my head around the idea that it had been Omar the whole time. LostAxis had been my friend. He'd made me laugh, and we'd played *Dragon Arena* so well together. We were completely in sync with each other. We were an amazing pair.

Maybe there was more to Omar than I had assumed.

Omar shrugged, his jaw still tense. "I think it's awfully convenient that you have this guy ready the moment you and Devin split. You were already playing with him before you and Devin even broke up. When did you first meet IRL? And what exactly did you talk *about* for so long online while you were still with Devin?"

I blinked. Wait. *What?* Was he accusing me of, like . . . *sexting* with LostAxis? Could it be possible that Omar's anger here had nothing to do with him actually being LostAxis, and was because he thought I'd *cheated* on Devin? With LostAxis? I snorted a laugh. "Um . . . you do know that Devin broke up with *me*, right?"

"Yes, but he's never really said why. Maybe he caught you talking to that guy. Or maybe not just talking."

That. Was. *Hilarious.* I laughed. Loudly. At least I knew he wasn't LostAxis, because then he'd know I wasn't sexting the guy.

"What's so funny?" Cass asked. Daniel and Cass were back, each with a plate of food.

I scooted to let them sit back down. "Omar thinks I cheated on Devin. With Daniel."

"I never said that," Omar said, still clearly furious.

I chuckled. "Yes, you did. And it's preposterous. I'm not even going to defend myself. Ask Devin why we broke up. And while you're at it, get him to explain it to me again, because your boy didn't make any sense. And he's the one who started hooking up with Hana while he still had jet lag." I was less amused and angrier the more I spoke. Because why shouldn't I be angry? After everything Devin did . . . did his friends honestly think I had cheated?

"What's going on here?" a voice behind me said. A voice I knew a little too well.

"Devin, this has nothing to do with you," I said. "Go back to Hana."

"I could hear you talking about me, so I think it *does* have something to do with me. Omar?"

Omar shook his head, giving me a look of distain. "It's all good, bro. Samaya and I were just talking."

"Whatever." I stood. Why had I thought coming to this party was anything resembling a good idea. "C'mon, Daniel, let's go check out that croquet game before the movie starts. It's kind of hockey-like, right? Sticks? Goals?" I was terrible at croquet. I was terrible at any sport that wasn't played with a controller in my hand and a screen in front of me. But I needed to get away from these people.

Daniel grinned widely. "Close enough. Nice meeting you, Omar. And *Kevin,*" he said as he led me toward the grassy area at the bottom of the stairs.

"It's *Devin,*" Devin called out as we walked away.

Daniel shrugged, but neither of us looked back.

The croquet game was set up in an area of the yard that had a lot of lighting, but it was still not exactly the best game for the dark. Of course, Daniel was excellent at it, anyway. The guy was a sports nut, and hockey and croquet were both pretty much using wood sticks to propel hard things into metal targets. But honestly? Daniel had been excellent at everything I'd seen him do. Like baking, and even talking about *Dragon Arena*. Hell, he wasn't even as bad as he thought he was at math.

And playing with him, especially after that mess with Omar and Devin, was *fun*. Fun was something I wasn't expecting to find at this party.

Daniel was so . . . entertaining. His commentary as he shot the ball (hit the ball? Lol, I knew nothing about sports) had me and the other players in stitches. He sounded like one of those hockey play-by-play reporters. And he had that trademark Daniel grin through the whole thing. He was having fun . . . and everyone around him was having fun because of him.

"And Ramos takes control, passes to Ramos . . . passes back to Ramos. We haven't seen stick handling this good since the playoffs. Ramos has the ball, setting up the shot . . . he shoots . . . he scores!" He made a sound that sounded like a stadium of fans going wild.

Kavita, who was playing with a friend against the two of us, elbowed me. "Your boyfriend is hilarious. Does he have any hockey player friends for me?"

Even I played better than I expected. With Daniel helping me with my form, of course. When I managed to get the wooden ball through the little metal hoop, I also got the excited hockey broadcaster treatment.

"Rookie player Samaya, the pocket rocket, Janmohammad shows us all that it's not size that counts! Keep an eye on this one . . . She's going to go far in the lawn sports world."

I got caught up in it, laughing. He whispered in my ear, "Permission to give you the highest of fives?"

I grinned, nodding, putting my hand up until he hit it. But he didn't slap my hand as expected. Instead, the second his hand came into contact with mine, his fingers curled around mine, holding my hand in his in the air.

Fine. We'd held hands earlier. He squeezed a bit, and our eyes locked for a second before he let go. That look, and that small action, sent a shiver down my spine.

I turned away, sure that my face was as red as the croquet bat (hammer? stick?) in my hand. That was when I noticed I was being watched. Not just by the other croquet players.

Devin was at the edge of the lawn, staring intently. The look in his eyes was . . . misery. Which, fine. I mean, I knew that it didn't feel too good for me to see his PDAs with Hana. But had Daniel seen Devin watching us? Was this why he'd held my hand?

I decided to ignore my ex and got back to the game.

We won croquet, of course.

Not long after our game, Hana finally lowered all the lights in the yard and set up the projector. In case anyone expected Daniel to sing along to the *Dragon Arena* movie, and so I wouldn't have to sit anywhere near Devin, I guided Daniel to one of the small round picnic blankets spread out on the grass. Each was big enough for two people, and a few blankets were already occupied by couples snuggling.

"This is good," Daniel said as he lowered himself on the blanket. It was one of those boho mandala-print ones with tassels around the perimeter. "I won't have to whisper here."

The movie was, of course, terrible. But being far from the crowd meant we didn't join in on the slagging, mocking, shooting the screen with water guns, or most importantly, the singing. We could just talk.

"Why'd you tell Omar earlier that we'd both go to Jayden's party?" I asked.

Daniel shrugged. "I thought we were being too defensive. It's good to agree to some things or they'll figure out we are lying. I won't actually go if you don't want me to. I can't believe he accused you of cheating."

I chuckled. "Yeah, I didn't see that coming. I was so sure he was going to admit he was LostAxis. Now I can eliminate him from my suspect list, I guess. If he was LostAxis, he'd know if I was fooling around with the guy. Or sexting him." My nose wrinkled at the thought of sexting Omar.

Daniel's eyes widened. "You were *sexting* this Axis guy?"

I laughed, shaking my head. "No! That's just what Omar accused me of. We only played together. It wasn't that deep. We didn't even talk of meeting up."

He shook his head. "Maybe I should go to that gamer party. Someone could accuse you of shit there, too." He sounded . . . protective of me. Which was sweet. "Maybe the catfisher will be there."

I shook my head. "We can't go. Here it's fine—we're just *talking* about the game. At Jayden's we'd be *playing*. You've never played *Dragon Arena* in your life."

He smiled mischievously. "Wrong."

I raised a brow. "You have?"

"I downloaded the free trial last night and started a character. And even woke up early to play before school. Addictive game."

My eyes were wide. "Seriously? What character class?"

"Dark Mage, of course. That's where I got the name IceMagic—that's actually my name in game."

I slapped his arm. "Why didn't you tell me?"

He laughed. "I wanted to tell you when no one else was around so I wouldn't have to share your surprised face with anyone. I think I want to start another character, though. I want to play as a Paladin . . . because he's like the center forward of a group, which is my position on ice. Dark Mage is like left wing, and Warrior is right wing."

"You have this all figured out, don't you?"

He nodded. "The Bard and the Weaver are defense. And you, the Light Mage, are the goaltender."

I snickered at that. "Well, unless you manage to level to fifty in a few weeks, there is no way we can go to Jayden's."

He frowned. "I'm already a five. How long would it take to get to fifty?"

"Months. Maybe a year. The early levels go quicker, but it slows down after fifteen."

"Damn. Too bad—that party wouldn't be so bad for you if we went together. I know you want to make your Tinker Bell game, and if going guarantees this guy will back down, then it would be worth it."

I looked at him. Did he really want to come to a party just to support me? I shook my head. "You're sometimes a little too nice, Daniel."

He grinned. "Impossible."

We watched the movie silently for a while. When the emerald dragon burst out into a love ballad (in the unique dragon language created for the movie), Daniel cringed.

"How many times have you seen this?" he asked.

"I don't know. A couple of times. Never by choice, though. I don't really watch a lot of movies, and I don't see the point of watching them ironically." I preferred playing games any day. Devin had always thought I was weird for that. "You don't have to watch if you don't want to . . . you're not going to be quizzed on it."

He chuckled, leaning back on his elbows, and looked at the enormous gray stone house. "This place is unreal. Is your house anything like this?"

I frowned. "What? No. Not even close. I mean, my house is nice. And my sister planted some stuff in the backyard—she and her boyfriend are into gardening. Our house used to be a one story, but we added a second level a few years ago. The construction was brutal. Hana's family is like . . . super rich, though."

"She still seems nice."

I shrugged. "She's *sometimes* nice. She's trying really hard to still be friends with me even though she's dating Devin. It's just guilt."

"Why are you going along with it? You don't have to be friends with her."

I shrugged. "She'd be too dangerous as an enemy."

Daniel looked at me, head tilted. In the flickering low light from the movie projector, I could see his sharp cheekbones. His lips were in a straight line, and his brows were furrowed. "Do you do that with everyone you know?"

"Do what?"

"Do you always assume people don't actually like you for *you*? That they have some other reason for wanting to be your friend? Maybe Hana just likes you and doesn't want to lose you as a friend because she's with Devin now."

I frowned. Did I always assume people didn't like me for *me*? Other than Cass and Aimee, all my friends *did* come through someone else . . . Devin. They were his friends. Everyone liked the school golden boy, so they liked the golden boy's girlfriend.

I looked at Daniel. He liked me for me, right?

"Habit, I guess." I didn't really want to explain it right now.

Daniel looked at me silently for a while before he spoke. "Do you think I passed tonight?"

"What do you mean?"

"Did I pretend to fit in here successfully?"

I was about to laugh when I looked at his face. The terrible CGI dragon on the screen was shooting flames that looked like they came from my dad's barbecue starter on the screen, so there was enough light for me to see his expression. He was unsure. Nervous. I wasn't used to that from Daniel.

"You didn't *pretend* to fit in. You actually did," I said.

Now I could make out one of his big-even-for-Daniel grins.

"Seriously," I said. "You did great. But it wasn't because of any pretending you did."

"What do you mean?"

I considered how to explain it. "Like, you pretending to be my gaming buddy was fine, but everyone here that liked you liked you for the *real* you. Not because of the things you were pretending to be into. Everyone except Devin and his bros, but who cares about them. People saw you as a great guy." That's why *I* liked him, too. I wished I had the guts to say that.

He shook his head. "Nah. I'm only a great guy when I'm with you."

I tilted my head, still looking at him. Was he really that self-conscious? It didn't make sense. Daniel was good-looking (like, OMG, there should be marble busts carved of that face), but more than that he was fun, really kind (which was super rare), and so optimistic he could put anyone in a good mood. And he was supportive. He had none of that toxic masculinity I'd assumed he'd have when I heard he was a hockey player.

"And there's no way anyone at this party would give me half the time of day if you weren't with me," he added.

"That's not true," I said. I meant it sincerely.

He shook his head. We were quite close together—we had to be so we could hear each other over the horrible orc screech-singing in the movie.

"But it is," he asked. "I'm only here because of you. I guarantee none of these people would *choose* to hang out with a baker who spends his free time in a family shelter, and who doesn't have . . ."

His voice trailed off. He didn't finish his sentence.

The tough thing was, what he was saying was technically true. He was here because of me, and I'd probably never have become friends with him unless he happened to own the face that LostAxis told me was his. Yes, I'd have met Daniel volunteering at the shelter. But without that LostAxis connection, I wouldn't have gotten to know Daniel in the same way. I wouldn't have developed this little crush.

To Daniel, I wasn't only the smart kid, or Devin's girlfriend. It didn't matter to him if I was winning the breakup, or what Earl's Whispers was saying about me. I felt safe being me. Maybe even a little bit more me than I could be with my friends.

I knew he liked me for *me*, and I liked him for him, too.

But I needed to keep reminding myself that Daniel wasn't doing all this out of the goodness of his heart, or because he was interested in me as more than a friend. He was doing it because he needed me as much as I needed him. And he didn't want to get too close—that's why he had that parameter.

I looked down, all of a sudden monumentally sad. I played with the tassels on the blanket, letting the twisted strands run between my fingers. Devin said he broke up with me because he wanted time to figure out who he was without me. But maybe he wasn't the only one who had lost themselves when we were together. Because I was so wrapped up in what people thought about me that I was pretending to be someone I wasn't *and* I was taking advantage of one of the best people I'd ever met, asking him to be someone he wasn't, too.

"You okay?" Daniel said. He'd leaned in close.

I nodded. "Fine."

"You had a look on your face. Sad."

I tried to smile. "Don't worry about it. Just an existential crisis."

"Ah. I hate those. In case it helps with your crisis, I should tell you that I'm having a great time tonight. I'm even enjoying this movie. Y'all are being too hard on it. Maybe they should have used some CGI to erase the wires the flying dragons are hanging from, but the story is kind of fun."

I blinked. "The dragons *are* CGI."

He laughed. "Really? The wires are to add to the camp! I love it!"

I smiled. "You're serious? I mean, you're actually enjoying yourself?"

"Absolutely. This is the most fun assignment I've ever had."

I exhaled. An assignment. That was all this was to him. Just the deal we'd made.

"That reminds me," he said. "You have five selfies left. Want a movie-watching shot?"

That was why we were here. I held my phone out in front of us.

He leaned close. "People are watching us," he whispered. "Should I put my arm around you?"

I looked around. People could see us. Hana, Devin, and some of the others. I nodded and Daniel scooted even closer and put his arm around my waist. It had been so long since I was this close to someone. I rested my head on Daniel's chest, the sweet smell of laundry detergent from the T-shirt I'd designed filling my senses, and I took the picture. But we stayed like that even after, since everyone was looking.

But also, because it felt so good. He was warm and he was solid, and even if it was fake, I could just be me. I turned off all the stuff that was always swirling around in my mind and let Daniel hold me up for a while.

Even if none of this was real, and even if there was an end date on this support, I needed it right now.

19

Real Talk in the Library

Earl's Whispers Instagram Photo:

Image: Back view of a couple watching a movie. The guy has his arm around the waist of the girl. He has straight short black hair. The girl is small, with wavy black hair falling to just above her shoulders. She is resting her head on the boy's chest.

Caption: Naysayers can weep their conspiracy theories to the stars, because Samaya Janmohammad's mysterious new flame had his coming-out party last night . . . and what a coming-out it was! Reports from the party ranged from "oooh, yum" to "he seems full of himself." Word is that he is neither an international pop star nor an NHL forward, but did possess some serious athletic abilities. He and Samaya dominated in a nail-biting game of croquet, where he wowed everyone with his obscure hockey trivia. Consensus is that these two are smitten, even if a little oddly matched. Will Samaya be bringing her Dark Mage boyfriend to the fall formal?

> Another question on everyone's lips is: How is Devin
> Kapadia feeling about his former girlfriend moving on
> so quickly . . . and moving on so well?

I zoomed in on the picture.

"This is . . . actually not bad. Who took this?" I said.

It was Sunday afternoon, two days after the party, and Cass, Aimee, and I were at the public library getting some work done on the game-dev project. This was the first I'd been able to work on it all weekend, since I'd gone with Daniel, Andre, and Muniba to the market again on Saturday. The game-dev meeting was Monday, and even though I'd reluctantly agreed to go to Jayden's *Dragon Arena* party in a few weeks so he'd let me be team captain, I still wanted to have the proposal done. I'd mostly agreed to go to Jayden's party because it seemed important to Aimee for some reason. I had no doubt her new boyfriend was bugging her to make sure I was there—or rather my Light Mage was there—and at the end of the day, Aimee was still my friend.

Aimee had done some character sketches of the fairies for the game digitally, and we'd spent the last few hours crowded around Cass's laptop at the back of the library trying to figure out how to animate them. It was tedious, frustrating work, so we'd taken a break to check what was happening on Instagram. Apparently, what was happening was more talk about me.

"Anyone could have taken this picture," Aimee said, frowning at the picture of Daniel and me on her phone.

Cass looked closer at it on their own phone. "I always thought Hana was behind Whispers, but this . . . this doesn't seem like something she'd write. Could have been one of her friends, though."

"I don't think it's Hana, either." I scrolled back to the Whispers post before this one, which declared Hana's supposed HD outdoor projector was really standard definition. Hana wouldn't have gossiped about herself. "Honestly, I have trouble believing the person behind Whispers is anyone from our crowd."

Cass shrugged. "Geeks can be gossips, too."

"Maybe," I said. "It doesn't matter, though. This post, finally, doesn't seem out to get me."

Aimee tapped her phone. "Oh, another picture was just posted."

Cringing, I opened the newest post. It was another picture from Hana's party, this one of Hana and Devin on one of those benches near the firepit. They were physically next to each other, but they looked totally distant emotionally, like one was in Vancouver and the other was in Prince Edward Island. Devin was gazing out into the distance, and Hana was scowling. I read the caption.

> Is there conflict brewing between Earl's hottest new it couple? Unconfirmed reports are that Devin Kapadia and Hana Dawar had a big fight after Hana's party. Maybe this unexpected trouble in paradise has something to do with Devin clearly not enjoying his ex Samaya flaunting her new upgrade among his friends. And Hana? Her wandering eyes were seen locked on to the rear-end region of Samaya's new man. The physics club president should be careful—Hana's type seems to be Samaya Janmohammad's castoffs.

Yuck. "Was Hana checking out Daniel's butt?"

Cass shrugged. "Not that I noticed. Daniel has a nice butt, though."

I glared at Cass. I mean, I'd noticed his nice rear end, too, but I hadn't realized everyone else was checking it out. "Yeah, but boys shouldn't be objectified for their body any more than girls should be. Patriarchy hurts males as much as females."

Aimee looked at Cass, and some unsaid communication passed between them. Finally, Cass spoke. "Um, Samaya, did you even read this?"

"Yeah. That's why I asked you if Hana was checking out Daniel's butt." This was the most conversation I'd ever had about any boyfriend's, or in this case, *fake* boyfriend's, butt. What had happened to my life?

Cass gave me a sideways look. "It says Devin and Hana were *fighting*. And yet the only thing you seem to be concerned about is Daniel's butt."

I frowned. Holding the phone closer, I read the caption again. It *did* say they argued after the party. "So what? I mean, no one actually thinks they'll last, do they? Devin was the president of the astronomy club last year, and Hana believes that if the school has an astronomy club, it should have an astrology club, too. For . . . *equality* reasons." I put air quotes around the word *equality*, mimicking Hana's high-pitched voice.

"Okay, yes, they're doomed to fail," Aimee said, "but, Samaya, maybe this means he wants to get back together with you?"

"Ew. I hope not." I made a sour face. "Besides. I have a boyfriend."

"A fake one," Aimee said under her breath.

I glared at them again. The library was pretty busy, and even though I didn't see anyone from Earl's, that didn't mean they weren't there to hear us. "But either way, I am not interested in getting back with Devin. Seriously."

Another look passed between Aimee and Cass. Clearly they'd had a conversation without me. "Cass and I were wondering . . . ," Aimee said. "Is there more between you and your fake boy?"

"More what?"

"More than . . . you know," Aimee said.

"More than lemon squares," Cass clarified. I was glad I'd told them our code name.

I frowned. "Well, yeah. We're friends. We spend hours together every week baking. And doing calculus."

"That's not what we mean, and you know it," Aimee said. "C'mon, Samaya. Just now, you were so wrapped up in the idea that others were looking at his butt that you completely missed the fact that Hana and

Devin are having trouble in paradise. Is it because you want to keep his butt to yourself?"

I looked at my friends, blinking. I'd always loved that these two could sometimes know what I was thinking even before I thought it myself. But it apparently was possible to have friends who knew you too well.

Because it was true. I had kind of, maybe a little bit, developed feelings for Daniel, even though I'd been trying hard to deny them. It was inevitable. He was a lot of fun. He was kind. And he was handsome. Like, almost excessively handsome.

And for those reasons, he was so out of my league he may as well live on Pluto or something.

"Samaya. Be real," Cass said. "I saw the way you two were sitting during the movie. What's really going on between you two?"

I was most definitely not ready to admit this to anyone. Even my closest friends. I'd been planning to ignore the crush until it went away.

But then again, these were my friends. I should be honest with them.

"Fine. Yes," I said quietly, so no one else in the library could possibly overhear. "I *like* him. But I'm not an idiot. I'm not planning on acting on it."

Aimee stared at me for several seconds before speaking. "Okay, two things. First, hallelujah you're not interested in that whiny man-child Devin anymore. Now that you're over him, I can call him that to your face. And two, why would you not act on your feelings for Daniel? You two looked so good together on Friday! Seriously. You saw the Whispers post."

"Yeah. We look good together because we were *pretending*. That was fake, remember?"

Cass gave me an incredulous look. "How was it fake if you admitted that you're into him?"

"Don't worry about my feelings. I'll tamp them down."

"What about *his* feelings?"

I fidgeted with the side of my phone. "Daniel does *not* have feelings for me. He's good at pretending, but also he's just . . . like that. He's excessively nice and friendly to *everyone*. Not just to people he's into. You should have seen him with the old people at the market. He thinks of this as a job, that's it."

Cass blinked at me a few seconds, then shook their head. "I disagree. He's into you."

"One way to find out," Aimee said, grinning. "Ask him. Tell him you'd be willing to take this fake thing real and see what he says. I agree with Cass. I think he'd be into it."

"No," I said.

"Why not?" Aimee said.

I waved my hands around in frustration. "Because we have parameters! And anyway, even if he was into me, which he's not, we would never work together as a couple. I mean, talk about oil and water. After this semester, when I'm done at the shelter, and he won't be in calculus, then what? What would we even talk about? Not to mention my parents worshipped Devin. He's the physics club president! Daniel is a hockey player who wants to go to culinary school. Which is fine, but . . . we're from different worlds."

"That's absurd," Aimee said. "That's no reason why you cannot be together."

Aimee said some other things about me giving it a shot, but I wasn't listening. I was watching Cass close their computer, a look of disgust on their face.

"What is it, Cass?" I asked.

Cass looked at me. I'd been friends with Cass a long time, and I thought I'd seen every expression they were capable of making. But I'd never seen this one. "I always knew you were a bit of an elitist, Samaya, and I get why. I have an Asian parent, too—I know the pressure they put on you to always be the best at everything. But do you even hear yourself? For months your only concern has been Samaya. Samaya's reputation at school. Samaya winning this breakup. And Samaya's happiness. You're giving up a chance with someone who you admit is one of the nicest people out there, because it messes with your brilliant reputation. Because Samaya Janmohammad, math genius, could not even think of lowering herself to date a mere hockey player. One who could actually make you happy."

They said all this while packing their computer in their bag, and all I could do was sit there and listen. Even Aimee stared at Cass, speechless.

"Cass," I said. "That's—"

"I don't want to hear it, Samaya. I'm leaving. You really need to figure your shit out so you aren't so needy with your friends."

And with that Cass took their bag and their computer and left the library.

I sat there with Aimee, blinking, not sure what just happened, when Aimee suddenly gasped. "Check the comments on your Earl's Whispers post, Samaya," she said.

GamesLost was back. They'd commented on the picture of me and Daniel.

Sometimes pictures do lie. Things aren't what they seem with these two. Soon enough, everyone will see who Sam really is.

20

Cass's Secret

Thanks to my best friend calling me needy, and the ominous message from GamesLost, I was almost shaking on my walk home alone from the library. What exactly did GamesLost mean by *Soon enough, everyone will see who Sam really is*? Whoever they were, it was clear they were trying to hurt me. Expose me. It was one thing when GamesLost was commenting on my own Instagram . . . but now they were posting on Earl's Whispers, too. Of course, they knew I wasn't actually dating Daniel—and that we were lying about how we met. Were they planning to tell Whisper's the lengths I'd gone to—actually asking someone to pretend to date me, just to win the breakup with Devin?

Or maybe it was just an empty threat—and their goal was to turn me into a complete basket case. If that was their point, they were succeeding.

When I got home, I told Mom I had a headache and went straight to my room. I needed to figure out who GamesLost was. But before that, I needed to process everything Cass had said.

I knew I had been wrapped up in my own crap since my breakup with Devin. I mean, I had a lot of crap to be wrapped up in. But was

I really *needy*? Too needy? I could feel my chest tighten. I hated that I had been a bad friend. I closed my eyes, massaging my forehead. I wanted to practice pi. Or maybe dig up some advanced trigonometry functions—I wanted to use numbers to escape this horrible feeling of hurting my friend.

But I couldn't. I couldn't sweep this under the rug and hope it would go away. And I couldn't deflect the blame on anyone else. I had been wrapped up in myself for the last few weeks. Focusing too much on unimportant things—like what Daniel would wear to Hana's party, or who was behind Earl's Whispers. When was the last time I'd asked Cass about how things were going with their family? Or had lunch with them, just the two of us? Now that I thought about it, Cass had been busier than normal lately—going out on weekends and doing something after school. Cass was a private person—but I hadn't once asked them what they'd been up to.

I loved Cass. I'd always supported them when they needed me. We'd been through so much together. I was there for them when they came out as nonbinary. I was there when they dealt with shit from their extended family. Cass was the calmest, steadiest person I knew. They were my rock, and I thought I was theirs.

But had I been taking more than I gave lately? That was not the person I wanted to be. I texted them.

Me: I've been a lot lately. I'm sorry.

I didn't expect Cass to write back, but they did. Immediately.

Cass: You have. And I should have told you off for it a long time ago.

Me: I wish you had.

Cass: I tried. A few times. I wanted to say

They didn't finish their sentence, I stared at my phone as the three dots appeared, then disappeared a few times. Finally, a text came through.

Cass: Can we talk about this tomorrow?

I really hoped that the talk wasn't going to be a friend breakup. I didn't know how I'd deal with that. But I had no choice but to agree. I knew Cass—they'd want to think through all their thoughts alone before bringing them to me. That was how they'd always been.

Me: Okay. Tomorrow.

Cass: And about Daniel—He's a good guy. If he's into you, which I think is, he doesn't deserve to be strung along. You need to figure out your shit.

I snorted. That was the Cass I loved. Telling me exactly what I needed to hear.

Me: I'm not stringing him along.

Cass: Make that clear to him.

Me: Okay. I'll talk to you tomorrow. Sorry again. I mean it.

Cass didn't respond. I wanted to say more—apologize again, ask them about their weekend, and hopefully get back to where we should be—but I didn't. I needed to give Cass space. As they had said, I needed to figure out my shit instead of burdening my friends with it.

I grabbed a notebook and a pencil and sat on my bed. I needed to figure out this LostAxis situation.

GamesLost had commented on three pictures: two on my own Instagram, and one on Earl's Whispers. All evidence pointed to GamesLost being LostAxis. The names were similar. And also, their reference to a hat trick. Their comment on my own account told me that LostAxis knew who I was IRL. Now, because they were commenting on a Whispers post, it was likely that GamesLost a.k.a. LostAxis was an Earl's student. They knew who I was, they knew my relationship with Daniel was fake, and they knew Earl's Whispers had been targeting me. Hell, assuming they read all the old posts on Whispers, they knew that I'd broken down into sobs begging Devin not to break up with me back in June.

A heaviness grew in my stomach.

Who could it be, though? I started listing the people in our *Dragon Arena* guild in my notebook. I'd already eliminated Jayden and Omar. But the guild was big—at its height last year, there'd been about twenty people in it. Maybe it was Arthur—a kid in grade eleven who'd been suddenly very friendly with me last year. Actually, he'd asked me last winter to do a duo quest with him, and I'd said no, because it was a quest I'd been wanting to do with Devin.

Then again, it was possible whoever it was wasn't in the guild. Hell, they might not even be an Earl's student.

I sighed. I had no idea how to figure this out. Or even if I should.

Maybe a clue could come from LostAxis himself? Before overthinking it, I logged in to *Dragon Arena* for the first time in weeks and searched for LostAxis, but he wasn't online. I unblocked the name. If LostAxis logged back in, he'd see me. And now he could contact me in the chat, too.

I stayed logged in all evening without playing, but LostAxis didn't show up. This was a waste of time. Maybe Cass was right—and it didn't matter who LostAxis or GamesLost was. So what if they exposed me? I hadn't done anything wrong. I was just hanging out with a new friend.

And maybe obsessing about this was alienating my friends. I needed to let it go.

~

It was raining on Monday morning. When I got to the bus stop at my regular time, I was surprised to see Cass in the bus shelter. I didn't know why I'd assumed they wouldn't be here, that they'd choose to be either early or late so they wouldn't see me first thing in the morning. But no. Aimee wasn't here, but Cass was. In their oversize jeans and vintage Frankenstein sweatshirt, and a knit beanie pulled low over their head. This was super awkward. I didn't know when they wanted to have our talk, but I wasn't going to force it if they didn't want to yet.

"I can wait outside if you'd prefer," I said.

Cass raised a brow. "And get wet?"

I shrugged. "I just . . . in case you didn't want to, you know . . . talk."

Cass sighed. "I told you I wanted to talk today."

Well, that was promising. "Good. I'm glad. I know I've been a bad friend, and I'm sorry. I shouldn't have sucked my friends into my shit. I'm sorry." I was talking fast and babbling, repeating some of what I'd texted yesterday. "Please don't think I don't appreciate you. You're the best friend I've ever had. I'll be better. I promise."

The bus arrived then, so we were silent as we climbed on and tapped our fare cards. We took two seats next to each other near the back.

Cass turned to look at me. "Are you going to tell Daniel the truth about how you feel?"

I sighed. "I'm not stringing him along. Honestly. There's something I haven't told you about our arrangement." I looked around to make sure there were no Earl's kids on the bus before continuing. I was pretty sure I was safe, but I lowered my voice anyway. "I told you about our arrangement, but I didn't tell you about his . . . parameter."

Cass raised one brow. "You told me about your parameters. Holding hands is okay, you were going to have three dates, eight pictures."

"Yeah, but there was another one." I told Cass about my parameter that the fake relationship would *never* be real, and Daniel's that he wouldn't be completely open with me like he would if this were a real relationship.

Cass looked surprised. "And he's been respecting that?"

I nodded. "Yeah. I really don't know much about him. He never talks about friends, or his childhood. He's mentioned his mother and some uncle he lives with, but the only person he really talks about is some aunt in Brampton who taught him how to bake. And he knows that I don't want to start actually dating."

"Okay, but now that he knows you better, he may want to renegotiate."

"I don't think so. He even said at Hana's that he sees this as a job. And, honestly, I don't think I want a relationship with Daniel. I'd be rebounding, wouldn't I? Plus, it would never work. We're nothing alike. He's into—"

"Do you actually believe that, or are you so convinced that he couldn't be interested in you that you keep telling yourself excuses so you don't have to try?"

I stared at Cass, blinking.

Cass smiled. "I get it, Samaya. Devin hurt you a lot. It's okay to admit you're scared to get in another relationship."

How . . . how exactly did Cass know exactly what I was doing when I didn't? I didn't know what to say.

"I'm talking to a guy right now who's nothing like me," Cass said, suddenly.

Wait . . . what? "What do you mean *talking*? Like, talking talking? Are you *dating*?"

Cass exhaled. "No! I don't know if he's into me like that. But we, like, talk a lot. Literally talking, not figuratively. We're friends."

I grinned. "How long?"

"Since July."

"And you're into him like *that*?"

Cass nodded. Their skin had turned completely pink.

Cass had a crush on a new guy since *July*, and hadn't said anything to me? "Why didn't you tell me?"

Cass shook their head. "You were pretty broken up this summer. I think the last thing you would have wanted to hear about was me pining over someone." They rubbed the back of their neck. "And since then, I tried to tell you. Several times. I actually could have used my friend's advice with this."

Ugh. I felt terrible. "Cass! I wish you'd bonked me over the head and told me to shut up. I'm so sorry. We've always been so close." I'd gotten so wrapped up in myself that I'd let this friendship go to shit.

Cass looked at me for a few moments before speaking. "I also didn't want to tell you because I didn't think you'd approve of him. He's a hockey player."

I cringed. Ugh. Now it made sense. I'd been going on for weeks about how Daniel being a hockey player meant me and him were incompatible. If Cass was into a guy who played hockey, then of course they wouldn't feel safe telling me about him. This was why they'd called me an elitist. "Does he, like, *accept* you?"

Cass rolled their eyes. "Not all hockey players are homophobes, you know."

"I didn't say that."

Cass shook their head, annoyed. "This is what I was talking about, Samaya. Okay, maybe you're not really an elitist, and your confidence in yourself was shattered by Devin, but you *have* always had these rigid categories about who people can be. You're the high-achieving nerd. Aimee is the artist. I'm the computer geek. Hana is the cheerleader. And hockey players are dude-bro jocks who are beneath us. Your first thought about someone is always based on their category in your head."

"That's not true."

"Isn't it, though? This whole thing with Daniel. Maybe I went too far in telling you off yesterday. But Daniel could . . . wait . . . not *could*, he actually *does* make you happy, and you won't even entertain the thought of keeping that in your life. As a friend, or whatever. Because he doesn't fit into the category you need him to fit into."

I let Cass's words sink in a bit. Was that really what I did? I exhaled, not at all happy about this mirror being put up in front of me. But that's what friends were for, right?

I asked the question that I should have asked as soon as Cass told me their news. "Okay, so forget about me. Tell me about your hockey player. What's he like? You really like him?"

Cass smiled kind of bashfully. And it was so cute. "Yeah. But he's confusing me. He's flirty and calls me all the time, we go for coffee, but that's it. I don't know if he's into me. He is pansexual, by the way. Out."

I grinned. "I'm *positive* he's into you. I want to know everything about him. Where did you meet? What's his name?"

"Owen." She paused. "He's actually my dad's coworker's son. We met at this family day thing at Dad's work. Also . . . I may have asked him if he knew Daniel when all this started with you. He doesn't know him personally, but he has a friend on Daniel's team. He said Daniel is a good guy and has a wicked slapshot. His team is playing Daniel's team on Thursday. Season opener."

"Oh, cool." I did know that Daniel had a game . . . or a practice, or a something on Thursday because we had to change our baking night to Wednesday this week. I should ask Daniel what he could tell me about this Owen.

"We should go to the game together," Cass said.

"Seriously? You want me to *meet* him? I've never been to a hockey game."

They shrugged. "I want to know what you think of him. And you can see your boy on the ice. I've never seen a game, either."

Cass had another one of those unfamiliar expressions on their face. We'd been friends for so long, and they had always been one of the most confident, self-assured, and wise people I knew. But there was something new there. Uncertainty. Nervousness.

It hit me . . . Cass wasn't asking me to go to the game so I could meet Owen, or so I could see Daniel play hockey. They were asking me because they were nervous to go without support.

From me. Cass wanted me there as their best friend.

Maybe it wasn't wise to go to Daniel's game, since I needed to get over this crush. And I wasn't even sure if he'd want me there—this might be overstepping. But Cass needed me.

"Let's do it," I said. "A new adventure for us. I can google hockey first. It's the game with bats and big rubber balls, right?"

Cass rolled their eyes but smiled, too.

That day after school we finally had the second game-dev meeting—the one where we would vote for the captain and game concept. And since I was the only one who actually had a proposal, I was officially elected team captain. Everyone was supportive of the forest-fairy concept, even Jayden, surprisingly. Aimee's art and Cass's rough animation of an intro sequence were big hits, and the team had great suggestions of what should happen in each level. I ended the meeting by handing out assignments to the team—including creating a script for each level, and a marketing and publicity plan. I left the meeting feeling great—my self-confidence *had* been low lately, but this game-dev club might be just the thing to get it back up again.

~

Daniel was extra cheerful on Wednesday at the shelter since Andre had finally given him the go-ahead to make a few pies as an experiment. Andre said if they sold well on Saturday, we could keep making a few pies each week.

"Oh, I need to ask you . . ." Daniel trailed off as he lined up butter, flour, salt, and sugar on the prep counter. "I have my season opener hockey game tomorrow, but can we do calculus after that? I'm pretty sure I'll be home by nine. There's a quiz Friday."

I had considered keeping going to his game plan a secret from Daniel so I could surprise him there, but I wanted to respect his parameter. "Or I could come to your game and we can go to a café or something to study after."

Daniel frowned. "You want to come to my hockey game?" he asked. "Don't you hate hockey?"

"Cass has been crushing on a guy that plays for the team you're up against. They want me to come with them to drool in person."

He laughed. "Really? For the Dolphins? Who?"

"Owen something."

"I know Owen. Wicked hook."

"He said you had a nice slapshot."

Daniel grinned proudly as he cut a block of butter into small cubes. "Is he a good guy?" I asked.

"I don't know him as a person. I've only ever played against him. He's never hurled racist insults my way, so there's that. I think that is the bare minimum for standard of behavior, though, not a selling point."

I cringed. "That doesn't really happen to you, does it?"

He nodded as he covered the bowl of cubed butter with plastic wrap. He put it in the fridge. "It doesn't happen often in Toronto with my current league. When I was in a more competitive league, I used to face off against teams outside the city. I was regularly called every slur for Asians you can imagine. And I was told to open my eyes on the ice."

I recoiled. "That's horrendous."

He shrugged. "It's life. It was a long time ago. And like I said, doesn't happen much here, and it's never happened with the Dolphins. There are other Asians on that team. I do have one question about you coming to my game, though."

I had anticipated this question—he wanted to make sure we wouldn't be pretending to date in front of his teammates. It was one thing to fake date for my friends, and Muniba and Andre, too, but I was sure he didn't want his hockey buddies to think we were dating. "Yeah, we need to talk about what we'll tell people."

"Um, no. That's not what I was going to ask. I wanted to know for sure . . . when you come to my hockey game, you are aware that I'll be playing *hockey* there, right?"

He said it with such a straight face that it took me a minute to realize that he was mocking me. I slapped his arm.

"Hey!" he said, rubbing his arm. "What happened to no physical contact without asking first!"

"Don't be a smart-ass then." I frowned. He had a point, though. Consent was parameter seven. "I will ask before I touch you next time, though."

"No need. Hit me whenever."

I laughed. "Okay, but seriously. I don't know what Cass told Owen, but if you want to tell your teammates that we're just friends—"

"I already told my teammates I'm dating you."

I raised a brow. "You did? Why?"

"You know, just in case someone from your school finds out. I haven't told anyone at all this is fake."

"Really?"

He nodded again. "Really."

"What about your family?"

"There is only my mother, who, by the way, also volunteers at the shelter sometimes. Yeah, *I* didn't tell her you're my girlfriend. *Muniba* did."

I cringed. Daniel rarely talked about his mother. I'd had no idea she also worked here, or I would never have let him tell Muniba we were really dating. "Oh my god, I'm so sorry. I've imposed way too much on you. Seriously, if you want to break up, I totally understand. I don't think we need to keep this going anymore."

He laughed. "We're not breaking up until after that dance, remember? I told you when we met that you're the perfect girlfriend to introduce to Mom. By the way, she'll be at the game. She comes to all my games."

I cringed. Meeting the mom. This fake relationship just got a lot more . . . real. What happened to his parameter? I bit my lip. "You sure you're okay with me meeting her?"

He shrugged as he started weighing flour into a big metal bowl. "Don't worry, I told her we're not that serious, so don't think she'll be like, I don't know, inviting you for family dinners or anything. Mom's cool. She gives me space. She hasn't told my uncle about you."

"He wouldn't approve?"

Daniel shrugged. "I have no idea. But he's a little judgy, so Mom and I don't tell him a lot."

I looked at him. He was quite focused on weighing all-purpose flour with a large kitchen scale. This was the most he'd ever told me about his family.

"I'm not the first girlfriend you've hidden from him, am I?" I asked, making sure the playfulness was there in my voice.

He laughed, shaking his head. "Perceptive. But you're the first bloodsucking vampire I've hidden. Now, are you ready for your first pie lesson, Count?"

I shook my head, laughing. He hadn't called me Count for a while. I'd kind of missed it. "I'll have you know I had pi memorized to a hundred digits before I was ten."

He rolled his eyes. "*Math nerds.* Pie. P-I-E. Here, take this. It's a pastry blender." He handed me a kitchen implement that I'd never seen before.

"Pie being a circular food, my pi knowledge is useful."

With Daniel's help, I made my first all-butter pastry. Basically, that meant I used the blades on the pastry blender to cut the cold butter into tiny pieces inside the bowl of flour, then added enough ice water to make a dough.

"So, all it took was a friend with a crush on a hockey player to get you to accept me as I am?" he asked as he was stashing the finished discs of pie dough in the fridge. He grabbed a bag of apples and handed me a peeler to start peeling them.

I cringed. I had already accepted him as he was, hadn't I? "If you're not comfortable with this, I won't come to the game. I know it's weird." I turned away to take an apple out of the bag.

Everyone he knew there, including his teammates and even his own mother, thought we were a couple. Which meant we'd have to respect our parameters, instead of just being us. Maybe he wouldn't want that when he was supposed to be focused on his game.

He took the apple I'd peeled and started slicing it. "I was kidding. I want you to come. I've always wanted a puck bunny."

I'd done enough googling last night to know exactly what a puck bunny was. I pretended to slap him but didn't actually touch him this time. "I am not showing up in your hockey jersey and booty shorts."

"Damn," he laughed. "Should have added that to the parameters."

21

My First Hockey Game

I stood in front of my sister's closet, more confused than I had ever been in my life about clothes. "What does one wear to a hockey game?" I held up Tahira's red *Super Mario Kart* sweatshirt in one hand and a black "ironic" wolf howling at the moon T-shirt in the other.

Tahira looked up at me from her sewing machine and made an expression that was exactly like the one she made on the weekend when she poured soy milk into her chai by mistake. "Ew, neither of those."

I frowned. I'd assumed a hockey game was a casual thing. When I googled this question, the standard advice was to wear a team jersey, and if you didn't have a jersey that matched one of the teams playing, then a pro jersey was appropriate. But that wasn't something that existed in this house. "What's wrong with these?"

"You're going to your boyfriend's hockey game for the first time," Tahira said. "You don't wear graphic sweatshirts for a date."

"It's not a date. We've agreed on three dates, and this doesn't count as one because no one from school will be there."

Tahira got up and went to her closet. "Yes, yes, so you said. All the same, even if you or he don't think it's a date, everyone else will." She started flipping through the clothes in her closet, which, since this was Tahira's closet, took a while.

"I don't think you should wear black," she said. "I mean, I like this nerdy-emo look of yours . . . but to meet his friends? And his mother? The point here is to make *him* look good."

"I don't look good?"

She pulled something out of her closet and handed it to me. "You look awesome. But there's always room for improvement."

The top she'd given me was a dark green, loose, boxy long sleeve. The bottom six inches or so had a busy floral print in shades of green and purple. The whole shirt was made of a silky, flowy fabric. It was exactly Tahira's aesthetic—modern and slightly unexpected.

"You made this?"

She nodded. "Custom fabric."

"Seems a little dressy for a hockey game, no?"

She shook her head. "Not at all. It's basically a sweatshirt. With your jeans and black Vans. Oh, arenas are cold." She handed me a long black cardigan. "Do you want me to do your hair?"

This seemed like a lot of work. Honestly, I hadn't even gone to this much trouble for Hana's party—and that actually *was* one of our dates.

But I supposed if his friends thought we were dating, then this was a date. And it did sound very date-like. All I could think about was what Cass said—maybe Daniel was looking to renegotiate the parameters of our relationship. But the problem was, I still wasn't sure I wanted to do that. On Monday Cass said I was resisting Daniel because I was afraid of getting hurt again. And I supposed it was true—because Devin had hurt me a lot. Not that I expected Daniel to ever hurt me that way.

But the more I cared about Daniel, the more it would hurt if things didn't work out. Or if he didn't feel the same way I did.

It was just safer for me to keep this professional. I could do that.

The arena was pretty far from our neighborhood, so Cass picked me up at five for the six o'clock game. I kind of expected them to be dressed differently, too, since they were pining for a player and all. But no. Standard Cass uniform, jeans and a sweatshirt. This sweatshirt was kind of funny—orange with the Cheetos logo on it. But even if they were dressed exactly as they always were, it was clear to me that Cass was nervous. As we drove to the arena, they kept pulling at the back of their neck. And they weren't really saying much.

Things had been good between Cass and me for the last couple of days. I'd been trying hard not to pour too much of my own drama on them. I hadn't even told them about that threatening comment from GamesLost on Earl's Whispers, and if they'd seen it, they didn't mention it to me. I tried not to obsess about that comment so much—my friends were right; I was focusing too much on things that were probably unimportant. Right now, my focus should only be on making sure my friend was okay.

"You good, Cass? You seem twitchy."

They shrugged, but their eyes didn't leave the road. "Nah, it's good. I'm not worried."

"Not worried about what?"

"Not worried about anything. It's fine."

I could see a tension in their jaw, the tension that usually only came out at exam time. Or that time they did the timed coding test at school.

"You and Owen dating yet?" I hoped they would have told me if they were.

"No. Just friends."

"He agreed to come to Starbucks with us after, right?" The plan was for Owen and Cass to join us at the café next door after the game so I could meet him, but then he and Cass would leave us alone when Daniel and I worked on his math. It was, of course, all arranged that way so Cass would have a reason to be alone with Owen.

"Yeah. But . . ."

"But what?"

"But I don't know." They were quiet for a while, staring at the road in front of them.

Cass was my best friend, and my best friend seemed to be anxious right now.

"Cass, talk to me. I'm here. I'm the one you're going to move to New York *and* Silicon Valley with, to take the tech world by storm one day."

They smiled, remembering our old pledge to each other. "With 100 percent more diversity in the CEOs."

"And 100 percent less unnecessary rocket ships."

"Fine." They sighed. "Owen said he wanted me to meet his friends. I doubt they are expecting . . . this." Cass's voice shook.

I raised a brow. "And what's wrong with *that*? Do you have any reason to think Owen has a problem with how you present?" I'd never known Cass to be self-conscious about their identity. But then I didn't really know what it was like to be them.

"No, I mean, he uses my pronouns fine. He's never had an issue."

"But you've never seen him with all his friends. His teammates."

Cass didn't say anything, which was enough answer for me. Had this guy avoided telling his friends that his new friend or whatever Cass was to him was nonbinary? Maybe I needed to stop automatically assuming anything about people anymore, but I remembered Daniel's comments about the racism he'd experienced. I doubted hockey was a bastion of LGBTQ2+ support.

But Cass said Owen was out. I looked at my friend. "Daniel said Owen's team is cool," I said. "And he's totally into you if he wanted his friends to meet you."

They shrugged. "I guess time will tell. Still nervous, though. How are you feeling about meeting Daniel's team?"

"Also nervous. Daniel told his freaking mother that I'm his girlfriend, and she'll be there." I looked over at Cass. "Glad you'll be there, too."

We were both silent for a while before Cass huffed a laugh. "How weird that we're going to hockey games for guys. We'll be wearing team jerseys by the end of the season."

"Daniel and I won't be fake dating by the time the season ends, so he might not want me coming to more games."

They chuckled again, then, after parking their car at the arena, turned to look at me. "Samaya Janmohammad, I adore you, and if you wanted to drop all your dreams and ambitions and move to New York or California with me right now, I'd go in a heartbeat, but you, my friend, are simultaneously the smartest and the dumbest person I know."

I laughed as I unbuckled my seat belt and opened the door. Cass was the only person who talked to me like that. "Why? Because I can't see someone like Daniel developing feelings for me?"

"No. Because you can't see that he has *already* developed feelings for you. He wants you to meet his mother, for god's sake. He's into you . . . I guarantee it."

I shook my head as I headed into the main door of the arena.

We climbed up into the stands and decided to sit near center ice since we were rooting for both teams. I hadn't been to an ice rink in years and had forgotten how cold they were. Which, duh, made sense. There was a lot of ice here. There were players skating fast around the rink in full hockey gear, the scrape of their blades on the ice echoing through the arena. Some players wore red jerseys and some black, so I assumed it was both teams warming up. I couldn't figure out which one was Daniel. I thought his team wore red, but all the players looked the same—like enormous, padded beasts. Not people. And none of them looked like my friend.

I looked around at the crowd. I didn't know what I was looking for—Daniel's mother should be there, but I had no idea what she looked like. Did she know what I looked like? Had Daniel shown her any of our selfies?

Cass leaned in close. "That's Owen's mother," they said, pointing out a white suburban mom-type a few seats over from us. She beamed and waved vigorously at Cass. Cass gave the woman an awkward wave.

"She likes me," Cass said.

I snorted. "That's an understatement. You've met his mother?"

Cass nodded. "I met them all at the family day at my dad's work."

I grinned wider. This was big—Cass already had parent approval. I had no doubt that this *friendship* was actually more than that. I couldn't believe how much of my best friend's life I'd missed lately.

"I think the three of us—you, me, and Aimee—are long past due for a dim sum brunch." It was time to resurrect our old weekend treat of dim sum at one of those Chinese banquet places with the old ladies pushing carts. Cass used to translate so we'd know what we were eating, and we'd gorge on shrimp har gow and black pepper short ribs until we couldn't see straight. We used to go every few months, but it had been a long, long time. I was deep in thought, wondering if Aimee would even come to brunch with us now, when I heard my name shouted.

"Samaya! You're here!" It was Daniel . . . at the edge of the ice near the railing (wall?), grinning ear to ear. Even with the wire cage thing from his helmet covering his face, I could see his wide smile. How could one person be so happy all the time? He was like the brightest ray of sunshine peeking over everyone else's dark cloud.

I couldn't help but grin back. "I'm here!" I shouted.

"Your very first hockey game!"

Of course, since Cass and I were sitting halfway up the stands, everyone heard what Daniel said. A bunch of people turned to look at me, curious what a person in Canada who'd never seen a hockey game would look like. We walked down the steps to talk to Daniel without spectators.

"I'll tell her the basics," Cass said. "I've already shown her where they hide the baskets between innings."

"Did you warn her to duck so she doesn't get hit by a flying bat after a touchdown?" Daniel asked straight-faced.

I rolled my eyes. "Ha ha, smart-asses."

Daniel laughed at me. "Want a pic for your social?"

I handed Cass my phone and stepped closer to Daniel. He took off his helmet for the picture, and I leaned my head into his. Cass showed it to us after they took it. It was perfect. The bright white of the ice behind us made us glow.

Daniel slipped his helmet back on. "I'll see you outside after the game? I'll shower quick. My uncle is going to bring my gear home so we can go study."

My eyes widened. "Your uncle's here?"

"Yeah, he drove Mom. Don't worry, it's fine." He looked at the ice. "I'm off. We should be starting soon."

"Do I say break a leg?"

He laughed. "Just good luck works."

"Good luck then."

Somehow, he beamed even wider. "With my small vampire lucky charm here? I'm unstoppable. See you soon!"

While heading back up to our seats, I posted the pic on my Instagram, adding the caption "Season opener vibes."

Just before I sat down again, a woman in the stands in front of us smiled at us. "You let me know if you have any questions about the game, dears. I know this is all new for people like you."

"Uh, thank you?" I said, not really sure what she meant by *people like you*. Brown people? Biracial Chinese nonbinary people? Canadians who'd never seen a hockey game?

Cass whispered in my ear, "Don't worry about her. Daniel seemed *excessively* happy to see you."

"Shush, Cass."

They started humming the wedding march, and I laughed. "Where's Owen?"

Cass pointed to one side of the rink. "He's warming up near the net. Number twenty-six."

I knew Daniel was number fourteen, but it hadn't occurred to me to look for his number on the back of his jersey when I couldn't spot him earlier. Now I searched for and found twenty-six. From this distance Owen looked like all the other players. Maybe a bit taller.

I found Daniel again and focused on him instead. His uniform was obviously really padded. I made a mental note to ask him why so much padding? Were flying pucks really that dangerous? Daniel looked . . . imposing. Burly. But weirdly nimble. He was skating around the ice smoothly. I'd skated a few times as a kid—I mean, I *was* Canadian. But I'd never been able to figure out how to balance, or how not to, you know . . . fall on my ass.

But Daniel . . . he seemed as comfortable on the ice as if he were wearing shoes on solid ground. Maybe even more comfortable. He seemed like he was flying, not skating. He glided gracefully across the length of the rink, taking the time to playfully tap one of his teammates, then turned quickly behind the net, his sharp skate blades sending a flurry of snow into the air. When everyone gathered in front of the net and took turns hitting the puck into it, Daniel's shot got through, even though the goalie stopped everyone else's. I couldn't look away. It was like the stick was an extension of his body.

This was weird. I was in awe. Completely mesmerized and admiring Daniel's ability at a sports thing.

I leaned into Cass. "Are they good?"

"Who?" Cass asked.

"Owen and Daniel. I don't know a thing about hockey."

"Owen is. I'll watch Daniel for a bit."

Now the players on Daniel's team were skating with a puck, taking it behind the net and around their side of the ice's edge. I had no idea how the hell Daniel could keep the puck stuck to his stick. While wearing skates. And going very fast.

"So is he good?" I asked.

Cass shrugged. "I have no idea. They all look good. I used to skate, but I could never do anything like that. And the last time I tried, I slammed into the boards and got a concussion. Wearing a helmet."

Possibly racist lady turned around. "Which player are you talking about?" she asked.

"Fourteen on the Geese," Cass said before I could tell them I'd decided not to engage with this woman. "We don't really know hockey."

"Oh, Ramos! He's excellent! Very fast. Good puck handling, too. There's a feel-good story there, right? We're all so proud of him. Should be one of those inspirational sports movies." She waved her hand in the air as if she were imagining a theater marquee. "A real Canadian hero. Too many sports movies are about American football."

Why was Daniel being on this team worthy of an inspirational movie? I remembered what he'd told me—about being a midrange player. I wonder if this lady realized that worshipping him for being pretty good at hockey despite being Asian was a microaggression. I smiled coolly at the woman.

The actual game started soon after, and it was immediately fast-paced and a little hard to follow, but after about ten minutes I could mostly understand the rules. I loved watching the players skate. They were *so* skilled. All of them. No one fell on their asses. Cass's crush was an excellent player, and even got a goal, which I was happy for, but I was also bummed because Daniel tried to get the puck away from him, but Owen was faster. Daniel didn't get a goal, but he did get an assist, which I figured out meant he was a good team player and helped the guy who got the goal. We cheered for both teams.

The three periods went fast. The final score at three minutes left of the third period was tied two against two, and I was at the edge of my seat. Both teams seemed to have found a store of awesomeness stashed away and played the last minutes with more intensity—clearly both really wanting to win. In the end, Owen's team got a goal, and Owen got an assist, so Daniel's team lost.

Daniel didn't look upset about it, though. He grinned up at me after shaking hands with the other team, or rather hitting his massive glove against each of theirs. When he took off his helmet, I finally saw his black hair shiny with sweat and his whole happy face. He skated over closer to us and called out, "Meet me outside, okay?"

Seeing him without the helmet, seeing his incandescent face, all that positivity shining right at me . . . I felt a warmth wash through me, even in the cold arena.

It was clear to me at that moment—this crush wasn't going away like I'd hoped. I needed a strategy . . . I needed to make these feelings go away. Maybe I shouldn't see Daniel more than I needed to. After tonight I should only see him at the shelter.

As Cass and I tried to make it outside with the crush of other spectators (well, not really a crush—this was a small recreational hockey league), Cass's phone rang. It was Owen, asking them to come back inside the arena to meet his team before heading to the café.

"You're okay, Cass?" I asked. "I can go with you."

Cass shook their head. "No . . . it's fine. You go see your boy."

"He's not my—"

Cass grinned mischievously. I rolled my eyes, but I was glad that they didn't seem nearly as nervous as they had on the drive here.

The moment I was outside, someone tapped my arm. I turned to see a small Asian woman with a warm smile. Behind her at a bit of a distance was an Asian man who seemed about ten years older than her. Daniel's family, I assumed.

"You're Samaya, aren't you?" she asked. "I'm Daniel's mother."

"Oh, hi. Nice to meet you," I said, putting my hand out to shake.

But she leaned in and gave me a tight hug instead. I tensed a bit, taken by surprise—I thought Daniel had told her we weren't that serious?

"I'm Christina Ramos," she said as we hugged, "but you can call me Chrissy."

She let me go. "Daniel has been talking about you so much! He'll be embarrassed that I introduced myself to you, but I wanted to make sure that I caught you before we left. I love that blouse! Very pretty. Did you enjoy the game? I know you don't know much about hockey."

"Oh, thank you. The game was great."

Daniel talked about me to his mother. What had he said? I peeked around her to see that the uncle was still looking at us stoically. Daniel's mother hadn't introduced us, and the uncle didn't seem to want to meet me anyway.

I was still talking to Daniel's mother about the game when Daniel himself appeared. He was grinning, of course, although he looked a little nervous that his mom and his fake girlfriend were talking without him. Which made sense—he had his boundaries.

His mom hugged him tightly, then ruffled Daniel's hair, which was wet from his shower. She said to him something in Tagalog, then looked at me.

"I'm sorry," she said. "I should speak English. I was telling him how proud I was of him for getting that assist."

Daniel said something to his mother in Tagalog, then told me he'd be back in a second and walked his mother and uncle to a silver SUV in the lot. He put his hockey gear in the back. I watched as he hugged his mother again, said something to his uncle, then came back to me. He still looked uncomfortable.

I smiled at him. "Everything okay?"

"It's all good," he said. "They'll bring my gear home."

On the short walk to the café, Daniel seemed to get over his discomfort. In fact, he was even more hyper and cheerful than normal. He kept talking about the game and some awesome maneuver someone on his team did that I hadn't even realized was awesome.

After we were sitting with frappé drinks, a muffin for me, and a scone for Daniel, Cass finally came in with a tall white guy with short red hair and dark-framed glasses. Owen, I assumed. Judging by the easy smile on Cass's face, meeting Owen's team had gone well.

Daniel grinned. "Hey, Cass! I hear you've been fraternizing with the enemy?"

Cass grinned. "Fraternizing with the winning team, you mean," they said.

Daniel laughed. "Ooh, harsh." He smiled at Owen. "Great goal there. You were flying."

Owen smiled. "Thanks, man. That was quite a fake out you did when you got that assist. I didn't even see Krebs there." He shook his head, in awe. "Wicked."

Cass and Owen joined us at the table, and Cass introduced us formally. I watched Owen and them both closely. Cass was definitely less anxious than before. Owen seemed nice and easygoing. Friendly. A bit like Daniel, in that he seemed like he could talk to people very easily. He wore a black turtleneck and slim jeans.

Owen gave Cass a mock scolding. "I still can't believe your best friend is *dating* Daniel Ramos," he said playfully.

"I did ask you if you knew him!"

"But you didn't say why. You were like, *none of my friends are into sports*, and yet . . ." He waved his hands between us to prove his point. "And of course I'd know him. If they play hockey in Scarborough, I know them."

Cass shook their head. "You can't possibly know all the hockey players in Scarborough."

Owen nodded proudly. "I've been on skates since before I could walk. Yeah, I absolutely have met them all. May not know them well. Definitely don't like them all." He nodded toward Daniel. "I like this one, though, even if the guy is playing for a shit team. He's got a decent slapshot, so it's all good."

Daniel laughed, and I rolled my eyes. But secretly, I was delighted with Owen. Not that I thought Cass would be into someone less worthy, but Owen was now the second hockey player who'd knocked down my jock stereotypes.

But mostly, I was so incredibly happy for Cass. Dating or not dating, it was clear that Owen was great for Cass.

22

Jocks Can't Play Video Games

Apparently, Owen got hungry after games, so he and Cass left soon after for the burger place next door. Cass said they'd be back for me in an hour.

"I like Owen," I said.

"Me too," Daniel said. "I don't know him that well, but I've heard good things." He looked down at his books. "We'd better get to this. I'm not sure I'll be able to make sense of it in only an hour."

We started going over his calculus. His test would be covering all the limits work he'd done in the last few weeks. After going over the principle of limits again, I gave him some practice questions I had prepared in advance. After he figured out the first couple of them, he gave me a proud smile.

"See?" I said. "I told you that you could do this."

"Yeah. Let's see if I can do it without you sitting next to me. I'm glad that I'll never have to think about calculus again, soon." He sighed. "I have to figure out how to tell my uncle that."

I was still a little weirded out that his uncle hadn't said hello to me outside the arena. "Does he still think you're applying to that engineering program?"

Daniel nodded. I didn't really understand it—if Daniel didn't want to study engineering, then why not just tell his uncle that?

"How mad will he be when you tell him you want to apply to culinary school?" I asked.

Daniel sighed. "He'll be pissed. I know I'll need financial aid and student loans for school, but hopefully he'll still let me live in his house. There's no way I'll be able to afford dorms without being in debt for the rest of my life."

"Isn't there some way of convincing him? Like, bake him a pie or something? No one can resist you with a pie in your hands."

He shook his head. "Would you believe my uncle doesn't like pie? Seriously. Never trust someone who doesn't like baked goods."

We did more practice questions until Daniel said his brain was shutting down from too much math. I could not relate. He seemed to be getting it, though. I asked him about his *Dragon Arena* progress as he packed up his stuff.

"I'm level twelve! I don't know why I've never played these RPG games before. I can't wait to play online."

"Soon," I said. You had to be level fifteen to play with others and do quests in parties.

"I wish I could catch up to you so I could come with you to that guy's party," Daniel said.

I shook my head. "Believe me, you *don't* want to go to Jayden's. He'd be harder on you than Omar was at Hana's. I don't even want to go." I picked up my frappé to take a sip.

Daniel tilted his head, looking at me curiously. "Do you . . . *like* your friends? Not Cass, but the rest of your crowd. Like that Jayden guy and the guy who accused you of cheating."

I paused, my iced drink frozen in midair.

"You don't actually have to answer that," Daniel said. "Remember, we don't have to be open if we don't want to be."

That was the first time in a while he'd even mentioned our parameters. And he'd been open with me lately—he'd even introduced me to his mother. He'd just now talked about his uncle.

"I don't mind answering. They're not really *my* friends. They're Devin's."

"And Devin is not your boyfriend anymore. I guess I'm trying to understand why you hang out with them still. You don't ever seem, I don't know, excited to do anything social with them. Why do you hang out with them all?"

"I hang out with them because . . ." Because we were a friend group at school—the smart kids. The gamer-nerds. Because when Devin and I were together, I'd felt like I belonged with them. And I had actually liked feeling like I belonged with them. I liked the feeling of them all respecting me.

But I wasn't that same person I was when I was with Devin. I knew I didn't like that crowd anymore. So why did I still care so much about what they thought of me?

~

I didn't sleep well that night. The hockey game had left me with an unsettled feeling. Partially because watching Daniel play made me realize this crush wasn't going anywhere. At the game, I couldn't stop focusing on him—on his speed, on his amazing agility on the ice. And on his smile, which I swear I could see clear across the ice, even through his caged face mask.

He was magnetic. And I was in trouble. And maybe everything Cass had been saying was true, and despite his so-called boundaries, maybe Daniel's feelings were heading in the same direction as mine. I mean, he told his *mom* about me. And his teammates, who, as far as I could tell, were his closest friends. That didn't sound like a guy keeping a girl at arm's length.

But the other thing messing with my mind was realizing I didn't even really like my friends anymore. If I didn't like anyone at school, why was I working so hard to make them respect me? Why did I care if Earl's Whispers made me into a fool?

And if I didn't need a fake boyfriend to help me get their respect, then why keep up this charade with Daniel? I had no intention of ending our tutoring, but did I need the selfies? The dates? The PDAs? If I wanted the crush to go away, then maybe it was time to end this fake relationship.

Daniel texted me Sunday morning to tell me he'd managed to get his character to fifteen, which didn't really surprise me. Like I'd told him, the early levels were easy—I'd originally leveled GreenEggsAndSam to fifteen in two days. The game really started at that level, since it was at that point characters could play with others online.

Daniel: So we can play together now, right?

I wasn't sure I wanted to do that. I should be ending this relationship, not finding yet another thing for us to do together.

Me: I'm not sure . . . you know I don't really play much anymore.

Daniel: Please? I'm not very good—I don't want to play online with strangers who'll laugh at me. C'mon, I really want to see an actual dragon in the game, and there's no way I'd survive long enough in a battle to get to a dragon without you.

Me: Okay, but I can't tonight. I have a bunch of schoolwork and game dev stuff to catch up on.

Daniel: Of course! I'm not going anywhere!

Me: Okay. See you Thursday at the shelter.

I'd wanted to keep my distance, but I found it very hard to say no to Daniel Ramos.

As I was walking into the game-dev meeting on Monday, I got an email from Mrs. Singh to tell me I had officially earned enough community service hours to graduate, so I didn't have to go to the shelter anymore.

I bit my lip after reading it on my phone. I could end all this now, and not even see Daniel at the shelter anymore.

But . . . I didn't want to do that. I'd made a commitment to Muniba and Andre to be there all semester, and I didn't want to disappoint them. Or the shelter staff and residents. And also? Just like when Daniel asked me to play *Dragon Arena*, I had trouble disappointing him. And I knew he would be disappointed if we stopped baking together every week.

I'd really been looking forward to our game-dev meeting after school today since our progress on the forest-fairy game was going so well. Cass and I had the opening sequence almost coded by now, and some others had updated me on their progress on graphics and scripts for the other levels. But about ten minutes into the meeting, I realized I shouldn't have been so optimistic. Jayden and Omar had been working on the script for level three, but I didn't know what they'd been planning.

Apparently, what they'd done was write the entire level as pretty much a sniper battle. With our forest fairies using semiautomatic weapons. *What?*

"You've turned the level into a first-person shooter?" I shook my head. "This is supposed to be an adventure game!"

Jayden crossed his arms in front of him. "This is way better. Trust me. This is how we win this thing."

"But it's a puzzle adventure game! In a forest!"

"I know it's a forest. That's why they're shooting squirrels and birds."

I cringed at the thought of bloody squirrels in our game. "Absolutely not. As team captain, I'm vetoing this. It goes against the entire vision for the game."

Everyone else started talking at once again, just like that first meeting. Most agreed with me—that a first-person sniper battle had no place in a puzzle adventure game. Others agreed with Jayden. I tried to get everyone to stop, but Jayden and Omar kept interrupting me to get the last word in.

"This is a democracy!" Omar said. "We should vote! How about everyone write a script, and we vote next week?"

I rolled my eyes, looking at Miss Zhao, to see if she could help me out. She was working on her computer, clearly keeping to her assertion that she'd be a hands-off adviser. That was probably a good thing—Miss Zhao would be evaluating my leadership abilities here—so it would be best if she didn't notice me losing control.

I needed to handle this. "We'll never get anywhere if we need to wait to vote on every tiny decision. We should keep with the puzzle adventure game play and not do a first-person shooter. Put your hand up if you agree with me."

More than half of the team put their hands up. "Good," I said. "Now, Cass, how goes debugging the code for the fairies' wings in the cave?"

That night after school I was working on the scripts for level four, when my phone pinged. It was a text from Aimee on the group chat with her and Cass.

Aimee: I know what you're thinking, and it wasn't Jayden. Also, my nails are REAL!

Me: What Are you talking about Aimee?

Cass: Samaya, check Earl's Whispers.

Oh god, not again. Dread settled in my stomach. I flipped to the Instagram app and found the picture in question. It was a picture of me, from the game-dev meeting.

Image: Very angry, short South Asian girl with black hair wearing a dragon T-shirt standing at the front of a classroom.

Caption: No one can be sure what Samaya Janmohammad's endgame here is, but word is that all her happy pictures at hockey games and farmers' markets are as fake as Aimee Whelan's nails. Apparently, there is a lot of turmoil behind the scenes between the math genius and her new hockey-playing himbo, and Samaya has been taking out her relationship woes on her game-dev teammates. Yelling at your teammates is not leadership behavior—although it was always questionable whether Samaya had the skills to match those of her ex, who everyone knows is a born leader. Whispers has learned that several of her teammates are considering speaking to the staff adviser of the club about her inability to be a real team captain. This account will be watching her closely to see what else cracks beneath her surface.

I stared at the post, reading it at least three times, while feeling like throwing up. Finally, I reopened the chat and wrote to my friends.

Me: What the fuck.

Before Cass or Aimee answered, a FaceTime call with both of them appeared on my screen. I answered it.

Aimee, looking extremely annoyed, was the first to speak. "What the fuck indeed."

"I think that's a good question for your boyfriend, Aim. How do you know he's not behind this? He's the one who wanted that sniper battle."

Aimee shook her head. "It wasn't him. He is not Earl's Whispers."

"I don't think he's Whispers," Cass said. "I do think he's the one who sent in the picture and tip, though."

"He would never," Aimee said. "You don't know him like I do. Plus, why would he make that crack about my nails? Jayden knows they're real."

"Maybe to deflect suspicion?" Cass suggested. "Honestly, I wouldn't put it past him. You need to see him for who he—"

"Can you guys stop?" I interrupted. "I'm really not in the mood for more arguing." My lousy day had just gotten lousier, and I wanted to go to bed.

Cass and Aimee were quiet for a moment. Finally, Cass spoke. "Samaya, we need to report this to the school. They're harassing you."

"How? By telling the truth? I'm not going to be the bitch who snitches after a tiny bit of pressure. The best revenge is living well, remember? I need to show Miss Zhao I can handle this. Lead the team to work together instead of fighting."

Aimee frowned. "But it's not true. You and Daniel aren't having problems."

I snorted. "Me and Daniel aren't real, remember? Just like the post says."

"Yeah, but no one else knows that. Why does—"

"Crap," Cass said, interrupting Aimee. "There's a GamesLost comment on it."

"What does it say?" I asked, bracing myself.

"She knows squirrels are the cause of most power outages, so why does she care about shooting some up."

Now I was sure I was going to throw up.

"What the hell does that mean?" Cass asked.

I frowned, the sour taste not leaving my mouth. "It means LostAxis must be in the game-dev team. The squirrels-causing-power-outages thing is a fact he once told me."

"Fuuuck . . . ," Cass said.

My sentiments exactly. I hadn't been trying to figure out who LostAxis was anymore—because as Cass said, it didn't matter. But now it did. If LostAxis was in the game-dev club, and was angry at me for blocking them and dating Daniel, could they sabotage the club? I was really enjoying the game-dev project—when the club was getting along. I didn't want to give up the forest-fairy game. And I *needed* the reference from Miss Zhao. This was my only extracurricular right now. As Mrs. Singh had told me, I needed the leadership experience for my scholarship applications.

"Who do you think it is?" Aimee said.

I bit my lip, thinking. "I really, really don't know. I've only elimi-nated Jayden and Omar. So that leaves"—I named the remaining members of the team—"Carson, Kavita, Nabil, and Alex. Wait, I doubt Kavita would be LostAxis. She played croquet with Daniel and I, and she seemed impressed with him. She didn't seem mad that he had stolen LostAxis's identity."

"What about the others? Did they talk to Daniel?" Cass asked.

I shook my head. "Carson was there when Omar accused me of cheating on Devin, but he didn't say anything. It could be him. Alex and Nabil weren't even at Hana's, were they?"

Aimee nodded. "Nabil was. Not Alex."

I barely knew these three—I couldn't believe one of them was LostAxis. But if GamesLost was at the game-dev meeting, it had to be one of them.

"Maybe bring Daniel to Jayden's party?" Aimee said. "Those three will be there. I am sure you and Daniel can focus on them and draw them out."

"I can't bring Daniel to Jayden's. His *Dragon Arena* character is level fifteen, not fifty."

"Buy him a level-fifty character," Cass said.

"Isn't buying leveled characters against the game rules?" Aimee asked.

"Yes," Cass said, "but that doesn't mean it doesn't happen. I know a place on the dark web where you can get one."

I shook my head. "Daniel's not experienced enough to play a level fifty. I've never even seen him play online before."

"So play with him. Figure out how skilled he is. If you think he could manage a level-fifty Dark Mage, let me know and I'll venture to the dark side of the internet and get one."

I cringed. This all sounded so shady. But maybe this was the only way to find out exactly who was out to get me. Because I didn't want to lose the game-dev club over this.

"Okay. I'll play with him tomorrow and see."

That settled one thing: I wasn't going to end this fake relationship with Daniel—at least not until after the party.

~

It took about six minutes of playing *Dragon Arena* with Daniel on Tuesday night to realize that no, there was no way in hell he could handle a level-fifty character. Since I'd met him, I'd been impressed with him so many times. His baking skills, his hockey skills—hell, even his skill with calculus was better than he seemed to think it was. But Daniel Ramos was a terrible, horrendous, complete newb *Dragon Arena* player. Questing with him was . . . challenging. He never paid attention to what I was doing when we were fighting together. Hell, he barely paid attention to what *he* was doing. Or to his own health bar. I spent way too many of my magic points making sure a low-level pixie didn't smoke his ass.

"Oh my god," I said as I used yet another crow feather to resurrect his dead body while blocking a centaur at the same time. We had a phone call on speaker so we wouldn't have to worry about typing on the chat while playing. "Don't start a destructive spell while I'm healing you! In hockey you watch what the other players are doing, don't you?"

I heard his chuckle. "There are no fire-burning dragons in front of me on the rink. Which is good, because then the rink would be a puddle."

The crow's feather had resurrected Daniel's mage by now, so I told him to head farther in but stay on the edge of the horde while hitting them with destructive spells. But he got too close, and soon the centaur leader was pummeling him again. I tried to keep up with my healing spells, but he kept locking on to other centaurs, which made them join the leader.

"Don't do anything while I'm healing you, then ready up a lightning on the leader," I yelled. "We can take care of the others later!"

He did the lightning spell right away. Before I'd healed him. Which meant my heal bounced off his spell and healed the centaur instead. Who then killed Daniel. Again. And I didn't have any more crow's feathers.

"Damn. This is way harder with two people," he said.

I moved my character toward his corpse. "Imagine it with a party of at least twenty at Jayden's on Friday." I had already explained to him what had happened the day before at school and on Earl's Whispers.

"I'll practice more. Tomorrow's Wednesday, so I have hockey, but I can do this some more after."

I exhaled. "Daniel, there's no point. I hate to break it to you, but you suck at *Dragon Arena*. Maybe with tons of practice you might get better, but there's no way you'll be able to play on Friday." I was doomed. "You can't come to the party."

He was silent awhile. With Daniel dead, and me not having the ability to revive him, I had no choice but to transport his body out of the cavern to the healer's hut, where he could be revived. We would not be completing this quest.

"Why don't you skip the party, too?" he asked.

"This is the best way to figure out who this GamesLost person is. Plus, I promised Jayden I'd go so I could be the game-dev captain. If I don't show, he'll be so pissed that he'll mount an insurrection."

"Your friend Jayden is an ass," Daniel said.

"He's not my friend. And anyway, every friend group has an ass, doesn't it?" I asked.

Daniel chuckled low, and it sent a shiver down my spine. Apparently being terrible at *Dragon Arena* wasn't enough to extinguish my crush.

I sighed. "Don't worry about it," I said as our characters made their way back to the village. "Our deal was two dates plus the dance. No one said anything about mastering a video game, or even helping me draw out a catfisher. I'll figure out some other way to identify them."

It was a while before Daniel responded. We'd reached the village and had to head to our own huts to log off. Finally, after I'd shut down the game, Daniel spoke, in a quiet voice.

"I don't mind. I like to do things for you," he said softly. "I've grown a little bit attached to you. You make me happy."

I was silent for a while. What exactly did he mean by that? Finally, I replied, even more quietly than him, "You make me happy, too, Daniel."

I didn't say anything more, but I couldn't believe I'd even said that. Seemed we were both in deeper than we'd expected.

23

Questing Again

The following evening, a solution to my problem of how to bring Daniel to the party fell into my lap—or rather fell onto Daniel's wrist. Daniel called me from the hospital while he was getting a cast put on the hairline fracture in his wrist.

He'd been at hockey practice and was stepping off the ice to hit the bench. He'd just taken off those big padded gloves, and literally seconds later, a hockey puck flew over the boards and hit him square on his arm.

"Ugh. I'm sorry," I said. "That really sucks. Does it hurt a lot?"

"Yeah. I used your pie trick to distract myself."

"You recited the digits of pi?"

"No, I thought about pie. Specifically, I considered the plausibility of a pineapple meringue pie. Worked well, thanks for the tip."

"How many games do you think you'll miss?"

"A couple. We have a bit of a break coming up anyway. But, Samaya, don't you see? This means I *can* come to that dude's party this weekend! No one will actually expect me to play the game with a cast."

I frowned. "You sound almost . . . gleeful about breaking your wrist."

"Well, I'm not actually *gleeful*. It hurts like hell, and yeah, missing games will suck. But this is a silver lining, isn't it? I can come, you don't have to go alone, and we can figure out who the catfisher is together."

I sighed. After our . . . confession to each other the night before, I'd been thinking all day that it was a good thing that Daniel and I weren't going to have another date after all. As much as I wanted to figure out who LostAxis was, I also still terrified of whatever was happening between me and Daniel.

"What if someone asks you to log in, though?" I asked. "Maybe you can get out of actually playing, but they still think you're a level fifty. You're fifteen."

"Sixteen," he corrected. "I played alone for a bit after you and I played. Honestly, I play better solo. Which is weird because I am usually a team-sports kind of guy. We can always come up with an excuse if someone wants me to log in. But it totally makes sense for me to come watch my girlfriend play even if I can't. This will work."

It could, possibly, maybe work. I sighed. "Fine. Jayden's party is officially a sting operation. We're going to smoke out a catfisher."

~

On Friday night Cass picked Daniel and me up at the shelter at eight to take us to Jayden's gaming party. I'd gone to the shelter after school because we needed more time to bake this week since Daniel was one-handed. I'd begged Tahira to go to the mall for me the day before to get Daniel a red *Dragon Arena* shirt from the gaming store since, once again, I didn't have enough time to mail-order one. I was also wearing a *Dragon Arena* shirt (my black obsidian dragon one), along with black jeans and my black Converse. Daniel had proclaimed me extra vampire-esque tonight. He was wearing the ruby dragon shirt with jeans and red sneakers.

Daniel's jaw dropped when Cass pulled up in front of Jayden's house. Jayden lived near Hana, in the posh Beach neighborhood of Toronto. And if Hana's house was impressive, Jayden's topped it. By a lot.

Daniel whistled low as we walked up the driveway. "This one is bigger than the last one. You sure your house isn't like this?"

"Hell no. Although"—I smiled, looking at the Audi in Jayden's driveway—"my mom has that car. She calls it her baby. Mom won't let Tahira drive the Audi. She's only allowed in Dad's Toyota."

After chatting with Jayden's mother for a bit—when she learned Daniel's cast was from a hockey injury, they bonded over the sport since she used to play in university—we headed downstairs to the gaming party.

"Jayden's mom seems awesome," Daniel said. "She should join the women's rec team that plays in the arena. They're always looking for players."

I nodded, following Daniel down the basement steps. "She is awesome. She was super nice the first time I came here. We ended up chatting here in the kitchen while everyone was playing. Whenever my parents meet any of my friends for the first time, Mom first asks what their parents do for a living."

Jayden's house was impressive, but the basement game room was really the best part. It was a large, open space with deep brown hardwood floors and warm gray walls. Jayden had set it up like he always did for our guild nights—with a long table (made up of two big wood folding tables) along the middle of the room, with seats all around it. There must have been twenty kids crowded around the table—mostly members of the guild, but some newbies we hadn't played with, too. Of course Jayden was there, as well as Aimee, Hana, Omar, and Devin. I also saw Kavita and Carson, but not Nabil or Alex.

The game was being projected on one wall, although everyone at the table was looking at their own laptop screens. A seating area near the table was also full—Daniel wasn't the only spectator here. Friends and dates of the players were already putting their feet on the coffee table. Daniel joined them. This was the biggest turnout I could remember for a gaming night. It looked like they'd been playing for a bit—some cans of Monster energy drink and small bags of Doritos were already scattered.

Jayden looked up from his seat. "Good. Here's another Light Mage—this one has an Obsidian Staff. Hope you brushed up on your healing combos, Samaya. Oh, you brought your Dark Mage . . . Slide over, Devin. Daniel can sit next to you. We'll be starting another round in five minutes."

I raised a brow. Jayden was barely even looking at us. I don't know what I expected, but with that Whispers post, I assumed people would be more interested in Daniel and I arriving together.

"Daniel's just here for moral support and to watch," I said, then pointed to his tie-dye-print cast. "Broken wrist."

Jayden stared at Daniel for a few seconds, then shrugged. "Whatever. We don't really need another Dark Mage anyway. We *need* the Light Mage." He patted the empty seat next to him. "These griffins are giving us a beating."

I set up my computer next to Jayden, even though I'd have honestly preferred to sit just about anywhere else. I looked at Devin on the other side of the table. He was sitting next to Hana, of course. She whispered something in his ear, and it made him smile. Huh. Maybe she *was* the one who'd taken that picture in game dev. I didn't think she was LostAxis, but I wouldn't put it past Hana to spread gossip about me.

Daniel was already chatting cheerfully with someone over on the couch. Because of course he was. That person was probably already becoming his next best friend.

"Hey, Samaya?" Kavita asked. She was sitting on the other side of Aimee. "What happened to your boyfriend's arm?"

"Hockey injury. He's really bummed he can't join the quest tonight."

Kavita pretended to fan herself. "I'm sorry, but that's *so* hot. *Hockey injury.* People into sports are so sexy. And he's into gaming, too?" She shook her head. "You really caught a live one, Samaya."

Yeah, I really didn't think Kavita was LostAxis. I glanced to see everyone else's reaction to what she'd said. Most were too focused on their screens to pay attention, but Hana scowled, and Devin stared straight at me.

A chair pulled up beside me. It was Daniel, squeezing in between me and Jayden. "I can't even see what's going on from over there," he said. "I'd rather be rink side."

I laughed, then whispered into his ear, "I'd rather you be closer, too."

Once I was logged in to the game, I joined the quest, and Jayden immediately started spewing orders.

"Okay, physical melee to the front, that's Warriors and Weavers. Dark Mages and Paladins led by me and Devin will be right behind you pounding with offensive magic, then Archers behind us. Light Mages and Bards can circle us. Focus healing on Dark Mages and Paladins, but don't forget to keep an eye on the melees. And for the love of god, keep the protective spells going!"

He gave a glare to a younger girl I didn't really know sitting across from him. I gathered she was a Bard or a Light Mage and was not playing to Jayden's standard. "We've already passed the silver griffins, which were no joke. Bronze comes next, then ruby. Both will make the silver ones seem like house cats. But the real enemy here are the diamond griffins—the dragon's nest will be surrounded by, like, thirty of them." He looked at Daniel. "With the extra high-level Light Mage, we might just survive this."

We started the fight. I could barely think with everyone yelling out commands. I did my best to keep the offensive players healed, and it was easier with the Obsidian Staff, but it was still tense. My jaw was clenched. I was getting a headache.

I knew I needed to be watching the others, and maybe even figuring out if Nabil and Alex were on their way here, but it had been a while since I'd played in such a big group, and I really needed to focus on the game so I didn't mess something up. But honestly? I wasn't enjoying it as much as I used to. Probably because these people in the guild weren't really my friends anymore. I wished I were back in the kitchen making pies with Daniel.

A hand was suddenly on my shoulder, rubbing gently. Daniel. "You got this. You're doing great, Samaya."

I took the strength he was giving me and channeled it back into the game, queuing up a complicated healing combo that burst from the tip of my staff in a shower of rainbows.

"Yes!" Jayden squealed. "That's what I'm talking about! Love that thing!"

I turned to thank Daniel for helping me, when I saw he was completely focused on the game projected on the wall. His lips were pursed a bit, and his eyes . . . his eyes were . . . intense. Of course, I'd noticed Daniel's amazing bone structure before. Those lips that could somehow portray anything from good humor to full-on joy with the slightest movement. But I'd never studied his eyes like this. They were round, and not as dark as they usually seemed. I could make out pale golden striations in the brown irises.

He must have realized I was watching him at that moment, because one side of his lips, the side closest to me, turned up the slightest amount. I'd spent so much time with Daniel in the last month that I knew his face. This was the same look he'd had when I tasted his apple pie last week.

"Samaya!" Aimee shouted. "Stop ogling your boyfriend and throw me a heal!"

I snapped back to the game, and healed Aimee, then Cass and Hana. My friends were almost dead because I'd gotten lost in Daniel's eyes.

After we finished off the final bronze griffin, we had a few minutes before the ruby ones appeared. A collective sigh erupted around the table. Some players took long gulps of their energy drinks, while others cracked their knuckles. This could be my chance to figure out the mystery of LostAxis's identity.

Carson was sitting across and to the right of Daniel and me.

"Hey, Carson," I said. "Nice job on that fight sequence."

He kind of recoiled when I said it, probably because that was the first time I'd ever complimented him. Carson was usually nice enough, but if I had to speculate, I'd say there was a closet incel hiding under the niceness. He barely talked to and never cooperated in game with the girls in the guild, and I'd heard him complain many times about not having a girlfriend in a way that made it clear that he fully blamed girls for that. I had difficulty believing he was LostAxis because I'd never got a sexist vibe from LostAxis, but I really didn't know him well enough to be sure. He definitely played well enough to be him.

"Okay?" Carson said.

"Have you met my boyfriend? Daniel, this is Carson. He's on my game-dev team."

Carson raised a brow. "Uh, yeah. We met at Hana's? I'm surprised you brought the guy here." He snorted, then looked at Devin and Hana, who were watching the conversation intently. "But clearly you like *playing* with Devin and this guy at the same time. Typical."

What the hell? That was the dumbest accusation I'd ever heard. Daniel wasn't even playing tonight. So Carson *also* thought I'd cheated on Devin with LostAxis, or with Daniel, or whatever. Carson couldn't be LostAxis.

But I glared at Devin. Why the hell was he letting his friends all think the worst of me? He could correct them at any point.

I turned to Jayden. "Hey, Jayden, aren't Nabil and Alex supposed to be here? I need to check with them about the level they're working on for the game dev."

Jayden nodded. "They'll be late. They're picking up Alina and Megan first. They should be here before we reach the dragon."

I sighed. The only thing I'd learned so far was that I didn't want to be here.

"You were awesome," Daniel said to me, clearly sensing my annoyance at everything. "You want me to get you anything?"

I smiled. "Nah, I'm good. I'm just a little tense. My shoulders always hurt after a fight like that." I rubbed the back of my shoulder.

"Here, let me." He took over rubbing my shoulder with his good hand.

I chuckled. "Thanks. Ooh, you're good at that. Yet another reason I'm glad you're here."

"I'm glad I'm here, too."

I turned to look at him . . . and his face was right there near mine. Daniel's eyes locked on to me as my breath hitched. It felt like we were alone instead of at a busy gaming party with at least thirty other kids.

I wanted to kiss him. Yes, I'd wanted to kiss him when we sat on the picnic blanket at Hana's party under the night sky, and again after seeing him fly across the ice at his hockey game, but no moment between us had ever felt as charged as this one. To be honest, I wanted to do a lot more than just kiss . . . but I'd start with a kiss. And I'd bet my limited-edition garnet dragon figurine that Daniel wanted the same thing. We were moving toward something that was far from the parameters we'd agreed on four weeks ago. I'd been convinced that he didn't feel this way, or it would never work between us anyway, but all those excuses and objections just melted away with that look in his eyes. It was ridiculous to fight something that felt this right.

"Ruby griffins are here!" Jayden yelled.

I scrambled my hands back onto my controller. I needed to focus on this fight now. The ruby griffins were harder than the bronze, but we all found our groove quickly and soon were smoking them, too. Hana spun webs around the griffins, allowing Devin to pound at them with his war hammer. Aimee was shooting flaming arrows on the ones that flew above us. After casting a wide healing spell over the entire party, I stepped back and enjoyed the symphony.

Things did get tricky—it was touch and go at the end thanks to a spectacular mistake the Bard made (they sang a cure-disease song instead of a top-up-the-party's-magic song)—but we still took out the last ruby griffin.

My adrenaline was pumping now. There was another wait before the final horde—the diamond griffins—appeared. I squeezed my fists on my lap. So many emotions were swirling through me. Euphoria. Adrenaline. Nerves. Joy. Attraction.

Yes, attraction, because I didn't think I'd ever wanted to be closer to another person—to the boy sitting next to me with his hand on my shoulder—than I did right now.

His hand moved from my shoulder to my knee. I reached down and intertwined my fingers with his. And we sat like that for several seconds, hands clasped under the table, as the other players chattered about the game around us.

What did this mean? My feelings were getting impossible to ignore. But did Daniel feel the same way?

Maybe for him, all this was for show? For the fake relationship?

Was it possible I was the only one who was feeling this way?

Daniel's phone rang.

"No calls during game," Jayden said as Daniel let go of my hand to pull his phone out of his pocket.

"He's not even playing," I said.

"The rule stands for anyone in the room."

Daniel looked at the call display, then looked at me, concerned. "It's Andre. Andre wouldn't call me at this hour unless it was important."

I cringed, looking at Jayden. "It's our boss . . . He needs to take the call. There's ten minutes before the next horde anyway."

"Rules are rules," Jayden said. Man, he really *was* an ass.

"It's not even a real job," Devin said. "It's just volunteer work."

"And it's not even a real boyfriend," Jayden added.

Wait, what did Jayden say? My head shot around, not to glare at Jayden, but at Aimee.

In all the gossip—people accusing me of cheating on Devin, people claiming that Daniel and I were in trouble, or that the joy in our pictures was fake, or, hell, even people claiming that Daniel was a pop star, no one had ever claimed that Daniel's and my relationship wasn't real in the first place.

Had Aimee told Jayden the truth?

I blinked. She was supposed to be one of my closest friends.

Daniel's phone stopped ringing, but his text tone rang. I watched his face as he read it. "Andre says I need to come to the shelter now. He's asking if you can, too," he said.

"Tell him Samaya's busy," Jayden said. "You're welcome to leave, though, hockey-boy."

Daniel stood up, looking worried. "He says it's an emergency," Daniel said. "I've known Andre for a long time—I don't think I've ever heard him call anything an emergency."

I nodded and shut off my computer. Andre was normally so laid-back. Whatever this was had to be serious. "We should go."

"What?" Jayden said. "Are you kidding? You can't leave before we fight the diamond griffins."

I glared at Jayden. "It's an emergency. This is a family shelter—with, like, kids and families. If there is an emergency there, it might be serious."

Cass closed their computer and unplugged it. "I'll drive you."

"Oh my god, why are you going, too?" Aimee asked Cass, voice full of attitude. "You don't even know if there is anything wrong yet."

Cass glared at Aimee. "I'm going because Samaya and Daniel are my friends, and if they say there's an emergency, then I trust that and I want to help."

Amid the chaos of them arguing, I zipped my laptop into my backpack. My heart was racing—I was scared for Andre and Muniba, and for everyone at the shelter.

"Everyone, everyone," Devin said, lowering his hands in a calm-down motion. "The griffins will be here in six minutes. And the fight will take, what, ten minutes? You can leave after that."

Jayden nodded. "Fifteen minutes won't make a difference. You made a commitment, Samaya." He gave me a look. He was probably already thinking about how he was going to get back at me if I left. "We've known you longer than he has, Samaya. You are supposed to be our friend."

I didn't even bother answering. Just stood up with my backpack.

"I'm going to call Andre," Daniel said, stepping away from the table.

Jayden looked at Aimee. "Told you she changed. She's been thinking she's better than all of us since Devin dumped her."

I glared at Jayden. I was almost positive now he was the one who'd sent that picture from game dev into Earl's Whispers. He wasn't the catfisher, but he was the one trying to ruin me.

Daniel came back to me, his face whiter than the ice he played on.

"What is it?" I asked. I put my hand on his arm just above the cast.

"Yasmin's missing." His voice cracked.

"What? What do you mean, missing? We just saw her today while baking. She said she liked my shirt."

"She was last seen at the shelter two hours ago. They've looked but can't find her. They're putting together a search party to check the forest. Andre wants my help because I've gone for walks with her there before."

My fists clenched. The forest that ended at the Scarborough Bluffs cliff. Yasmin was just a baby—only five years old. She shouldn't be alone out there.

I stepped away from the table, looking straight at Jayden. "Yasmin is a five-year-old girl from the shelter where we work. You can't possibly be so heartless to stop us from going now."

No one said anything.

"Let's go," Cass said, heading to the stairs. "I can join the search party, too."

I squeezed Daniel's arm. I'd never seen him like this. He looked terrified. I knew Daniel had worked at the shelter a lot longer than I had, and I knew that he and Yasmin had a close bond. Yasmin *had* to be okay.

"Cass and I are going to do whatever we can to help, okay, Daniel? Let's go. We'll get there quickly."

Aimee stood. "I'm coming, too. To help find the kid."

"For fuck's sake," Jayden said. "So we're going to *abandon* the mission?"

Everyone ignored Jayden's outburst. Daniel and I followed Cass to the stairs with Aimee close behind me. When I looked back, Hana, Omar, Carson, and a bunch of others I didn't know very well were heading to the stairs as well, saying they wanted to join the search party, too. I didn't see Jayden's expression as his quest went up in dust. And I didn't care that I wouldn't find out who LostAxis was now. None of that mattered.

We needed to find Yasmin. Now.

24

Tea and Hugs

Daniel and I sat in the back seat of Cass's car on the way to the shelter. Aimee was in the front passenger seat. Daniel looked so upset—eyebrows furrowed. Normally smiling mouth in a straight line. I needed to stay close to him. I wished there were something more I could do.

When we got to the shelter, Andre was in the front lobby talking to a police officer with four men I didn't recognize. He held a bunch of flashlights.

Faduma, Yasmin's mother, was in the common room with some other women from the shelter, along with her two oldest children. She called out to me, so I went to her. She was wearing a black hijab tonight, with a sweatshirt and long brown skirt. I'd had a few chats with her in the last few weeks and met her older children. I liked them all.

"Ah, Samaya." Faduma reached out and took my hand. She'd clearly been crying but smiled faintly at me. "Yasmin loves you so much. Thank you for being her friend."

I nodded and sat next to her on the couch. "Of course. I'm sure we'll find her. Did she tell you where she was going?"

Faduma shook her head. "No, but I know. She wanted to look for fairies. That girl and her imagination. She will be a storyteller one day, eh, Shanta?" she said to one of the other women, who nodded.

Muniba came into the common room. "Oh good, you're here, Samaya. I was about to make tea for the residents. They're all so worried. Are you going with the others to search the forest?"

Faduma was still holding my hand. "You stay with us," she said, squeezing. "Daniel will find her."

I agreed to stay behind to help support Yasmin's mother. I was worried about going out into the forest with my tree allergies anyway. I excused myself to say goodbye to Daniel.

"You'll be okay?" I asked after telling him I was going to stay behind with the mothers.

He nodded, then leaned down and kissed me on the cheek. "I'm sorry your night was ruined."

I shook my head and squeezed Daniel's hand. "Go find her."

It was weirdly quiet in the shelter after the search party left. Muniba and I went to the kitchen, and she put a big pot of water on to boil.

"I'll make masala chai as well as the regular stuff," she said. "The residents always say my proper chai is the most soothing thing in the world. Put out some of the treats you made earlier, too. We can spare some."

I took a big serving tray and started filling it with teacups. And I grabbed a plate of the iced sugar cookies Daniel and I had made earlier that evening. That seemed like so long ago, now. My heart clenched as I put the cookies on a plate. These were Yasmin's favorite.

I brought the tea and cookies out to the common room.

"You know," Faduma said when I handed her a mug, "Yasmin told me that she wants to be like you and make her own fairy game one day. You've made a big impact on her."

"She's my favorite," I said. I really didn't know what else to say. "She is a special kid. I hope they find her safe and sound."

250

She nodded, then touched her hand to her chest. "My girl is strong." She looked into my eyes. "But, my dear, if you are a praying type, please say a prayer for her."

I nodded and said a silent prayer as I handed out the tea. I wasn't very religious, but I wanted to do everything that might help. When I took the tray back to the kitchen, I found Muniba vigorously cleaning the counters. She smiled sadly at me. "I clean when I'm stressed."

"I practice pi. I think your habit is more productive." I took a sponge and started cleaning the pot we'd made the chai in, reciting the digits of pi in my head as I scrubbed.

"You know," Muniba said after a few minutes of silent cleaning, "I've worked here for seven years now, and I've never lost a child that young."

"They'll find her."

She nodded and turned back to the counter. "Families that end up here are often at the tail end of their hope. We try to make it welcoming for kids of all ages, but there is only so much we can do." She sighed. "I doubt anyone looks back at their time here with fond memories."

"I know Yasmin loves you," I said. "I think she feels welcomed here."

Muniba nodded but kept cleaning. "The kids have been through too much. Too much trauma. Too much uncertainty. They've built walls around their feelings to protect themselves. Many times, we can't get through these walls to really reach the kids—they're too hurt. But when we do? They make all this worthwhile. They stay here." She touched her heart. "Even after they leave, they leave their mark."

"You feel like you got through to Yasmin?" I asked.

She shook her head. "Yasmin didn't put up walls. It isn't in her nature. Daniel's like that, too. He's an open book. That's why he bonded so well with Yasmin. It's why he keeps coming back months after he moved out of here."

But no. Daniel wasn't an open book. Not with me anyway. He wanted his parameter. But . . . I dropped my sponge. What did she say? "Daniel . . . *lived* here?"

Muniba turned quickly to me. "Shit. I wasn't supposed to tell you that. He didn't want you to know."

I was confused. Daniel had a home with his mother and uncle. The shelter was for families without homes. "But . . ."

Muniba tilted her head. "Families end up here for many different reasons, and it's not my place to divulge why. I'm sorry I told you." She furiously started cleaning the stainless counter again.

Daniel had experienced homelessness. This was the secret he hadn't wanted to tell me. Even though we'd become so close. I blushed, remembering how much I'd wanted to kiss him at the party. Now it totally made sense why he'd wanted that parameter. It wasn't because he didn't like me enough to be open, or because he didn't want a relationship with me. It was because he was hiding a secret that was too big to tell me. A secret that would have betrayed his mother's privacy if he'd told me, too. I went back to scrubbing the pot. "I won't tell him you told me."

Just then I heard a commotion at the entrance to the shelter. I dropped the sponge and rushed out, Muniba close behind me.

A big group of people from the search party were coming back into the building, led by Daniel, who was holding Yasmin in his arms.

"Yasmin!" Faduma yelled, rushing past everyone to get her daughter.

"Mama!" Yasmin put her hands out toward her mother.

"She's fine," Andre said. "She's tired, and she says her leg hurts."

Faduma took her daughter in her arms and sobbed. Muniba put her arm around the woman and guided her to the common room sofa. "The ambulance will be here soon," the police officer said, following them into the common room. "We need to get her looked at."

Daniel stood in the hallway outside the common room, looking a little empty after Yasmin was taken from his arms. Tears were streaming down his cheeks, but his face . . . his face as he watched Yasmin and Faduma showed pure relief. Not a surprise, really—there wasn't a dry eye in the place. I was sure my eye makeup had run into my sad-raccoon look.

I went to him. "Thank god you found her."

"I knew where to look. Fallen trees. It's where she thought the fairies lived. She told me the book said they welcomed visitors on full moons."

I cringed. "I shouldn't have given her that book."

Daniel shook his head. "She wanted to ask them if they had a house big enough for all her brothers and sisters to have their own rooms. She said she tripped because it was too dark, so she decided to wait under a tree until a fairy, or I, came to help her."

"You?"

He nodded. "She said 'there you are' when she saw me." His voice cracked again.

I couldn't just stand there anymore. I took two steps toward Daniel, and wrapped my arms around him, holding him tight. He hugged back, burying his face in my neck. "She's okay," he whispered again.

"She is," I said.

And then neither of us said anything for a few minutes. Just stood there, in the lobby of the family shelter, clutching each other tightly. I wasn't sure what to say. I didn't fully understand how he was feeling right now because I didn't fully understand him. Or his life. I had no idea what it would be like for someone like Daniel—someone so positive, optimistic, happy—to find himself without a home. There were so many questions swirling through my head. How long had he lived here at the shelter? What was his time here like? Did any of it have anything to do with his strained relationship with his uncle?

But I said nothing. I didn't want to intrude. Even if this hug had nothing to do with our fake relationship, and even if I'd left my own parameter far behind me, I'd respect his privacy. All I could do was be here for him, like he was always there for me. I could do that.

~

The paramedics arrived and were taken straight in to see Yasmin in the common room. The rest of the search party returned to the shelter. Everyone was laughing and smiling with relief, slapping Daniel on the back when they heard how quickly he had found the girl. The police began conducting interviews, so Muniba and I made more tea for the search party. And Andre pulled out some celebratory brownies and passed around the plate.

The paramedics said Yasmin seemed fine other than a twisted ankle, but they wanted to take her to the hospital for X-rays. When they were getting her ready to go, she said she wanted to get a colored cast like Daniel's. Then she started telling the paramedics all about the fairies in the forest.

"I always wondered why you came here so much, like more than you needed to," Cass said as they followed me into the kitchen to pack up some sugar cookies for Yasmin to take to the hospital. "I get it now."

"What do you mean?"

"You look at home here," Cass said. "Like, you're comfortable. Daniel is good for you. And this place is good for you, too. Anyway, Aimee wants to head back to Jayden's. I think he wants to restart the diamond run. There's probably enough time. Can I assume you're staying here?"

I looked out into the common room. There was still a pleasant celebratory mood in the air, now that Yasmin had been found and was okay. The other kids from Jayden's party had left, so it was pretty much just shelter staff and residents here now. Daniel was sitting with the other staff and volunteers, but his face no longer showed relief, or joy, but a kind of melancholy acceptance. It broke my heart a little bit.

"Yeah, I think I need to stay with my friend."

Cass nodded. "Yeah, I think you need to, too. I can swing by and get you when I go home from Jayden's."

"Yeah, or I could call my family. You go. And . . . thanks, Cass."

They smiled. "Anytime, bestie, but don't grow too attached to that *friend* label for Daniel. I'm pretty sure that's about to change."

I chuckled as I took the cookies out to Faduma in the common room. She thanked me for the package before heading out to the ambulance with Yasmin and the medics.

Then I moved to sit next to Daniel. I squeezed his arm gently. "You good?"

He looked surprised that I was still here. He blinked a few times. "Can we talk? Outside?" he asked.

We went to the kids' play structure and climbed onto the little metal platform at the top of the big slide. It was pitch dark out and getting colder. I zipped up my hoodie. Thank god Daniel had found Yasmin when he did. She hadn't even had a warm coat on.

I wrapped my arms around my knees.

"What's up?" I asked when he didn't say anything.

He still didn't speak. His legs were crossed, and he was trailing his fingers over the raised bumps on the metal of the floor of the landing.

"Thank goodness you found her," I said, mostly to escape the silence. "And thank goodness she's okay. I think you will forever be a hero to Faduma. And to Muniba. Actually, to everyone here."

He nodded again, then looked up at me. "Muniba told me that she told you," he said. When I didn't respond, he clarified: "She told me she slipped and said I used to live here."

I nodded. "Yeah. She didn't mean to say anything. She was scared about Yasmin."

Daniel looked down again.

I wanted to reach out and squeeze his knee, reassure him that it didn't matter, and that he didn't have to talk about it. I would respect his parameter. He seemed so closed in on himself, like he didn't want to be talking about this.

He took a breath. "I knew it would be awkward if I didn't say I knew Muniba told you. So that's why I'm mentioning it," he said. He paused. "But you don't have to treat me different or feel sorry for me. It doesn't need to change anything." He paused again. "But if you want out of our deal, I understand."

I shook my head. "Why would I want out of our deal? You're supposed to be my date for the dance. I'm helping you with calculus. I still want to go ahead with our arrangement."

That wasn't completely true. Our arrangement was that he would be my fake boyfriend. And maybe a few days ago I'd wondered if I should end it because I was growing too attached, but right now I wanted out of it because I wanted this to be as real as it felt.

He shrugged.

But I didn't want to say that yet, because right now, this was about him, not me and my feelings. "Daniel, I understand why you didn't want to tell me this. But . . . I wouldn't have treated you differently if I knew. I would have still asked you to be my fake boyfriend."

He shook his head, not making eye contact. "As if I could tell you that I used to live in a shelter. That my mom couldn't afford rent anywhere and we had no one else who would let us crash at their place. You, whose friends live in multimillion-dollar houses and whose mother drives an Audi. You said your parents loved your ex because his parents are a cardiologist and an engineer. My mother is a glorified babysitter. How could I have told you?"

He sounded bitter . . . and all I could think of was when Cass called me an elitist. Was this really what people thought of me? Were they right?

I shook my head. "Okay, that might be true about my friends and my parents, but why do you think I care about any of that? None of that matters to me."

He turned away. "I'm not smart like your friends. I'm not rich like them. I can only play hockey because a right-to-play charity covers the cost. I barely passed my classes last year because it was impossible to get any studying done at the shelter. Today you said that the first thing your parents ask your friends when they meet them is what their parents do. My mom is a personal support worker. Basically, a nursing assistant—not even a real nurse. And my uncle that we live with? He's not even my uncle, but my mother's *employer*. Mom cares for his mother. I live in his only spare bedroom, and Mom sleeps on a cot in the old lady's room. The reason I have to do whatever he wants is because Mom's afraid if I don't, he'll decide I can't live there anymore once I turn eighteen."

"Daniel, look at me," I said. He turned to me, and thanks to the bright lights at the shelter door, I could see his eyes were glistening. I shook my head. "I don't care about any of those things. I'm really sorry I gave you the impression that I wouldn't like you for *you*. Just the way you are."

He blinked. "You wanted me to pretend to be someone I'm not."

That was true. But that was because I needed Daniel to pretend to be LostAxis.

But . . . he was kind of right, too. Deep down, I didn't care about how much money his parents had, or about how he did in school. But on the surface, I sure looked like I cared about that stuff. A lot. I was so wrapped up in my image—in showing the kids at school that I could move on from Devin to someone smarter, and better-looking, that I turned this amazing person into someone who I thought everyone else would find perfect. And deep down, the whole time I knew he was perfect just as he was.

What if LostAxis hadn't existed? What if Daniel was just a cute boy I'd met at the shelter, instead of the person my online friend was pretending to be? We would have probably still become friends. I would have still helped him with calculus after we baked each week. Of course I would have thought he was hot. But I probably wouldn't have used

Daniel to get back at Devin. The point was to look like I was winning against Devin. And no matter how gorgeous Daniel was, to my friends or to the gossips at school, a pie-obsessed hockey player wouldn't have been an upgrade from Devin.

I put my hand on his knee. "I'm sorry," I said. I knew it wasn't enough. "You probably thought I was a horrendous snob. I . . . I don't even know what to say. I'm sorry I didn't make you feel comfortable enough to tell me about your life. And I'm sorry if I made you think I had any problem at all with the real person you are. Because I happen to like the person you are. A lot."

His eyes were locked on my hand on his knee. He was mesmerized by it. So was I. I tried to tamp down the warmth I felt radiating from where we were connected.

"I didn't think you were a snob," he said. "I thought you were brilliant. And funny. And kind—the way you talked to Yasmin, and to the other residents. You were patient with me even though I suck at calculus. You didn't make me feel like an idiot, and it didn't feel like you were pretending." His eyes were still on my hand on his knee.

I thought about how *not pretend* this had been for me for a while now. Sitting in each other's arms at Hana's party. The way I felt watching him play hockey. The almost-kiss at Jayden's. Holding hands in the car on the way to the shelter tonight. Him crying into my neck after he brought Yasmin back. For the last few weeks, my feelings for Daniel felt as real as if we'd been in a real relationship. Did they feel as real as the feelings I'd had for Devin?

I was fifteen when Devin first asked me out. At first, I was . . . starstruck. I couldn't believe that Devin, the smartest kid in the school, who somehow was also super popular, would want to be with *me*. And then we dated for so long, I kind of got used to him. And used to being Devin Kapadia's girlfriend.

But did I ever ache inside simply because I liked him so much? Did I see something in a window and feel overcome with an urge to show it to him, the way I did with Daniel when I saw a pie? Did Devin ever open my eyes to something new, something I would never have thought I could enjoy? Like baking lemon squares named after a random lady named Rose. Or watching a skilled hockey player taking practice shots at a goal.

Time slowed down when I was with Daniel, but I also felt like I never had enough time with him. And he was so generous—I couldn't imagine anyone else staying up late power-leveling in *Dragon Arena* so he could come with me to a party because I'd been dreading going alone.

I may have ignored almost all our parameters lately, but I couldn't ignore the most important one: that, although we didn't always need to be completely open with each other, when we did speak, we would only ever speak the truth.

I exhaled. "The truth is," I said softly, "this, you and me . . . it hasn't felt fake for me for a long time."

His eyes lifted to look at my face. There was a tiny smile on one side of his mouth. "I thought I was imagining that."

I shook my head. We looked at each other for several long seconds.

The fingers on his good hand wrapped around mine. "I think we're failing at the fake part of this arrangement," he said. "But . . . this is complicated."

"That's okay. I like complicated stuff, remember? Complex equations are my jam."

He chuckled. "That day I met you—"

"I made a fool of myself and powdered myself like a jelly doughnut."

He shook his head. "You were *adorable*. Honestly, I've always had a thing for very smart vampires covered with sugar."

I laughed.

He kept talking. "But then I got to know you and realized you weren't really my type. Because my type couldn't be someone so brilliant. So together. Someone with so many friends, and a stable family. Someone cool enough that gossip columns actually talk about her."

I leaned in closer, because how could I not? His smile widened. After a few more seconds of grinning at each other like fools, he raised his hand and slipped it behind my neck. "Permission for physical contact. I'm thinking about kissing you."

I grinned. "Permission granted."

And it was perfect. Not fireworks, or goose bumps, just absolute perfection. His lips were warm, and soft, and he smelled like the sugar cookies we'd been eating.

He pulled back and looked at me.

"That was okay?" he asked.

I nodded, smiling. "More than okay. In fact, any chance you want to kiss more?"

He grinned widely and uncrossed his legs so he could pull me closer. I came willingly and put my arms around his shoulders. Then Daniel and I were kissing again. Really kissing this time. And this time there *were* fireworks. I had no idea it was possible to feel so comfortable and so excited at the same time. This felt so right.

All the differences between us didn't matter, because we *fit* together. Right now, Daniel and I fit better than I had ever fit with anyone . . . ever.

I knew then that I loved Daniel Ramos. I wasn't going to say anything yet, but the feelings were there. And they didn't scare me at all. I was all in.

25

A Shift in the Parameters

Of course, we couldn't stay at the top of the playground making out all night. Even though I really wanted to. But this was a *family* shelter. We needed to keep our interactions family friendly. Also, we really needed to talk about this change in our relationship status before we got too carried away. Because even if this felt extremely right, I wanted to make sure we were on the same page. We had to agree on what we wanted from each other.

Daniel was leaning on the railing around the little platform, and I was sitting next to him. His good hand was tracing patterns on my jeans. "What happens now?" I asked.

"What do you want to happen?"

"I don't know." I turned to face him. "I want to do this . . . be with you. But I don't know what to tell people."

He grinned. "Telling people is the easiest part. Did you forget that everyone thinks we're already dating?"

"I know, I know, but we've been *lying*." I looked down. I didn't know how to explain this to him. I took a breath. "We were *pretending* to date. Which didn't scare me at all because it's just, you know. Pretend. But this. This is different."

"And you're scared now?"

"I trust you." I bit my lip. "But I *just* got out of a long relationship. It was a messy end—I'm realizing that I kind of lost myself in that relationship. And that's why the breakup completely wrecked me."

"Do you think you're rebounding?"

Good question. It certainly didn't feel like I was. Devin was not even a blip on my radar anymore.

"No. I think I'm ready to move on. But I'm kind of scared to jump into something serious. Especially since everyone thinks we've been . . ."

"We've been going at it for a month," he said.

I nodded.

"C'mon. Put your head here." He guided me to sit between his legs with my head on his chest. He loosely encircled my waist with his arms. It was the most amazing feeling in the world to be completely surrounded by Daniel. And . . . it was strangely easier to talk about this while not looking at his face.

"Are you afraid of getting dumped again?" He smelled like the forest, and a little bit like pie.

"It's not that I don't trust you. It's just . . . we can't exactly take it slow at this point."

He chuckled. "That train left the station a long time ago."

"Yeah," I said softly.

"Why don't we just stick with our original deal, then," he said. "The dance is in a week. We don't commit now to anything beyond that. No pressure. We agreed on two dates plus the dance, and eight pictures. We fulfill what's left—that's one dance and three pictures. Then, we see how we feel. Decide what we want to come next. Deal?"

One more date didn't sound scary. I wouldn't be committing to anything more than what I had already committed to. I could do that.

"Okay. We keep all the parameters except for the first one, that the relationship will be fake dating only, and then we reassess when we're done."

"Exactly." He tightened his arms around me more. I was pretty sure there was no way in hell I would walk away from this next week, but it felt better to know I could if I needed to. But right now I wanted to stay like this forever.

"Can we change one parameter, though?" I asked.

"I hope you're going to say the physical-contact one."

I laughed. "Yup."

He leaned down and kissed the side of my neck, sending a shiver down my spine.

"Um, Daniel?" I asked.

"Hm?"

"Please don't think you have to, but are you comfortable telling me . . . how . . . ?"

"How we ended up living here?"

I nodded.

"Yeah, okay. I'll tell you." He sighed. "My mom moved here from the Philippines before I was born. She became, like, all involved with the Filipino community here, and used to go to church a lot. She met a man there. Whirlwind affair, or so she says. I love my mother, but she has terrible taste in men."

"He wasn't a nice man?"

"He was married. Mom said she didn't know, but my aunt told me that Mom knew the whole time. Anyway, he was, like, an important man in the church or something, so Mom hid the pregnancy. And then some people found out, so she stopped going to church and, like . . . left the community. She kept in contact with my aunt, Tita Maria, the one with the bakery, but no one else. She's actually Mom's cousin, but insisted I call her Tita. Anyway, the man denied I was his. It was apparently a mess."

"Ugh, that's horrible. How did your mom get by? With a baby?"

"She worked as a home care nurse for this agency. But yeah, it had to be hard when I was little. When I was five, she got a permanent job in a family's house caring for the wife's mother. We both moved in there. The Browns. They were cool—and super rich. They were great to me and Mom. They even paid to put me in hockey with their own son. But then the couple split up, and it was messy. The wife couldn't afford live-in care for her mother anymore." He shifted a bit, so I took the opportunity to rest my cheek against his chest so I could hear his voice reverberate through his body.

"Mom and I moved in with Tita Maria, and Mom got a job in a nursing home. Tita Maria tried to convince Mom to go to church again, but Mom was stubborn. The man, technically my father, was still, like, important there. She thought she'd be shunned. When I was old enough, I helped out at my aunt's bakery.

"Then Mom met another man—this white widower. He promised her he'd take care of us both, and she wouldn't need to work. And he promised he'd pay for my college when I was ready. We left Tita Maria's to live with him. But . . . he also turned out to be not so nice. He was abusive." Daniel's arms tightened around me.

"Oh, Daniel. I'm sorry."

He sighed. "We were stuck there, though. We couldn't go back to Tita Maria's. She and Mom had gotten into a huge fight when Tita Maria tried to warn Mom about her new boyfriend. One night things got scary and I called the police. A social worker eventually helped us get out of his house. But since we had nowhere to go, we ended up at the shelter."

"I'm so sorry."

He shrugged, looking over to the front door of the shelter. "You've seen the place—it could have been so much worse. Because of my cooking background, I started helping Andre in the kitchen. We came up with the farmers' market idea together. And I became close to some of the residents. Muniba connected me with the hockey charity so I could start playing again. After a while Mom reached out to Tita Maria again and started going to a Filipino church near here—one where people didn't know her history. That's where she met Edwin Uncle.

He's Filipino, too. His mother has a disability, and he needed a live-in caregiver. Mom can speak to her in Tagalog. It's been working well for Mom."

"Are they . . . good to you?"

Daniel shrugged. "Edwin is a bit . . . controlling. No, that's not the right word. He's very religious, and sometimes I think he sees helping us as some sort of service. I don't know."

"And he wants you to be something you're not."

"Yes. He said he can help me with engineering jobs. Mentor me."

"Why don't you tell him you don't want to do that?" I asked.

He sighed. "It's easier to just keep the peace. Mom's happy there. She loves caring for a Filipino patient. She's started getting involved with the Filipino community here. She has new friends. It's a good place for her to land, after everything she went through."

I got the impression things were a lot worse for him and his mother before they ended up at the shelter than he was letting on. "And what about you?"

"After everything Mom and I went through, it's nice to have someone other than Mom who actually cares about my success." He chuckled. "I'm not used to that. Also, I'm seventeen. My situation there is short term. Mom's more important. If he doesn't let me stay after high school, it's not that big a deal. I'll get a job. Or maybe after I show him my excellent calculus mark, he'll be so happy he'll get off my back." He hugged me tighter. "Mom and I are taking one day at a time. And right now I just want to hold you like this."

I liked that idea, too. It had been a heavy night for him. And if holding me comforted him, I'd happily be there for him.

Eventually, of course, we had to go home. To avoid inconveniencing Cass, I texted my sister. She was leaving a party and said she and Rowan could pick us up and they'd drop off Daniel, too.

Daniel and I went in and said good night to everyone who was still in the common room. Tahira and Rowan arrived soon after. When

Rowan dropped him off, I saw Daniel's, or his uncle's, house for the first time. It was a small, standard Scarborough bungalow. Kind of similar to ours before we renovated.

When I finally got home, utterly exhausted after the long and emotional day, I changed into a T-shirt and flannel pants and got into bed right away. My phone buzzed with a text.

Daniel: I've never texted you good night before. But there's something I've always wanted to ask you.

I grinned. What?

Daniel: Do you count sheep to help you sleep, or are numbers way too exciting for you to relax to?

I laughed.

Me: Sometimes I practice pi to help me sleep. But I don't think I'll have trouble falling asleep tonight.

Daniel: I don't know if I should feel insulted by that. Don't tell me I bored you?

Me: OMG no. Not boring at all. I won't have an issue sleeping because

I paused. We were supposed to be going slow. I wasn't supposed to admit how much I was into him already.

Daniel: because what?

Me: Because I don't think I've been this happy in a long, long time.

He sent a smiling emoji. Then a heart emoji.

Daniel: I'm going to say good night on that high note. Good night Samaya.

Me: Good night, Daniel.

26

Whispers Is Whispering Again

Daniel was helping Andre and Muniba at the farmers' market the next day, and I almost went and joined them because all I wanted to do was spend time with Daniel. I still had that warm, goose-bumpy feeling come over me whenever I thought about what had happened last night. I wouldn't mind more of that. Not the scared-about-Yasmin part of the night, but the closeness-with-Daniel part at the top of the slide. The kissing part, too.

But instead, I decided to do the smart thing and spend Saturday and maybe Sunday, too, studying for my physics midterm test coming up on Monday. Without studying I would probably be fine . . . but I was Samaya Janmohammad, and I had no intention of letting this shiny upgraded relationship affect my grades.

Daniel did text me a few times over the course of the day. Sending me pictures of the lemon squares we made the day before, plus some pictures of the pumpkin pies one of the farm stands was selling. He let me know that our bars outsold Andre's cinnamon rolls again. And he texted me some other silly Daniel-type observations and jokes, just like he'd always done. In fact, none of his messages were any different from the ones I'd always got from him.

Which . . . why? Maybe I imagined that closeness last night? Maybe in his eyes things weren't really changing? I mean, we did agree that we were going to keep most of the relationship parameters the same until the Nerd Prom. Just (hopefully) with more kissing.

Ugh. I was tied up in knots worrying about this.

But near the end of the day, after I had done a fair bit of studying for physics and finished my functions and English homework, another text came through from Daniel.

Daniel: Okay so I've been trying to play it cool all day . . . but I haven't been able to think about anything but seeing you. Can we video call?

I grinned huge and opened the call right away.

"Hey," he said, his voice a little low. Okay, that was different from how he normally sounded when we FaceTimed.

"Hey, yourself." I didn't know what else to say, so I just looked at him. He was so gorgeous. I couldn't believe he was into me.

But . . . this was awkward. We couldn't stare at each other all evening, could we? My nose wrinkled. "What are you wearing?"

He frowned looking down at his T-shirt. "I'm thinking that wasn't a suggestive"—his voice lowered to a growl—"'what are you wearing' but a more disappointed 'what *are* you wearing.'"

I laughed as he moved his phone away so I could see his whole shirt—it was Mickey Mouse in full gear playing hockey.

"Now that I've actually trapped you," he said, "I can let myself go a bit and wear my cartoon characters in hockey uniform shirts."

I must have looked horrified, because he laughed. "Kidding, kidding, Samaya. I don't have any more cartoon character shirts. And I only wear this one at home. This lady who used to work at the shelter bought it for me because I liked hockey. Sweet lady. Very creepy Disney obsession."

I laughed again. "They really spoiled you there, didn't they?" Now that I knew that Daniel had once been a resident there, the way everyone treated him at the shelter made more sense. Whenever I'd seen him with staff and even some residents, they were protective of him. He was clearly a favorite because of his . . . well, his amazingness, but also, everyone looked out for him like he was one of them, because he had been.

"What can I say? Mom-types love me."

As soon as he spoke, I could tell he regretted it. And I thought I knew why. Last night he'd said he'd never imagined I could be into him because my parents wouldn't approve of me dating someone who didn't come from a professional, high-achieving family like Devin's.

And the conversation was awkward again. Why was this harder now? We'd never had trouble talking before. I bit my lip.

"Hey . . . ," Daniel said. "Wanna play *Dragon Arena*? We can try that Ruby quest again. No pressure this time, just for fun."

"Your hand okay for that?"

"Yeah, I think so. If it hurts, I'll watch you play."

But I honestly needed a break from *Dragon Arena*. I smiled. "Or maybe you can teach me to play *HockeyStars*?"

He laughed, then nodded. "Yeah, let's do that. You'll love it. Just imagine the opposing team are unicorns or elves or something."

~

Like old times, Cass and Aimee were waiting for me at the bus stop on Monday. I immediately told them about how much fun I'd had playing *HockeyStars* on the weekend.

"Seriously, the game is amazing. There's this tournament mode and—"

"So, one cute boy and you're, like, *done* with *Dragon Arena* and switching to sports games?" Aimee asked, giving me her trademark eye roll.

"Uh, no. I was just trying something new. And I enjoyed it, so I decided to tell my friends about it."

"Yeah, well, you can't completely give up *Dragon Arena*," Aimee said. "We didn't finish the Diamond run, so Jayden's rescheduling. He was so pissed that we couldn't get it done on Friday. He'll need you as Light Mage again."

I raised a brow. Last year, getting Aimee to join us for *Dragon Arena* parties was like pulling teeth, but now that she was dating Jayden, she was telling me when my services as Light Mage were required? And she accused *me* of changing for a guy?

Had Aimee's loyalties always been to the boy she was dating rather than her oldest friends?

"So what exactly happened after we left the shelter anyway?" Cass asked. "And how did it lead to you playing hockey video games with your fake boyfriend this weekend?"

I blushed. "Yeah . . . um, we're not exactly *not* real anymore."

Cass raised one brow. "English, Samaya."

"Fine. Daniel and I are kinda sort of really dating now."

"So you got all hot and heavy after rescuing a lost kid?" Aimee asked. "At the shelter? That's weird."

"We kissed. Long after he found Yasmin. And he admitted he'd caught feelings, too."

Cass smiled. "Of course he did. I've been telling you that for a while. This is amazing . . . I'm so happy for you." Cass gave me a knowing look. They were probably thinking this meant we would go to hockey games together more often. Last I'd heard, Cass and Owen were still frustratingly pretending to be just "friends."

I was kind of excited to go to more games though. Daniel and I had talked about it while baking on Friday, and decided that we'd go to Owen's next game with Cass. Since Daniel couldn't play until his wrist healed, he wanted to watch as many games as possible for his hockey fix.

Aimee huffed. I wasn't sure why she seemed so put out by me actually dating Daniel. Then I remembered Jayden's comment that Daniel wasn't *really my boyfriend*. I'd forgotten about it because of all the commotion. Was that something Aimee had told him?

I didn't even ask her. I didn't want any dark clouds over my head today. So I let it go and read over my physics notes for my test the rest of the way to school.

I had physics second period and finished the test before anyone else, so the teacher excused me from class early. I was sitting alone in the quad working on English when Cass suddenly sat next to me.

"There you are. I left calculus to find you. Why's your phone off?"

I frowned, turning my phone back on. "Whoops. I had it off for a test."

"So . . . you haven't seen Instagram?" they asked.

"No, like I said, physics test." I opened Instagram, but I didn't have any notifications. Then I saw it.

I cringed. "Whispers, again? I thought they were done torturing me." I'd blissfully almost forgotten the account existed. I looked at the picture.

It was me and Daniel at Jayden's on Friday night. I didn't even remember anyone taking this shot. Daniel was sitting next to me at the big table, and I was looking in his direction with total disdain. I knew I'd been looking at Jayden, who was sitting on the other side of Daniel, and probably yelling at me that I was too slow for a level fifty-five Light Mage or something. But the picture really looked like I was making that face at Daniel.

"This is ridiculous," I said. "Who took this picture? This is completely out of context!"

"Read the caption, Samaya." Cass looked like they were barely controlling their rage.

If there's one thing we pride ourselves on at Earl Jones high school, it's integrity. And we expect it more from the upper echelons of our student body more than anyone.

"Who the fuck writes this drivel?" I asked.

"Keep reading, Samaya."

Samaya Janmohammad was once poised to be a grade-12 darling at the school. Together with Devin Kapadia, she was in the physics club and the math club last year, and some even suspected the pair would be made co-valedictorians. But after an emotional public breakdown after her breakup with Devin Kapadia last spring, Samaya had a rocky start to this year. That all changed when she was seen in the company of a hot new stranger. And her new guy seemed to out-Devin Devin. Claimed to be a top academic student and top *Dragon Arena* player. Plus, a gifted hockey player who volunteers at a family shelter in his free time. He seemed too good to be true. Well, it turns out that we've all been had. He is too good to be true. A trustworthy source has confirmed that this new boyfriend of Samaya's is 100 percent made-up. He's not an honor student. He doesn't even play *Dragon Arena*. The source tells us that Samaya has been paying a teenager who lives in a homeless shelter, Daniel Ramos, to pose as her boyfriend. You heard that right—she has been exploiting a homeless guy for her own gain.

All this just to get back at Devin for breaking up with her? Apparently, hell hath no fury like Samaya Janmohammad scorned. Once the golden girl, it seems she has resorted to cruelty to maintain her relevance. Disappointing.

Fuck. I stared at the picture. They were accusing me of hiring Daniel to pose as my boyfriend. And they were outing him for having experienced homelessness. I closed my eyes.

"This is . . ." I exhaled. My heart rate was speeding up.

"It's BS," Cass said.

I took several deep breaths. "We need to shut this down . . ."

"Read the comments, Samaya."

The top comment, with the most likes, was by Cass.

This post is the real cruelty, even for an account as evil as this one. To claim someone who doesn't even go to this school is homeless just for the sake of gossip? For entertainment? You have no clue what the nature of these two people's relationship is. And you have no right to put a person's private family and social situation on the internet. And his name, too. This isn't gossip, this is doxing, and it's wrong. It's high time someone doxed the horrible, privileged person or people behind Earl's Whispers. I am disgusted that I go to school with you.

Many comments agreed with Cass. A few disagreed, but several people also called for anyone who knew the identity of Earl's Whispers to come forward. Several people wrote that they would be blocking the account.

I looked up at Cass. "Thank you, but . . . it's true, though," I whispered.

Cass gave me a curious look. "I know you were fake dating, but—"

"It's true," I repeated. "Daniel . . . he and his mother lived in the shelter for a while last year. But how did anyone know that? I only found out on Friday."

Cass exhaled. "Fuck. Poor Daniel. I didn't know."

"Not many people knew. Only people at the shelter, really, but even that . . . I've worked there for months, and no one said anything. They're big on privacy there. Ugh—someone in that other car that came to help find Yasmin could have overheard Muniba. Or maybe someone else at the shelter told one of them. Maybe told Aimee."

Cass cringed. "Yeah. I think Aimee or Jayden definitely have something to do with this."

"Or Hana," I said, shoulders slumping. The whole school had seen this. "We need to get this taken down. This isn't fair to Daniel." I didn't leave a comment on the post myself. I knew that would only add fuel to the fire. But I refreshed the post and saw more comments had been added calling for a boycott of Earl's Whispers.

"They'll delete the post because of this backlash," Cass said. "I guarantee it. Whoever this is can dish it, but they can't take it."

Probably. I took a screenshot in case they did. I might need this as evidence or something one day.

The quad started filling up then, and I could feel everyone looking at me. A couple of people yelled out support, a few others gawked. I felt so exposed. Humiliated. Just like I did last spring when Earl's Whispers posted that picture of me reacting to Devin dumping me.

But was this different? Maybe I deserved to be humiliated for what I'd done? There were a lot of truths in this post. Daniel and I were together now, but we'd faked it for weeks. I may not have paid him money, but I was tutoring him in exchange for his deception. And Daniel wasn't living there now, but he had lived in the shelter at one point.

But whoever was behind this had no right to bring Daniel's past into it. They could have outed me for faking the relationship without mentioning his family situation.

Cass gave me a look, then took my arm and guided me out of the quad. We hid out behind the school, where no one could stare at me, for the rest of lunch. I emailed Miss Zhao that I couldn't come to game dev after school while Cass messaged the team that the meeting was canceled. I didn't want to face them all today.

By the time we went back inside for third period, the entire Earl's Whispers account had been deleted. If nothing else, at least I wouldn't have to deal with their vendetta against me anymore. But I was afraid the damage to Daniel had already been done.

As I was leaving my last class of the day, Hana cornered me in the hallway. "Samaya, can we talk for a few?"

I didn't answer. Just glared at her.

She clasped her hands at her chest in a begging motion. "Two minutes. That's it."

"Fine. Two minutes."

We ducked into a nearby alcove. I crossed my arms and waited.

"I know you think I'm the one who sent in those tips about you to Earl's Whispers, but I'm not," Hana said. "I would never do that to you."

"Okay. I'm not sure why I should believe you, though," I said.

"You don't have to believe me, but it's the truth. No one sent in a tip this time. Earl's Whispers discovered the stuff about your boyfriend herself. I know who she is."

"Who?"

"Kavita."

I blinked. *Kavita?* I barely knew Kavita. She was in the guild and the game-dev team, but she was in grade eleven, and I'd never had a class with her. Why would she do that? "Holy shit. *Kavita* is Earl's Whispers? How did you find out?"

"She told me after the post went up today. She thought I'd—I don't know—be on her side or something."

"But *why*? Why would she do that to me? I've never done anything to Kavita."

Hana shook her head. "It was just gossip, Samaya. She wasn't out to get you. She was doing it for fun. You were apparently prime gossip fodder. She gossiped about me, Devin, and the rest of the school, too."

I felt like I was going to throw up. She probably got a high off the likes. That account had caused me so much hurt going back to last year. When those pictures went up on Whispers in June of me crying and pleading to Devin not to break up with me, people were mocking me in the hallways until the last day of school.

And Kavita had done it all not to hurt me or anyone else, but just for fun. I didn't know what to say.

I really, really hated this school.

"Devin told the principal," Hana said.

"What?"

"Devin turned Kavita in. She'll probably be suspended for cyberbullying."

"*Devin* did."

Hana nodded. "He was so pissed when I told him it was Kavita. Like . . . he was going to punch someone. He said he never wanted to see you hurt like that, and he'd do anything to go back and do it differently." She blinked, looking up at the empty stairwell.

"Seriously?" I couldn't believe he would say that to Hana—his actual girlfriend. I was over Devin—was it possible he wasn't over me?

Hana nodded. "He said, 'We used to be duo goals, now look at us.' I have no idea what he meant by that. He told off Jayden, too."

I frowned. I was glad that he'd reported Kavita, at least. "Why did he tell *Jayden* off?"

Hana met my eyes. "It was Jayden who sent in the picture of you at game dev. He apparently sent more than one tip to Earl's Whispers about you. Jayden told Devin all about it today. I have no idea if Aimee knew."

Aimee. My so-called best friend.

"I'm sorry, Samaya," Hana said. She sounded sincere, at least.

I looked at Hana. "Thanks for telling me." I did feel bad for her—she clearly thought her boyfriend still had feelings for me, yet she still told me all this. But I wasn't about to comfort her.

I turned away and walked right out of the school.

I spent the entire bus ride home reciting pi in my head. I knew I would need to deal with everything, and I had every intention of telling Daniel about the Whispers post, but I just needed to escape it for a little while. I texted Daniel as soon as I was home, and told him I needed to talk to him. He called me right away.

"What is it? Did something happen in your game-dev meeting again?"

"No. Hang on, let me show you." I sent him the screenshot of the Whispers post.

"Shit," was all he said. I agreed wholeheartedly with his sentiment.

"I'm *so, so* sorry, Daniel," I said, sitting on a stool at the kitchen counter. "The account has been deleted. The post wasn't up for very long—maybe an hour. And the person behind the account will probably be suspended from school. There was a huge backlash against Whispers." I told him about Cass's comment and everyone boycotting the account. I didn't tell him it was Kavita the whole time. Or that my so-called best friend's boyfriend had been sending tips to Whispers for weeks.

Daniel didn't say anything for a while. I felt terrible. This whole fake-dating arrangement had been a mistake. Daniel was pure, generous, kind, and so much fun, and we'd *used* him. First, LostAxis used his picture, and then *I* used him in a much worse way.

"Daniel, I'm sorry. If you never want to see me again, I understand. I shouldn't have asked you to pretend to be my boyfriend. I was using you."

"No, Samaya," he said immediately. "Did you forget that we had a mutually beneficial deal? I am passing calculus, which is a miracle. We weren't using each other; we were helping each other."

"Yeah, but you're doing much more for me than I am doing for you. You took me on those dates, plus the selfies, and the *Dragon Arena* leveling, even though that ended up being pretty much unnecessary. And now this. If I'd known about your family's issues, I totally wouldn't have asked you—"

"Hold up. You said that me living in a shelter didn't matter to you. Don't coddle me as some poor unfortunate that needs special care now that you know."

"I'm not." I wasn't. Was I?

"Then the fact that my mom had to stay in the shelter for a while should not have made a difference to whether you made this deal with me or not. You were not *exploiting* me. And the post isn't even true. It says I *live* in the shelter—well, I don't. And it says we're *fake* dating, which . . . that's not what we discussed on Friday. Or did I imagine that kiss?"

His voice lowered to that rumble that made my insides melt. Daniel Ramos was cheerful, and optimistic, and incredibly sexy, too.

And he was right. The fact that his family once stayed in a shelter didn't have anything to do with our arrangement. I was not *exploiting* him. We were friends helping each other. I sighed. "I didn't want to bring all this into your life."

"You're worth it," he said.

I shook my head. I wasn't sure I believed that. "But, Daniel, they doxed you. You're a private person . . . why aren't you madder at me?"

He shrugged. I wished I could see him in person—instead of over this video call. "I can't say that I'm happy about it. But you said it's been taken down, and that most people didn't approve of the post. It will probably blow over."

"But what if people you know saw it?"

"I probably shouldn't be hiding this anyway. I haven't done anything wrong."

I exhaled, exasperated. "Daniel, do you have to be so perfect all the time?"

He laughed at that. "Seriously, Samaya. I'm okay. I don't even go to the school—it doesn't bother me that much that people are gossiping about me there."

"Ugh. Don't remind me. I *do* go to that school. Mom told me to stay out of drama . . . well, this is drama. It better not screw up my teacher references for scholarships."

He frowned. "I don't get why it will do that."

I shrugged. "It shouldn't. But if I lose respect in game dev, then Miss Zhao might not give me a reference for awards or scholarships. Hell, if any teachers believe this stuff, they might not respect me anymore."

"Can you afford university without those scholarships?"

"Well, yeah. My parents have saved. But—"

"Samaya, don't be shocked that I don't have a ton of sympathy for you whining about money you don't even need."

That shut me up. *Fuck.* He was right. I was so blind to my own privilege. But it was hard to shift all my focus like that.

"Look, I get it," Daniel continued. "You've been in the middle of that competitive academic world *forever*. I *get* the pressure. I know a lot of it comes from your parents." He snorted. "I've recently discovered what that's like. But I think you've wrapped up your self-worth in this stuff too much. You can achieve your goals without losing yourself, you know?"

I chuckled. "You're being a wise old boomer again."

"Seriously, Samaya. You're a *good* person . . . but that's not because everyone at your school likes you, or because you're the head of all your school clubs or because of your grades. You're good because . . . you're still coming to the shelter even though you don't have to anymore. And you're always patient when you're teaching me calculus or reviving my idiot Dark Mage. You're a good person because you brought Yasmin a book about forest fairies that you knew she'd love. Because you came to my hockey game to support Cass, even though sports is like a hellscape to you."

"I don't really mind hockey anymore."

He chuckled. "The people who actually care about you don't care about what everyone else thinks about you."

He was right. But it was so hard to let go of what I'd thought was important for so long. I exhaled. "Daniel . . . I am so glad that I met you."

"Right back at you, Count Von Count. You have time for some *HockeyStars*? I can teach you how to play goalie?"

Strangely, I turned out to be quite good at playing goalie in *HockeyStars*. Like . . . really good. Weird.

27

The Return of the Gamer-Boy

After playing for about an hour, Daniel had to leave for hockey practice. He still liked to skate with the team even though he couldn't hold a stick yet. So I went downstairs to see what was happening for dinner.

Tahira was standing in front of the open fridge. "Mom called," she said. "She's got a late meeting or something. We're on our own again." She closed the fridge, a handful of vegetables in her hands. "I'm making an omelet."

I shrugged. I didn't have that much of an appetite.

Tahira tilted her head, concerned. "What's wrong? Rough day?"

I exhaled. "You don't know the half of it."

"What happened?" she asked as she took a knife out of the drawer.

I sat on the stool at the breakfast bar in the kitchen and told Tahira everything while she cut up mushrooms, peppers, and onions.

"Holy shit," she said. "I can't believe Jayden would do that. And that girl Kavita. I can't believe any of these people would do any of this."

I nodded. "I know. I don't even know what to think."

"What are you going to do about your game-dev team?"

I shrugged. "I don't know. Kavita obviously isn't welcome anymore. I think Aimee might leave if I kick out Jayden, and I have no idea how we can continue without her art." I sighed. I needed to talk to Aimee about this. "Shockingly, Hana seems to be an okay person. I can't believe Devin turned in Kavita. Hana seemed pretty sure that Devin is still hung up on me."

Tahira snorted as she took the eggs out of the fridge. "*Is* Devin hung up on you?"

"I have no idea. But he told Hana he never wanted me to get hurt, and we were *duo goals* or something." I paused, thinking. "'Duo goals' is a weird thing to say, isn't it? Isn't the common phrase *couple goals*?" A realization hit me. A major, horrendous, revolting realization. *"Fuck."*

Tahira raised one brow. "What? You've gone all white."

I blinked. "When Devin and I were together, he never, not once, called us *couple goals*. Or duo goals. But *duo* is what you call a two-person party in Dragon Arena. You know who used to say we were *duo goals*?"

"Who?"

"LostAxis. *Devin* is LostAxis."

Tahira put down the carton of eggs. "Holy crap."

"I need to go to Devin's."

Tahira took the plastic wrap out of the drawer. "Screw omelets. I'll drive you. I have the car."

The Kapadia family lived in an enormous house about fifteen minutes from ours. Tahira pulled into the empty driveway. I hadn't been here in months. I used to love this house. I'd spent hours here—sometimes with Devin's parents, but most of the time alone with him. He and I studied together. Watched movies in the living room. And we'd spent hours hanging out . . . alone . . . in his bedroom.

It was weird being here now. I didn't feel like I belonged anymore.

"Want me to come in?" Tahira asked.

I shook my head as I unbuckled the seat belt. "Nah. I can handle it."

"Okay. I'll go pick up shawarmas for dinner. I'll be back in about twenty."

I got out of the car. When I rang the doorbell, Devin answered the door immediately.

"Samaya. What are you doing here?" He glanced behind him. "My parents aren't home."

"That's fine. I need to talk to you," I said.

He just looked at me, not letting me in, which was weird. But seeing him in the doorway felt just like old times. He even looked like the old, normal Devin. I'd noticed he'd pretty much given up on that worldly, sophisticated Indian look he brought back from South Asia and was back to his geeky shirts and jeans (today's was a Loki shirt), and his hair was now too long to be called cool.

He'd always been the right amount of nerdy mixed with handsome. He just wasn't the kind of handsome I had any interest in anymore.

Devin finally moved out of the way. "Fine. I'll get you a chai. I'm doing my homework."

He looked tense as he walked toward the kitchen. Did he know why I was here? I took off my shoes and headed into the dining room. The table was strewn with books, a half-full mug of chai, and Devin's laptop. Devin had always done his homework in the dining room—his parents preferred to watch him work. I sat, eyeing the plastic container of his mother's nan khatai cookies on the table.

A few minutes later, he handed me a mug of chai and sat on the chair in front of his computer. "I have a big bio essay due tomorrow," he said.

Now that I was here, I didn't know how to get him to admit he was LostAxis. "So . . . Devin. As you know, I had a day from hell—"

He interrupted me. "I had nothing to do with that Whispers post. It was Kavita."

"I know. Your girlfriend told me all about it. She also said it was Jayden who sent in all the other tips to Kavita."

He frowned. "*Hana* told you?"

I snorted. "She didn't seem happy with you. You might need to do some relationship damage control. I doubt you two are going to last."

He cringed. His eyes were sad. Resigned.

He rubbed the back of his neck. "I'm sorry, Samaya. About everything. I really didn't want things to turn out this way. You were . . . my best friend."

I narrowed my eyes at him. I didn't want his apologies right now. I took a cookie and bit into it, the flavor of cardamom and butter bursting on my tongue. I needed to get Daniel one of these—he'd love them.

So, what now? Maybe I should just ask him outright if he was LostAxis. I was about to open my mouth to do that when he suddenly looked up and blinked. "My parents were the ones who told me to break up with you," he said.

I nearly spit the cookie out. "What?"

He nodded. "They thought we were getting too serious. I told my mom we were going to . . . you know."

Wow. "You told your *mother* we were planning to have *sex* while they were in India?"

We'd been planning it for weeks. I was ready. He said he was, too. Tahira had even taken me to get birth control. His parents were going to India, and he was staying home, and we were going to have sex for the first time. But then he dumped me and went with them to India.

"So they told you to break up with me because I wouldn't be pure and virginal?" I asked. I'd liked Devin's parents. They'd never seemed that backward to me. "Why would you even tell them?"

He shook his head. "No. No . . . you know they're not like that. Mom asked me if we were sexually active, and I couldn't lie to them. They hadn't realized we were that serious. And they didn't think you were"—he made air quotes—"'long-term material.'"

Two years sounded pretty long-term to me. "Why not?"

"They said I needed to think about the future, and I'd be happier with an Indian girl. Someone with a higher-profile family."

I blinked, looking at him. I must have misheard. "What? I *am* Indian. I'm literally having nan khatai and chai right now."

"They mean *Indian* Indian. Your parents were born in Canada. And your grandparents are from Kenya. And you're Muslim, not Hindu. My parents suggested we break up. And they convinced me to come with them to India to see what real Indian girls are like."

"Your parents convinced you to dump me because my ancestors left India in the 1800s." When he didn't answer, I shook my head. "I take it you didn't find a good meek Indian girl in India? What does 'a higher-profile family' even mean?"

He shrugged. "My dad's the chief of staff at the hospital. So something like that."

Seriously? My dad was a lawyer, and my mom was VP of HR for a huge company, and that wasn't high profile enough for them?

I cringed. "Wow. I never realized what horrendous snobs your parents are."

"No . . . it's not like that, Samaya. They just saw how stressful it was for me to be with you."

"Stressful because I'm not Indian enough. Also, Hana's not Indian, either. She's *Pakistani*! I can't believe you actually agreed with your parents about this."

"I didn't. I mean . . ." Devin ran his hand through his hair. "Honestly, forget I said the Indian part—that's not what was stressing me out about our relationship."

"So, what was so stressful?" I asked. And why hadn't he ever told me about it?

He stared at me, then sighed. "Fine. It's because you're smarter than me. My parents could see how stressed I was that you're smarter than me. That's why they called the camp and had you transferred."

For the love of god. "What the hell, Devin? You and I are both smart. We're the top students in our grade! Both of us! Why would they ruin my summer job because I'm smarter than their precious boy? To sabotage my success?"

"No, *you* are the top. I'm second best. Last year after the Math Olympics, they saw how hard I studied, and I still scored lower than you. They knew it would stress me out to be in that math camp with you all summer. After breaking up with you."

I shook my head. Poor fragile masculinity. "So your parents convinced you to dump me because I'm smarter than you, but also a little bit because I was a double migrant who was about to lose her virginity. Nice, Devin. You're painting you and your family in a lovely light here. No wonder you were too embarrassed to tell me this."

He sighed, running his hand through his hair. It was a stupid habit. That's why his hair was probably so shiny—it was greasy. "It sounds horrible when you say it."

I shook my head. I couldn't believe I had been in love with him. So much time—and so many feelings—wasted. I loved his ambition, I loved his focus, and I loved the way he made me feel . . . worthy. But . . . I was starting to see now what went wrong. There'd been plenty of cracks in our seemingly perfect relationship.

Things had changed in the last months before we broke up. We didn't spend as much time together. We didn't play *Dragon Arena* just the two of us anymore. I hadn't thought we were growing apart; I'd thought we were just . . . growing. Finding new interests. Making choices for what we wanted to do after high school. There was no question in my mind that I wanted to stay with Devin, and it was fine that we were going through a phase.

But I also remembered how detached he was when we were alone. I remembered working hard to get him to open up to me. I remembered how worried he was about the Math Olympics results. I'd even held off on telling him my results because I thought he'd feel bad about me scoring higher than him.

Now I was furious at myself for doing that. I'd hidden my own accomplishments—minimized my success because I'd worried he'd feel bad about himself instead of happy for me. I'd supported him much more than he'd ever supported me. How had I not noticed it before?

"It wasn't your fault," he said, as if he knew what I was thinking. "I was under a lot of pressure."

I sighed. "I understand pressure." I *was* mad at him—he was too fragile to be with someone smarter than him? Ridiculous. But I sympathized, too. Devin's parents were extremely ambitious. Only the best schools. Only the top grades. My parents could be intense, but Devin's had the force of a pressure cooker.

But just because I sympathized . . . *understood* . . . didn't mean I was letting him off the hook for being a terrible boyfriend. Or for catfishing me, for that matter. I took a breath. It was time to find out if my ex-boyfriend was LostAxis.

"Devin, I'm glad you told me all this, and that we're finally talking about why you broke up with me. But that's not why I'm here. I had three mysteries to solve these last few weeks. First, who was Earl's Whispers. Two, who kept giving them gossip about me."

When I didn't go on to identify the third mystery, he blinked a few times. I knew this guy. I knew him very, very well. And I could tell from his reaction he knew what I was talking about. He didn't say anything, though. Just stared at me.

"Log in to *Dragon Arena*," I said, gesturing at his laptop.

He sighed and pulled the computer toward him. After a few moments, he turned it so I could see the character on the screen.

A level-fifty Dark Mage wearing a high-level black cloak and carrying an Obsidian Staff in front of him.

LostAxis.

I came here because I was sure Devin was LostAxis, but seeing the character on the screen felt like a punch to my gut. LostAxis. My old gaming buddy. My friend. "Why . . . why did you do this? Create a whole fake character . . . just to play with me? I don't understand, Devin."

He ran his hand over the back of his neck. "I don't know. It just kind of happened. I started the character secretly so I could play anonymously. Like, without everyone from school, to get away from it all sometimes. Then on that message board, I saw your character, and you were looking for a Dark Mage for a duo . . . and I wanted to play with you. No pressure. No parents' influence, no friends. Just you and me, having fun together." He looked up at me, eyes glistening. "I know I should have told you who I was a long time ago. It snowballed."

"You shouldn't have lied to me in the first place," I spat out. "We were dating then. I would have been thrilled to play with my boyfriend as a Dark Mage. If you didn't want to play with anyone from the school, then why did you play with me?" He'd been pulling away from me then in real life.

He shrugged. "I always loved playing with you. You're an amazing player. And it was just . . . fun without all the real-life crap getting in the way."

"The real-life crap being the fact that I'm better at math than you."

He blinked, saying nothing.

I shook my head. "Why did you send me a picture of Daniel, though?"

He shrugged. "I saw him volunteering at the shelter that day we went to build a playground. There was this chef man yelling at anyone with their camera out, so Jayden, Omar, and I started secretly taking pictures."

"That was Andre. He's amazing. Why'd you take a picture of Daniel?"

"He was standing there for a while in that pose that looked exactly like a Dark Mage in game. Even holding a staff. I thought it was funny, so I took a pic, thinking I could make it a meme or something. Like I'd found a real-life Dark Mage."

"Okay, then why'd you send *me* the picture?"

"You asked me what I thought LostAxis looked like IRL, and this is what I thought he would look like."

"Come on, Devin. You had to know I'd assume the picture was of you. You didn't even correct me."

He shrugged again. "I kind of didn't mind you thinking I was him. I watched the guy that day . . . he was *cool*. He smiled so much, and he talked to people so easily. It was like he didn't have any problems in the world. I'm not even making sense. I'd gotten into a huge fight with my parents about the Math Olympics the night before, and I wished my life was as effortless as that guy's."

If Devin actually knew what Daniel's life had been like, then he wouldn't be saying he wished his life was like that.

"But Daniel lives in Scarborough! What were you planning to do if I ever ran into the guy?"

He nodded. "I know. I wasn't thinking."

"Clearly, you and your parents are right—I *am* smarter than you. Also, why were you—as LostAxis—always spewing shit about squirrels and moose?"

He shrugged. "I don't know. Animals are neat. I said one fact once, and you seemed to find it funny, so I kept with it."

I shook my head. This was unreal. He'd created a whole new person as if he were creating a video game character.

"And anyway," he said, "I didn't think you'd go looking for the guy in the picture."

Teeth gritted, I shook my head. "I didn't go *looking* for him. Honestly, finding Daniel was random. Were you GamesLost, too? Commenting on my Insta?"

He nodded. "Yeah. It really messed with me to see you all over that guy all the time. I just . . . I had to do something. But I know I shouldn't have. I'm sorry."

"You were jealous of Daniel—when you knew you were the one who'd sent me the picture of him in the first place. How did you know about the fairy snipers shooting squirrels? You're not even in game dev. Did all your friends know you were GamesLost?"

He shook his head. "No, no one knew it was me. But Jayden and Omar are my best friends. They showed me what they were working on for your game. I thought their ideas were dumb, by the way. Why would there be snipers in a forest-fairy game?"

I blinked, shaking my head. "I don't even know what to say, Devin. You broke up with me . . . You had no right to be jealous that I was with someone else."

He nodded. "I thought you were trolling me by showing up everywhere with him. I thought maybe you knew I was LostAxis. I gave you so many opportunities to come clean that you were messing with me, but you never said anything."

"I had no clue it was you! You should have been the one to come clean to me!"

He said nothing. I kept silently scrolling through the stats and quest logs of LostAxis. The chat logs with me were so long. "You manipulated me. You lied to me," I said.

"But you lied, too, didn't you?" he said. "You pretended to be dating him. You don't have to do that anymore."

I chuckled. "You're right. At first my relationship with Daniel wasn't real. We were just friends. But it's very much real now. You were also right when you fixated on him at the shelter—he *is* cool. And honest. And so supportive of me. Daniel would *never* do something like this to me. He's twice the person you are."

I stood. I didn't want to be in front of him anymore. Hopefully, Tahira would be back by now. "I'm leaving. For your sake, and mine, I would rather you didn't tell anyone about this. I really don't want people to keep talking about me and you. And never speak to me again."

He nodded, without looking at me. "Okay," he said. "Samaya. Again. I'm sorry."

I put my shoes on and left without another word.

I was so completely done with Devin Kapadia. Forever.

28

Home-Baked Cookies Are No Consolation

For probably the first time in my academic career, I skipped a day of school on Tuesday. Well, it wasn't exactly the first time—I mean, I didn't go to school the day after breaking down at school last June after Devin dumped me. I'd been sad, and confused, and completely shocked.

But this time, I was skipping school because I was just angry. I couldn't face them all. Face Aimee and Jayden, face everyone who saw the post and now knew personal information about Daniel that he hadn't even wanted me to know. And I didn't want to see Devin again after finding out everything he'd done and why.

Ugh. I still couldn't believe Devin was LostAxis. LostAxis! The guy I'd secretly stayed up all night with to fight unicorns and orc hordes with. The guy with the quirky animal facts—though I still didn't get why he'd told me so many of those. LostAxis was the guy who helped me forget the pain Devin caused. It was Devin all along! It didn't make sense to me.

And now, school was a nightmare, and Daniel was doxed. My final year of high school was already an epic disaster, and I wasn't even two months in.

At least I still had Daniel. I hadn't told him about Devin being LostAxis yet. He hadn't texted me after his hockey practice last night, so I assumed he'd gone out with his friends afterward. I spent the day catching up on homework and tinkering with the game-dev code, glad I had work to keep my mind off everything. I texted Daniel a few times over the course of the morning and the afternoon, too, but didn't hear back. Which was fine—he couldn't always text when he was at school.

Mom got home around five. I'd told her and Dad I needed a personal day. I wouldn't dare tell why—that I was still reeling after learning that Devin, their perfect boy, had lied and catfished me.

Mom had just started making dinner when there was a knock at the door. I figured it was a delivery or something, so I was surprised to see Cass and Owen in the doorway.

"Oh, hey, Cass, you have homework for me or something?"

Cass shook their head. They had a grave look on their face. They glanced at Owen a moment, then looked at me. "Have you talked to Daniel today?"

Had something happened to Daniel? I clenched my fists. "What's going on?"

"Let's talk outside," Cass said, glancing over my shoulder at my mother cooking. I guided them to my backyard. It was pretty warm for October, and someone, probably Tahira, had put out massive pots of fall flowers on our deck. I'd actually spent a ton of time here with Tahira and Rowan this past summer when I wasn't working at the ice cream shop. Rowan was really into gardening and had inspired Tahira to put some effort into the backyard, even though she was allergic to a lot of plants. But she called this garden *allergy proof*, because she'd done some research and chosen plants with fewer allergens.

Owen and Cass sat at the outdoor sofa. I took the seat opposite them.

"Okay, tell me."

Cass looked nervously at Owen, then at me. "Why weren't you at school?" they asked.

"I texted you why. I needed a personal day. After the fucker . . ." I stopped. I did like Owen, but I hadn't known him that long. He didn't know about the history between me and Devin, and I wasn't sure I wanted to get into the whole thing now.

"So it's because of Devin?" Cass asked.

I nodded.

"You haven't heard from Daniel? You don't know where he is?"

I shook my head. I was starting to get scared. Really scared. "What's going on?"

Cass sighed and looked at Owen again. "You tell her."

He nodded at Cass, then looked at me. "So I have a good buddy on Daniel's hockey team, yeah? Austin. I got a call from him—he knew that I knew your best friend, and he thought I might know where to find him."

My spine straightened. "Find him . . . Where is he? He had hockey practice yesterday."

Owen shook his head. "Apparently yesterday on their team's Discord, Daniel told them all that he wouldn't be coming to practice. He said he was quitting the team and moving."

"What? Why?"

"He said he got into a fight with his uncle about some Instagram post, and left home. No one has heard from him since."

My hand shot to my mouth. "Oh my god. Where is he?" I picked up my phone.

"Austin said he hasn't responded to texts or their group chat all day," Cass said. "His team is worried."

I texted Daniel.

Me: Please respond. I'm worried about you. I heard what happened with your uncle.

There was no answer.

"Where do *you* think he is?" Cass asked.

I chewed my lip, thinking. "One of two places. With his aunt, who has a bakery in Brampton, or at the shelter." I thought about it for a moment. "The shelter is closer. We could start there."

I texted Andre.

Me: Hey Andre, sorry to bother you, Is Daniel there?

Andre wrote back right away.

Andre: Yeah, and I'm glad you texted. I wanted to call you, but Daniel asked me not to. He's here. Making pies.

I exhaled a long sigh of relief. "He's there."

"Want me to drive you?" Cass asked.

"Yeah, let's go."

After telling Mom I was going out with Cass and probably wouldn't be home for dinner, Cass, Owen, and I headed to the shelter.

Cass didn't come in after dropping me off, saying they'd wait in the park with Owen so they could bring me home. I gave them an awkward hug. "Thanks. I mean it, Cass. I probably don't deserve you."

"You don't, but you got me anyway."

Yasmin was sitting on a bench right inside the lobby of the shelter, staring outside longingly. Her leg was in a cast.

"Mama said I was supposed to say sorry to you for causing so much trouble," she said to me when she saw me rushing in.

I was impatient to speak to Daniel, but this was the first time I'd seen Yasmin since she'd gone missing. I smiled at her. "Apology accepted. How's your leg?"

She shrugged. "I'm not allowed to ride my bicycle. I only wanted to see the fairies in the forest. I was going to tell you what they look like for your game."

I crouched in front of her. "Thank you for thinking about my game. Did you find any fairies?"

She shook her head. "No. But I saw some trees that had holes at the bottom. Were those fairy doors?"

I shrugged. "I don't know." I didn't want to encourage Yasmin to look again. "I think we might be able to get some fairies to move in here at the shelter, though." I pointed to the little garden out front that was visible through the window. "I'd bet if we built a fairy house and put it there, they'd move in for the winter. We might not see them, but we'd know they were there."

Yasmin's face erupted into a huge grin. "Will you and Daniel help me build one?"

"I absolutely will. I need to go talk to Daniel about something else right now, but I'll come back in a few days so we can do this as research for my game. And I'll give you consulting credit for the game."

"What's consulting credit?"

"It means I'll add a note in the game letting everyone know you helped me. But I want you to promise you'll listen to your mother and not leave the shelter without a grown-up again. Okay?"

Yasmin's enthusiastic nod made my heart melt a bit. "Okay. I think Daniel is mad at me."

"Why? I don't think he is."

"He didn't say anything when he got here today. And he doesn't want me to sit in the kitchen and watch him bake." She had a solemn look on her face.

I tilted my head. "Sometimes big people need to be alone to think."

She glanced toward the kitchen, then back at me. "You can help him. I think he likes you better than anyone else here."

I patted her leg. "I think he likes you second best."

I found Daniel alone in the kitchen. He was scooping cookie batter onto baking sheets. He looked rough—dark circles under sleepless eyes, and no sign of his normal cheerfulness. It hurt my heart to see him this way.

He barely looked up when I walked in. "I know you can't abide raisins in cookies, but how do you feel about currants?" he asked.

I frowned as I walked over to him at the prep counter. "A currant is the same thing as a raisin, isn't it?"

He shook his head. "Completely different fruit. Raisins come from grapes. They grow on vines. Currants, those are grown on little bushes." He leaned over and took a handful of small black, wrinkled things out of a plastic container and held them out for me.

I took one and carefully ate it. "It's different." It was more floral. Sweeter. "I like them."

"Good." He went back to scooping the dough. He seemed closed off—like he didn't want me to know how he was feeling.

"Owen heard from your teammates that you had a fight with your uncle," I said.

Daniel nodded stiffly. There was so much tension in his body. I'd never seen him like this before. "More gossip about me." He sounded so wooden.

"Your teammates are worried about you. They care." When he didn't say anything and kept scooping the cookie dough, I added, "I care, too. I'm worried. You haven't answered my texts all day."

"I don't have a phone anymore." He took the tray of cookies to the oven. He had to set it down to open the oven, since he still had a cast on one wrist. "It's technically my uncle's phone, not mine. Nothing is actually mine."

I put my arm on his when he came back to the counter. "You could have used Andre's phone."

"Maybe I wasn't feeling like talking to anyone."

Including me? I let go of his arm. "I can go, if you want."

He finally looked at me. I couldn't read his expression. Yes. There was sadness there. And anger. At me? If it was the Earl's Whispers picture that his uncle saw, then it was my fault. All of it.

I didn't know how to get him to open up, but I wasn't going to stop trying. I put my hand over his. His gaze shifted to our connected hands. "What happened, Daniel?" I asked. "What did you and your uncle fight about?"

Daniel sighed. "He saw the Whispers post."

"How?"

Daniel gave an angry little snort. "He looked at my phone while I was packing my hockey gear."

Shit. I'd texted him a screenshot. "He knew your phone password?"

Daniel nodded. "It's technically *his*. And he's paying for the service. But I had no idea he ever looked through my texts."

"Daniel, I'm so sorry I sent that to you." I put my hand on his arm, but it didn't look like he wanted it there, so I took it away.

"I knew he wouldn't approve of our arrangement," Daniel said. "But he *just* came into my life. I've never had a father. My mother cares about me, but she *trusts* me. I've never had to tell anyone *everything* I do. It's like he's trying to be a savior or something to a poor disadvantaged youth. Anyway, I got a lecture about my priorities and about lying. And about how hard it would be for me now that everyone knew about my unfortunate past. I told him that you were helping me with calculus, and somehow that made him even madder, because I'd told him I was getting help from a teacher. He said I should have gone to him for calculus help instead of some juvenile delinquent, and I'm not supposed to be playing violent video games anyway."

I frowned. "Am I the juvenile delinquent?"

He nodded. "Because of the way you dress . . . and because you introduced me to the blasphemous video game."

"That's ridiculous. I'm an honor student, not a delinquent."

He shrugged. "He doesn't want me dating you. And I have to stop working here. If I agree, he'll let me continue hockey."

"What does volunteering at the shelter have to do with anything? Is it because I'm here?"

He shrugged. "He said I can volunteer at the youth programs at his church, instead."

"What does your mom say?"

"She disagrees with him—Mom's on my side. She said if he kicks me out, she'll quit and move out, too, and we can rent a place. But I don't see how we can afford anything decent."

"So, what are you going to do?"

"Don't know yet." He started wiping the flour off the counters with a kitchen rag. He seemed to be pretty good at working with one good hand by now. "My aunt said I could come work in the bakery and live with her. Then Mom could keep her job."

I shook my head. "But you can't leave like that! Why can't your mother put her foot down—she's your parent! In a few months you'll be an adult, and you won't have to do what anyone says anymore!"

He looked at me. "Samaya, you have no idea what it's like to not really have a home."

Of course I didn't. I'd lived in a house—the same house—my whole life.

"This isn't just him telling me what to do because I'm a kid," Daniel continued, wiping down the counter again. "It's because he's *giving me a place to live*, but with strings attached. And you know what? Maybe the strings are worth it. I don't agree with him on most things. But I like living there. I have my own room. He drives me to hockey. I like the neighborhood—I have new friends and a social life. My mom is happy. She's treated well, and the woman she takes care of is nice. They reminisce about the Philippines, and my mom cooks her favorite foods for her. If I go back to my aunt's, I'll be back to sharing a room with my eight- and eleven-year-old cousins. If I move out alone, I'll have to work full-time to afford rent, so I won't be able to go to college."

"But if you stay, he's going to insist you study what he wants you to study, like computers or engineering or something. You won't be able to go to culinary school."

He sighed. "I'll figure it out. If I do what he wants, then maybe in a few months he'll let go on that. I need to decide what compromises to make." He tossed the towel in the sink.

I blinked, looking at him. "You mean me."

He stared at me for several seconds, then nodded. "Yeah."

"You're breaking up with me."

"Samaya, we haven't even started dating yet, remember? We have no commitment after your dance."

"But you're backing out of that." I couldn't believe this.

He shook his head. "We both know we don't fit together anyway. We're mismatched. Like putting chocolate on lemon squares. What will your parents say when they meet me and you tell them, 'I know my old boyfriend's family were millionaires with homes in Canada and India, but here's my new guy! He failed grade-ten math, is a pretty good hockey player, but not like NHL quality or anything, and his mother is a home care nurse. He lived in a shelter for a while, but some man took them in out of pity. Isn't he hot?'"

There was venom in his voice. It was so unlike Daniel that it pierced my heart. "I told you, none of that matters to me. And if my parents didn't approve of you, that wouldn't change the way I feel. But seriously, my parents wouldn't care about what your parents do, or what you want to study. They'll care that you're a good person." The best person.

Daniel looked at me. He was standing next to me at the food prep counter, but now he took half a step away. "Don't *you* care, though, Samaya?" he said. "What about everything you made me pretend to be?"

"We've gone over this. That was only because you had to pretend to be LostAxis!"

"Okay, but would I have been enough for you if I was just me?"

I studied his face, but couldn't read the expression on it. "Of course you would have been enough, Daniel. I didn't know you when we made that deal, but I've loved getting closer to you since then." I sighed, stepping close to him. "I know I was wrong to make you pretend to be someone else. I wish I could turn back time and redo it all. I had all these . . . assumptions about who I was. About what was important. And about who you were, too. I was traumatized, and way too wrapped up in what other people thought. But other than those two parties where I asked you to pretend to be LostAxis—I've *always* accepted you. When we've been at the market, or baking, or working on your math, or playing games online, or even at your hockey game . . . I've liked you for *you*."

I'd loved him for him. The guy who seriously considered the merits of cake vs. pie, without being able to choose one over the other. Who took a little girl to the forest to look in hollowed-out logs for fairies. Who taught me to play croquet and cheered like a whole arena when I scored a point. Who made oatmeal cookies with butterscotch chips because I didn't like raisins. Daniel had always been enough for me personally. More than enough.

When he didn't say anything, I sighed. There was really no point in arguing. Daniel deserved to be happy. He deserved to be baking pies, playing hockey, living with his mother, and studying to make an even better piecrust. And . . . if I was getting in the way of Daniel being happy, then I didn't belong in his life.

Didn't mean I liked it, though. "This situation is blatantly unfair."

Daniel shrugged. "Life isn't fair. We do the best with what we have." The timer went off. "Cookies are done," he said.

He put on the oven mitt and took the trays out of the oven. The smell was almost too much. Warm butter, brown sugar, and currants. I knew I was forever going to associate the smell of freshly baked oatmeal cookies with this heartbreak.

Daniel took one of the cookies, blowing on it a bit to cool it, and handed it to me. It was hot, but I took a bite, not even wiping the tear that was falling down my cheek as I ate it. It tasted . . . delicious. The currants were small enough that it didn't feel like my cookie was all fruity, but at the same time, their slight acidity cut through the richness of the butter.

It was the best, saddest cookie I'd ever had.

Daniel packed the rest of the cookies in a plastic container and handed it to me. "Don't put the lid on until they're cool. They'll get soggy."

I took the container, frowning. "These are all for me?"

He nodded.

"How did you know I'd be here?"

"I knew you'd find me. If you didn't, I was going to leave them here for you with a note."

"You were planning to break up with me with a note and a box of breakup cookies?"

He shrugged. "I didn't want to. I'd rather give you this with the cookies." He stepped closer to me and slipped his hand behind my neck. My breath hitched when his lips touched mine. The kiss was soft, and sad, and I wanted it to never end. I pulled him closer. When we broke the kiss, he just hugged me for a few seconds, and I savored it. We fit so well for two people who didn't really fit at all.

"Goodbye, Daniel. I hope we can be . . . friends again one day." I took my sad cookies and left.

29

Well, Yeah, It's Complicated If You Put It That Way

Well?" Cass said as I approached.

Cass and Owen were sitting on a park bench near the start of a walking path. I'd texted them as I left the shelter, and they'd told me where to find them.

This was the same forest where Yasmin had gone searching for fairies on Friday. I sat between them with the box of cookies on my lap.

"Daniel's fine. He left his phone at home."

"He's moving out?" Owen asked.

I shook my head. "No." I took a deep breath. I couldn't believe this was happening again. "But he dumped me."

"What?" Cass sounded shocked. And pissed.

I was not pissed. I was monumentally *sad*. I didn't fully understand *why* Daniel would go along with what his uncle wanted instead of fighting to live his own life, but I did acknowledge that his life wasn't mine, and what I would do was different from what he would do, and he had to do what he felt was right. I leaned back on the bench. "We were officially dating for only four days, and I'm a mess. Pathetic, right?" I wiped a rogue tear.

"What? I thought you guys were together for almost two months?" Owen asked.

I let out a sad chuckle. That was at least one good thing about this—people wouldn't question why I was so heartsick over a days-long relationship because, in the world's eyes, it had been months, not days.

And it hurt like it had been months, not days. "Thanks for keeping my secrets, Cass, but it's not really necessary anymore."

"What do you want to do now?" Cass asked. "Dye your hair? Get a piercing? I know a tattoo shop that doesn't ask for ID."

"Honestly, I just want to eat these cookies." I offered the container to Cass and Owen first, then took a cookie for myself.

"That I can get behind," Cass said.

We ate cookies while Cass and I gave Owen the briefest backstory of my situation. "So let me make sure I have all this," Owen said after we'd explained. "Your ex broke up with you and went to India all summer, and when he came back, he started dating your friend. All while you were talking to a guy online and playing *Dragon Arena* with him. Another friend does some photo editing of a picture of online-guy with you, so the school thinks you're really dating online-guy, not just online friends with him. It turns out that online-guy gave you a fake picture, though, and it's actually a picture of Daniel, who you randomly were volunteering with. You ask Daniel to pretend to be online-guy and pretend to date you because a gossip Insta is claiming your ex was winning your breakup. But then you and Daniel started dating for real until the gossip account called you out for fake dating, and Daniel's uncle went through his phone and saw the post and forbid him from seeing you or he wouldn't let him continue hockey?"

"Yeah, that's pretty much it." Then: "Oh wait—the online-guy turned out to be my ex catfishing me the whole time. And his parents told him to dump me in the first place because I'm smarter than him. And not Indian enough for them."

Cass gave me an incredulous look. "What? Are you serious? *Devin* was LostAxis?"

I chuckled, nodding. "Yup. I figured it out and went to confront him last night."

Owen looked over me at Cass. "When I asked you out, you told me you couldn't date me because your life was too complicated."

What? I glared at Cass. "Owen asked you out? I've tried to give you space, Cass, but you should have told me this! What did you say?"

Cass rolled their eyes. Clearly, I needed to have a talk with them about their relationship with Owen. Preferably when Owen wasn't with us.

"My life is just complicated," they said. "Samaya's life is a complex calculus equation. But seriously, I can't believe LostAxis was Devin the whole time. What a dingus."

"This is the best love square that turned out to be a love triangle I've ever heard of," Owen said.

I winced and took another cookie. At least I had these.

"My life is a disaster," I said after swallowing. "I totally get why Daniel's uncle doesn't want Daniel anywhere near me."

Neither Cass nor Owen spoke for a while, which gave me time to finish the cookie. And to eat another one. I was firmly #TeamCurrants now.

Finally, Cass spoke. "Two things, Samaya. First, let's put the blame for most of this situation on one person—the one who manipulated you."

"Devin?" I asked.

"Yes, Devin. Want revenge? I can spread the word that he was catfishing you. I'm sure Hana would love to know that when she was getting busy with Devin, he was still talking to you. Just not as himself."

I frowned. Devin's whole scheme reeked of desperation, and if the student body knew, Devin would be the one getting the stares and the whispered mocking at school instead of me. I could even tell people that he broke up with me because I was smarter than him. Or worse, that his parents thought my family wasn't "high profile" enough.

I could destroy my ex. And considering none of this would have happened if it hadn't been for him, I was sorely tempted.

But why? Would it make things better for Daniel? Would it make it possible for us to be together?

"No," I said.

"No?" Owen asked. "Why not? He deserves it."

I nodded. "He does, but I don't care. I don't care if the whole school hates Devin, or if he continues on as the golden boy."

I thought about that while Cass and Owen continued eating their cookies. I quite honestly didn't want to get revenge on Devin. And not because I still cared for him. I just knew revenge would only make me feel worse in the long run. I wanted this whole situation—all the gossip, and the competitiveness, and the backstabbing—to go away, not dig myself deeper into it.

There was no winning or losing here, and I was losing touch with what was important during the fight.

And also? I was in *love* with Daniel. And, thanks to Daniel, it had finally been drilled into my head that the person I was inside was much more important than the person people thought I was. And there were way more important things in the world to spend my time on than winning a breakup. I'd much rather be helping kids like Yasmin, or working on my mobile game, or supporting my real friends.

"I don't care what anyone at school thinks of me anymore, either," I said. "Let them hate me, let them think I'm a snob, or crying about Devin, or whatever. All that's important is to be the person I want to be." I turned to Cass. "Cass, do me a favor and smack me upside the head if I lose sight of that again."

Cass snorted. "With pleasure, my friend. Be your amazing self. Now, eat another cookie."

~

The first thing I did when I got home was tell Tahira to cancel my dress order for the fall formal. She was annoyed, since it had been a bit of work for her to get the wholesale deal, but she understood. She also said she would take back the menswear samples she'd borrowed from her school for Daniel to wear. Even without a date I could still go to the dance, but I didn't want to. That had nothing to do with me not wanting to be seen alone, or even because I didn't want to see Devin and Hana together.

I just couldn't bear being there without Daniel after we'd been talking about going together for so long. I wouldn't have fun.

But I wasn't hiding from my classmates, so I did go to school the next day.

I was sitting alone on a bench in the hallway at lunch reviewing my functions lesson when someone stopped next to me. It was Hana.

"Was Devin with you yesterday?" she asked.

I looked up at her with a raised brow.

Hana looked upset. "Was he?" she asked again.

I shook my head.

Still frowning, Hana sat next to me. "He's not answering my calls. I heard you were at his house on Monday. I assume you two are back together."

I huffed a laugh. Why would he ghost Hana now? Unless his parents were sticking their noses into this relationship, too? "That assumption is so far off the mark it's practically in Fiji. Yes, I saw him Monday, but I didn't see or speak to him yesterday."

"I don't know if I believe you."

I turned back to my book. "I don't care if you don't believe me, Hana, it's the truth. I'm sorry you two are having issues, but I haven't done a thing to cause them." I sighed. "I'm going to study now." I ignored the existence of Hana Dawar. Frenemies were too much work.

After a few seconds, she got up and left.

Miss Zhao had switched the game-dev team meeting to today after I didn't show up on Monday, which was thoughtful of her. But I wasn't sure anyone would show up. Kavita was suspended—so I knew she wouldn't be there, and I doubted Hana or Jayden would come. But no one had told me they were leaving the team. And I had certainly no intention of giving up on it. I was genuinely enjoying building the game and wanted to see it through.

When I got to the tech lab, I surprised to see the whole team—except Kavita, of course. But Aimee, Cass, and Jayden were there. Even Hana. Miss Zhao was already at the side of the room working on a computer. She smiled when I walked in.

I stood at the front, took a deep breath, then asked everyone for their progress on their duties for the game. I was relieved by their responses. Everyone was still taking it all seriously. Hana had done some market research, and she showed us the marketing plan Kavita had done. Aimee had put together some advertising mock-ups. Cass was still coding the first two levels, and Alex had been helping them debug an issue in the code that was turning the fairies' wings upside down whenever they walked into a cave.

Apparently, I hadn't lost the team. At least until I asked Jayden how level three was going. Hopefully he'd let go of his forest-fairy sniper-battle idea.

Jayden smiled a smile I didn't trust. "You'll love this. Omar and I have a full script and battle plan." He showed us some mock-up he'd drawn.

And no. There were no snipers. Instead, there were . . . alien mechas? "Jayden! Why the hell would fairies be fighting giant robots from space?"

He shook his head. "They're not fighting *against* the mechas, they're fighting *in* them. You said it needed to be a puzzle adventure game.

Well, getting in and controlling the mechas will be the puzzle. And mechas are always an adventure."

Omar laughed.

I glared at them both. "Okay, but why would there be mechas from another world in the forest?"

"This will appeal to a wider demographic," Jayden said. "I know what gamers like, and they'll like mechas a hell of a lot more than fairies ice-skating with grass tied to their shoes. We're trying to make a game here—not preschool playtime. Maybe you need to stop hanging out with children so much."

Cass turned to Jayden. "You're being an asshole for no reason."

Nabil and Carson jumped in, defending Jayden's idea, and Hana told them to shut up, that their idea was stupid, and he should listen to me because I was team captain.

Jayden turned to look at me, then very obviously turned away. "Not even sure you should be the captain anymore. We need teamwork to win. You seem to care more about your 'boyfriend' than the team." The air quotes he made around *boyfriend* sent Omar, Carson, and Nabil laughing.

"Plus, she'll probably go crying to the principal if she loses, like she did about Earl's Whispers," someone else said. I didn't see who. Jayden snorted a laugh.

I was livid. It wasn't even me who'd gone to the principal; it was their buddy Devin. "Why do you have it in for me, Jayden?" I tried to keep my voice calm. I needed the team to respect me. I was supposed to be a leader here.

Jayden's eyes narrowed. "Pretty full of yourself to think that I care at all. Why don't you step aside and let the actual gamers run this game-dev team?"

I stood there, blinking at my team for several seconds. Respect went both ways, and I was done busting my ass to get respected by people who I didn't respect in return. I *wanted* to lead a game-dev team. And I *wanted* to make this forest-fairy game. But these guys on the team had already decided not to respect me as the captain, and nothing I did was going to change that. So we were never going to win the competition together. Hell, I doubted we'd even get a game made. It just wasn't going to work.

I picked up my backpack and put it on my shoulders. "I'm out."

"What do you mean, out?" Aimee asked.

I shrugged. "Just out. I don't want to be in this team anymore. Go ahead, Jayden. Make your shooter game. You can be captain."

"So, you're not going to do game dev?" Jayden asked.

I paused. This team had been my idea. And this game was for Yasmin.

I looked at Miss Zhao, who wasn't paying attention to the meeting. "Miss Zhao, do you have an issue with me leaving this team and forming a new one?"

Miss Zhao shook her head, frowning with confusion. "No. The school can have as many teams as they want to enter."

I smiled. "Cass?"

Cass got up from their seat. "I'm with you."

"You can't take Cass!" Jayden said. "They're the best coder in the school!"

"She's not *taking* me," Cass said. "I'm *leaving*."

We headed toward the door. Cass and I had the skills to do this on our own.

"Wait," a voice said. Aimee. "I'm leaving, too."

"What the fuck!" Jayden said, shocked.

I raised a brow at Aimee. She was literally dating Jayden, and she was abandoning his team?

"That is," Aimee said, "if you'll have me, I mean."

Aimee and I had been friends for over a decade. As long as Cass and me. Aimee had done all the concept art for the fairies, so it would be better if she were still on my team.

"You sure?" I hadn't forgiven her for letting her boyfriend send that picture to Earl's Whispers. But I did want the chance to repair our friendship.

She looked back at the guys. "Absolutely."

On the way home, the three of us made plans for how to enter the competition as a new team. And the next day, we sent out feelers for new members, telling them we'd be meeting Monday after school. In a surprise twist, Miss Zhao stopped me in the hallway and told me she was jumping ship, too, and wanted to be our adviser. She explained she'd roped Mr. Patel into being adviser for Jayden's team. She also was planning to speak to some math and science teachers to see if they had any students who would be interested in joining us.

Thursday morning I got a call from Muniba. She didn't tell me much about how Daniel was doing but said that his uncle had allowed him to stay in the baking project—as long as I wasn't working with him. I had all my volunteer hours—so I didn't *need* to work at the shelter anymore. But Daniel did need them, so I agreed to walk away from the baking project. I asked Muniba if I could still volunteer there— maybe in another role, and when Daniel wasn't present—and she said absolutely. She would ask around in the other areas to see where I was needed, and she'd call me next week.

By the time our new game-dev team met on Monday, we had nine kids from all grades—all either girls, nonbinary, or LGBTQ2+ kids. After our first meeting, I could already see it was a hell of a lot more fun than working with the old team.

I heard Kavita wasn't planning to come back to Earl's after her suspension, which was wise since the backlash over Earl's Whispers final post—the one outing Daniel for having lived in the shelter—was still going strong. In fact, a grade-eleven girl who'd come to the shelter that night to help find Yasmin started a new club at school to fundraise and donate a backpack full of toys, books, and school supplies to each kid at the shelter. They also planned to donate a purse filled with makeup, skin care, and feminine products for each woman there. I joined the club immediately.

Earl's Whispers may have been gone, but Earl's was still full of gossip. In fact, someone told me early in the week that Devin and Hana had broken up. Strangely, however, Jayden and Aimee were still together. Aimee didn't mention Jayden when I was with her, but then we didn't really talk about anything other than the game-dev team. I found I didn't miss my old friend group at all.

But despite things going well at school, I was still sad. I missed Daniel. So much. I'd texted him so many times, but there was never an answer. I assumed his uncle didn't give him his phone back. I wasn't sure I'd ever see him again.

~

Thursday after school, Cass and I went to a local café. "You're looking longingly at cakes again," Cass said while we were waiting for our drinks.

"Those are blondies. Which makes them a square, not a cake. Not a cookie, either." Was my chest going to clench like this every time I saw squares and bars from now on?

When we were seated at a table with our coffees, Cass gave me a look. "Have you heard from him at all?" they asked.

"Who?"

"Um, Daniel? Duh."

"No."

They narrowed one eye. "I've been trying to figure it out. You've been so different from when you broke up with Devin. I wondered if maybe you weren't as invested in the relationship with Daniel or as into him as you were with Devin and that's why this breakup is easier."

I shook my head. "I *was* into him. A lot. I know we weren't together long, but I never felt like that about anyone." I was in love with him, but I didn't want to admit that out loud.

"But you're coping better. I haven't had to smack you upside the head once this week."

I laughed. Cass was right. I *was* coping. Why? The easy answer was that it wasn't really a breakup. Daniel and I had agreed not to commit to each other until after the dance. Plus, I wasn't mourning a long-term relationship, just the potential for a future together.

But there was more to it.

"When Devin broke up with me, it felt like I was losing more than just a boyfriend. I was losing an identity I'd kind of grown attached to. I'd been Devin's girlfriend. One half of the Earl Jones power couple. I was upset because I felt like I'd lost that. Or lost the person I wanted everyone to see me as," I said. "This time, I lost the guy, but not my own identity." I paused. "I am upset, though." I glanced over at the display case of pies and other baked goods at the counter. "I will probably burst into tears the next time I smell a pie baking."

Cass smiled. "Who needs therapy when you can figure this shit out on your own?"

I chuckled. "But seriously. I *miss* Daniel, and I am so, so utterly sorry that I messed up so much for him. And I am so, so grateful to him for . . . for being *him*, right when I needed it. I wish I could tell him how much he helped me put everything into perspective."

"You *should* tell him."

I frowned. "Maybe when you tell Owen how you really feel about him? Did you agree to go out with him yet?"

Cass blushed. "You're changing the subject, Samaya."

"Cass! You can't be cagey with Owen forever! You know he's into you, and you admitted you've been into him since, what . . . July?" I paused. "I said you could smack some sense into me when I start acting irrational. Can I do the same with you?"

They tilted their head. "This isn't about me . . . it's about *you*. Tell Daniel how much you care. This is *Daniel* . . . he's a big ol' emotional sap. Things might be a mess for him right now, but I think hearing about how well you're doing will make him feel better. He's a helping-people kind of person."

I sighed. It was possible that Daniel wanted nothing to do with me. Or maybe Cass was right, and hearing I was doing okay would make him feel a little bit better. If that was true, I wanted to give him that.

I could send him an email. Emails were noninvasive. If Daniel didn't want to hear from me, he didn't have to open it. And I doubted his uncle was screening his school account.

"Okay, fine. I'll message Daniel if you agree to go out with Owen. Like a real date. Not as friends. Deal?"

Cass frowned at me for several long moments, then shockingly, they nodded. "Fine."

I chuckled. That was too easy. Apparently, Cass had wanted that little push.

That evening, I wrote to Daniel.

Daniel,

I know you said that we could someday be friends again, and it's only been a few days so this might be way too soon for that. But it still feels like we are friends. I guess it's hard for me to turn off my feelings. If you never want to hear from me again, tell me now and I'll be gone forever. Or tell me it's not someday, yet. Or you can ignore me, and I won't hate you for that. I don't think I could ever hate you, anyway.

You're right that I could never understand what it's like to be you, and I shouldn't judge your choices without walking in your shoes. I don't want to be the friend who doesn't let you do what you know is best for you. I would rather be the friend who you go to when things are amazing, and when you want to play games, or go to a dance, or make pies. Or be the friend you come to when things are hard, and you want a shoulder to lean on without judgment. I wish I could be that friend for you.

I'm rambling. I've had an intense, stressful, hard, and good couple of days since I saw you, and I can't seem to think straight. Really the reason I'm writing this is to tell you two things.

First, I started my own game-dev team without Jayden and his crew. We're doing Yasmin's Forest Fairy game, and I'm totally going to credit her as inspiration. The new team is amazing and collaborative, and joyful, and it's so exciting and I hated that I couldn't tell you about it.

And second, I wanted to thank you. I'm going to get real and talk about you and me and feelings, now, so if you don't want to hear it, stop reading.

I'm not sure you're fully aware of how confused and messy my life was when we met. I had been Devin's girlfriend for so long I didn't know how to be anything else. And I think I was scared that I didn't have much value outside that identity. But you liked me for me—not for my grades, or my parents' status, or for who my friends were. You made me realize that what's really important is being true to my real friends, seeing people for who they are, not what they are, and helping people who need it . . . no matter why they need it. And that it only mattered what the people I cared about thought of me, not anyone else. I figured out so much about me, and even though I miss you . . . like, really, really miss you, I wanted to tell you that I'm pretty proud of me. I wanted to share that good news with my friend.

I know I wasn't as helpful to you as you were to me, and I'm really sorry for that. But I know you, and I know that helping people means a lot to you, so I thought you might want to know how much you helped me.

I won't ever forget you.

Samaya

I sent the email. And by the time I went to bed, I didn't have a response. Which, fair. I myself said he didn't have to write back.

I did hold out hope that one day he would, though.

30

The Belle of the Ball

D id you go and get yourself another date for the dance without
telling me?"

Tahira had poked her head into my room Saturday afternoon while
I was on my computer trying to fix the fairy-wing problem in the game's
code.

I stared at her and frowned. "No. I'm not going. Why?"

"There is a very tall red-haired boy with glasses downstairs. He's
wearing a tie and holding one of those flower boxes you get from the
florist. Handsome dude. Do you think he'd model streetwear for me?"

I only knew one tall redheaded boy. "Owen? What did he say?"

"Nothing. He asked for you, so I came to get you."

I rushed past Tahira and headed downstairs.

The moment I saw him, I understood why Tahira wanted him to
model her designs. He cleaned up nice. Wearing a slim blue suit, a pale
pink dress shirt, and a blue tie, with his bright hair slicked down instead
of flopping over one eye, he looked perfectly nerdy-cool.

"Owen. What are you doing here?"

"Um, I'm here to drive you and Cass to your dance? I know I'm
early. I was expecting a big line at the florist because of the dance.

But no one was there. Do people not give flowers to dates for dances anymore? My dad said this was what Cass would expect." He tilted his head. "Is that what you're wearing?"

I looked down at my leggings and my WHICH CAME FIRST, THE DRAGON OR THE EGG? sweatshirt. It wasn't my favorite. And no, this wasn't what I would wear to the school dance. Because I wasn't going.

Clearly something was going on here.

"Oh, okay, um, why don't you come in? I'll be right back. This is my sister, Tahira. She'll probably ask you who you're wearing. If she asks you to model, she's not being creepy—she's studying fashion and is always looking for tall people."

Even before I was upstairs, I had a FaceTime call open with Cass. "Can you tell me why Owen is here to drive us to the dance?"

Cass cringed. "Damn it. He called my bluff."

"Um, what bluff?"

Cass sat on their bed. They were in their room wearing a gray dress shirt, with the top two buttons open. "He's sooo stubborn. That's bad in a relationship, right?"

I sat on my own bed. "Cass, it's time for you to actually talk to me about what the hell is going on between the two of you. And somewhat quickly, too, because right now he's in the living room alone with Tahira. I give her about thirty minutes before she's convinced him to get his whole hockey team here to model her new sweatshirt line."

Cass shook their head.

"Spill, bestie."

Cass sighed. "Fine. I did what you said—I told him I'd go on a date with him."

"OMG! Yay, Cass! Finally! So why did you say he called your bluff?"

Cass shook their head. "I tested him—I said I'd only go on this date if it met my parameters."

I raised a brow. "Parameters?"

"I learned from you. I said our first date had to be the fall formal, and you'd be with us, too. He'd have to wear a suit and everything. And I'd be wearing a suit, too. And we'd have to slow dance, and post at least three pictures of us on each of our Instas where it's obvious that we're on a date."

I laughed. "These parameters are perfect. He looks very good in a suit. Why'd you think he wouldn't agree to all that?"

"You don't get it, Samaya! I told him this, like, an hour and a half ago! He doesn't own a suit that fits him since he had a major growth spurt last year."

"Well, the one he's wearing now fits him well. Really well."

"How the hell did he get a suit so fast? I can't even imagine someone willing to do all that."

I laughed because it was so funny to see normally stoic Cass freaking out. "Of course he's willing! That boy is completely nuts for you. Cass, why are you so scared of Owen?" That was the burning question. Cass had dated people before—even before I'd started dating Devin, actually—but not since coming out as nonbinary last year. "Is it the hockey? He's already introduced you to his team. And I thought he was out, anyway."

"He is. But, I mean, I met them all as his friend. And it's not just them. I think it's one thing for him to have a nonbinary friend and totally another to date them, right? He's, like, I don't know. A catch. He can get anyone. Why deal with my weirdness?"

I smiled. "I happen to adore your weirdness. Maybe you should let Owen decide what he's willing to deal with?"

Cass sighed.

The thing was, even though Cass didn't like to talk much about what they were feeling, I *knew* them. And I knew Cass wasn't only reacting this way because they thought Owen wasn't ready to date a nonbinary person. Cass themselves was also nervous to start dating with their brand-new gender identity. And I knew they'd become quite close with Owen, even if just as a friend, so taking it to the next level was a big risk. "And clearly Owen's decided he *wants* to deal with you. And he looks like a complete snack. He's even got a boutonniere for your suit."

"Damn. He doesn't even like flowers."

"You can't go back on your word now. I sent Daniel that message, so now you have to go out with Owen. Hey, why did you tell him to pick you up here, anyway?"

Cass raised one brow. "Um, because I'm supposed to be there in, like, fifteen minutes to pick you up? You and me are going together, aren't we? Why aren't you dressed?"

"I'm not dressed because I'm not going to the dance!"

"What are you talking about? Of course you're going to the dance!"

"Did you forget that Daniel and I broke up?"

"So? That means you're not going? Daniel doesn't even go to Earl's! You're going to get a bunch of awards, aren't you?"

I frowned. I'd told Tahira I wasn't going when I asked her to cancel the dress, but now that I thought about it, it was possible I'd failed to tell anyone else. "Yeah, but—"

"Samaya, you told me to smack you if you started to lose your perspective again. I need to put on my tie and comb my hair, then I'll be there to deliver that smack."

"But I—"

"Samaya, this is the *academic* banquet, and you are *you*. I get it. You don't want to go because you're sad about Daniel, and because of the people you don't like who will be there. And those are valid reasons to stay away. But tonight isn't about your popularity, or your boyfriend, but about celebrating how hard you've worked for your accomplishments."

I sighed. Cass was right. Not caring so much about what people thought of me didn't mean I couldn't be proud of my hard work. Because I'd worked freaking hard. I deserved to celebrate my achievements. This was my last academic banquet before graduation. If I didn't go tonight, I'd probably regret it one day.

"So you want me, you, and Owen to go together?" I asked.

Cass nodded. "Yes! You and I were always planning to go together. So what if you don't have a date anymore? And also? Now Owen is coming, and I'm completely freaking out. You *cannot* leave me alone."

I frowned. "I don't have a dress. I canceled my dress order."

"What did you do that for? Don't you have anything else?"

I stood and opened my closet door. I wasn't really a dress person—it was mostly T-shirts and sweatshirts in here.

"Nothing nice enough. Except my dress from last year's dance." Something bright caught my eye. "I could wear the lehenga Devin bought me in India." I laughed at that idea. But then I thought about it. I did love that lehenga. A lot.

I pulled it out of my closet and put the camera in front of it so Cass could see it. "Should I wear it?"

Cass shrugged. "It's gorgeous. If you like it, wear it. Who cares where you got it? It's just clothes—it's not that deep."

That was such a Cass way of looking at it. But they were right. I loved the outfit. Why should I be deprived of it because Devin was a disaster? "But accessories and hair. We'd need to leave, like, now, right?"

"Can you do this in half an hour? I'll get there as soon as I can to help you."

"Maybe? I'll give it a shot."

I disconnected the call and texted Tahira that she needed to help me get dressed in that lehenga in half an hour for the dance.

Tahira must have flown up the stairs because she burst into the room almost immediately. "Leave this with me," she said. "That outfit is *gorge*. I have just the jewelry for it."

Tahira and Cass managed to get me into my outfit and jewelry, and my makeup done, with time to spare. I was in the bathroom adding some intentional, smooth waves to my normal unruly waves while Cass, in a three-piece gray suit, sat on the edge of the bathtub, watching a YouTube hair tutorial and telling me what to do. Owen was apparently talking to Dad in the basement family room.

Tahira poked her head in, singing "It's Raining Men."

"Is Owen getting antsy?" Cass asked.

"Nope. Dad is pretending to know what the NHL draft is. But there is *another* cute boy at the door. Shall I send this one away or bring him in like the last one?"

I lowered the curling iron, annoyed. "What are you going on about, Tahira?"

"That cute pie-making boy of yours is here. And he has a pie, which makes him even cuter. Most people bring flowers for their date before a dance, but who am I to argue with nonconformity?"

There was only one pie-baking boy in my life. Which meant . . .

Daniel was here.

I unplugged the curling iron and pushed past Tahira to rush down the stairs.

Cass followed me but went straight to the basement door. "I can give you ten minutes. I'll stall Owen."

I opened the front door, and there he was. He was also wearing a suit, but no tie. His dress shirt had the top button open, the rich blue glowing against his tawny brown skin. I could see a stretchy bandage where his cast used to be. His hair was brushed and styled, instead of his normal messy but ridiculously shiny look.

And his eyes . . . but wait. Daniel's eyes looked dark in the dimming sun. They didn't have their normal twinkly-with-joy look. Instead, he looked anxious. His lips were in a straight line, his posture seemed stiff, and his brows furrowed. He leaned forward ever so slightly in the doorframe.

And he was, indeed, carrying a pie. In a box.

I stared for several seconds, not sure I remembered how to form words with my mouth.

"I wrote you an email," I finally blurted out. *Real smooth, Samaya.* My heart was racing. I squeezed my fists.

Daniel seemed to find communication challenging right now, too. He looked down nervously, then back at me. "I know. I read it. You look . . . amazing. I made you a pie. This pie."

I peeked into the little plastic window on the pie box, but all I could see was that it was a double-crust pie. "What kind is it?"

"It's pie."

"I can see that. What kind of pie?"

He tilted his head, and I could see the slight beginning of a Daniel smile there. "Can I show you?"

I nodded and motioned him into the house. I didn't know why he was here. But if he wanted to come in wearing a suit and give me a pie, I wasn't about to stop him. In fact, I'd find a way to keep him here as long as I could.

After taking off his shoes, he followed me into the kitchen. He'd never been to my house before, and I couldn't help but wonder what he was thinking. It wasn't really anywhere near as impressive as Hana's or Jayden's houses, but the kitchen was pretty nice. The gleaming quartz countertops and stainless appliances clearly weren't cheap.

Was he resenting all this? Did seeing it make him think we were further apart?

He placed the box on the kitchen island and opened it. I watched his hands carefully. Daniel, of course, wasn't small. He was a hockey forward and built like one. But his fingers were long and narrow. Almost delicate. Hands made for making pastry and piping buttercream roses for little kids' birthdays.

After sliding the pie out of the box, he placed it on the counter. I looked at it carefully . . . then burst out laughing.

"I asked you what kind of pie it was, and I thought you said *pie*—not *pi!*"

Around the perimeter of the pie were little numbers cut out of pastry. The numbers 3.14159265359, to be specific.

"It's a pi pie," Daniel said.

"You made it for me?"

He nodded, looking a little shy. It was adorable. "You said things were intense and stressful. And you told me once you recite pi when you get stressed. I make pie to deal with stress. I thought this might be a way we could . . . meet in the middle?"

I shook my head, still chuckling. I loved this. "What kind is it?"

"Cranberry apple."

I grinned and looked up at his face. He was grinning, too, and it was so much better than that unsure look he had earlier.

"Should I cut us some?" I asked, opening the kitchen drawer to get the pie lifter and knife.

He took the utensils from my hand. "I'll cut it. I don't want you to make a mess on that dress. You look gorgeous. When do you need to leave for the dance?"

I checked the time on the stove. We needed to leave now. "I can eat pie first. You look nice, too. Are you dressed like that because . . ."

"Because I wanted to ask you if you still needed a date."

I smiled. "Really?"

He nodded. "I borrowed this suit from a guy on my team. I got your email, and I didn't know how to say this in a message, so I came to see you in person." He put the knife down. "This week, even before I got that email from you, I decided I wasn't willing to give you up as a friend. Every time something happened to me, I hated that I couldn't text you about it. When I saw Krebs get this total once-in-a-lifetime goal in the game Tuesday, when I got a B+ on my calculus quiz, when I found out I didn't have to move no matter what I studied in school—"

My face erupted with a wide smile. "What did you say?"

His face flashed a luminous smile as he finished cutting the pie. "Krebs got this amazing goal at our last game! It was *wicked*. I hope I'll be cleared to play again really soon. This thing is annoying." He pointed to the bandage on his wrist.

"No, not that part. The other part."

"My grade on the quiz?" He knew exactly what I meant but was toying with me.

"No. You not having to move."

He grinned. "Me, my mom, and my uncle had this big, long discussion. I told him I planned to go to culinary school. And my mother told him we'd both move out if he overstepped his authority again. She got me my own phone today." He held up a new phone to show me.

"Wow. And your uncle agreed?"

Daniel shrugged, handing me a slice of pie on a plate. "He didn't have much of a choice. Edwin Uncle's mother said she wasn't letting Mom go. She technically owns the house, and she said me and Mom can stay as long as we want."

"And he'll still take you to hockey?"

Daniel shook his head. "Nope. But his mother is letting me borrow her car. That's how I got here."

"What?" I was shocked. Daniel . . . drove? "I didn't even know you knew how to drive!"

He nodded proudly. "Andre taught me last year."

"That's amazing." I was sure my face would split open from smiling. I couldn't believe he was here. I didn't know what it meant for us, but at least I had my friend back. I took a bite of the pie. It tasted perfect, of course.

He looked down at his pie, avoiding my eyes. "Samaya, I've done a lot of thinking, and you were right. I should have fought back. I'm a people pleaser, but I shouldn't sacrifice the things I love, hockey, and baking, everything, to please others. It's *my* life. And what I want from my life is—"

Cass and Owen came up the stairs talking loudly. Before they could say anything, I put my hand up. "Give us five more?"

Cass grinned. "Got it. Let's wait in the car, Owen."

Owen waved happily at Daniel, and then Cass and Owen put their shoes on and left.

"Go on," I said to Daniel.

He stepped closer to me. "What I want in my life is you. Like I told you before, I resisted this for so long because I was so sure you wouldn't be interested in me if you knew about all the crap in my past. I didn't think there was a place for someone like me in your fancy life."

"There is," I said.

He smiled. "I know. I was selling myself short. I decided that you couldn't possibly like me for me . . . even though you clearly did. You, my beautiful little vampire, were always fighting for what *you* deserved, even when you were a little misguided about what that was. And what you said to me last week, how could I expect others to value me when I didn't seem to value myself much . . ."

I frowned. "I said that?"

He nodded, grinning. "I think so. It's what you meant, at least."

"So . . ." This was too much. He was here, and he said he wanted me in his life. "Does this mean we're back to being . . . friends?"

He tilted his head, looking at me. He took a step closer. And then another. He was so close I could feel his warmth radiating off him. He came even closer and reached down to touch my cheek. "You, Samaya Janmohammad, are the smartest person I've ever met. And funny. And you're patient with my dumbass self for mixing up fractions and functions. You're generous. You're just . . ."

"I'm me," I said softly.

"And that's perfect," he whispered. He was about to kiss me. In my kitchen. With a pie he made for me. A pi pie.

But he was going too slow. I reached out and put my hand around the soft skin at the back of his neck and pulled him closer.

And we were kissing. And everything was right again in my world. He was strong, and solid, and we fit together perfectly. His kiss intensified as his arms came around my waist, his cool hands on the strip of bare skin between the lehenga skirt and the cropped blouse. I wanted to get closer. If I could alter the time-space continuum and eliminate any space between us, I would do that in a minute.

The loud sound of a throat clearing pulled us apart. Tahira was in the doorway. "I didn't tell Dad you have a date here, too, Samaya. So unless you have time for a father interrogation, you should probably leave. I'll clean this up. Hi, Daniel. I'm going to need you to model for me one day, soon, by the way."

Daniel laughed. "Sure, if you say so." He looked down at me. "So you're going with Cass and Owen?"

"*We're* going with Cass and Owen. Cass needs me with them for reasons. People go to dances with a group of friends all the time."

"Is that what we are? Friends?"

I grinned and pulled him tighter. "Not if I have anything to say about it. You and I are friends . . . plus more. But we should probably go before Cass gets scared and runs or Dad comes upstairs." I pulled his arm and guided him to the door.

"Be good, kids," Tahira said, handing me my coat and purse. "Don't do anything I *would* do."

~

The dance was being held in a banquet hall near an industrial area on the edge of town—the same place it was last year. As expected, we were late. We had to park at the far end of the lot.

"Samaya?" said a voice the second Cass, Owen, Daniel, and I walked into the lobby of the building. Damn it. Devin.

I turned. "Devin." Daniel helped me take off my coat.

He was standing alone near the entrance. And he was staring at me. "You're wearing the lehenga I bought you," he said.

"Don't read anything into that," I said. "You gave it to me, and I like it. I'm here with Daniel. Daniel, you remember Devin."

Daniel grinned and nodded. "Nice to see you again. Love the suit."

Devin looked confused to see Daniel. "I'm surprised you're here."

"Why are you hovering near the door, Devin?" I asked.

"Everyone was gossiping about me." Devin stepped closer. "Can we talk for a second?"

I rolled my eyes, but I considered it. I hadn't forgiven him, but to be honest, since Devin confessed he was LostAxis, I'd started to sympathize with him more. The pressure his parents put on him had to be hard. I knew they thought he was perfect—a real golden son. And he'd been raised to obey like a good Indian child. I wasn't surprised he snapped and did something ridiculous. And if I stripped it all back . . . LostAxis *had* helped me. My summer would have been so, so much worse without LostAxis.

So Devin didn't deserve me to hear him out, but maybe LostAxis did. "Fine. Talk," I said.

"We can wait inside," Cass said. "We'll get a table."

I nodded. "Yeah, I'll be there in a second."

Daniel looked at me, concerned. "You sure? I can stay."

I smiled at him. "Nah, go ahead. I'm fine. Save me a seat."

Once Daniel, Cass, and Owen were inside the banquet hall, Devin guided me to a bench near the door.

"Okay, what do you want?"

He sat, then ran his hand through his hair. He motioned for me to sit next to him, but I stayed standing.

"I . . . uh . . . ," he stuttered. "How are you?"

I couldn't help it. I laughed. "Really?"

"I . . . I just . . . Can you sit, Samaya? You're looming over me."

"I'm barely five feet tall. I've never *loomed* over anyone in my life."

"You figuratively loom all the time."

Still chuckling, I sat next to him. "Okay, so what did you want to say?"

He sighed. "It's just, we're both getting awards tonight."

"Yeah, I know." We were the top two kids in our grade. We always had been.

He ran his hand through his hair again. He was going to have to wash it after the dance. "It'll feel weird if we don't clear the air first, don't you think?"

Clear the air? Really? "Devin, where's Hana? Oh wait, you dumped her, too. Did your parents tell you to? And did you obey like a good, obedient son? Should I tell Hana that if any strangers slide into her DMs, it's probably you?"

He recoiled at my words, then looked down. "I deserved that."

"Hell yeah, you did."

He met my eyes again. "I don't know what else I can say. I'm sorry. I shouldn't have lied to you. Samaya, I miss you."

I shook my head. "Devin . . . you know we would never have lasted anyway, right? All the issues we had would have gotten worse as we got older."

"I know."

"And the whole you-catfishing-me thing proves that you're in no way mature enough for a real relationship."

"I know that, too. That's why I broke up with Hana." A loud voice came through from inside the banquet hall, stating dinner would be served soon. "Look, Samaya, you never have to talk to me again if you don't want to. All I wanted to say is I'm sorry. Again. I'm sorry I hurt you. And lied to you. I was hoping we could be friends again. But I'll leave you alone."

He stood and started to walk inside. "Wait," I said. I paused. He'd meant the world to me once. I took a deep breath. "Let's go in together."

He blinked, surprised. "Really?"

"Yeah, really. This is the Nerd Prom. It's to celebrate the biggest nerds of last year. That would be you and me." I smiled. "I'm still mad at you, but I think we should walk in together."

I wasn't sure I was ready to forgive Devin, or ever be friends with him again, but the truth was, he was such a big part of my past. And I hated the idea of all those memories being tainted forever.

So I did it. I walked into the Nerd Prom with Devin Kapadia by my side. My past.

And then I left him to be with the guy who was my present, and hopefully my future—Daniel Ramos. The person who made me happier than I ever imagined. Who made me want to be the most genuine me I could be.

Daniel leaned in after I sat down. "You looked so amazing walking in. Five stars. The smartest and most gorgeous person in the room. I've said it before: you are way out of my league."

I shook my head. "Not even close. We are both exactly in the same league. Together."

Daniel gave me a soft kiss on the forehead. Then he whispered into my cheek, "I am so in love with you, Samaya Janmohammad. I hope you realize that."

I wrapped my fingers around the back of his head and whispered into his ear, "I love you, too, Daniel Ramos."

EPILOGUE

May—seven months later

The forest-fairies game won second place at the National Youth Developers Mobile Game Competition. Our team lost to a first-person shooter game, which was annoying, but at least it wasn't Jayden's team's alien mecha sniper-battle game. But still—coming in second out of eighty entries was pretty cool. Andre threw us a barbecue in the park to celebrate our win. But I think he mostly threw the party for Yasmin, because we'd named the game *Yasmin of the Forest* after the main character: a little brown-skinned fairy who went on adventures and solved puzzles in the forest.

"How come the fairy doesn't have earrings?" Yasmin asked me. We were sitting at a picnic table, and she was playing the game on my phone for the first time. She'd recently had her ears pierced, and most of her conversations lately were about her earrings. That or her new kitten. Yasmin's family had moved out of the shelter about a month after Yasmin had gone missing that night last October. Now they were living in a basement apartment nearby, and Yasmin attended the shelter's after-school program while her mother worked, so Daniel and I still saw a lot of her when we were volunteering there.

"The game is meant to be played on phones, so it's very small," I explained. "No one would see her earrings."

Yasmin thought about that for a moment. "She shouldn't wear earrings, I think. She couldn't go swimming in the river until they healed."

I nodded. "That's a very good point."

Aimee shook her head. "I think earrings would have looked cool. I mean, in-game graphics don't need earrings, but we could have put them on the character sketches. Their ears are big enough. I'll add them for the sequel."

I snorted. After the long hours working on this project on top of all my other schoolwork, plus volunteering, I had no intention of making a sequel. Aimee, as I expected, wasn't dating Jayden anymore. She was on to a new guy—someone she'd met in photography class. Aimee and I weren't really close friends anymore, though. She was only here today because she'd been on the game-dev team.

Cass was, of course, still my best friend. They were here at the park, too, playing ball hockey with Daniel, Owen, and some of the others from the shelter and game-dev team. I wasn't surprised Cass and Owen were still together. But I was shocked that Cass had joined an introductory gender-inclusive hockey program and was now totally obsessed. I had no intention of joining in with my friend's and boyfriend's obsession. I watched their games, and I now knew what *offside* meant, and that was enough for me. I loved Daniel; I didn't need to love everything he did.

I looked over to him. He and the others had finished their game and were heading toward an empty table. Daniel smiled and waved me over when he saw me looking. I went to join them and sat next to him.

He put his arm around my waist and nodded toward Yasmin. "How's she liking her namesake game?"

I chuckled. "She can't seem to get past level one." Which made sense. It was created for ages fourteen and up. Yasmin was six. Her little brow was furrowed as she focused on the screen.

"She's smart. Give her some time. When do we need to head to your parents' to help with dinner?"

I checked my watch. "Soon. Mom wants you to make brownies for dessert."

He chuckled. "I swear, she only invites me to Sunday dinner so I'll make dessert."

I laughed. He knew that wasn't true. My parents *adored* Daniel—which didn't surprise me. He was very likable. They did ask him what his parents did for a living when they met, but they weren't judgmental at all about the answer. And they didn't care that Daniel wasn't an academic student—as long as he was driven to follow his own dreams. Sunday dinners at the Janmohammad house were big, noisy affairs lately, with not only Tahira's boyfriend but now Daniel having open invitations. Also, sometimes Daniel's mother came, too. Mom said she wanted to spend as much time as possible with us all together since I'd be leaving in a few months.

I had been accepted into the computational mathematics program at University of Waterloo, and Daniel had been accepted into a pastry arts program at a different college also in Waterloo. We were both going to be living on campus at our own schools.

Daniel hadn't planned on going to a school outside Toronto—he'd wanted to stay in town to save money by living at his uncle's house. And he didn't want to leave his mother alone. But though things were somewhat better for him at his uncle's, he still wasn't completely comfortable there. And when his mom realized that he was only staying in town for her, she held an intervention—she told him she was fine, and she needed him to do what he felt was right for *his* life, instead of hers. So he applied to the excellent pastry arts program at a community college near my university. Andre and Muniba found him some grants and scholarships, and he lined up a job in the campus food services.

Even though I knew we'd both be so busy that we probably wouldn't see each other as much as we did now, I was happy we'd still be in the same city. I felt better knowing he would be near me.

"I asked Mom to get lemons, too," I said. "I want lemon squares." Daniel had once said that like chocolate and lemon squares, he and I didn't fit together. He was wrong, though. I happened to think the two flavors went together beautifully.

Daniel tightened his arm around me and rested his chin on my shoulder. His lips grazed my neck, which even after all these months sent shivers down my spine. "Lemon squares remind me of our parameters. I'm glad we stomped all over those."

I made a happy noise as I held his hands around me. "Best thing we ever did. Our new ones are so much better."

"There are no parameters, anymore," he whispered. "Just endless happiness. Love you."

"Love you, too, Daniel."

ROSE'S LEMON SQUARES

- ½ cup butter at room temperature
- ¼ cup confectioners' (icing) sugar
- 1 cup and 2 ½ tbsp flour, divided
- ¼ tsp salt
- 2 eggs
- 1 cup granulated sugar
- 1 tbsp lemon zest
- 3 tbsp freshly squeezed lemon juice
- Extra confectioners' sugar for dusting

Preheat oven to 350 degrees.

Make crust: cut butter, confectioners' sugar, flour, and salt together and pat into an 8x8 ungreased pan. Bake for 15 minutes.

While crust is baking, make filling by beating eggs, granulated sugar, lemon zest, flour, and lemon juice.

When crust is baked, use a brush to lightly grease the sides of the pan above the crust, then pour filling over crust. Bake for an additional 15 to 20 minutes until filling is set.

Let cool completely. Sift additional confectioners' sugar over lemon squares before cutting.

ACKNOWLEDGMENTS

No book is created in a vacuum, and this one, like all my books, would not have been possible without the support and encouragement from my family, my friends, and my colleagues.

My biggest thank-you goes to my friends who beta read an early version of this story: Roselle Lim, Lily Chu, Namrata Patel, and Laura Heffernan. This book would not have been possible without your help, and I can't thank you enough. I will always be in awe of your generosity.

Thank you to my agent, Rachel Brooks, who is always excited and supportive of my work. Thank you to my acquiring editor at Skyscape, Carmen Johnson, for her unwavering passion and commitment to this project. And thank you to the rest of the team at Skyscape, from the editors, copyeditors, production editors, and proofreaders, to the art team, publicity, sales and marketing—it was comforting to know I was in such good hands for this book.

Thank you to my kids, Khalil and Anissa, for understanding that Mom's head isn't in the real world very often anymore. Thank you especially to Anissa, for being the best brainstorming buddy a writer could ask for. My nerdy little gamer-girl was written for her.

And to Tony, who was patient and let me rant, vent, cry, and talk through every issue in this book whenever I needed it. Behind this author is a husband holding her up, letting her vent, and making sure she's getting enough sleep.

ABOUT THE AUTHOR

Photo © 2021 J. Heron

After a childhood filled with Bollywood, Monty Python, and Jane Austen, Farah Heron constantly wove uplifting happily ever afters in her head while pursuing careers in human resources and psychology. She started writing her stories down a few years ago and is thrilled to see her daydreams become books. The author of *Tahira in Bloom*, *Accidentally Engaged*, and *Kamila Knows Best*, Farah writes romantic comedies for adults and teens full of huge South Asian families, delectable food, and most importantly, brown people falling stupidly in love. Farah lives in Toronto with her husband and two teens, a rabbit named Strawberry, and two cats who rule the house. For more information, visit www.farahheron.com.